Dark Days at the Beach Hotel

Francesca Capaldi has enjoyed writing since she was a child, largely influenced by a Welsh mother who was good at improvised story telling. She is a member of the RNA and the Society of Women Writers and Journalists. Francesca currently lives in Kent with her family and a cat called Lando Calrissian.

Also by Francesca Capaldi

Wartime in the Valleys

Heartbreak in the Valleys
War in the Valleys
Hope in the Valleys
Trouble in the Valleys

The Beach Hotel Series

A New Start at the Beach Hotel
All Change at the Beach Hotel
Dark Days at the Beach Hotel

Dark Days
at the
Beach Hotel

Francesca Capaldi

hera

First published in the United Kingdom in 2024 by

Hera Books
Unit 9 (Canelo), 5th Floor
Cargo Works, 1-2 Hatfields
London SE1 9PG
United Kingdom

A CIP catalogue record for this book is available from the British Library.

Print ISBN 978 1 80436 137 5
Ebook ISBN 978 1 80436 136 8

Look for more great books at www.herabooks.com

Printed and bound in Great Britain by Clays Ltd, Elcograf S.p.A.

1

Dedicated to Carmela, Peter, Giovanna, Jack, Luca, Phynn and Seren

Prologue

'There it is!' said Helen Bygrove with great excitement, as her husband Douglas drove down South Terrace in Littlehampton.

He brought the two-seater Wolseley-Siddeley motorcar, which he'd borrowed from a friend, to a halt next to the tennis court, opposite the large edifice known as the Beach Hotel. 'I just hope this lives up to expectation.' He leant down a little to look sideways at the building from under the fabric hood.

'Cousin Eleanor seemed to think that it was splendid inside,' said Helen. 'She reckoned it had a lot of business potential. I've passed it numerous times, both in a motorcar and whilst out walking, but have never visited it before. Mother says that she and Father did in their younger days.' She felt a sadness creep over her, thinking of her father.

Douglas got out of the motorcar, then headed around to Helen's door to open it.

'Thank you, dear.' He was ever the gentleman. It was one of the first things that had attracted her to him. She smiled at him now, taking in his tall, wiry body and neat, light brown hair, which was currently oiled and slicked back. He wore a smart sack suit with wide lapels and a bowler hat. 'Eleanor says these tennis courts belong to the hotel too.'

'Splendid.' Douglas grinned broadly, smoothing his moustache unnecessarily with a forefinger and thumb. 'I like a spot of tennis myself.'

'I know you do,' she chuckled. She took his arm as they stood on the opposite pavement, considering the red brick structure. Being tall, she was almost the same height as him.

She shaded her eyes as she considered the hotel. There seemed to be three sections to the main building, all with numerous windows. The centre section had several white beams, creating a pattern, similar to a Tudor house. In the centre was a large canopy, likely to be the entrance. There was a selection of smaller and larger gables on the second floor at the top, and several chimneys. The first floor on the right-hand side had a balcony running around the building, with a tiled canopy over it. The first-floor balcony, in turn, created a canopy for the ground floor terrace around the building. Both were held up by props that looked like tree branches.

On the left was an almost separate building with a clock tower, which she understood was a public house, owned by the hotel. The whole area, way beyond the buildings on the right-hand side, was surrounded by a stone wall.

'It's a lot bigger than anything else we've seen,' said Helen.

'So it has a lot of promise. It's been on the market a while. I reckon we could negotiate on the price and bring it down a little. Either way, we'll still have some money left for any changes or modifications needed.'

'Thanks to my mother. How wise she was, keeping her inheritance in her own name and not putting the money in a joint account with my father. I dread to think what would have become of it, had he got his hands on it.'

'It was your grandmother who was wise. She was the one who made the proviso in her will that your mother would only inherit the property if it, or any money resulting, remained in her name alone.'

'Yes, you're right, dear.'

Her mother, Lady Rose Wright, had come into the money only two years back, when her own mother had died and left her a manor house in Lyminster. That had been a surprise to Lady

Rose as her mother had hinted at leaving it to a male cousin. After the manor had been sold, she'd deposited the money into a bank account of her own, as directed by the will. This had caused many arguments between her parents, her father asserting that no one could take the money now it was hers, but her mother wouldn't back down. Helen experienced another brief wave of sorrow. Her father, Sir Ronald Wright, had died only a year ago. He might have caused a lot of problems, but he had still been her father.

'I hope Mummy is coping with Dorothy and Arthur, especially with him being so young.' She pictured her daughter, soon to be two, and her sweet little four-month-old son. 'And Mummy isn't in the best of health.'

'I'm sure she's coping admirably.'

'I'm feeling a little lost without them, if I'm honest.'

'You'll have to get used to that if you're going to help me run the hotel, as you have expressed a wish to. Even if it is in a supporting role, we'll have to employ a nursemaid for them.'

'I suppose we will.' The prospect made her exceedingly sad, but she was determined to help Douglas in this endeavour, especially if they took on something this large.

'Shall we cross over?' Douglas pointed towards the hotel.

'One moment.'

She looked down at her olive green suit, smoothing down the skirt past the row of ornamental buttons, to make sure it was neat.

'Am I presentable?' she asked, patting lightly at the front of her copious blonde hair, which had been coiled around her head. On top she wore a wide brimmed hat trimmed with ostrich feathers.

'Of course you are. You always are, my dear.'

'Thank you, my darling. I do want to look my very best for visiting this hotel.'

She took his arm once more, and they waited until a horse and cart from the dairy had gone past.

Douglas opened the gate for her, and they walked across a courtyard to the grand open brick porch. Passing beneath it, they reached the double door of wood and etched glass.

In the foyer, they were greeted by a young porter in a mid-blue uniform with a peaked, circular hat.

'Good afternoon, sir, madam. How may I help you?'

'We are here to see Mr Edwards,' Douglas said in a rather superior tone. It must be an attempt to stamp his authority on the place from the beginning, thought Helen.

An elderly gentleman came out from a door to the left of the desk.

'Here he is now,' said the porter, before walking over to him. He said something they couldn't hear, but it put a smile on the old man's face as he looked over at them.

'Mr and Mrs Bygrove, and so prompt too, so prompt. Welcome to the Beach Hotel. I am Mr Edwards, the current owner and manager of this splendid establishment.'

He shook hands first with Douglas, then Helen.

'Thank you, Mr Edwards. I always like to arrive at an appointment when I am supposed to, and I would rather be early than late. Manners maketh the man, and all that.'

'Quite so, quite so,' agreed Mr Edwards.

While they were talking, Helen turned a full circle to take in what would be a first impression for guests, as well as herself. It was elegant, with its cream walls and beige marble floor with pearl-coloured veins. There was a large crystal chandelier in the centre and crystal wall-mounted lights around the foyer. Next to the cloakroom, which itself was next to a lift, was a grandfather clock. As she spotted it, it chimed four times.

The reception desk, at the far wall in the centre, was of dark oak. It was manned by a middle-aged man with short, neat hair that looked darker than it probably really was. He looked over at them in a rather pompous manner. Behind the desk was a curving marble staircase, wide and grand, with ornate black and gold railings.

'Impressive, isn't it?' said Mr Edwards.

'It's certainly a good start to our viewing,' said Helen, hoping the rest of the hotel lived up to this initial promise.

'We will make a judgement when we've seen it all,' said Douglas.

'Let me show you around the ground floor public guest rooms first. Afternoon tea is just finishing, so now would be a good time, while it's not too busy.'

'You have plenty of trade here still then?' Douglas asked.

'Oh yes, yes. It's one of the top premier hotels here on the Sussex coast, with a *very* good reputation.'

'We are aware of that, of course. In which case, why are you selling it?'

Helen felt a little embarrassed by her husband's doubting and slightly patronising tone. It was almost as if poor Mr Edwards were in the dock, but no doubt Douglas wanted to make sure everything was in order.

'Good question, good question, Mr Bygrove. But, as you can see, I am not exactly a spring chicken any more.' He stopped and indicated himself with a downward sweep of his hand. 'Mrs Edwards and I would like to enjoy a bit of retirement in Devon before we shuffle off this mortal coil, so to speak.'

Douglas nodded, as if satisfied with the reply.

Mr Edwards headed off once more and they followed on, Douglas drawing himself up to his full six feet whilst clasping his hands behind his back.

The first room they came to, situated behind the foyer and stairs, was a dining room, currently empty. There was a maid there in a black dress with a white apron and frilly white cap. She was polishing a dresser, and Helen detected the scent of lavender polish.

It had a view over the back lawns and a rockery replete with flowers. The part of the room nearest the garden, about a quarter of it, was under a glass roof. Outside, the awnings had been rolled down against the bright day. The curtains, pulled back now, were of William Morris fabric patterned with birds and flowers. The tables were fully laid with spotless white cloths and silver cutlery.

'Are these Chippendale?' she asked, admiring the mahogany dining chairs with their claw feet and padded leather seats.

'Indeed, indeed. You can spot quality when you see it.'

'As can we both.' Douglas smiled thinly. 'I have worked in hotels for many years.'

'Yes, of course.' Mr Edwards tipped his head in a brief bow.

Oh dear, she hoped her husband wasn't offended by the manager's words to her; he could be a sensitive soul at times.

As the two men spoke of guest numbers and mealtimes, she wandered around the tables to admire the view once more.

'Let's move on to the conservatory now.'

Mr Edwards walked to a door that led to a room that was three quarters under glass. This room, like the dining room, faced south, and the awnings were drawn down outside here as well. The room had the same view of flowers and lawns, but Helen also spied a greenhouse to one side, on the edge of the building. There were venetian blinds pulled across the glass ceiling. At the windows were net curtains, which had been tied back. The room was filled with large pot plants, including a variety of palms with wide and narrow leaves and some variegated. There was also a yucca, a weeping fig and a dracaena. Four of the tables were still occupied.

'This is where we serve afternoon tea.'

Helen was about to make a remark when she thought better of it. She would let Douglas speak first, as this was his field of expertise.

From one of the smaller tables next to the window, a distinguished-looking gentleman, somewhere in his sixties, rose. He had a full head of greying hair and a gingery-grey handlebar moustache. He smiled when he spotted the manager.

'Mr Edwards, old chap. It's a lovely afternoon, what? Showing some new guests around, are you?'

'Good afternoon, Major Thomas. Yes, in a manner of speaking.'

'That was a delicious repast, as always, especially the meringue Genoese. Compliments to the chefs.'

'I'll pass them on, Major.'

After the old man left, Douglas said, 'I'm guessing that he's a regular.'

'A permanent, you might say,' quipped the manager. 'The hotel has become his home. And a very nice gentleman he is, too.'

'I suppose it guarantees a regular income from at least one room, what?'

'Quite, quite.'

Helen spotted a china tea set on the table of two older women. It was cream with a green and gold gilt edging and decorated with pink roses. Such a pretty and elegant tea set in beautiful surroundings. She pictured herself sitting here with Douglas, partaking of afternoon tea. Ironically, if they bought the place, that was unlikely to happen.

'Are you waiting for us to leave?' called a rather haughty voice from the table with the two women. The owner's attire was somewhat dated, though still elegant. The lady with her was in a plainer outfit.

'Indeed not, indeed not, Lady Blackmore. You and Miss Cecelia must take as long as you like.'

They left the conservatory. As Mr Edwards closed the door, Douglas said, 'Are they permanent guests too?'

'Oh no, no,' he laughed. 'But Lady Blackmore and her companion, Miss Cecelia, live only down the street on Empress Maud Road and are regular guests... Let me show you the ball-room next.'

They entered the foyer once more, but turned left, past the lift, into a short corridor. Mr Edwards pushed open some double doors with a flourish to reveal a large, white room with long windows and outside doors on two sides. The embossed walls had pillars, with arched mirrors in between. From the ceiling hung several intricate crystal chandeliers. The floor was similarly spectacular with its walnut and oak parquet in the shape of hexagons and stars.

Helen could tell that Douglas was impressed, but he played this down by saying, 'Not bad. Do you hold many balls here?'

Mr Edwards looked a little crestfallen by her husband's understated reaction. 'Not as many as we used to, as they have fallen a little out of fashion, but we hold other functions here, like large private parties and musical soirees. Recently we hosted a string octet, all ladies. Very popular it was.'

'I'm sure, I'm sure,' Douglas said, in the repetitive manner of Mr Edwards. He often seemed to imitate the important people he met. She supposed it was a method he'd learned during his years in the hotel business.

'We have a smaller, private dining room next door, on the other side of the cloakroom, for more intimate events.'

'I see, I see.' Douglas lifted himself up onto the balls of his feet briefly. It's what her father used to do too, when considering a matter.

They headed to the room in question for a brief look at it. He pointed at the fireplace here, the grate of which was empty. 'We have a few fireplaces in the hotel, but not many. You may have noticed that much of our establishment is heated by radiators.' He pointed at the cast iron one on the inner wall. 'All of the guest rooms have them now, though a few of the large rooms retain a fireplace as well.'

'It's good that the guests get a choice.' Douglas looked around the room.

'Let me show you the staff area now, and then we'll look at some of the guest bedrooms.'

They headed across the foyer, to a door on the opposite side, and entered a corridor. It was lit only by a length of high windows. It was lighter at the opposite end, where Helen guessed that the window lites looked out onto the dining room and conservatory.

They visited the staff dining room first. It contained a large table that filled much of the room, bordered by several bench seats. On the far side was a large fireplace that was not currently in use.

There were three middle-aged women sitting at the table, with several young women in maid's uniforms, and another young porter.

'Let me introduce you to Mrs Leggett, the housekeeper, and a most important member of our staff,' said Mr Edwards.

A slender woman sitting at the nearest end, who looked to be in her mid-forties, stood. Her light brown hair was pulled into a tight bun. Her clothes were neat but from the early part of the century. Her serious expression made Helen wonder what she would be like to work with.

'This is Mr and Mrs Bygrove,' the manager continued, 'who are considering buying the hotel and managing it.'

'I would be the one managing it,' said Douglas. 'Though my wife would be involved in some capacity.'

Mrs Leggett looked them over, her expression not exactly impressed. 'Good afternoon to you both.'

Before Helen could reply, Mr Edwards said, 'And these two ladies here are Mrs Norris, the cook...'

''Ello there, me ducks,' said the tall woman. She was broad and stout, her expression neutral.

'...And Mrs Turnbull, the storekeeper.'

'Good day and welcome to you. It's right grand of you to consider our lovely hotel.' The woman with white curls pulled into a loose bun on top of her head was all smiles. Helen really did feel welcomed by her.

'Is that a Northumberland accent?' She had once stayed in the area with her cousin Eleanor.

'That's right. Newcastle, to be exact.' Her smile became even broader and she seemed inordinately pleased that Helen had recognised her accent.

'Ladies, would you accompany us on the tour of the staff areas?'

The housekeeper, storekeeper and cook followed them out, and between them and the manager held a commentary as they visited the scullery, stillroom, office and various store cupboards.

The kitchen was filled with the savoury aroma of roasting meat. It made Helen feel hungry. Mrs Norris led them around as a lofty young man with a head of thick black hair turned from one of the work surfaces to survey them.

'This is me son, who's head chef here,' the cook said proudly. 'These good people might be buying the hotel, Joseph.'

The chef's expression went from a frown to a slight grin. 'Welcome to our kitchen. We only create the very best food here.'

'So true, so true,' said Mr Edwards. 'Only haute cuisine is served here. Never known a better kitchen team in all my days in the hotel business.'

The housekeeper and storekeeper left the room as Helen and Douglas were given a tour of the kitchen. One side was filled with stoves and ovens, while most of the other three sides had cupboards, shelves and worksurfaces. From the ceiling hung a variety of pots and pans, mostly copper. There was a door to a store, and in the middle of the room, a large table. After explaining a little about their typical day, Mrs Norris showed them various menus that had been prepared in the previous weeks.

Next, they were guided up a narrow staircase to the manager's quarters on the first floor.

It was the most disappointed Helen had felt during the whole visit. There was a sitting room that also contained a dining table. Next door was the main bedroom. Both faced the shorter area of common on the left of the hotel. Beyond she could spy fields, and in the distance, the large convalescent home in Rustington. She could only spot a tiny bit of the coast. It also looked over the white Georgian buildings on the eastern side of South Terrace. Two smaller bedrooms and a bathroom faced the front, with a view only of houses. That was it. The furniture within, which Mr Edwards had already informed them would be left behind, was old fashioned to say the least, even if it was good quality.

This would be the first time they had owned their own home, always supposing they bought it, and so far they'd possessed nothing but second-hand furniture. Still, it was only one tiny mark against the hotel so far, and she was sure they could modernise it themselves. If they had any money left to do so.

A visit to some of the staff bedrooms on the second floor was followed by a tour of a selection of the twenty-seven guest bedrooms on the first and second floors. Some had the same vista as the manager's quarters. The best ones though, at the back and on the right-hand side of the hotel, had views of either the sea or the larger part of the common and River Arun. There were even two small rooms, albeit with magnificent views, on a tiny third floor.

Helen was standing now in a room on the second floor, by a triple window, overlooking the promenade and beach, about a hundred-and-fifty yards away. The sea looked turquoise today, with the bright blue sky reflecting off it. It shimmered in the sunshine. The beach and promenade were teeming with people. The tents and huts on the sand, providing provisions and entertainments, seemed to be doing a roaring trade. In the distance on the right, she could spy the bandstand, and further away, the coastguards' cottages, windmill and the river mouth.

Next, they walked around the extensive outside area, with its lawns, flower beds and sunken garden. They were introduced to Mr Hargreaves, the head gardener, who continued the tour.

Afterwards, Mr Edwards showed them back to the foyer.

The porter who had welcomed them earlier came forward. 'Anything I can do, sir?'

'Yes, Mr Cobbett. Please show our guests to the conservatory.' The manager turned towards them. 'I trust I can treat you to tea and pastries while you discuss your impressions in private?'

'That would be agreeable,' said Douglas.

Helen said nothing but was delighted, after her earlier thoughts about having tea here.

The porter showed them through to a table by the window that had been laid up ready. The guests who'd been present when they'd first visited had now departed.

'So, what do you think?' said Helen, after the young man had left.

'The fact that it's been on sale a while and that Mr Edwards is keen to retire will probably work in our favour, price wise.'

'I meant, what do you think of the hotel?'

'It lives up to its good name, though some of the bedrooms are rather… Victorian. They could do with updating. Which should also work in our favour in bargaining.'

'Yes,' she sighed. 'The manager's quarters were rather old-fashioned too.'

'We can remedy that easily enough,' he said.

She took his hand. 'Of course we can.'

'Some of the staff will have to be taught to show a little more respect. It's not acceptable for the cook to refer to us as *me ducks*.' He said the last two words pointedly. 'I don't know how Mr Edwards puts up with it.'

'She was probably only trying to make us welcome. We're not the owners yet.'

'I suppose so. That housekeeper though, she looked like a sour mare.'

'Douglas!' She tapped his hand playfully and giggled.

He laughed too. 'Well, she did. If she keeps that up, I'll be tempted to replace her with someone who looks a little more cheerful.'

'Let's not judge them until we get to know them. If we do.'

A tray containing the tea set Helen had admired earlier arrived, brought over by a gentleman with a German accent. Shortly afterwards he brought in a silver salver of sumptuous yet delicate-looking pastries, more than they could hope to eat.

Around half-an-hour later, as they were finishing the last of the tea, Mr Edwards returned and stood by their table.

'I hope you've enjoyed your little impromptu afternoon tea.'

'Most delicious,' said Helen.

'Indeed, indeed,' Douglas agreed.

'And, um, what do you think about the hotel?' He looked hopeful.

'I think it might be time for a little negotiation,' said Douglas. 'Although luxurious, the hotel needs a lot of work to modernise it and is not worth the asking price.'

Mr Edwards sighed. 'Make me an offer, and we'll work from there.'

Helen and Douglas left the building smiling. They hadn't got it at the first price Douglas had suggested, which hadn't surprised Helen, given how ridiculously low it had been. But they had soon found a compromise that had satisfied both parties.

'Let us walk to the promenade and view the hotel from there,' Douglas said.

She took his arm and they made their way to the back of the hotel. All the while she looked up at the top floors of the building, visible above the surrounding wall.

Reaching the other side of it, they kept walking across the common towards the beach, passing an ornate stone fountain on the way.

'How thrilling it will be for us, to own a hotel,' she said. 'Especially one so grand. I am sure Mummy will be pleased with our investment.'

'Indeed, and so she should be, though we did agree that it will be in my name.'

'I know. Mummy did point out that women can own property now. They have been able to for some years. So we *could* own it together, in joint names.'

'But you know, well, you know I like to be the man of the house. Having it in joint names would make me feel somehow... emasculated.'

He looked down at the ground as they walked. Despite his outward confidence, she had always detected an inner lack of confidence in him. Maybe it was his humble beginnings as a blacksmith's son.

He regarded her now, his face sad. 'Do you not trust me? I'm not a gambler and a wastrel like your father was, frittering away his fortune and South Court Manor on drinking and gambling.'

Yes, her father had done exactly that. Their lovely home in Rustington, not far from the sea, in which her parents had lived since before she was born, had been sold six years before her father had died, and they had gone to live with his cousin, Eleanor, in

Arundel. Mummy had asked her own mother for accommodation, but Grandmama would only agree to accommodate Helen and her mother, not her father. Mummy would not agree to that.

'It was a good job your grandmother was wise enough to insist that your mother keep her inheritance in her own name.' He paused before continuing with, 'But that won't be necessary in our case.'

'Of course I trust you.' She gripped his arm more tightly for a moment.

She thought back to the day they met, on a visit to Arundel Castle, back in 1903. Helen had been immediately attracted to Douglas's kindness and charming manners. She had been afraid that her parents would have something to say about her walking out with someone below their station. Her father, however, had still felt too wretched from losing their home to be bothered about anything else. Her mother, Lady Rose, with her husband's disgrace, and not knowing at that time that she'd inherit her own money, had come to terms with the fact that Helen would inevitably marry below her station. And she'd liked Douglas, detecting his ambition and believing that he would be the best prospect her daughter could hope for. And so, they'd married in St Nicholas' church in Arundel in June 1905.

'It's our fifth anniversary next week,' said Helen.

'So it is. What better present for us both than acquiring the hotel. Though I'm sure I'll be able to rustle up another little present for you.'

He squeezed her hand affectionately and a contentment spread through her body.

They reached the promenade and turned to survey the Beach Hotel. There was a breeze, warm yet insistent. Helen enjoyed its gentle caress against her cheeks.

'It looks magnificent from here.' She felt a bubble of excitement, thinking of the years ahead.

'It certainly does. And I'm sure we can make it even more magnificent.' He lifted his chin as he sniffed in and adjusted his already neat tie.

Her dear Douglas, who had worked so hard as the manager of the Bridge Hotel in Arundel. He was an ambitious man, dedicated to his work. She was sure they'd make a real go of it.

Chapter One

Helen Bygrove was on desk duty in the foyer, adding a detail to the reservation book, when she heard the front doors of the hotel open, along with voices.

Lady Blackmore swept in with her companion, Cecelia, who was being talked down to as usual. Her ladyship was wearing a long, dark brown coat, undone to reveal a matching dress that was a few years out of date with its lengthy skirt, laced front panel, high neck and pinched-in waist. Around her neck was an extensive string of pearls. On her head sat a large hat with several long, curved feathers flowing out of a silver taffeta rosette. Cecelia's plain, wool coat, in black, was done up, but Helen could guarantee she would be wearing a plain blouse and skirt beneath, as she always did.

'Come along, Cecelia, let us get to morning coffee before the morning is over.'

'Sorry Lady Blackmore. My ankle is still sore from my fall.'

Poor Cecelia! Being harassed by her employer seemed to be part of her job description. Helen closed the reservation book, making her smile ready to greet these regular outside guests.

'Good morning, Lady Blackmore, Miss Cecelia.'

'Ah, Mrs Bygrove, I am so glad that you are on duty today.' Her ladyship strode to the desk, a black umbrella hooked over the arm of her coat. Cecelia trotted behind, limping a little.

'What can I do for you, my lady?'

Was this going to be some complaint about the decline of standards, or about there being less choice of fancies with coffee? Or, alternatively, a comment about what a shame it was that Douglas had been conscripted, and how on earth was she managing without him? Such comments from guests had been rife after he'd been sent away in June. They had dwindled over the summer, thankfully. However, these remarks had started up again after Douglas had been home on leave in the middle of September.

But Lady Blackmore had so far said nothing of the sort in the four months he'd been away, training at the Shoreham-by-Sea camp.

Her ladyship reached the desk. 'I was just saying to Cecelia here, how well the place has been run since Mr Bygrove went away, wasn't I, Cecelia?'

'You were, my lady.'

'Not that it was poorly run before, of course. But I was not very hopeful that you would be able to carry on without your husband. However, I have to say that, despite the increasing shortages, if anything, things seem more organised. And we don't get him in the conservatory every few days, fawning over those he deems to be *important*.'

'Lady Blackmore—' Cecelia started, in a slightly cautionary tone.

'No, Cecelia, I will say my piece. Despite my title, Mr Bygrove clearly considers me insignificant. You on the other hand, Mrs Bygrove, treat all the guests with equal importance. And you are doing an excellent job.'

Helen was stumped for a few seconds. Was Lady Blackmore suffering a bump on the head, or early signs of senile dementia?

'Well, um, thank you, my lady. I'm lucky to have a very dedicated staff.'

'I agree. I was sceptical when the men started to enlist and women took over their posts, but, I have to admit, they're doing an equally good job. If not better, in some cases. Is that not right, Cecelia?'

'It is, my lady.'

'I cannot help but agree about the women,' said Helen.

'I did not think that anyone could do as good a job of head waiter as poor old Günther, or Mr Smithson who followed him,' said her ladyship. 'But Lili has filled their shoes admirably.'

'Does anyone hear from Günther?' Cecelia asked.

Helen nodded. 'Phoebe, the deputy head waitress, writes to him at the internment camp in Newbury. He is apparently being treated well.'

'That is something.'

The doors opened once more. This time Helen's heart really did sink.

It was Isabella Harvey, a friend of Douglas's from the tennis and bowls club. She owned Selborne Place Guest House, an establishment two roads back from South Terrace, and was someone for whom Helen had little regard. She was certain the woman felt the same about her.

Unlike Lady Blackmore, Miss Harvey, despite being in her mid-forties, was now up to date with her couture, though it had not always been the case. Her navy-blue suit, with its ankle-length, full skirt and flared jacket with a high waist was very stylish, as was the saucer brimmed hat on her fair hair.

'Oh dear, not *her*,' muttered Lady Blackmore. 'How tiresome she is.'

Helen noticed Cecelia look down and half smile.

'Good morning to you, Lady Blackmore,' Miss Harvey pronounced effusively. She ignored Cecelia completely.

The answering, 'Good morning,' was said rather stiffly.

'I don't suppose you approve of the tennis courts being dug up any more than I, especially as you live nearby on South Terrace.'

Not this again. Both Lili Probert and Phoebe Sweeton, had reported this complaint from Miss Harvey on several occasions after she'd been in for either morning coffee or afternoon tea.

'What a *mess* it looks,' the woman added.

'*Actually*, I live on Empress Maud Road,' said her ladyship, looking down her nose at Miss Harvey.

'It's all the same, isn't it?' said Miss Harvey, laughing. 'That's just an old name for that part of the road. They're all numbered as if they are one road.'

'No, it is *not* the same.' Lady Blackmore looked most affronted. 'The houses between Pier Road and Augustine Road still belong to Empress Maud Road, and South Terrace does not start until after the tennis courts.'

'Well, I have it on good authority, from one of the councillors, that they consider it out of date and are thinking of changing the name to make it all South Terrace.'

'Not while *I* draw breath!'

Miss Harvey no longer looked so sure of herself. For someone who always liked to flatter those with titles and position, she had chosen a very contentious subject on this occasion.

'And as for the tennis courts being dug up, I think it was a jolly good idea. And Cecelia agrees, don't you, Cecelia.'

'Yes, my lady, for it's—'

'What Cecelia was no doubt about to say is that the gardeners have done a splendid job of planting up a vegetable garden, which, I am sure, will be needed by the hotel with the current shortages, which, I am certain, will only get worse.'

'That's right,' said Helen, determined to have her say. 'The vegetables we grow there have been a boon to the hotel.'

'And why, for *goodness* sake, would anyone be wasting their time playing tennis when there is work to be done towards the war effort,' said Lady Blackmore. 'I, myself, am now on several committees for raising funds for various good causes. And what encouraged me was Mrs Bygrove's excellent example, with all the charity events she has organised here at the hotel.'

'I *think* you'll find that *Mr* Bygrove organised those,' said Miss Harvey, looking smug.

Douglas would have told her that, and no doubt everyone else in his little golf, tennis and bowls groups.

'No no! I have it on good authority, from Miss Sophia Perryman no less, who runs the committees I'm on, that it was *Mrs* Bygrove here who organised them. Is that not right?'

She turned to Helen, who felt she had temporarily replaced Cecelia.

'That is correct, my lady. Douglas, my husband, trusted me to arrange things.'

She'd added the last bit in case it got back to him. She was convinced that Miss Harvey was writing to him. It was generally thought, among the staff, that she had a crush on him. They didn't know she knew, but she'd overheard Fanny Bullen and Gertie Green joking about it once to some of the others. It wasn't as if she hadn't suspected it herself. In fact, she had wondered, on more than one occasion, whether there was more to it.

'Well, I, um, was—' Miss Harvey stuttered.

'And instead of complaining about the lack of tennis courts,' said Lady Blackmore, 'you might, instead, think of joining one of our fundraising committees.'

Miss Harvey, composed once more, said, 'I will give it due consideration, my lady.'

How interesting, that both these women were difficult, yet clearly did not see eye to eye. But the fact they were both so trying was likely the reason for it.

Several uniformed men entered the hotel, all officers who had visited before. Helen was keen to greet them, as much to end the current contentious conversation as to welcome them.

'Good morning, gentlemen,' she called as they approached the desk.

'Good morning, Mrs Bygrove. I assume we can go through to the conservatory for coffee?'

'Of course, Captain Harries.'

As the men moved on, Helen was hoping the ladies would take their lead, but Miss Harvey stalled them with, 'Have you heard about those letters received by some people in Beach Town?'

'No, I haven't,' said Helen.

Lady Blackmore turned to face them once more. 'What letters are these?'

'Oh, *dreadful* missives, sent to some of the guest house proprietors, including myself, and also to Mr and Mrs Johnson at the dairy and the landlord of the New Inn. They are absolutely scandalous, sent by an anonymous person. They claimed either that the sendee was an awful person, or that someone of their acquaintance was and that they should not socialise with them. And there are a lot of...' She leant forward to whisper, 'Profanities.' Straightening herself up once more, she continued with, 'The language was *quite* shocking. If the secrets they are revealing are true, there will be *many* reputations ruined. And if they are not true, then whoever is sending them will find themselves in court on many counts of libel, and their own life ruined. Presumably, neither of you have received one then?'

'What reason would they have to send *me* one?' Lady Blackmore made herself taller as she frowned at Miss Harvey.

'None, of course not, and neither did they have reason to send them to me or the other recipients. It was just plain unpleasantness. I've reported it to Detective Inspector Toshack and made sure the others did so too, those whom I know have received them. There may be others. I will ask around.'

Cecelia stepped forward timidly. 'Is this Detective Inspector Toshack the replacement for DI Davis?'

'That's correct. It took them long enough. From north of the border, by the sound of him,' Miss Harvey said dismissively.

Cecelia was about to speak once more, when Lady Blackmore said, 'I'm sure this Inspector Toshack and Sergeant Gardner will get to the bottom of it. In the meantime, I would like a cup of coffee. Come along, Cecelia.'

'Yes, Lady Blackmore.'

Despite the two women heading away, Miss Harvey stayed put, much to Helen's disappointment. She glanced at the grandfather clock. Ten twenty-seven. Edie should be here any moment to take over.

'How is Douglas getting on? Have you had any correspondence?'

Helen certainly wasn't about to tell this woman of his constant complaining and showing off in his letters, so simply went with, 'Fine, fine. He's due to go overseas in the new year, I believe.'

Didn't she already know this? Maybe she was wrong about them corresponding, yet how else had he found out about her having the tennis courts dug up? Or perhaps she was writing to him, but he wasn't replying? She was surprised to realise that she didn't really care either way. That, in turn, made her sad.

'It is *such* a pity he was called up. He was the beating heart of this hotel.'

Beating heart?

Helen had no time to consider this familiar phrase because a well-dressed man in a blue striped suit, navy mackintosh and a grey fedora entered the foyer. His appearance gave her quite a start, but in a pleasant way. She wasn't sure why.

After looking around the foyer and seeming impressed, he approached the desk, frowning. Helen noted the dark brown hair, the large blue eyes and the dimples. She would have thought him handsome indeed, had his countenance not been so serious. He was tall, likely well over six feet.

Miss Harvey greeted him with a smile. 'Why, Inspector. Fancy seeing you here. We meet again.'

'Good morning, Miss Harvey,' he said, somewhat shortly. He turned his attention to Helen. 'I am Detective Inspector Toshack. Could I speak to the manager, please?' There was a Scottish lilt to his accent.

'Good morning, Inspector. I am currently the manageress, as my husband is now in the army.'

'In that case, I would like to speak to you.'

'Of course, in one moment, as my replacement on the desk is due about now. In the meantime, Miss Harvey, do go through to the conservatory.'

The woman looked disappointed. She hesitated before moving off without a word.

DI Toshack, meanwhile, was tapping the fingers of one hand on the desk, somewhat impatiently. 'How long exactly, before your replacement arrives?'

The door to the staff corridor opened and Edie emerged, a few seconds before the clock chimed the half hour.

'Here she is,' said Helen. 'Perhaps we could conduct this conversation in my office?'

He held out his hand. 'Lead the way.'

'Edie, I will be in the office, should anyone need me.'

'Very well, Helen.'

'Edie Moore is my undermanageress,' she told Toshack as she led him to the staff corridor. They turned right part way down, into a smaller, narrower passageway, which led to the office.

Inside, she sat at the desk, indicating that he should take the seat on the other side.

'I'll stand, thank you.'

'Is this about the anonymous letters some people have been receiving?'

'You know about them then?' He narrowed his eyes.

'Only since five minutes ago, when Miss Harvey informed me of them.'

'You haven't received any yourself?'

'I have not, no.'

'That's surprising, given that many of the proprietors of the bigger guest houses in the area have received them.'

'Is that just in Beach Town? Miss Harvey hinted as such.'

He blew out impatiently. 'Since I have *no* idea what this *Beach Town* refers to, I can't answer that.'

'It's a local name for the area around the beach and the streets behind South Terrace, as opposed to the area around the river and the town.'

'It doesn't matter where exactly they've been received, only who has received them, and, ultimately, who has sent them.'

'I can help you with neither I'm afraid, Inspector.'

'You may be able to.'

'How so?'

He pulled a face, as if in pain, and held onto the back of the chair, lifting his left leg a little. When he was composed once more, he said, 'How many employees do you have here at the hotel?'

'Twelve live-in staff, and twenty-five live-out staff, including gardeners, plus the attendant who looks after our private hotel garage and lives in the cottage next door. Thirty-eight in all.'

'I will need samples of all their handwriting.'

'I will certainly try, though one or two may not be terribly literate.'

'Then it won't have been them who wrote the letters, will it?'

Normally she'd have been happy to cooperate with the police, but his tone was making her feel rebellious. 'May I ask why my staff are being singled out? Are others being asked to produce samples?'

'Some, yes. But there are things written in the letters received, implying that someone in the immediate vicinity, and working in an establishment such as this, has sent them.'

Helen felt a little annoyed by this accusation. 'Why would any of my staff have reason to do that? If anything, the fact that we're the premier hotel in the area is more likely to provoke jealousy and make *us* the target.'

'But you haven't received any letters.'

'Not yet, no.'

'I will call back in a couple of days to collect the samples.'

'Not everyone will have been in work by then.'

'Then you must do your best. And I will need your handwriting too.' He looked her squarely in the eyes, almost as if he were… accusing her?

'Of course.'

'Thank you. I'll find my own way out.'

As he turned, she asked, 'May I enquire whether you are DI Davis's replacement?' even though she knew he was.

'Aye, that's right. Good day to you.'

He walked slowly towards the door, turning only briefly to consider her, before he opened the door and left.

That was an *interesting* introduction to the new inspector, she thought. Although DI Davis could be firm, he'd always been charming. She didn't know what to make of this man. It was as if he resented doing his job. Or resented being in Littlehampton?

Yet... There was something else she couldn't quite put her finger on. She pictured his face, his expression. Sadness. Was that it? Or had she imagined it?

She chuckled at the fanciful notion, rising to go to the drawers. From here she took a few sheets of writing paper with the hotel crest and address on and several pencils.

Beating heart. That was it! She knew she'd heard the expression Miss Harvey had used somewhere recently. It was when Douglas had appeared before the tribunal, to apply for an exemption from conscription, back in June. He'd described himself to the panel as the *beating heart* of the hotel.

Was it a coincidence that Miss Harvey had used the same expression?

Either way, Douglas's claim had not swung the tribunal's decision in his favour, and he'd had his application for exemption turned down. And then he had blamed it on her, saying she hadn't supported his claims enough. Maybe he'd been right, but she hadn't wanted to lie, and she had been certain that they had already made up their minds.

Remembering a meeting she had planned with her cook, Mrs Norris, she placed the pencils and paper on the desk and headed for the office door. The handwriting samples would have to wait until later.

—

It was the start of the late afternoon tea break when Helen finally walked into the staff dining room. With her were two new members of staff. The pens and paper she'd brought in she placed on the dresser.

They'd only just started lighting the large fire in here again, after the summer and early autumn. The scent of it always reminded her of the fires in South Court Manor.

At the table were Nelly Norris, head waitress Lili Probert, storekeeper Bridget Turnbull and head portress Gertie Green.

Imogen Leggett, the housekeeper, was sitting at the head of the table, as always.

Fanny Bullen, the head chambermaid, was sitting opposite the housekeeper, her six-month-old baby Elsie on her lap, sleeping. As she looked down at her lovingly, she pulled the cap from her tawny bun.

Since Douglas had been conscripted, Helen had taken to joining the staff in the dining room more often. Not too often, as she didn't want them thinking that management was watching them, but for one tea break every couple of days. It was interesting to hear their thoughts on aspects of the hotel's running.

And it was nice to have some adult company. She had lost touch with most of her friends since marrying Douglas.

'Good afternoon, everyone,' Helen began. 'I'd like to introduce you to Ada Saltmarsh and Jessie Jessup, our two new live-out chambermaids. I've been showing them both around.'

Ada was short, with a small build, her blonde hair piled up into a neat hairstyle. Jessie, on the other hand, was tall and broad shouldered, her dark brown hair in a long, thick plait down her back.

'Jessie Jessup?' said Mrs Leggett. 'That's rather a lot of Js and Ss.'

'Only two Js,' said Jessie, frowning. 'And four Ss. My teacher used to say it rolls off the tongue 'cos it's alliteration.'

'They'll both be starting work tomorrow,' Helen put in quickly, afraid the housekeeper would take umbrage at the new chambermaid's forwardness before she'd even started the job. 'We'll join you for a cup of tea, if you don't mind. That way, Ada and Jessie can get to know you all a little. Sit down ladies and help yourself to tea and biscuits.'

Ada seemed a little hesitant, but Jessie was straight in, with a 'Don't mind if I do.' Helen only hoped her directness wasn't going to be a problem with the others, especially Mrs Leggett.

'It's a shame all your young men have gone off to war,' said Jessie. 'I'd have liked to have got to know them.' She gave a cheeky smile. 'I knew your porters, the twins, Stanley and Leslie, a bit. They live on my street. Or did, before they were conscripted.'

'Your jobs would be carried out quite separately,' said Mrs Leggett, 'so you would *not* have seen much of them.'

'But I'd have seen 'em at breaks and mealtimes.'

'You ain't missing much,' said Gertie, chuckling. 'But some of them are still 'ere, on the desk, or in the kitchen—'

'But they're quite, well, *old*,' said Jessie.

'I was gonna say, and Jack, also in the kitchen. He ain't old. He's only nineteen.'

'Bit young for me. I'm twenny-three.' Jessie giggled, then looked serious as she asked, 'Is he a pasty facer, or something?'

'A *what*?' said Mrs Leggett.

'A pasty facer. A conchie.'

'A conscientious objector?' said Gertie. 'No, he ain't nothing like that.'

'Why ain't he at war then?'

'Flat feet.'

'Anyway,' said Helen, pointing to one end of the table. 'This is Fanny, our head chambermaid.'

'That's me,' she said, beaming. 'I'll be showing you the ropes tomorrow and guiding you through your duties. Have you done this work before?' She looked at each of the newcomers in turn.

'Nah, I worked in me dad's shop, but he retired last month,' said Jessie.

'I have,' said Ada, putting a hand up timidly, as if she were in school. 'Only in a guest house, though.'

'That's a start,' said Fanny. 'And Jessie, I'm sure you'll pick it up soon enough. Edie, who's now our undermanageress, had never done any cleaning before she became a chambermaid, and she soon picked it up.'

'What, Miss Moore, what's on the desk right now?' said Jessie. 'She looks too posh to be a cleaner.'

Various members of staff glanced at each other before Helen said, 'That's a story for another time.'

27

'Anyway,' Fanny continued. 'If you have any problems while you're working, I'll be there to 'elp you.'

'What a sweet baby,' said Ada, who'd taken the seat next to Fanny. 'I suppose her daddy's at war, poor little mite.' She looked sad, making Helen wonder if she was thinking of her own sweetheart or a member of her family.

'Um, yes, that's right,' said Fanny, whose smile had slipped a little.

While it was true that Elsie's father was at war, it was also a fact that he and Fanny were not married. He'd broken up with her when she'd told him she was pregnant. But the new members of staff didn't need to know that.

'I hear that new detective inspector came in today,' said Fanny, maybe to change the subject. 'I'm told 'e's quite 'andsome.' She lifted her eyebrows twice.

'He certainly came in,' said Helen. 'Whether you think him handsome is a matter of taste, I suppose.' Even as she said it, she realised that she was being a hypocrite. Hadn't she thought the same? But any good looks he possessed had certainly been diminished by his curtness.

Lili passed the teapot to Helen. 'Edie spent a couple of hours with her friend Julia Nye this morning, who's engaged to the previous detective inspector. I spoke to them before they went for their walk. Julia said the inspector was invalided out of the army and apparently has a false leg.'

'It didn't look like it when he walked in and out,' said Helen. Though, thinking about it, there had been that moment in her office when he'd shifted his leg and had looked a little in pain.

Jessie leant forward and considered Lili. 'Where's that accent from then? Scotland?'

Lili pulled a face. 'Scotland? No. South Wales, isn't it.'

'Oh. Don't know no one from there.'

'You do now,' said Lili, her dark eyes shining as she beamed.

There was a tap at the dining room door, which was unusual. People normally just strolled in.

'Knock knock,' came a female voice. The door was pushed open a little more. 'Hello Mrs Bygrove, I hope I'm not disturbing you. The scullery maid said you were in here and to just come through.'

'Oh Miss Nye,' said Helen. 'How strange. We were just talking about you.'

Julia looked a little alarmed.

Helen laughed. 'Don't look so worried. Come and sit down and have a cup of tea. You know you're always welcome. Lili was telling us what you said about the new inspector being invalided out of the army with a false leg.'

'That's right. He was a DI in Hartlepool before the war. He apparently had a short spell in Horsham recently, before being sent here.'

Mrs Norris leant over to offer Julia one of her own homemade biscuits. 'Can't see him being no good at running after criminals.'

'He's got Sergeant Gardner for that,' said Gertie.

'He's not getting no younger neither.'

'Sadly,' Julia started, pausing before carrying on. 'His wife was apparently killed during the German bombardment of Hartlepool, back in December 1914.'

Helen glanced at Mrs Turnbull, as did several others there. She had lost a brother-in-law and nephew in the same raid.

'Aye,' said the storekeeper. 'Too many good folk were lost that day.'

'I'm sorry, Mrs Turnbull,' said Helen. 'I don't suppose you needed to be reminded of it.'

'I am so sorry,' said Julia. 'Of course. Edie did tell me about your loss at the time.'

'Don't worry yoursel' pet. It's not like I can ever forget it.'

'Have you got menfolk in the war?' Gertie asked, regarding the two newcomers.

'Me four bruvvers,' said Jessie.

'That must be a worry, pet.' Mrs Turnbull patted her hand and she nodded glumly.

29

'I don't have any siblings,' said Ada, whose accent was a little more genteel than Jessie's. 'And my father's too old for service. But a couple of my cousins are in the army.'

Helen wondered, not for the first time, about Ada's likely middle-class roots, and why she would want a job as a chambermaid. But then Edie had been the daughter of a baron when she'd joined the hotel just before the war. She still was, of course, but she never used her 'honourable' title and was estranged from her parents. Not that any of them had known that in the beginning.

'These are our two new chambermaids, Ada and Jessie,' Helen told Julia.

'I remember you,' said Jessie. 'You taught my youngest sister, Rosie, at East Street School.'

'Would that be Rosie Jessup?'

'That's right. Fancy you remembering, Miss.'

'Of course I do. She was very good at arithmetic.'

'Yep, that's our Rosie. Doing accounts at Dando's she is now, as the man what was doing it's gone to war.'

'Returning to the subject of DI Toshack,' said Mrs Leggett. 'Why exactly did he come in? Just to introduce himself?'

Helen took a deep breath before telling them, adding what Miss Harvey had told her about the anonymous letters.

'I heard about the letters from one of the mothers in school, who lives on Western Road,' said Julia. 'She reckoned that some of the so-called revelations were quite... indecent.'

'That's a good point,' said Helen, turning towards Ada. 'You live on Western Road, don't you? Have you heard about these letters?'

'I can't say I have.'

'I 'eard about them when I went to the shops on Norfolk Road, a coupla days back,' said Gertie.

'You didn't tell us,' said Fanny.

'I musta forgot. I wonder who could be sending them?'

'I wouldn't be surprised if it weren't Miss Harvey herself.' She and Gertie giggled.

Mrs Leggett tutted. 'This is *not* a laughing matter. And claiming such a thing is as libellous as the letters themselves. Well, slanderous, anyway, since you said it rather than wrote it.'

Fanny raised her eyes heavenward.

'Indeed,' said Helen. 'And at the moment, everyone is open to suspicion, which is why the inspector has requested samples of handwriting from everyone who works here. And that is why I've brought the pencils and paper.' She pointed to the dresser.

'As if the person responsible couldn't hide their writing,' said Mrs Leggett.

'I don't disagree, Imogen. However, if you'd please each take a piece of paper and write... well, the inspector didn't specify anything in particular. Write your full names and then – maybe a couple of sentences of anything you'd like. A poem, perhaps.'

'I don't know no poems,' said Gertie.

'Whatever you like then,' said Helen. 'Just a few lines. The inspector wants to collect them in a couple of days. Please tell the rest of the staff when you see them, in case I haven't caught up with them.'

Lili leant over and picked up the teapot to pour herself another cup. 'Major Thomas was telling me at afternoon tea about a German destroyer raid in Dover Straits.'

'That's not that far from here,' said Mrs Turnbull. 'And they're right by the coast, like us.'

'We're not quite as accessible here to destroyers as Dover is,' said Julia. 'It faces more to the east than Littlehampton does.'

'But the navy's using the river 'ere,' said Gertie, 'and that might encourage the Germans to come this way.'

The last thing Helen needed was for her staff to start panicking about attacks. 'There's no point fretting about it at the moment. I'm sure Miss Nye is right. And a lot of people have escaped the east coast to come to us, in the belief that they're safer here. And I'm sure they will be.'

'That's right,' said Mrs Leggett. 'Let's not frighten our guests with unlikely scenarios.'

'Well, young Ada and Jessie, you've certainly had a taste of breaktimes 'ere at the Beach,' said Mrs Norris. 'We're indeed ones for discussion and chatter 'ere. 'Ope we 'aven't put you off.'

'Nah, it's always been like that in our family,' said Jessie. 'What wiv us ten children. Got five sisters too, see, and I'm the third youngest.'

'Thought having two older brothers and two older sisters was bad enough, I did!' Lili said, chuckling. 'I can't imagine having even more.'

'I'm an only child,' said Ada, 'so it's very quiet in my house. But I think I'm going to like it here.'

'Me too,' said Jessie. 'It'll be a real 'ome from 'ome.'

Mrs Leggett stood, clapping her hands. 'Tea break is over. Time to get back to work.'

'And I must get back to my lesson preparation,' said Julia. 'I only dropped by to bring a book I said I'd lend Dorothy. She told me today that she couldn't find it in the library. Her reading is coming on tremendously, so I'm sure she'll manage it fine.' She took a copy of *Dorothy and the Wizard of Oz* out of her wicker basket and laid it on the table.

'That's very kind of you,' said Helen. 'She certainly whizzed through the first three of Mr Baum's Oz books quickly. I think she imagines she *is* Dorothy, having the same name.' She chuckled. 'I will make sure she looks after it.'

'I'm sure she will. She is the tidiest of my pupils.'

'Wouldn't mind reading that meself,' said Fanny, tipping her head to look at the cover.

'You're welcome to borrow it, when she's finished,' said Julia. Fanny looked pleasantly surprised. 'Oh. Thank you, Miss Nye.'

With the tea break over, and Julia leaving, Helen took that as her cue to show the new recruits the rest of the staff area.

Chapter Two

It was a beautiful Sunday morning as Helen stood at the desk in the foyer, considering it was nearly the end of October. She had a couple of hours free soon, before the busy lunchtime, and was looking forward to taking a walk out with the children and their nursemaid, Vera.

She checked her watch. Only ten minutes before Mr Watkins, the head desk clerk, came to replace her. He'd been at his mother's house in Lancing since Friday and was due back today. Hopefully his train wouldn't be late.

Hearing the entrance doors open, she made her smile ready to welcome a current guest or a morning coffee visitor. Her heart sank. It was Detective Inspector Toshack.

She'd suspected that he'd be back today and had placed the required handwriting samples, pinned together with a paperclip in a card folder, on the lower ledge of the desk. Attached to it was a piece of paper with instructions that the folder was to be handed to the inspector when he arrived. She had hoped that it would be on someone else's shift. With any luck, he wouldn't delay her departure.

'Good morning, Inspector,' she said, as he approached the desk. 'I assume you've come for these?' She lifted the folder, ready to hand to him.

He stopped just short of the desk, not taking the samples at first.

'That's very organised.' He pointed to the folder.

'I have to be, running a hotel, particularly with paperwork.'

'Aye, I suppose you do.'

As he took the folder from her, their hands touched briefly. His skin was soft and warm. Helen realised it had been a long time since she'd touched a man's hand. The thought saddened her for a moment.

Mr Watkins entered the foyer from the staff corridor, holding open the door for Vera as she pushed Elsie out in the perambulator. Behind them came Dorothy and Arthur.

They all approached the desk as Helen said, 'I was wondering whether people could disguise their handwriting, therefore making the samples... insufficient evidence?'

'Even if they've tried to disguise it, there's often some little clue that gives them away.'

'I see. If that's all, Mr Watkins has come to take over, and I'm off for a pre-prandial walk with the nursemaid and children.'

It occurred to Helen that Mr Watkins's handwriting would not have been included in the samples, but the thought that he might be the perpetrator of the scandalous letters was laughable.

Elsie, lying under a mass of blankets, started making a fuss.

Inspector Toshack looked awkward. 'Well, I'll leave you to your walk, since your baby is anxious and would probably be happier moving.'

'Oh, Elsie is not my baby, though the other two are my children. Elsie belongs to one of the live-in staff.'

'I see.' He gazed at the children for a moment, his mouth down at the corners. He seemed to come to, then shuffled a few steps back. 'Good day, Mrs Bygrove. I may well be in touch again.'

'Good day, Inspector.'

He twisted around and headed for the exit. Now she looked, there was something slightly awkward about his gait, though it wasn't anything she would have noticed had she not been told about his false leg.

Turning towards the head desk clerk she said, 'Thank you, Mr Watkins, for being so prompt.'

'You know me, Mrs Bygrove, I hate being tardy. Now, you enjoy your walk.'

Vera lifted Elsie into a sitting position, something the baby had been able to sustain for the last month.

'There you are, lovey. Is that better?' said Vera.

As if in reply, Elsie stopped crying immediately and giggled.

'I think you have your answer,' said Helen, as they set off towards the exit.

When they reached the hotel's front courtyard, Inspector Toshack was just leaving via the front gate. Helen recalled the expression on his face when he'd regarded the children. Lili had mentioned his wife, but not whether there had been any offspring. If so, could they also have been lost in the Hartlepool raids? How very sad, if that were the case.

'Which way, madam?' Vera said, as they exited the gate.

'Let's go left and enter the common that way.'

As they turned to do just that, a tandem passed by with two young ladies on it, cycling in the direction of the river. Dorothy started singing, *Daisy Bell*, and Arthur soon joined in.

'*Daisy, Daisy, give me your answer do...*'

Helen spotted the inspector once more, waiting for the tandem to pass before crossing to the other side of the street. They'd reached the right side of the hotel's surrounding wall now, and turned left to head across the grass of the common, as the children ended the song with, '*On a bicycle made for two.*'

'Mummy, will there be any donkeys or goat carriages to ride today?' asked Arthur.

'I think it unlikely, being the end of October, but you never know, with the weather being so nice. If not, I see Vera has brought a bag of buckets and spades, and you can also have a paddle. The sea shouldn't be too cold yet.'

'All right, Mummy.' Arthur sounded disappointed yet accepting of the situation.

Helen glanced once more in the inspector's direction, as he disappeared down Beach Road.

Now she could forget him and the infernal writing samples and enjoy this time with her children.

'I have brought the toy yachts as well,' Vera said, holding up a second bag.

'Then perhaps we could head to the Oyster Pond first, and visit the beach on the way back.'

'Hooray!' Arthur called, turning right and running westwards, followed by his sister.

Being a Sunday, and a warm one at that, the common and promenade were busy with people taking a stroll. Helen looked over towards the bandstand as they passed it, which was close to the beach. There was a brass band getting ready to play, but it would likely be the last day they would perform here, until the spring. The performances of the Pierrots and the commercial tents and huts of the beach had already shut up shop for winter.

It always saddened her when the season came to an end, even though the hotel would still have plenty of custom from the wealthy visitors. But it wasn't the same as the bustle and glee of the ordinary holiday makers, here for a short time on a well-appreciated holiday.

They neared the buildings close to the river, the coastguards' cottages, windmill, tearoom and Casino Theatre, on the eastern end of the common. The children had already reached the large, round pond on the right, once a place to store oysters, and now popular for sailing toy yachts. Vera hurried towards them, then removed the boats from the bag and handed them one each as Helen caught up with them.

They'd been sailing the boats for about fifteen minutes, when Arthur stood bolt upright.

'Look Mummy, one of those navy dazzly ships.' He pointed towards the river.

'It's called dazzle *camouflage*,' Dorothy corrected. 'And they're very *common* here now, since the *Admiralty* took over the harbour.'

Oh dear, she sounded rather pompous, like her father, heaven forbid, thought Helen.

'I still like to see them,' he said, undaunted by her superior attitude. 'They're weird, like something out of a fairy tale.'

'They're just ships painted to confuse the enemy when they try to torpedo them, silly.'

'I know that.' Arthur raised his eyes heavenward.

'Enough of that now,' said Vera. 'We don't want to get into an argument on our nice walk out, do we?'

'Shall we gather up the yachts and head to the beach?' Helen suggested.

'Yes please!' the children both called.

With the boats collected, they strolled up the slight incline to the wide path by the river. Helen glanced to the right, inland, down Pier Road, where the fishermen kept their boats and nets on the shore side, opposite their cottages. Further down she spied the warehouses on the river's edge.

They turned left, towards the river's mouth, strolling past the windmill, theatre and old gun battery mound, towards the small pier and the beach. Arthur, having initially skipped ahead, fell back to take Helen's hand. His skin was warm and soft, reminding her of the sensation of touching Detective Inspector Toshack's hand earlier. She had a brief image of walking along here, holding a man's hand.

What man though? Douglas hadn't been one for holding hands for a long time. And she'd certainly never be holding the DI's hand. What a thought!

'Oh look, someone's actually selling ginger beer today,' said Helen. 'Let's get some before we head onto the sand.'

And hopefully she'd forget any daft and unlikely scenarios, like holding a man's hand.

–

Helen opened the door into the dining room on the first evening of November to carry out her usual inspection before dinner. It was a relief to get out of the cramped office, where she'd been double checking the accounts and reviewing staff rotas.

The young waiters, Simon Lane and Dennis Ward, were laying up the tables, while Lili was standing by the dresser, polishing cutlery.

'Good evening, Mrs Bygrove,' said Lili, laying down a fork.

'It's all looking splendid in here, as usual.'

'Especially since you had the walls painted pale yellow.'

It had taken a while to find decorators who hadn't been conscripted, but there were still a few older gentlemen in business. She'd had to wait a while before the one she'd chosen could fit the hotel in, with them all being in demand.

'We've had a lot of compliments about it,' Lili continued. 'People say it's more… cheerful than the grey.'

Douglas had chosen the insipid shade of grey there before, saying it was sophisticated and showed class. She'd never been fond of it. Goodness knows what he'd say when he came home next, but it wasn't as if they could keep things here the same forever. No doubt he would be cross that she hadn't asked his permission, but if she did that about everything in the hotel, she'd be forever writing to him and getting nothing else done. She had to think what to do in the private dining room next.

'I'm glad people like it. I'll leave you to it, as it's only half-an-hour until dinner begins.'

She left the room and walked through the foyer on her way to the private dining room. It would be empty this evening, as it was most days, although she had taken a number of bookings for the Christmas period.

In the dining room she looked around at the pastel green walls and the long, mid-green curtains. There were wooden panels on the bottom half of the walls. They'd re-painted this room when they'd first arrived, as they had much of the hotel. By *they*, she of course meant *he*. Douglas had let her have little say in the updated décor. It was tempting to change the colour in here, just because she could. But she liked this green. It could do with a new coat of paint, but she would opt for the same colour. Besides, she didn't want to have to change the curtains, which matched it beautifully.

She wondered whether this room might be better employed as a lounge for the guests. She'd mentioned the lack of one to Douglas on more than one occasion, but he'd always said that the guests' rooms *were* their lounges, and they could always sit in the conservatory when it wasn't serving morning coffee or afternoon tea. It was something to think about, nevertheless.

Helen stepped back into the foyer, just as Sir Lucas Finlay and his wife, Lady Serena, reached the bottom step of the sweeping staircase. He was attired in an evening suit, underneath his wide, unbuttoned swagger-style coat. Her ladyship was wearing a mink coat. Helen glimpsed the bottom of her sateen dress, with its long, loose overskirt that was divided in the front. Her pleated hat had a narrow brim with a cascade of silk roses over the front of the crown.

'Good evening, sir, my lady.'

'Good evening, Mrs Bygrove,' Sir Lucas replied. 'I'd just like to say what a splendid luncheon we had here today. Given the shortages and whatnot, your chef is doing a marvellous job. And the room is top notch.'

'I'm glad it has your approval,' said Helen. 'And I shall pass your compliments on to Mrs Norris in the kitchen.'

The couple had reached the middle of the foyer, when he stopped, looking surprised. 'A woman chef, eh. Well, needs must, I suppose, in these days of war. A jolly good job she's doing too. Full marks.'

Several words, like *condescending* and *chauvinistic*, came to Helen's mind, but she simply replied, 'Thank you.'

Gertie came through the front doors, announcing, 'Your motor taxi has arrived, sir.'

'Excellent. Thank you, Gertrude.' He turned back to Helen. 'We're off to a little soiree at Arundel Castle, with the Fitzalan-Howards.'

'I'm sure you'll have a wonderful time.'

He held out his arm and Lady Serena took it, before they marched out of the doors, opened for them by Gertie.

Helen made her way over to the desk. 'Everything all right, Mr Watkins?'

'Everything's fine, thank you, Mrs Bygrove. We're in a bit of a hiatus at the moment, but I dare say it will get busier as people come down, and in, for dinner.'

'Yes. I believe we're fully booked tonight.'

'Indeed, madam.'

Helen glanced at the grandfather clock in the foyer. She'd better go back to the office to pick up the list of items she wished to discuss with Edie and Mrs Leggett in a while. Then she just might get some time with the children before they went to bed. And later, she had a meeting with all the staff to discuss some Christmas ideas.

Many of the live-in staff, and a few live-outs, had gathered in the staff dining room for the late meeting. Helen was waiting now for Mrs Leggett and Mrs Turnbull before she began, as they'd been delayed in the storeroom for some reason that they seemed to think was important.

'Another year without fireworks,' said Fanny, looking sad. 'I do miss 'em. I 'ope the government lifts the ban, once this war's over.'

'Didn't you used to do them here, at the hotel?' asked Ada, sitting next to her.

'Oh yes,' said Alice Twine, one of the scullery maids. 'They did a real good show 'ere.'

'It was for the guests,' said her sister, Annie, 'but people used to come from all over town to see 'em.'

'I remember 'em,' said Jessie, sitting with the sisters, with whom she'd become quite friendly. 'Me mum and dad used to bring us all down 'ere to see 'em as kids.'

'It was Mr Edwards, the previous owner, who started the tradition,' said Helen. 'Douglas – Mr Bygrove – and I, decided it was worth carrying on.'

'I think they got even better when you took over,' said Mrs Norris. 'Never mind, it won't be too long before the 'otel will be getting all Christmassy.'

'I'm really looking forward to it,' said Fanny. 'Elsie's first Christmas.' She sniffed loudly, her face creasing a little, before she pulled a handkerchief from her pocket to dab her eyes.

'What on earth is wrong?' said Helen, leaning over the table to take Fanny's hand.

'Oh, nuffin', really. Just grateful to you, that Elsie and I 'ave an 'ome 'ere. And Vera's lovely with 'er when I'm working.'

'Didn't you 'ave an 'ome with 'er dad?' asked Jessie.

Fanny looked awkward. Helen was wondering what to say to cover up the situation when Fanny replied with, 'When 'e went away, I couldn't afford a place on me own.'

The second half of that was at least true, and the first part could mean a few things. Though the two newcomers were bound to find out the circumstances eventually, hopefully it wouldn't be until they'd worked here long enough to have some loyalty.

Mrs Leggett marched into the room at this point, with Mrs Turnbull not far behind.

'I'm sorry we're late,' said the housekeeper, standing to attention. 'Miss Bullen reported that certain cleaning products had gone missing, and I was helping Mrs Turnbull look for them.'

'Did you find 'em?' said Fanny. 'I'm sure they were there yesterday. I check the supplies twice a day.'

'No, we didn't,' said Mrs Turnbull. 'And I'm sure you're right about the quantity what was there, pet, for I have it all written down.'

Helen experienced a wave of stress. Just as things seemed to be going reasonably well, she didn't need a new problem. 'What has gone missing, exactly?'

'Two canisters of Vim, three bottles of Jeyes fluid and three bottles of linseed oil.' Mrs Leggett sounded as peeved as Helen felt. 'I know it doesn't sound like a lot, but they have been in shorter supply in the shops of late. And I suspect it's not the first time this has happened, though I can't be sure. Recently I suspected that tins of bees' wax had gone missing.'

'It would be a nuisance to have to keep the stores locked the whole time,' said Helen, 'but you might have to.'

Mrs Turnbull's brow creased and she looked dismayed. 'But it's handy for cleanin' staff to be able to pop in and fetch what they need without havin' to come and find me every time.'

'Mrs Leggett, Mrs Norris and I also have keys, of course, but it might be handy if Fanny had one too, as head chambermaid, and the most senior of all the maids.' Helen glanced at Fanny, noticing her grin. 'Go to the locksmiths tomorrow to get her one cut, Bridget.'

'Aye, that's a grand idea,' said Mrs Turnbull, smiling now.

'I hope this is not the start of a spate of pilfering.' Mrs Leggett looked around at the staff there, her eyes narrowed.

Helen hoped not too. She also wondered whether it had been wise mentioning it in front of the two newest members of staff. Might one of them be responsible? Jessie came from quite a poor family, but she shouldn't jump to conclusions. And she needed to move things along.

'Let's start this meeting, before it gets too late… I'd like to discuss ideas for Christmas, particularly involving fundraising. Our concert last year, to collect money towards Christmas boxes for the men abroad, was a big success, and Mr Janus has agreed to organise the acts again, if we hold it in the ballroom once more.'

'Mr Janus?' Jessie queried.

'He's the owner of the Casino Theatre up by the windmill, and of much of the entertainments on the common in the summer, including the Pierrots.'

'Oh 'im, right.'

'Some of the chamber and other maids have helped at these events, welcoming patrons to their seats and giving out refreshments in the interval.'

'I'd like to do that. I like to think me bruvvers are being looked after in the war, especially at Christmas.' Jessie looked sad.

'That's why we do it,' said Helen.

'It's a great idea,' one of the housemaids called out.

'I've also had another idea,' said Helen. 'I'd like to open up the hotel during December, two lunchtimes a week, for cheap meals for anyone to come and eat. Good hearty stews and soups, that kind of thing.'

'That's what we'll end up serving to our regular customers if the shortages keep going,' said Jack Sinden, the young second chef.

'Not on my watch,' said Mrs Norris, standing by the fire, her hands folded under her bosom. 'I can make the plainest food look fancy, and I've got a good, skilled team in the kitchen, including you, Jack, so don't you go putting yourself down. And I'm sure we can make them hearty stews for ordinary folk special too, especially with the winter veg we're growing and our pantry full of our own dried 'erbs.'

'For how long though, if meat and whatnot gets even more in short supply, or starts to be rationed?' said Alice, sitting near her. 'Maybe the posh folk need to lower their expectations.'

'Let's cross that bridge when, and if, we come to it,' said Helen, wanting to make her staff feel less negative. And herself too. 'And at least we can still offer comfortable and luxurious accommodation, and this we *must* keep to the very highest standards.'

'I shall make sure of that,' said Mrs Leggett, still near the door, standing tall.

'Me too,' said Fanny.

'I'm going to leave some paper on the dresser—' Helen started.

'The inspector don't want more handwriting samples, does he?' said Alice, slumped in her seat.

'No, no,' Helen laughed. 'It's for you all to write any ideas you have about Christmas activities to raise money. We also had a short carol concert last year, as some of you will remember, given by members of staff, led admirably by our head waitress here.'

She pointed to Lili, who went all coy, looking down at her hands.

'I thought, this year, we could make it more of an event and collect money for a children's charity. We've lost a couple of our singers to conscription, so anyone who has a good voice, please do volunteer... Now, I want to say a big thank you to you all. We've had a lot of compliments recently about how well the hotel is run, and about how attentive and competent the staff are. When my husband was conscripted, I think a lot of people felt that the hotel's standards would slip. But I think it's safe to say that it is thanks to you all that we have managed to keep them as high as they were.'

'If the hotel's success is down to anyone, it's down to you, Mrs Bygrove,' said Edie. 'You are a natural leader, and you treat us all with respect.'

'Hear, hear,' said Mrs Turnbull.

Helen wasn't sure how to reply to this, and wondered whether it would have been better to have said nothing in the first place. After all, Edie was inferring that she was managing better than Douglas had done. Whether that was true or not, it wouldn't do to let the staff foster a low opinion of him, for he would have to return and run the place again one day. But she didn't want to think of that now.

'Thank you, Edie, but I believe you've all played your parts. Now, it's getting late and some of you need to head home. Good night everyone.'

There were various calls of farewell as the live-out staff dispersed, and some live-ins took the vacated seats at the table. Edie got up and went to Helen, who was now standing near the door. Once the room had emptied out, leaving only the live-ins, the pair of them headed into the corridor.

'I was wondering,' said Edie, 'whether one of the new chambermaids might be responsible for the missing items.'

'My thoughts too. But, as I told myself, we mustn't jump to conclusions. We've taken on a few staff members in the last few months, and it could be someone taking advantage of the fact that we might accuse the newest members.'

'I suppose so… It looks like the staff are still happy to help with the charity events, anyway, and liked the idea of providing the cheap meals. I'm sure it will go down well with the community.'

'Although not with Douglas when he finds out.'

'How will he find out?'

Helen looked sidelong at Edie with a mirthless smile. 'How do you think?'

'Isabella Harvey? If she *is* writing to him.'

'I'd lay good money on it.'

'By the way, someone from White and Thomson Aircraft Company in Middleton made a telephone enquiry earlier about hiring a room for an evening in December for a meal to celebrate Christmas. They're the ones who make the flying-boats. I presume we could accommodate them?'

'Of course. I'll leave you to sort that out, and I'll work out some dates for our events and go to the newspaper offices tomorrow to book some advertisements in.'

She only hoped Detective Inspector Toshack didn't turn up to accuse anyone of writing the letters.

–

'Good afternoon, Inspector.' Helen made her lips smile as she stood up from her desk, but it didn't dispel the apprehension she felt at his appearance. His navy mackintosh was covered in a light scattering of rain.

Edie, who'd showed the inspector in, lingered, looking at Helen pointedly, as if enquiring whether she needed company.

'Thank you, Edie. I'll speak to you later.'

'Very well, Helen.'

As Edie shut the door, Inspector Toshack said, 'Good afternoon, Mrs Bygrove.' He lifted his hat briefly. 'I've come about the writing samples.'

This did not bode well. He wouldn't have bothered coming back if there was nothing to report.

'Please, take a seat, Inspector.'

He hesitated for a moment, but finally pulled out one of two chairs opposite her and sat down somewhat awkwardly. Helen felt a moment's sympathy, wondering whether his reluctance had been because he knew he couldn't carry out the action gracefully.

'So far we've found nothing in the letters to implicate anyone at the hotel,' he said.

'That's a relief, though—'

'However, I believe there to be an omission. This Mr Watkins, for instance, who turned up to replace you on the desk when I collected the samples. There was nothing with his name on.'

'But Mr Watkins has worked here for years, Inspector. I'm sure he wouldn't—'

'So have many of your staff, Mrs Bygrove, but that's not the point. We can't let some people off just because *you* think they're not the sort to do such a thing. No doubt, when we find out who it is, people will say the same about them.'

He looked at her sternly and she was reminded of the rector at the church her family had attended in her childhood. He'd been fond of piercing various members of the congregation with accusing glares during his sermons on death and damnation.

'Of course. I really don't think many of them would be capable, but it doesn't mean anyone should be let off handing in a sample of handwriting,' she said.

'You don't think *many* of them would be capable? Does that mean you think some would?'

Why did he have to take her words the wrong way? This was getting tiresome. 'No, Inspector, that is not what I meant. I just don't know all of them well enough to make a judgement.'

'I have a list here of the names of those who submitted samples. Could you please confirm that all staff members have been included?'

She took the list from him as he leant over with it. 'They should be. I made sure that even the part-timers not due in came to write a sample. Apart from Mr Watkins.'

'I'd appreciate it if you checked it anyway.'

She kept her impatient sigh to herself. 'Very well.' The names weren't in any kind of order, which didn't help, but she took a pencil and ticked them off, one by one, as she considered each category of staff. 'Yes, all present and correct.'

'Would you write next to each what their role in the hotel is?'

About to question the reason once more, she decided against it. The quicker she fulfilled his requests, the quicker she could be rid of him. She took her fountain pen this time to complete the task, which took some minutes.

'There you are, Inspector. All done.' She handed the sheet back.

'Thank you.' He turned slightly awkwardly on the chair, before pushing himself up. 'I'll leave you in peace now.'

Helen almost fancied that he smiled slightly as he said this, but she couldn't be sure. It could be a grimace from the pain in his leg.

He was about to walk away when there was an urgent knock on the door.

She called, 'Enter,' only to be faced with an alarmed Gertie.

'Mrs Bygrove, Miss Harvey is in the foyer, causing a stink. Good job you're still 'ere, Inspector.'

'It's that bad?' said Helen.

'She says she's received another anonymous letter, something about Fanny and this awful 'otel. 'Er words.'

'Fanny?'

'Edie's doing her best trying to calm things down, but lots of people are in the foyer listening.'

Helen rose and followed Gertie out into the narrow passageway, turning left onto the main staff corridor, which led to the door into the foyer. The inspector followed on. Sure enough, Miss Harvey was in the foyer, shouting and waving pieces of paper around. Several patrons, presumably those leaving the dining room after lunch, were gathered, wide-eyed, listening.

'Please, Miss Harvey, can't you see that this is just someone trying to cause trouble?' said Edie, standing in front of the desk. 'Why would anyone from *here* write these letters about us?'

'To throw people off the scent, that's why!'

Inspector Toshack went ahead. 'Miss Harvey, I would advise you to calm down. This is not the way to deal with the situation. You should have brought the letter down to the police station.'

'I did that with the first one, as did others, and what's happened? Nothing! I'm not having some wanton piece writing to insult me.' She lifted up one of the sheets. '*Fanny the chambermaid is a dirty disgusting slut, with her bastard child—*'

Several onlookers gasped, including Lady Blackmore and Cecelia.

'That's right, that's what it says. And then it goes on to say, *And you are just as bad if you continue to patronise the hotel. No wonder you remain unwed, you old cow.*'

'That is enough, Miss Harvey. Let me have that.' Inspector Toshack snatched the letter from her hand, folded it and put it in his coat pocket. 'We don't need to upset all and sundry now, do we? And Miss Moore may have a point. Why would someone from here write about their own hotel?'

He was sticking up for them now? Helen couldn't make the man out. Not five minutes ago he'd seemed determined to prove it *was* someone from here writing the letters.

'Like I said, it's a red herring.' Miss Harvey pinched her lips together. 'And they're using this excuse to call me horrible names, and to say that I'm a degenerate because I come to a place where people like, like… certain women, who are no better than trollops, are sheltered.'

Major Thomas, stepped forward from the group looking on. 'I think you need evidence before you start bandying around these accusations, madam. I've lived in this hotel a good number of years now, and I've never seen any evidence of underhand activity. And who exactly is supposed to be the target of this letter? I'm a little confused. Is it you, or those in the hotel?'

'Thank you, Major,' said Toshack, 'but I'll handle this.'

The major bowed his head in deference, then stepped back.

'It is not for you to decide who is guilty, Miss Harvey. We will gather evidence at the police station.'

But Miss Harvey did not seem inclined to let this go. 'What of this accusation about Fanny the chambermaid? I presume that's true. It has been noted that the nursemaid from here has been seen with a baby in a perambulator. I assumed it was a guest's, but now—'

'It's nobody's business, you old busybody,' said Gertie.

'So, it is true then?'

'I didn't say it was. I said it was none of ya business.'

'Miss Green,' Helen warned. 'Let us deal with this.'

Gertie strode off to the staff door, her expression dark. The lunch guests who had gathered started murmuring among themselves.

Lady Blackmore now stepped forward. 'If this is true, why would you have such a woman working at this prestigious hotel? *That* sort should be sent to the workhouse in East Preston, along with her progeny.'

'That wouldn't be a very kind solution,' said Cecelia, speaking in a firmer voice than usual.

'Do be quiet, Cecelia.'

Lady Blackmore's companion took several steps back, her eyes lowered.

'It is shocking, keeping on such a woman in what *used* to be a first-class hotel,' said Miss Harvey. 'And it's all *her* fault.' She pointed at Helen. 'It wouldn't have happened under Douglas's management. He would *not* have allowed the hussy to stay.'

She smiled smugly, clearly thinking she'd scored a point. But Helen wasn't going to allow her the upper hand.

'Actually, Miss Harvey, the mother in question gave birth *before* Douglas was conscripted, and he *did* allow her to stay.'

She wasn't going to admit that he'd initially demanded that she should be sent to the workhouse. He had changed his mind when Helen had pointed out that throwing her out made it more likely that the news would get around.

'And we decided to take care of them both since the mother had been taken advantage of and the poor girl was too inexperienced to know what was happening.' This was almost certainly not true, and although Helen hated lying, she felt it was in a good cause.

Miss Harvey no longer looked so superior.

'Whatever the truth of the matter, this is nobody's business apart from those involved,' said the inspector. 'It's the writer of these letters who is committing an offence, so let's concentrate on finding the real criminals, not blaming the victims.'

'Well, *I'm* not staying a moment longer in a place with such low moral standards,' said Lady Blackmore. 'Come along, Cecelia.'

Cecelia looked at her employer as she strode to the door, getting her umbrella ready to open. She turned towards Helen, calling a quiet, 'Sorry,' before following on.

'I still think it's someone from the hotel sending these libellous letters,' said Miss Harvey. 'For who else knew that this Fanny had given birth to a by-blow, as you'd all kept it secret, by the looks of it? And I wouldn't mind betting that the father of the baby is a staff member.'

'A staff member could easily have mentioned it to someone else,' Helen countered. 'And the father in question, who was never a staff member, is now at war.'

'It's excuse after excuse.' Miss Harvey narrowed her eyes before pointing a forefinger at Helen. 'And it's your fault Douglas was conscripted, because *you* didn't stand by him at the tribunal.'

She lunged forward, jabbing her finger further ahead. Helen stepped back with a small cry, afraid the woman was about to poke her. As she did so, the inspector leapt between them, almost overbalancing in the process, causing Miss Harvey's fist to knock into his chest. He pushed Miss Harvey back as she declared, 'What on earth?' The audience once again gasped and muttered.

'I'm cautioning you to calm down, Miss Harvey, or be arrested for attempted assault.'

'I did nothing of the sort. The only reason I made contact with your person is because you got in the way. I was only using my finger to emphasise my point.'

'I suggest you make your way home. If you receive any more letters, bring them straight to the station. And if you hear of anyone else doing so, tell them to do the same. Do you understand?'

'Oh yes, I understand. You're placing the blame on the innocent.' She looked at him and Helen with contempt. 'What, is there something going on between the two of you, and that's why you're defending her?'

'You're skating on thin ice, Miss Harvey. Go. Home.'

'I wouldn't want to stay a moment longer in this, this, den of iniquity. Douglas should have placed someone else in charge. I, for one, would have made a much better job of it.'

With that, Isabella Harvey gave Helen one last withering glance before clip-clopping purposefully towards the door in her Louis heeled boots.

When she'd disappeared, the inspector turned to the gawping audience. 'Please, do make your way to your destinations. And I would advise you all *not* to spread any of Miss Harvey's accusations, for that would be slander. Thank you.'

Helen, Edie and the inspector watched as the guests either filed out of the door or made their way to the stairs and lift.

When they'd all disappeared, Toshack turned to Helen. 'I'll await the remaining sample, as quickly as you can get it to me, please.' He lifted his hat briefly, then made his way to the exit.

So much for him defending the hotel, thought Helen. Edie joined her.

'I've no idea where Gertie got to. She seemed very upset though. Bert's gone on an errand for a guest, so I have no porters here at the moment.'

'I'll go and find her,' said Helen. 'It's the late staff lunch now, so she may be telling them of the revelation about Fanny.'

'Oh dear.'

'Indeed. And Fanny is going to be most upset when she finds out.'

As Helen had feared, Fanny was in tears when she reached the staff dining room, her grizzling baby on her lap. Gertie, Annie Twine from the scullery and the head stillroom maid, Hetty Affleck, surrounded her where she sat.

'Let me take Elsie until you calm down,' said Mrs Leggett. 'Your tears are upsetting her too.' She lifted the baby from Fanny's lap and carried her out of the room, joggling her up and down.

'Oh, Mrs Bygrove,' Fanny whined, when she spotted her. 'I'm sorry I've caused all this trouble.'

'It's not your fault… Gertie, Edie needs you back in the foyer.'

Gertie nodded and headed off.

Fanny placed her chin in her hand and leant her elbow on the table. 'I think someone in the hotel must have told someone about Elsie, otherwise how would they know?'

'I think that's highly possible,' said Helen. 'But it doesn't mean someone at the hotel has written the letters, just that someone they know has.'

'Or perhaps they told someone, who told someone, and so on, and *they* wrote the letter,' said Hetty.

'Indeed. I suppose it was unlikely that this situation was never going to be discovered.'

'I know,' sniffed Fanny. 'But to say such *horrible* things about me, and especially about Elsie, who ain't done nothing wrong.'

'I agree, Fanny.' Helen took the seat next to her. 'But whoever has written these letters does not sound in their right minds. You must pay them no heed.'

'But others will. They'll think the letters are true. There have been a lot of letters sent, by the sounds of it. I wonder what else she's said in them, the writer.'

'Why are we assuming it's a woman?' said Annie. 'Could just as easily be a man.'

'Dunno. Seems more the kind of thing a woman would do. And there are more women around now than men.'

'Inspector Toshack is considering both,' said Helen, 'as he asked for samples of handwriting from everyone.'

'Will I have to go to the workhouse now?' said Fanny. 'And give Elsie up?'

Helen took her hand. 'No, of course not. I made it clear that we're looking after you both here, and that you weren't to blame and were put upon.'

'But I wasn't reall—'

'That doesn't matter. Elsie's father left you in the lurch, so, in that way, you were put upon.'

Fanny nodded glumly.

Helen stood up. 'Now, I believe some of you have shifts to get to. Do you need some time before you go back to your shift, Fanny?'

'No, Mrs Bygrove, thanks. I'd rather keep doing something. I'll just take Elsie back to Vera, and I'll get on with it.'

'That's probably for the best.'

Helen wondered what *she* could do for the best, for the hotel. She guessed she'd just have to see what impact the letter and the scene in the foyer had over the next few days, before she decided.

—

Helen was exhausted by the time she got to bed that night. So far, there had been little impact on the hotel. Nobody coming in from outside for afternoon tea or dinner seemed to be any the wiser about the accusations. Those staying had even murmured words of support and sympathy to Lili, Phoebe and the young waiters, Simon and Dennis. Lili had been sure that Major Thomas had played some part in this, for which Helen was grateful.

All this went around and around in Helen's head, as she struggled to get to sleep. She snuggled into the clean sheets, breathing in the scent of Sunlight soap. It reminded her of her early wedded days to Douglas, snuggling up to him at night, the macassar oil on his hair being the dominant scent back then. But such affection had disappeared long before he was conscripted.

Her mind wandered to the incident where Miss Harvey looked about to push her. Whether she really had been only pointing her finger for emphasis, Helen had been surprised when Inspector Toshack had come to her rescue. She'd seen a different side to him, not the always slightly annoyed, gloomy detective, but someone more thoughtful.

The earlier scene floated into her mind as she became a little drowsy. It was almost like she was viewing it on the screen at a picture house; like one of those romantic adventure films where the hero comes to rescue the damsel in distress. Fanny had said that someone had described him as handsome, and she'd thought so herself. If things had been different, and Douglas hadn't been around... Not dead, but maybe had run away with Miss Harvey. She emitted a small chuckle. And if Inspector Toshack was a little more in manner like Inspector Davis... And, and... What had she been thinking about? Oh yes, Inspector Toshack. She wondered what his first name might be...

Almost sleep, she suddenly jerked awake once more. What on earth was she doing? Making up her own romantic adventure? Goodness knows why: she was firmly disillusioned with the idea of romance. Douglas had seen to that. He'd been so tender, so attentive in the beginning. But if she was honest, they hadn't owned this hotel long before she'd started to see the change in him. She'd been in self-denial for so long, thinking she could summon the old Douglas back eventually.

Had that Douglas ever really existed? In the beginning, yes. The change had been subtle at first. Maybe it went back even further than them first owning the hotel, to when Grandmama had died in 1908, and left Rustington Manor to Mummy. Of course, there'd always been a possibility she would, even though she'd threatened to leave it to a cousin. Had Douglas been relying on that? Had her main attraction been the possibility of him getting his hands on some money?

Either way, she was finished with romance.

Chapter Three

Over three weeks had gone by since Miss Harvey's outburst, and it was now the first of December. Helen was walking to East Street School to pick up Dorothy and Arthur. This was a treat for her, as Vera normally carried out this task, and although it was gloomy and cold, she relished an opportunity to escape the hotel for a while.

As she passed Smarts chemist, on the corner of High Street and East Street, she checked her wristwatch. Five minutes until the children finished school. It was only part way up the street, but she'd better put a spurt in her step.

During the walk, she'd thought about the music concert they were holding that evening, with Mr Janus's help. They'd sold plenty of tickets through various stores and businesses in town, much to her relief. They hadn't charged too much, hoping people would also donate money at the end, giving the wealthier an opportunity to maybe give a little more than those with less.

Whatever Miss Harvey had hoped to achieve by blaming her for the libellous letters, and revealing Fanny's secret, it had back-fired. Despite her and Lady Blackmore no longer patronising the hotel, plenty still came from the local area for meals and coffee. Many who'd mentioned the affair had been sympathetic. And the major, from what she'd heard, had spared no time in telling people that the accusation of anyone at the hotel being responsible for the missives was nonsense.

As far as Helen knew, there had been no more letters. Perhaps the person responsible had heard of the trouble, and the police being involved, and had decided it was too risky to keep on sending them.

Helen hadn't long entered the school gate when she saw Arthur rushing down towards her, closely followed by Dorothy.

'Mummy, you came to collect us today,' said her son, wrapping his arms around her.

'Miss Nye told us it's December today.' said Dorothy. 'Will the shops have Christmas things in them now?'

'They won't yet, sweetheart. Not until later in December.'

Both the children looked crestfallen.

'Mrs Bygrove, good afternoon. How lovely to see you here.' It was Miss Nye, walking among the crowd of departing children.

'Good afternoon, Miss Nye. All the children seem very excited.'

'I do apologise. They're supposed to walk out of school quietly, in a neat line, but as it's Friday the prospect of the weekend off does make their little spirits high. I must say, I'm quite excited myself, for I've bought a ticket for your concert this evening. I've seen some of the performers in the past, and they were most talented.'

'How splendid,' said Helen, genuinely pleased that she was coming. It was likely Edie had persuaded her.

'All the teachers from here are coming, including Miss Boniface, the headmistress. I believe Mr Janus is helping to organise it once more?'

'That's correct. And Miss Sophia Perryman, who's in charge of so many of the charities in the area, is coming to introduce it. We've had a marvellous response, and that will be largely because of the two of them.' This was another thing she'd been grateful for, after the trouble caused by Miss Harvey.

'I will no doubt see you later then. Good afternoon, Mrs Bygrove.'

'Good afternoon, Miss Nye.'

She took the children's hands. Arthur's were sticky, but she didn't mind at all. They left the school and headed back towards the town.

'Is our headmistress coming to the hotel?' Dorothy asked. She looked a little anxious at the prospect.

'Apparently so,' said Helen. 'But it's nothing to be worried about. She's just coming to see the entertainment.'

'Can we see them too?' said Arthur.

'Not this time. It's more for the grownups. You can come to the carol concert later in the month, when our hotel choir will be singing.'

'And when can we put our tree up, in our sitting room?'

'Not until a couple of days before Christmas, sweetheart.'

'And can we go to Worthing again, to look at toys, like we did last year?'

Helen laughed. 'My goodness, Arthur, you are full of festive questions today. Yes, I'm sure we can take a few hours out one Saturday to do that.'

'Will Daddy come this time?' Dorothy asked.

Last year he was supposed to have taken them to Worthing himself. He'd failed to turn up due to having been invited to lunch by someone he'd described, hesitantly, as a *good customer*. She had wondered a few times since, whether it had been Miss Harvey.

'I'm afraid he can't, Dorothy, as he's in the army.'

'But he's only in Shoreham-by-Sea. Won't he be home for Christmas?'

'It's unlikely.'

Dorothy was right. He was only about a dozen miles away, and yet seldom seemed to be able to come home even on a day's leave. She hated to admit to herself that she was relieved about this. It wasn't the way she wanted to feel, but… there it was. Despite the increasing difficulties that the war created for the hotel, and the recent trouble, she had a sense of peace these days that she hadn't felt for many years. She knew it was because Douglas wasn't there to boss her around and overturn any good decisions she made for the hotel. Or take the credit for any he did allow that were successful. She didn't have to keep wondering when he'd turn up from his various activities at the golf club or with his tennis chums, or more recently, with the bowls club.

'Mummy,' said Dorothy, as they reached the end of East Street and headed onto Beach Road, 'one of the big girls in the playground today said that there'd been German air raids on London by an aeroplane. Will the aeroplane fly here and drop bombs too?'

'I don't think so, sweetheart. London is an important city, that's why the German aeroplane would have picked it. We're just a quiet little seaside town.' With plenty of admiralty shipping going up and down the River Arun, Helen added to herself, but she didn't need to say this. 'Now, when we get home, how would you two like to play a few games of Ludo.'

'Yes please, Mummy,' they choroused together.

The children chattered about their day at school as they passed the shops on the first half of Beach Road, then crossed over to the residential part of the street. The gloom was drawing the day to a close even earlier than it would have done normally, but Helen was content.

This contentment lasted only until they were passing St Catherine's church, when she spotted Miss Harvey coming out of Selborne Road, where she had her guest house.

What should she do? Ignore the woman? Impart a civil greeting, and leave it at that? She didn't want to stoop to Miss Harvey's level.

However, as she was about to open her mouth, the woman crossed over Beach Road and entered the public gardens. Helen sighed with relief. It wasn't long before they reached South Terrace and turned left towards the hotel. With any luck, that would be the last time she'd see Miss Harvey for a while.

–

As Helen and the children entered the staff corridor, Mrs Leggett came out of the kitchen.

'Ah, Mrs Bygrove. A letter has come for you from Shoreham-by-Sea.' She reached into her skirt pocket and pulled out an envelope, before handing it to her. The expression on her face reflected what Helen felt about receiving it.

'You go upstairs and get the Ludo board ready,' Helen told the children. 'And ask Vera to fetch us all some refreshments. I'll be up in a moment.'

Dorothy and Arthur scurried off, racing each other up the staff stairs.

'I'll leave you to your letter.' Mrs Leggett entered the stillroom.

Helen stared at it. She could read it now or ignore it and wait until the children had gone to bed. Or until after the concert this evening. That would make it quite late before she got to it. Better to get it over and done with.

She tore the envelope open none too delicately. She hadn't got more than a sentence in when she let out a huge sigh. There wasn't even a 'dear' written before her name, after which Douglas had placed an exclamation mark.

He'd started with, *What is this I hear about you holding yet another silly concert?* She closed her eyes, reminding herself that there was nothing he could do about it, before she carried on.

> *There is enough to do with looking after our guests without occupying our diminished and hopeless staff on trifling matters. Let others worry about charitable affairs. After all, I am doing my bit in the army. It's no wonder that people are complaining about the fall in standards in the hotel.*

Fall in standards? If only he knew how many compliments they'd received about the service and the hotel generally. Either he was assuming that, without his presence, everything had gone downhill, or *somebody* had given him that impression. And she had a fair idea of who that could be.

She read to the end of the short missive, giving her advice that she didn't need. *Teaching your granny how to suck eggs*, is what Mrs Norris would have called it.

If Imogen Harvey had written to him about the concert, wouldn't she have mentioned the libellous letters too? Maybe he was saving that up for another time. She folded the letter and stared at it for a few seconds. Today should have been a happy one, spending some time with the children and selling so many tickets for what promised to be a splendid concert this evening. And, even from a distance, he'd still managed to spoil it.

She took hold of the letter and tore it into tiny pieces, before charging around to the office and depositing it into the wastepaper bin there.

Now she could forget it and get on with enjoying the rest of the day.

—

The turnout for the concert was even better than Helen had anticipated, as she greeted guests in the foyer. The audience contained a mix of people that were only found in the hotel on these occasions, but she rather enjoyed that. It certainly hadn't happened before the war, and, sadly, probably wouldn't happen after it had finished. But, for now, the wealthy and titled staying at the hotel seemed, on the whole, unfazed by the presence of those they might deem to be lower than them in society. At least for these occasional short periods. There was a feeling among most that they all had to pull together during these difficult times.

While greeting Sophia Perryman's parents, who were regular diners at the hotel, she spotted the navy mackintosh and grey fedora of Inspector Toshack. Her heart gave an involuntary jolt. No, she mustn't get anxious: if he'd come to arrest anyone, he'd surely have had other police officers with him.

'Good evening, Inspector,' she greeted him. 'I trust you've come for the carol concert?'

'That's right. For a change.' He grinned.

'I'm pleased to hear it.' She had a moment's panic, hoping he didn't think she meant she was pleased to see *him*.

'I suppose it makes a change for me to be here for pleasure, not business.'

'If you'd like to leave your coat with Mrs Turnbull at the cloakroom, just over there –' she pointed towards it, '– you can then go through to the ballroom, where you'll be shown to a seat.'

'Thank you.' He tipped his fedora briefly before setting off.

He'd only taken one step forward when Helen let out a little, 'Oh no!' causing him to stop.

'What's wrong, Mrs Bygrove?'

'Look who has come in.' Helen indicated with her head towards Miss Harvey, who was striding through the foyer, looking straight ahead, as if on a mission.

'Um, Miss Harvey,' the inspector called, as he took several steps towards her, causing her to come to a standstill. 'Have you come for the concert, or for some other reason?'

'For the concert, of course,' she said curtly. 'I'm a great philanthropist and wanted to help raise money to allow our poor men in the trenches to have some Christmas cheer. That's the *only* reason I'd step in *here*.'

Philanthropist? Helen thought of her as the complete opposite: someone only ever looking out for her own interests. She'd seen no signs of generosity towards others.

'Then enjoy the evening,' said Toshack, stepping away to allow her to carry on.

She said nothing in return but did carry on a little more slowly to the cloakroom.

The inspector returned to Helen, who'd been listening in to the exchange even though she was greeting a morning coffee regular.

When the guest had moved on, Toshack said, 'Miss Harvey is here for the concert, but I will, nevertheless, keep an eye on her.'

'Thank you, Inspector. I wouldn't put it past her to cause a fuss somewhere where she'd have a large audience.'

'Not if I can help it.' He lifted his hat once more and headed to the cloakroom.

When the flow of people into the foyer had tailed off, Helen left the porters on duty, Gertie and young Bert Wiston, to greet any latecomers. She headed down the short corridor next to the dining room that led to the ballroom and entered to see most people now seated. Inspector Toshack was still standing at the back. Helen went over to him.

'Inspector, there are still seats available.'

'Aye, I know, thank you. I was just wanting to see where Miss Harvey sat before I took a seat. She's near the back over there.' He pointed to a row on the right side of the aisle. 'If I sit here, at the back, I'll be able to keep an eye on her.'

'I hope it won't spoil your enjoyment of the concert.'

'I'm sure it won't. Unless she starts anything, then it will spoil it for everyone. But I will try to nip it in the bud.'

Helen nodded, not knowing what else to say.

'This is a lovely room,' he said, pointing at the arched mirrors and beautifully embossed walls with their pillars, then up at the elaborate crystal chandeliers.

'Yes, we're very lucky. It hasn't been used for many balls since the war started, sadly, but it's been a blessing for our charity events... Ah, it looks like they're about to begin. Please, do take your seat, Inspector.'

He gave her a smile and a small nod of his head, before complying with her request. Helen stood at the back of the room, along with the rest of the staff present.

–

The first half of the concert was going well. So far, they had been treated to a monologist reciting a portion of *Hamlet*, a harpist and singer performing 'Early One Morning', a wonderful soprano singing 'O Solo Mio', and a rendition of the Major-General's song, from *The Pirates of Penzance*.

As the audience applauded the latter, Helen saw somebody rise from the audience. It was Miss Harvey. She made straight for the doors, speaking to no one, and disappeared. Inspector Toshack turned to look at Helen, who promptly indicated that she'd follow her.

By the time she'd reached the foyer, Miss Harvey was nowhere to be seen.

'What was all that about?' said Gertie, who was still on duty there with Bert. 'Why did she bother coming if she wasn't gonna stay?'

The inspector was in the foyer by this time too. 'She's left the building then?'

'Indeed,' replied Helen. 'Gertie, if she returns, please let me know forthwith.'

'I certainly will, Mrs Bygrove.'

'Please, do return to your seat, Inspector. I believe there are more marvellous acts to come.'

'After you, Mrs Bygrove.' He put out his hand, inviting her to go first.

On their way, he said, 'There is a spare seat next to me, if you wish to take it.'

'No thank you, Inspector. I like to stand and get a better view of the audience, to make sure everyone is all right.'

Back in the ballroom, he took his seat once more, but she noticed him glance at her and smile, before directing his attention at the stage. Helen felt that, once again, she'd seen a different side of the inspector. Perhaps, settling in a little more to his new surroundings, he'd taken on a more relaxed manner? Time would tell.

Not that she wanted to spend time in his presence to find out, but if she must deal with him, it would be less daunting on this more friendly footing.

–

A couple of days later, the hotel was holding the first of its cheap meals for those who couldn't normally afford to patronise the hotel. On this occasion it was a Sunday lunch.

'I can't believe how successful this has been,' Helen said to Edie, as the pair of them stood in the doorway of the private dining room, watching the young waiters, Simon and Dennis, serve the full tables.

'People who can't afford to stay or dine here normally probably want to see what the food is like. Even though it will be simpler than that we normally serve, I'm sure they'll appreciate how well it's cooked.'

'I'm only sorry that we had to turn some people away. If we had more tables and chairs, we could serve them in the ballroom.'

'I think Mrs Norris might have something to say about all the extra work,' Edie chuckled. 'And we only have just enough waiting staff to serve those who are here.'

'You're right. We can only do so much.' Helen sighed. 'It's a shame we could only serve them compote of pigeon, but we do need to save the other meats we can still obtain for our elite guests.'

'And it would be too expensive for them. Anyway, Jack, who prepared the compote, allowed me a small taste of it, and it was delicious.'

'I'd expect nothing less from my kitchen team.' Helen beamed. 'I'm going to get an apron on and help clear away plates as people finish. That way, Simon and Dennis can get on with serving the apple pudding for dessert.'

'And I've got to relieve Grace on the desk so she can go for lunch.'

'She seems to have settled into the job now,' said Helen.

'Yes, and it's been a relief to have someone else on the rota for the desk. It was good of you to "muck in", as Mrs Norris would put it.'

'I always have done.'

'But you're the manageress now.'

'All the more reason to make up any shortfall and keep things running smoothly.' Unlike Douglas, who had done less and less over the years, even resenting working on the desk in the foyer.

'I'll see you later.'

–

As it transpired, Dennis insisted on clearing up the main course plates so that Helen could help serve dessert. The customers seemed very taken with the idea that the manageress was serving them, and Helen certainly enjoyed passing the time of day with them. She felt that some of the hotel's more select clientele could learn from the good manners of those they would deem to be lowly.

An old lady in a black bonnet breathed in deeply as Helen placed a bowl in front of her. 'Hmm, smells fruity and buttery. Lovely!'

Helen was sure there would be no butter involved, and more likely margarine had been used for this dining room's fare, but she was happy that it was so appreciated.

'I hope you enjoy it, madam.'

'Madam! Not often I get called that.' The old lady beamed.

Helen had just served the last bowl in her hand to a middle-aged gent in a suit that had seen better days, smiling at a compliment about how lovely the hotel was, when she saw Edie standing in the doorway. Her expression did not fill Helen with confidence. She hastened to the door. 'Is something wrong?'

'Detective Inspector Toshack is here and says he needs to speak with you.'

Helen looked around the room. The two waiters were coping admirably. 'All right, I'll come and speak to him.' She indicated to Simon that she had to go and he nodded.

As she walked down the short corridor to the foyer, she removed the apron and cap. 'Would you put these behind the desk, Edie. I'd better be presentable to any guests who might be around.'

'Of course.'

In the foyer, Helen was alarmed to see that Sergeant Gardner was with him. Standing behind him were WPC Amanda Love-lock, who used to be her bookkeeper, and Constable Twort, who'd retired originally a few years before the war. A feeling of dread crept up her body and she had a bitter taste in her mouth.

Surely they hadn't concluded that someone from the hotel had written the letters. Could it be one of the new chambermaids, as Edie had suggested? Did Miss Harvey know something, and was that why she'd turned up at the carol concert?

'Inspector,' she greeted him. 'How may I help you today?'

The inspector opened his mouth to respond but was cut short by both front doors being pushed open. Lady Blackmore was fussing as she entered, along with around a dozen people Helen recognised from the businesses in Beach Town. Cecelia was nowhere in sight. The looks on their faces suggested they weren't here for pleasure.

Lady Blackmore opened with, 'Well, that decides it. The hotel crest was on my latest letter. Now try and tell me the letters did not originate from this hotel.'

'And on mine!' cried Norah Johnson, who as Norah Daniels had once been a chambermaid at the hotel. Before the dairy farmer's son had made her pregnant and they'd had to marry. 'Just because I used to work 'ere and had to marry my Jim, don't give you no permission to send me letters calling me names like *trollop*.'

'That's what I was about to tell you,' Toshack told Helen. 'More letters have been received, but this time on hotel note-paper.'

'And what have I ever done to you?' said Mrs Riddles, the postmistress from Norfolk Road. 'Calling me a stinking cow of a liar, just because I took my last letter to the police station.' She pointed towards Helen.

'I've never done any such thing,' said Helen, feeling a weight in her chest. 'And why on earth would I send anonymous letters on hotel paper.'

'But they're not anonymous,' said the landlord of the New Inn, also on Norfolk Road. 'They're signed H.B. That's you innit?'

'That's even less likely then,' said Edie, coming forward.

'No, it's to double bluff people, Miss Harvey here reckons,' said Norah Johnson. 'And it makes sense. It'd be the best defence in a courtroom.' She pulled her body upright, taking on a pose with a prim face. '*Oh no, my honour, I wouldn't send rude letters with my own name on them,*' she chirped, in a badly rendered imitation of an upper-class accent. She fluttered her eyelids.

'That's enough of that now,' said Inspector Toshack. 'If you'd all kindly leave me to carry out my job—'

'We want to make sure you *do* carry out your job,' said Miss Harvey. 'Not like last time.'

'I used to think you were a decent sort,' said Norah, 'when I worked for you. Thought it was ya 'usband what was the silly bugger. I guess now 'e's gone away you've taken over his meanness too.'

'That's enough of that, young woman,' Sergeant Gardner warned.

'And this accusation about her ladyship,' said the landlord. 'What proof have you got that her companion is her daughter.'

'We don't need to mention the details,' Lady Blackmore whimpered, her hands covering her cheeks.

'Mine had that ridiculous claim too,' said Mrs Riddles. 'I can quote it exactly, I can. *Lady Millicent Blackmore can't keep her vile secret any more,* it said. *We can all see the likeness between her and Cecelia, and we know that she's really her bastard child, born out of wedlock when she was a slip of a girl.*'

Lady Blackmore let out a strangled cry of anguish. 'Of course that's not true! I am only ten years older than Cecelia. How could she be my daughter? Whoever heard of anything so absurd?'

'I agree,' said Helen. 'And I would *never* say such a thing.'

'Not to our faces,' said Norah. 'Makes me wonder what you said be'ind our backs when I was working 'ere.'

'I'm warning you,' said the sergeant.

'What, only me?' said Norah. 'What, 'cause I'm the trollop 'ere, eh? And my letter also said that they're 'arbouring conchies at the 'otel now.'

'Mrs Bygrove is hardly going to claim that in a letter now, is she?' said Edie.

'Like I said, double bluffing.'

It seemed to Helen that the scene before her was diminishing, and the sound fading. She had an acid taste at the back of her throat. Was she still in bed, dreaming?

The gathering mob started to talk over each other, provoking both Sergeant Gardner and Inspector Toshack to censure them. The sergeant went with, 'Quiet now!' while the inspector went with the more polite, 'Would you all calm down now.'

The double instruction had the desired effect and the incensed chatter ceased immediately.

'Now, unless you want to be arrested for disturbance of the peace, I suggest you all vacate the hotel,' said the inspector, stretching up to his full height. 'And if I receive any reports that you've returned to cause trouble, I will spare no time in sending one of my officers to your abodes. Is that clear?'

There were several mumbles of assent, before each of them turned to exit. Lady Blackmore charged out of the door first, almost knocking Norah Johnson over. The rest followed on, subdued, apart from Miss Harvey. She stood, defiant, for several seconds, glaring at Helen. She was the last of them to leave.

Helen was grateful that nobody had emerged from either dining room during this scene, though she had no doubt that the throng that had gathered today would soon pass around news of the latest letters.

'Mrs Bygrove,' said Toshack. 'Mrs Bygrove?'

'Hm?' She came to. 'Sorry, what did you say?'

'I said, could we go somewhere more private.'

'Of… of course. Edie, I'm leaving you in charge.'

'Yes, madam.'

Helen took a deep breath, determined to pull herself together. But she was badly shaken. 'Come this way.' She led the four police officers to the staff area, stopping in the corridor. 'We'll go to my office.'

'No, this will suffice,' said the inspector. 'WPC Lovelock, you know the building. Show Sergeant Gardner the way.'

68

'Yes, sir,' she said with little enthusiasm. She opened the door to the stairs, that led to the staff living quarters.

'What are they doing?' said Helen.

'Carrying out a search.'

'But my children are up there, with Vera, their nursemaid.'

'I'm sure WPC Lovelock will escort them elsewhere. Constable, you search the office, down this passageway on the left.'

Twort performed a short salute before obeying the command.

'Why are you doing this, Inspector?' Helen asked. 'Why would anyone here use the hotel writing paper for anonymous letters?'

As she finished the sentence, the door to the stairs opened once more, and Vera appeared, with Elsie in her arms. Dorothy and Arthur came just behind her.

'Shall I take the children into the staff dining room, madam?'

'That would be best.'

When they'd gone, Toshack was about to speak, when Alice Twine and Hetty Affleck came out of the stillroom and went into the dining room, laughing, and Lili came in from the guest dining room to get to the kitchen.

'On second thoughts, is there somewhere more private we can go?'

She was about to reply facetiously, *the lavatory*, but thought better of it. 'No, there isn't now the constable's in the office. Anything you wish to say to me, you can say here.'

He shuffled a couple of times, looking down at his feet, before saying, 'As you've probably gathered, there's been a new wave of letters sent. Unfortunately, looking more carefully at the hand-writing, it does have a lot in common with one certain person's.'

'And the first wave didn't?'

'Maybe it was better masked the first time. Mrs Bygrove, the writing is a lot like your own cursive script.'

'I've already said, I did *not* write them. I find it interesting though, that you're echoing Miss Harvey's allegations. Given her interest in my husband, she'd have a lot to gain by me being arrested.'

'They were having an – an… affair?'

'I don't know about that, but they certainly seemed to spend a great deal of time together, and she's always saying how marvellous he is and how the hotel has been ruined since I took over.'

'Which might give you a motive for sending such letters to her.'

'But not to anyone else. And why would I make it obvious it was from me? Discounting the double bluff nonsense. My point was that it would be in Miss Harvey's interest if I were accused.'

'You're saying she's the one who's written them?'

'No, only that it would be in her interest to use the opportunity to get me locked up. Then the real perpetrator would get off scot-free.'

'I see. We can only work with what evidence we have, Mrs Bygrove, and we have none that implicates her, or anyone else. And if we find nothing here, then I doubt there'll be much of a case to implicate you either, with just the similar writing.'

'Good. Because you will find nothing.'

'Which post office do you use?'

'The one in Norfolk Road, of course. It's the closest.'

'That's where the letters were sent from.'

'Everyone in Beach Town probably posts their letters there.'

If he had any reply to this, it was halted by Sergeant Gardner.

'Sir, we found this in Mrs Bygrove's living quarters, in one of the drawers.' He handed him some used blotting paper. 'Some of the words that have been blotted are legible.'

Toshack examined it. 'I see.'

'What does it say?' Helen asked.

'Something we've seen in the letters. You don't need to know what.'

'Then it's nothing to do with me. I don't even keep blotting paper in the drawers upstairs.'

'I'm sorry, Mrs Bygrove, but I am going to have to arrest you on the charge of criminal libel.'

'But I've done nothing. And what about my children? And I have a hotel to run.'

'I'm sorry, but the evidence I've been presented with leaves me no choice. You've got a nursemaid and enough staff.'

Helen's breathing became rapid and she felt a rising panic. 'I need to tell Edie what's happening.'

'I'll go and find her,' said WPC Lovelock, who'd just emerged from the stairs.

As she left the staff area, Constable Twort appeared from the passageway to the office. 'I've just found these, sir. Letters started but scribbled out, in the bin. They're like the others.'

'What?' said Helen. 'They must have been put there by someone else.'

Toshack took the two sheets of crumpled paper and read them briefly. 'I see. I think we have enough,' said the inspector.

Edie came running through the door, with the WPC behind her. 'Helen, they can't arrest you.'

'Just stop there,' said Toshack, holding up his hand. 'I'm afraid that I *will* have to arrest Mrs Bygrove. You'll have to take her place until something more permanent can be sorted out.'

'But the children—'

'Edie, could you please tell the staff what's happened, and ask Vera to take charge of the children until I return.'

'Of course. Helen, what can we do?'

'Contact my solicitor, Edie. Mr Burtenshaw, on Arundel Road.'

'That's a good idea,' said the inspector. 'He might be able to sort out a surety for bail.'

'Edie, you have access to the hotel account. You may give whatever money is needed to the solicitor.'

'Very well, Helen.'

'Come along now,' said Toshack. 'We'll take the staff entrance out, to minimise embarrassment.'

'Can't I say farewell to my children?'

He halted a while, his brow knitted. 'I, um… I think it's probably better if you don't for now. If you get bail, you'll be home soon enough.'

Sergeant Gardner went ahead, with WPC Lovelock and Constable Twort behind, as Inspector Toshack led Helen out. At least they hadn't placed handcuffs on her. But her children, oh her children. Her heart broke as she thought of them, wondering what had happened to their mummy, and after their daddy had been sent away too.

And she was innocent. Innocent! She had to keep hold of that thought. And the staff would vouch for her.

But how had the blotting paper and scraps got into her quarters and the office wastepaper basket? It had to be someone in the hotel.

She saw the police motorcar on the road as they took the path down the side of the hotel. Her innocence would win the day. It just had to.

–

Inspector Toshack had locked Helen up in one of the small cells at the police station and was now back at his desk. He rubbed his bottom lip with his forefinger, as he examined what had been found at the hotel. It did seem all rather convenient. Why would an intelligent woman write such things, let alone make it obvious it was her? Yes, making it a double bluff might be a clever thing to do – but risky. And she just didn't seem the type.

Yet how much did he really know her? His accurate judgement of people had held him in good stead in many cases. But… Could it be, on this occasion, that his – what? Attraction to her? Whatever it was, could it have skewed his judgement?

There was a knock on his office door and Sergeant Gardner stepped in. 'Sir, I hope you won't think I'm talking out of turn—'

Toshack leant back in his seat. 'Even if I do, I'm sure you'll say your piece.'

The sergeant placed his hands behind his back and looked down. 'Yes, you're right.'

'Spit it out.'

'Sir, despite the evidence, I'm not convinced of Mrs Bygrove's guilt. I've known the family a while, and she was always the decent one. It's something I wouldn't have put past Mr Bygrove, if I'm honest, but not her.'

'Perhaps he's put her up to it?'

'I doubt she'd have agreed. From what I've heard, she seems to be relieved that he's gone. That's only between us, mind. Alice and Annie Twine what work in the scullery at the hotel, their mother's my wife's second cousin, and that's apparently their opinion. And I've been acquainted with Mrs Bygrove and her mother since they moved into the hotel in 1910. Always a very pleasant pair. Unlike him, Douglas Bygrove.'

'Her mother?'

'Lady Rose Wright. She died in 1912. Heart attack, if I recall correctly.'

'Mrs Bygrove is from a titled family?'

'Her father was Sir Ronald Wright. He owned South Court Manor in Rustington, until he had to sell it to pay off debts. He died, oh, back in 1909, having been bedridden for a while. Alcoholic he was. Rumour has it that it was Lady Rose what gave the Bygroves the money for the hotel. She was moneyed in her own right, as her mother left her a manor house in Lyminster.'

'How do you know all this?'

'I have me sources, like all good police officers.'

'Aye, I suppose. I did have a theory that maybe Mrs Bygrove was missing her husband and the trauma of it had sent her a little – deranged?'

Gardner laughed. 'More likely she'd be deranged with him there. Like I said—'

'She's relieved he's gone. Be that as it may, Sergeant, the evidence is piling up and it's not looking good for her. And could it be that, being under her husband's thumb in the past, no one has seen the real person?'

'WPC Lovelock used to work for her as bookkeeper, and she says there's not a cruel bone in the woman's body.'

'I thought she didn't look very happy when we arrested Mrs Bygrove.'

'No, she still isn't, sir. She went off on her beat around the town looking very miserable. We need to gather more evidence. If the person who's sending the letters doesn't realise that Mrs Bygrove's been arrested, they might trip themselves up by sending more letters. I wonder if we could do a little surveillance of the pillar box.'

'I wouldn't mind betting that if it is someone else then they do know. And I'm not sure we have enough officers for night surveillance, which is what it would no doubt have to be.'

'I could have a look at the rota, sir?'

'Mm. But I can't see it being worth doing unless Mrs Bygrove gets bail and goes home anyway.'

'You're probably right, sir. And whoever's responsible might not use that post office any more, in case they're caught.'

'Anyway, until something else comes up, the evidence is a little overwhelming, so I can't ignore it. I wonder if we need to get more writing samples, maybe from the people who've received the letters? Miss Harvey mentioned the accusation against the hotel being a double bluff, but surely an even better one would be to make out you'd also received a letter.'

'Exactly sir. If Mrs Bygrove was that cunning, she would have sent some letters to the hotel.'

'But if she didn't send them, how did the blotting paper and the scrapped sheets get into her office and living quarters?'

'There's lots of people moving around the hotel all the time, sir. It'd probably be easy to get in, say a delivery person, a friend visiting, someone fixing something.'

'Or, someone who already works there?'

'Yes, sir, that too. And I have to say, the writing in the later letters was more like Mrs Bygrove's than the original ones, almost as if someone had found something written by her and copied it.'

'It's a possibility.'

'I'll ask Twort to get writing samples from anyone who's received a letter who hasn't already done one, just to make sure.'

'Thank you, Sergeant. Tell him to tell them it's just for elimination purposes, so we don't have anyone complaining.'

'Righty ho, sir.'

After Gardner had left, Toshack rested his elbows on the desk and pressed the fingers of each hand together. He was keen to acquit Mrs Bygrove of the charges. Not that he'd admit that to Gardner. But was it simply because he found her – attractive – or whatever it was?

Attractive. He'd thought of no woman like that since his wife had died. His poor, dear Olive. He took the photograph out of his wallet, the last one she'd had taken. She'd just been starting to show she was with child. Their unborn child, who had perished with Olive in the attack on Hartlepool. He put the photograph away.

He had to admit it, what he felt for Mrs Bygrove, Helen, *was* attraction. There was no other word for it. And admiration. The way she'd taken on the burden of the hotel, with professionalism and competence, was impressive. Her cool head reminded him of Olive, who had run a draper's shop for her father with efficiency.

He had been aware of these feelings from the beginning, and it was no doubt why he'd been harder on the woman, at least initially, than he would have been. His guilt at feeling anything like that for another woman had been the cause. And now, just as he had become more comfortable in her presence, this had to happen. Not that there could have been any kind of relationship, apart from friendship. Maybe not even that. She was married, after all.

Perhaps he should look for a new woman: that's what a couple of colleagues during his time at Horsham had said. But he'd had no heart for it since Olive's death. It had taken her four years to fall pregnant, and then…

He screwed his eyes up tightly. No, he couldn't wallow in that pain now. And he couldn't be soft on Mrs Bygrove just because she was pleasing to the eye and gave the impression of being a respectable woman.

He opened the bottom drawer of his desk and pulled out a brown paper bag in which was the cheese sandwich he'd made himself that morning. He had wanted to buy some sliced meat yesterday, but the grocery store had run out by the time he'd got there.

He took a bite from the sandwich and started to make a note of things he needed to do. It tasted all right, war bread notwithstanding. Not a patch on the meals at the hotel, he would imagine. It was a shame he'd arrested the manageress, as he could quite fancy having a meal there, from time to time. No doubt it would be expensive, but what else – or who else – did he have to spend his inspector's salary on?

There was another knock on the door before the sergeant put his head around it. 'Sir, there's been a burglary reported on Fitzalan Road. Owners were away the last few days and came back to find a back window broken and quite a lot of valuables taken.'

He put the sandwich back in the bag. 'Let's go then, Sergeant.'

Chapter Four

When Edie entered the staff dining room for the late afternoon break, she was presented with a table full of glum-looking colleagues. Hardly anyone had touched their tea. There was Lili, Fanny, Gertie and Phoebe, on the far side, resting their arms on the table. Mrs Turnbull and Mrs Norris were unusually quiet. Jack, the second chef, sat with his head on his palms, his elbows resting on his knees. Even Mrs Leggett was slightly slumped in her seat at the head of the table.

The housekeeper looked up at Edie. 'We can't let this miscarriage of justice take place.'

'I rang Mrs Bygrove's solicitor at home earlier. He didn't appreciate being disturbed on a Sunday but was happy to talk once I had explained the problem. He's going to sort out a surety so she can get bail.'

'That's good,' said the housekeeper. 'She'll still ultimately need some proof that she's innocent though.'

'We need to do something,' said Lili. 'But it's going to be difficult, being December and the hotel so busy.'

'If we carry on being busy after this,' said Fanny. 'People were willing to overlook the accusations against the hotel before, you know, about 'aving conchies 'ere and me, you know, 'aving a baby, but now...'

'I think that conchie was supposed to be me, wasn't it?' said Jack, sitting up. 'I'm the only male left in the hotel of conscription age.'

'Everyone knows you're not a conchie,' said Phoebe.

Mrs Norris patted him on the back. 'That's right, lad. You did your best to enlist.'

77

Gertie held her hands up. 'But what can we do?'

Edie took a seat. 'While it's just us in here, I do have an idea. This is just between us.'

They all leant in, like conspirators.

'What's on your mind?' said Mrs Leggett.

'WPC Amanda Lovelock popped in to see me about an hour ago. She came to say she wasn't happy about the arrest and was sorry she had to take part. She also said that they knew that the letters were being posted at the Norfolk Road pillar box.'

'How would they know that?' Phoebe asked. 'The postmark would only say Littlehampton. It could have been posted in the town.'

'Because Mrs Riddles the postmistress remembers seeing the same handwriting on a few letters she took out of the box. She's received two herself, which she found among the letters when she was sorting them, and realised they must have been posted by the same person.'

'How does this help us?' said Phoebe.

'Amanda said that she wasn't aware that any surveillance had been organised. She felt it was an easy arrest and they may not bother. It seems obvious now that someone has set it up to look like Mrs Bygrove is responsible.'

'That's obvious,' said Gertie.

'If the police aren't going to do any surveillance on the pillar box—'

'Then we should?' Lili finished. 'But if they have set Mrs Bygrove up, they're not gonna send letters while she's locked up.'

'Good point,' said Edie. 'We'll have to wait until Helen's back. However, it wouldn't hurt to have a snoop around, because someone is guilty, and I'm sure as I can be that it's not Helen.'

'The thing is,' Gertie started. 'I don't really like to accuse anyone, but this has happened since Jessie got here, especially as she was the one what asked if Jack was a conchie.'

'I did wonder the same,' said Phoebe. 'Jessie has been terribly forward, always listening into conversations and asking questions, like she's trying to find out things. She's terribly nosey.'

'Jessie might be the one who wrote the letters,' said Gertie. 'Like Phoebe said—'

The door swung open, hitting the wall, causing everyone to look around. There in the doorway was Jessie, coat done up and hat in hand.

'What're you sayin' about me? I just came back for me 'at and there you all are accusing *me* of sending the letters!'

Edie stood up. 'I'm sorry Jessie, we were just working through several theories and—'

'I don't care about your bleedin' *theories*. It weren't me! If that's the way you feel about me, I'll get a bleedin' job elsewhere.'

Ada came through the door, doing her coat up. 'Whatever's the matter?'

'They're only bleedin' accusing me of sending them letters.'

'Jessie, we weren't actually—'

'And they were rude about me!' She stormed off and another door was heard being slammed.

'Oh dear,' said Ada. 'I did wonder about her. She has asked me a lot of questions about people here. I had to tell her I didn't know most of the answers. Because I don't.'

'I'm sorry,' said Gertie. 'I should have made sure no one was listening before I said anything.'

Soon yet another door was slammed, and Alice stood in the doorway, a face like thunder. 'You've no right accusing Jessie of sending them letters. She's nice, is Jessie. She might be talkative and nosey, but that don't make her no criminal.' She stomped off.

'I'd better go,' said Ada. 'I'll see you all tomorrow. Hopefully it will be less fraught.'

'Amen to that,' said Mrs Turnbull.

When Ada had gone, Mrs Leggett stood up and peeped out into the corridor, looking up and down. She came back, closing the door behind her before sitting back down. 'We need to be careful what we say where and keep things to ourselves. It is unfortunate that Miss Jessup overheard, whether she's guilty or not. I think we should tell the police about her though, just in case. In the meantime, let's make a plan for our own investigation.'

'It's all very Sherlock Holmes,' said Mrs Turnbull.

'Or Father Brown,' Gertie piped up.

'We might have included Alice and Annie in our investigation,' said Edie, 'but they do seem to have become good friends with Jessie.'

'What about Ada?' said Jack.

'No, better not. Let's just keep it between us,' said the housekeeper. 'Now Jack, why don't you fetch in some coal, and we'll build up this fire again. Then we'll have a think about this surveillance idea, and what to do next.'

Helen had endured an uncomfortable night in the cells. She'd slept little and cried a lot. Her stomach ached with the stress of thinking about the children. She was used to solving problems at the hotel, and was good at it, but every time she'd tried to think around this problem, she came back to the same thing: if she were locked up, the children might be sent to an orphanage. Her poor, precious children. What would it do to them? And when she came out of prison, would she be allowed to have them back?

It was an immense relief, halfway through the following morning, to see her solicitor, Mr Burtenshaw, come through the door with Inspector Toshack. He was obviously riled. Helen stood but stayed next to the poor excuse for a bed. She picked up her coat, which she'd used as an extra blanket, and put it on.

'And I assure you, Inspector, that you have the *wrong* person. You need to do your job more thoroughly.' The solicitor stepped into the middle of the small cell.

'It's an ongoing investigation, Mr Burtenshaw, and—'

'Then you should have completed it before arresting anyone.'

'To be honest, I do wonder if being locked up here last night was actually safest for Mrs Bygrove, given how angry the crowd that came to accuse her was.'

'She'd have been quite safe enough, locked inside the hotel.'

'Except that the front doors are unlocked much of the time.'

The solicitor huffed impatiently, turning to Helen. 'Are you all right, Mrs Bygrove?'

'I've had better days.'

'Quite, quite. The surety and bail have been sorted out, so you're free to go home.'

'For now,' said the inspector. 'We'll do our best to turn up any new evidence, but if nothing else comes to light, you can expect to appear before the justice of the peace in the new year. They'll decide whether there's a case to answer.' It was said without expression.

Helen picked up her hat and arranged it on her head with the pins. Her hair must be a mess, but she had no mirror to tidy it by.

Toshack led the way out to the reception area.

At the desk was Sergeant Gardner, looking at her sympathetically. At least he didn't seem to think she was guilty. Mr Burtenshaw carried on to the exit without addressing any more comments to the inspector. Helen followed him.

'Good day to you, Mrs Bygrove,' said Toshack.

She looked back at him, tempted to retort with, *It's hardly going to be that*. Instead she said nothing. His face twisted a little as if he were in pain and she found herself feeling a little sorry for him, despite what had happened. After all, it wasn't his fault that someone had gone out of their way to make her look guilty.

Out on the road, which was behind the railway station, she saw a train pull in. How she wished she could escape on one somewhere with the children. Worthing or Brighton, or further away, far, far from the troubles here. What day was it? Monday, of course. Usually the least busy day of the week, but there was still plenty to organise at the hotel, with Christmas coming. She felt no inclination to do any of it.

'I've brought the motorcar to give you a lift home,' said the solicitor.

'That is much appreciated, Mr Burtenshaw, for my back is aching from the terrible bed and I'm sure I look a sight.'

'We'll soon have you home, don't you worry.'

But she would worry, for, unless contradictory evidence was found, the worst was yet to come.

Chapter Five

Four days had gone by, and Helen had slowly got back into the swing of things. Her staff had been so kind, making sure she was all right, asking if there was anything they could do to help her. They must have seen the weariness in her eyes.

The children had been told that mummy had gone to visit a cousin, the night she was in the police cell, so were still blissfully unaware of what had happened. But she wondered how long it would be until some whisper or other reached their ears.

As she'd expected, the custom from those in the Beach Town area had dwindled, and four rooms of guests, hearing from someone outside what had happened, had checked out.

She and Edie were now sitting in the office, discussing what could be done to limit the damage.

'We still have plenty of people from other parts of the country booked in between now and New Year,' said Edie.

'As long as they don't hear in the meantime what has happened and cancel.'

'I don't see how they would.'

'Unless they know somebody who lives here. Or it gets into the newspapers. I am worried, for if we manage to secure the food we need, and that is getting more difficult and expensive, but there's nobody to eat it, we shall quickly lose money. Quite apart from the terrible waste, what with the shortages.' Helen felt a wave of helplessness wash over her. 'Oh Edie, if it goes on like this, we will lose a lot of money and I don't know how we'll carry on. And then Douglas will have all his worst fears realised and probably say he knew all along I would fail.'

Edie stood up and went around the other side of the desk, placing her hand on Helen's shoulder. 'Douglas is the least of our worries.'

'I know, but I wanted so much to prove I could run the hotel proficiently. Even more proficiently than him. I know that sounds petty.'

'Helen, you were already running it more proficiently than him, even before he left.'

'But now it will look like it failed because he wasn't here.'

'You mustn't think like that. We will get to the truth and find out who is really responsible. Some of the local staff have been getting family members to nose around and ask questions. Only those of a select few though.'

'Really?' It was the first Helen had heard of it.

'Yes. Gertie, Phoebe, Mrs Norris and Jack all have family nearby. We thought it better if the staff themselves weren't involved, as whoever's responsible might catch on.'

'That's very kind of them, to put themselves out.'

There was a sharp rap at the door, and Helen called, 'Come in.'

The door opened to reveal young Bert, the porter. 'Madam, Miss Harvey's in the conservatory, causing a stink.'

Helen stood abruptly, making the chair scrape along the stone floor. 'Not again!'

'I tried to stop her in the foyer, but she can't 'alf move, that woman.'

'What on earth is she up to now?' she said, running to the door.

'She reckons she's had another letter.'

'I thought that might happen,' said Edie, following them into the corridor and through the door leading into the dining room.

They could hear the shouting even before they reached the conservatory. Inside, the rain was tapping against the glass. There were only two tables in for afternoon tea.

'Oh, here she is.' Miss Harvey was standing in the middle of the room, an envelope in her hand. 'It didn't take you long to start again, did it?'

'Madam, your presence here isn't welcome,' Mr Perryman barked.

'Hear, hear!' called Marigold, one of the three artists who regularly came to stay at the hotel. With her were Ebony and Hazel.

'Bert, ask Grace to ring the police, please,' said Edie.

'Right away, madam.' He hurried off towards the dining room.

'You needn't waste your time,' said Miss Harvey. 'I've already informed the police that you've started again. And I'm not the only one to have got a letter.'

Mrs Perryman, on a table by the window with her husband, was already standing. 'And what proof do you have? Apart from this claim that Mrs Bygrove has signed the letters and made it obvious it's her? I've never heard anything so ridiculous in all my born days. As if she would be so stupid.'

'It's a double bluff, so that you would come to just that conclusion.'

'So *you* say.'

'No, someone else suggested it. But it makes perfect sense.'

'Who, who suggested it?' said Helen. 'It was you who first came out with it. And you've always disliked me, so what makes perfect sense to me is that you're using it to blacken my reputation, instead of allowing the police to catch the real culprit.'

'I don't need to blacken your reputation. I've been doing a little investigation of my own and discovered from your cousin, Eleanor Wright, that you're from a disreputable family. Your father, Sir Ronald Wright, threw away his fortune, along with your home, South Court Manor in Rustington, on gambling and alcohol, and who knows what else. You are clearly a chip off the old block.'

'It is true that my father wasted his fortune, but had you dug a little deeper, Miss Harvey, you would have discovered that my mother did not waste hers. She gave most of it to me, which is how Douglas and I bought the hotel.'

Looking around, Helen could see astonishment on the faces there.

'Oh, I always assumed that you and Mr Bygrove managed the hotel for the owner,' said Marigold.

'No, we own it.' *Or Douglas does*, she thought. Now, more than ever, she wished that her name was on the deeds too.

'Helen, you are not obliged to tell this woman anything. You have done nothing wrong.'

'I have nothing to hide, Edie. And I also know that Eleanor would say no such thing. Quite apart from the fact that she has been visiting her sister in Kent for the last fortnight.'

'Well, um, she, of course, she told me a while ago.'

'I doubt that, otherwise you would have already revealed it.'

'Anyway, Miss Moore here is hardly in a position to defend your reputation, being the daughter of Baron Moreland and reduced to this.' She held up her hand to indicate the building. 'I wonder what disreputable thing you did.' Miss Harvey looked smug, as she surveyed the room, but nobody was surprised about this and her thin smile soon disappeared.

'First of all, that is hardly a secret any more,' said Edie. 'And hasn't been for a while. Secondly, I didn't do anything *disreputable*. I just didn't want to be part of that world any more.'

'But you are still part of that world, except now you *serve* them.'

'Which is much more to my liking.'

Footsteps were heard near the door. Helen looked around to see the major entering, a newspaper in his hand.

'What the devil is going on here?' he said. 'Oh, it's you, Miss Harvey. Are you responsible for this?' He held up the *Littlehampton Gazette*.

'What's in the *Gazette*, Major?' said Helen, fearing the reply.

'I'm afraid they got wind of the police arresting you, Mrs Bygrove. Jolly bad business, if you ask me.'

'Nobody did ask you,' said Miss Harvey. 'And no, I'm not responsible for it. Now, I've said my piece, so I'll be off.'

'And we'll all be thankful for that,' called Ebony.

86

Once she'd gone, Helen looked around at those present. 'I am so sorry that you've had your afternoon tea spoiled.'

'That's not your fault,' said Mrs Perryman.

'Indeed not,' Ebony agreed. 'She should be reported to the police forthwith for disturbance of the peace.'

'Don't worry, we will inform the police when they arrive. And to make up for the disruption, your afternoon teas will be on the hotel. And yours too, Major Thomas, if you wish to partake.'

'That's very generous of you.' He bowed his head.

Helen and Edie left the conservatory, wandering through the dining room.

'Surely the police aren't going to allow Miss Harvey to keep making such a fuss,' said Edie. 'Maybe it's time they locked *her* up.'

'If only. No doubt she will be going around the town telling all and sundry of the latest misdemeanours. There must be something that can be done.'

'You could take out a charge of defamation. I'm sure Mr Burtenshaw would be able to advise you on that.'

'Except I doubt I'll be able to do that unless I can prove I'm innocent of the charge.'

'And where did she get the information about you being Sir Ronald Wright's daughter from?'

'Where do you think? Eleanor and I have always been good friends. She would never have done that to me.'

'Ah, your husband again. Would he have told her to blame your cousin?'

'The fact she knows that Eleanor Wright is my cousin suggests that, apart from anything else.'

They reached the foyer in time to see Inspector Toshack enter with Constable Twort.

'Good afternoon, Mrs Bygrove, I—'

'Once again, Inspector, there is nothing good about it. And I'm afraid you have missed Miss Harvey, who, once again, came to accuse me of writing more letters.'

'More have been received?'

'Apparently so.' She told him what had taken place in the conservatory.

'Twort, did you… Twort? Twort!'

The constable jerked, as if in shock, then coming to, said, 'Yes sir.'

'Are you all right, Twort?'

'Yes, sir.'

'The samples of writing you took the other day. Did they include Miss Harvey's?'

'No, sir. Just Mrs Riddles', the postmistress, as she had the best access to the letters.'

'But I requested samples from all those who'd received letters who hadn't already given one.'

'But I didn't think it likely—'

'You weren't told to make a judgement, Constable, just to carry out the task.'

'Yes, sir. Sorry, sir. I'll get onto that when we get back.'

'We'll go one better and fetch it on our way back to the station. We'll have to call around to speak to her anyway. Then tomorrow, please carry out the rest.'

The constable simply nodded his head and fiddled with his large, grey moustache, looking sullen. Helen did feel a little sorry for him, being told off in front of them. Still, he didn't seem to be concentrating on the job.

'And there's another thing, Inspector,' said Helen. 'News of my arrest appeared in the *Littlehampton Gazette* today. Have you any idea how that happened?'

'If you're suggesting that I might have tipped them off, you're wrong. I certainly wouldn't stoop to such measures, and I hope my officers wouldn't either. What do you say, Constable?'

'No sir, certainly not.'

'Did you check out Jessie Jessup,' said Edie.

The inspector looked confused. 'Jessie Jessup?'

'I came to the station three days ago and informed Constable Twort here about her. How she started working at the hotel just before the letters started and how nosey she'd been, asking about people.'

He turned towards the constable. 'Twort?'

'Ah, yes. It's on the list, sir.'

Toshack sighed. 'Then make sure you get onto it when we get back, Constable.'

'Yes sir.'

'We'll leave you to get on.' He jogged the arm of the constable, who seemed to be miles away once more, indicating that they should go.

He hadn't got to the exit when the door to the staff area opened. Dorothy came running out, crying.

'Dorothy, I told you to wait until Mummy returned,' Vera called, running after her. 'I'm sorry, madam.'

'That's all right, I— What on earth is wrong? Why have you a plaster on your face?' She hunkered down and looked more carefully. 'And a bruise. And your lip's swollen... Oh, Miss Nye, what are you doing here?'

'I thought I'd better come and talk to you about this.'

The inspector came forward, leaning over to take a better look. 'How did this happen?'

Dorothy, sobbing now, told the story haltingly. 'A big girl – in – in the, the – playground, she – she said her mummy told her that you were a bad person and had been locked up in gaol. So – so, I pushed, h-her, and she, she thumped me.'

'It happened during afternoon playtime. The school nurse attended to her,' said Julia. 'The girl concerned has been disciplined, and Miss Boniface said she'd speak to the parents.'

'Oh, my poor Dorothy.' Helen felt like crying as she cuddled her, but she wouldn't with the inspector there.

'I will visit the school on Monday and speak with Miss Boniface,' said Toshack.

'Very well, Inspector,' said Julia.

'Now we really must go. I hope you're feeling better soon, Dorothy.'

Helen didn't reply or look around as he left.

'You two see to the children,' said Edie. 'I'm going to get this sorted out. Julia, seeing you has given me an idea. Could you spare five minutes?'

'Of course.'

'Excellent.'

Helen didn't question what it might be. She trusted Edie and she was happy to wait until this evening to find out what she had in mind.

–

'There's one good piece of news at least,' said Lili, as Edie entered the staff dining room, at early supper.

'What's that then?' Edie took a seat.

'Mr Lloyd George has taken over as Prime Minister from Mr Asquith. Maybe some progress will be made in the war now.'

'I don't see how,' said Mrs Leggett, the only other person in the room so far. 'It's not like he can conjure up more troops, or better weapons, or has some magic powers.'

'Doesn't hurt to hope, does it?'

'Terrible business, what happened earlier,' said the house-keeper. 'Both Miss Harvey turning up, and poor little Dorothy being beaten up like that. I blame Miss Harvey for that too, for if she hadn't gone shouting her mouth off about Mrs Bygrove being responsible for the letters, I doubt word would have got round so quickly.'

'No, it's most unfortunate,' said Edie. 'But I have made some progress on our plans to get to the bottom of it.'

'I'm all ears, Miss Moore.'

'It occurred to me, when Julia Nye turned up earlier with Dorothy, that her rooms, being on the first floor in Norfolk Road, are within view of the post office. Julia has agreed to let a few of us take turns in watching from her sitting room, whoever is not on duty at the time. I'll do it tonight. It will be much better than our original idea of hiding in a doorway or dark corner.'

'I still have reservations. I'm not sure the person watching will be in a fit state to work the next day if it happens in the middle of the night.'

'We won't watch all night, of course. Whoever is posting them probably doesn't want to be up in the middle of the night either.'

'I think we're making a lot of assumptions,' said the house-keeper. 'We don't know if this round of letters was posted in Norfolk Road, like the last. We have no idea what time the perpetrator might post them.'

'I know, Mrs Leggett, but we have to do what we can, otherwise there'll be no jobs for us to be in a fit state to do.'

'Yes, yes, you're right. When the shifts have finished this evening, I'll gather our little group together and tell them the plan, while you're at Miss Nye's.'

'Good.'

The door opened, and Annie Twine entered with Ada Salt-marsh. Mrs Leggett put her forefinger to her lips and the other two nodded.

–

'Thank you,' said Edie, as Julia placed a cup of tea for her on the windowsill.

They sat together, in the darkened room, on two dining chairs, looking out of the bay window.

'We're lucky that the moon is three-quarters full,' said Julia. 'It does make it easier to see the street.'

'When the clouds aren't drifting over it.'

'This is exciting. I feel like I've taken on some of Philip's work, now he isn't the detective inspector here any more. He will laugh when I write and tell him. Maybe he'll have some suggestions.'

'Did he do a lot of surveillance work here?'

'Not that he told me about. The new DI does seem to be happy to take the easy route though. You would think they'd have had someone here, watching.'

'Maybe there is, and we can't see them,' said Edie. 'After all, what would be the point if we could?'

'True.'

'And I hate to remind you, Julia, but DI Davis did take the easy route to begin with, when it came to assuming that our fellow lodger was our erstwhile landlady's killer.'

'You are right, of course, he did. He has said so himself and regrets it.'

'How is he, Philip? I do find it strange, calling him that.'

Chuckling, she said. 'So did I to begin with.' Then she became serious. 'He's hating the training, and not looking forward to the prospect of fighting. He says it's his job to prevent crimes, and he feels like he'll be perpetrating them.'

'My Charlie felt the same. Now he's in the thick of it, out in France, I do worry about him.'

'I can understand that.'

Edie peered out into the darkness. 'It's very quiet out there. Apart from the odd man going in or out of the New Inn.'

'Wait. Who's that there, on the corner of Selborne Road?' She pointed out of the side of the bay window.

'It's Constable Twort.' Edie studied him more carefully, squinting. 'Yes, I'm sure it is. He's even in uniform.'

'Do you think they've sent him to watch?'

'If they have, he's not being very secretive about it. If the guilty party were to come here to post anything, they would spot him and be put off. Oh, what a bother. You'd think if they were going to do any surveillance, they'd do it properly.'

'He may only be on the beat, of course. And if someone did post a letter, they may be perfectly innocent.'

Edie took a sip of her tea. 'I know. But if we can make a note of those we recognise, then it's a start. And the guilty party might act, well, guiltily.'

'You know, it could be someone who's received a letter. Even Miss Harvey herself.'

'We have talked about all sorts of possibilities at the hotel. But if it were her, she'd be unwise to make such a fuss and draw attention to herself. We've even wondered if it could be someone wanting to buy the hotel and thinking that if Helen were gaoled they'd get it cheaply.'

'It's certainly not beyond the bounds of possibility,' said Julia. 'It looks like Constable Twort is staying put. If he were on the beat, he'd surely keep walking. And he does seem to be watching the post office.'

'He does. If you don't mind though, I will stay a little longer. I don't know what it is about him, but he doesn't seem very alert.'

Edie and Julia chatted as they looked out of the window. For forty minutes, Constable Twort did not move.

'You don't have to stay with me all evening, if you have other things to do, Julia. Or if you want to get to bed.'

'I will probably go soon, but I'm all right for now. Oh look – the constable is moving off.'

'What, that's it? If that was surveillance, it was very poor. He hasn't even been there an hour.'

'No, he hasn't.' Julia stood up. 'I will get myself off to bed now, if you don't mind.'

'Of course not. I'm just so grateful to you for letting us watch from here. I'll probably only stay another half-hour myself, as I have an early shift tomorrow.'

They wished each other good night, and soon Edie was alone. She watched for the time she'd stated before putting on her hat and coat and letting herself out.

–

It was four days after she'd been let out of gaol that Helen received the letter from Douglas.

She was standing in the office now, reading it over again, a little confused. There was nothing about the accusations or about her arrest.

There was a knock on the door.

'Come in.'

Edie put her head around the door, and started to say something about the butcher, but stalled, continuing with, 'Are you all right? You look… confused.'

'It's another letter from Douglas.'

'Oh dear, he found out.'

'That's just it. It's not a nice letter, but there is nothing about the libel letters and the arrest. I don't understand it. If Isabella Harvey is writing to him, you'd have thought that she'd have jumped at the chance at getting me into trouble.'

Edie stepped in properly and closed the door. 'That is rather strange. What does it say? Sorry, it's none of my business.'

'On the contrary, I think it is. Listen…

I hear that the number of guests at the hotel has dropped dramatically. It should be booming at this time of the year! You are a complete imbecile, and I should never have left you in charge of the hotel. Even that idiot Fanny could have done a better job than you. However, I currently have no choice but to let you carry on, since the authorities here don't seem to think this is a good enough excuse to take leave.

'This is followed by a whole list of instructions. Well, more demands.'

'What's Miss Harvey's game?'

'Maybe it isn't her telling him things after all. Maybe, whoever it is, has some plan they think will work to some advantage.'

'That could still be Miss Harvey.'

'Oh, I don't know, Edie. I think I'll just tear this one up, the same as I did the last one… Anyway, I'm due on the desk for a short shift now. What were you saying about the butcher?'

'Just that he's able to deliver most of what we asked for, and he'll send it in an hour or so.'

'That is some good news at least.'

—

As Douglas's letter had implied, trade had become even slower at the hotel, when normally, being nearly halfway through December, it usually picked up. Helen surveyed the reservation book as she stood at the desk. There had been three more cancellations from staying guests, so word must have got around. They were still half full though, so that was something. However, even fewer outside guests had come in for meals, morning coffee and afternoon tea. Even the cheap meal that they'd put on yesterday had attracted far fewer people.

How long before the rumour spread further and wider and the business started losing money?

And what if they found no evidence to acquit her? What if she went to gaol? This thought haunted her several times a day. She shivered as a cold chill of dread surged through her. What would happen to her children? Would they be sent to a home, or the workhouse? Could Vera keep on looking after them, and the staff keep running the hotel, on their own, with Edie in charge? The dreadful possibilities of what could happen made her feel sick.

The front doors opened, and a couple with three children and what looked like three maids and a chauffeur entered. Helen composed herself. She needed to keep going, not buckle under the worry of this dire situation. All was not lost – yet.

Ah yes, she recognised them now. She put on her most welcoming smile. 'Lord and Lady Glanville, how nice to see you again.'

'Good afternoon, Mrs Bygrove. I'm glad to see that it looks as splendid as ever here, the war notwithstanding.' He indicated the foyer.

'We do our best, my lord, despite the troubled times.'

'I was wondering what the food would be like now.'

'Still up to our usual standard, my lord. There is less to hand, that is true, but our kitchen makes excellent use of what there is.'

'I don't doubt it at all. It's good to get away from London, get some good sea air, even at this time of the year, especially after the recent air raid.'

'I read about that, my lord. Very worrying.'

She proceeded to check them in, reminding them of mealtimes and answering her ladyship's questions. The servants would be accommodated in smaller rooms, except for the nursemaid, who would sleep in the children's room.

As she dealt with them, she didn't feel part of the proceedings. It was as if she was watching herself from a distance. It was most disconcerting, but it was how she'd been feeling for the last few days.

'Here are Gertrude and Wilfred,' she said, as the two porters on duty returned from errands. 'They will show you to your rooms and carry your luggage.'

'Thank you, Mrs Bygrove.'

The group moved off, following the porters. Lord and Lady Glanville and the children took the lift, while the rest headed to the stairs.

Helen wrote something in the reservation book, leaving it open for the ink to dry, before glancing at the grandfather clock. The children should be home soon, and Grace English would be here to take over at the desk shortly after. There were things to organise, but she'd eat with the children and spend a little time with them first. It was something to look forward to.

She must try to look on the bright side, to be optimistic. She wasn't guilty of the crime for which she'd been arrested. The truth would out, and everything would get better. She closed her eyes, breathing out slowly through her mouth, calming herself.

There, that was better. The three artists, Hazel, Ebony and Marigold, entered the foyer from the stairs, all in a different colour and style of corduroy coat, each with a fur collarette and a turban hat.

'We're just off for a walk on the promenade, while it's still light,' called Ebony. 'Although the wind is a little bracing.'

'At least the sun is shining,' Helen replied.

'Indeed.'

As she was checking the clock once more, the door from the staff corridor opened. It was slightly too early for Grace to be relieving her.

'Vera, so you're home. Grace will be here soon and then I'll—'

'Madam, it's Dorothy.'

'What is wrong?'

Mrs Leggett appeared behind Vera. 'I'll take over from you until Grace arrives.'

'Has something happened?' She left her post and the housekeeper stepped into her place. 'Has someone picked on her again?' She hurried to the staff door.

'No, madam,' said Vera. 'She's not well. She's in the scullery.'

'The scullery?'

They hurried through the stillroom, where Hetty had hold of Arthur's hand and Annie was rocking the perambulator with Elsie in it. In the scullery, Miss Bolton, the hotel nurse, was hunkering down, talking to Dorothy, who was sitting on a stool there.

'What is it, sweetheart?' said Helen.

'Don't feel well, Mummy.' She coughed.

'She has a high temperature, and this…' Miss Bolton lifted the little girl's dress and vest, to reveal a rash.

Helen put her fingers to her lips. 'Oh my!'

'I believe it's measles.' The nurse placed the child's clothes back in place.

'There've apparently been two serious cases of it in Dorothy's class, reported today,' said Vera.

Helen found it hard to swallow. She'd had a cousin die of measles. 'V – Vera, please ring Dr Ferngrove.'

The nursemaid rushed away.

'We must get her to her bedroom and away from the staff, until we find out who's had it and who hasn't,' said Miss Bolton. 'We don't want this spreading around the hotel. I had it as a young woman, so I'm immune.'

'And I had it as a child, so I will take her and look after her. I'll need you here, on duty, in case others get it.'

'Of course, madam. We will also have to isolate Vera, Arthur and Elsie. We can put Elsie's cot in Arthur and Dorothy's bedroom.'

'It's not ideal, but I suppose it will have to do.'

Helen knelt and hugged her daughter. Dorothy started sobbing. Helen felt herself tear up but held her feelings in.

'Come on sweetheart, let's get you to bed.'

She led her out of the scullery and stillroom, to the corridor, and then up the stairs to their rooms. It was then she let the tears fall, silently. Her poor, poor Dorothy. If anything should happen to her...

She couldn't think that way. She would do her best to nurse her daughter and get her through it.

Chapter Six

'The doctor has confirmed that it is measles,' Edie told the staff at early supper.

'Poor Mrs Bygrove; that's all she needs,' said Gertie, taking off her porter's peaked hat and undoing her bun so that her auburn curls fell down her back.

'Dorothy's not too poorly at the moment, but the doctor says she's to be given plenty of water, and he's left some laudanum for the pain. And Arthur, of course, has to stay away from school.'

Fanny thumped herself down at the table. Her mouth was turned down at the corners and her eyes were sad. 'I can't see Elsie for the next few days, even though I've had the measles. It's in case she sneezes or snivels on me and I carry it on my hands or clothes or whatnot and infect someone.'

'That's sensible, pet,' said Mrs Turnbull. 'You wouldn't want to be givin' it to no guests.'

''Spose. But Elsie will wonder where I am. And I don't want her forgetting me.'

'She won't do that, pet.' The storekeeper leant over the table and patted Fanny's hands.

'Is there anyone here who hasn't had measles?' Edie asked. 'I'm making a list.' She looked around at Gertie, Fanny, Mrs Turnbull, Phoebe and the head stillroom maid, Hetty.

'Don't think I have,' said Hetty. 'Unless I had it when I was very young and don't remember.'

'Hopefully it won't be a problem,' said Edie, 'if we all wash regularly and vigorously, and keep well away from the children.'

'Ooooh,' said Fanny, distressed.

'I know Fanny, it must be hard, but it won't be for long. With Helen out of action, the shortage of food, and this libel case hanging over us, it's not going to be easy. And trying to keep up with our surveillance is going to be hard too.'

'We'll manage,' Gertie said decidedly. 'By the way, I meant to say. During my turn at Miss Nye's last night, I did see Constable Twort as well, just for a while, watching the post office.'

'That's odd,' said Hetty. 'He was there for just half-an-hour when I did my stint. Do you think they have some information about the letter writer only turning up at a certain time?'

'I don't see how,' said Edie, 'but who knows? Unless the constable's been asked just to hang around for a while on his beat...' She shrugged.

'It's a good job we're on the case,' said Gertie. 'Hey, maybe we could speak to Amanda again, see if she knows anything.'

Edie nodded. 'That's not a bad idea. I'll pop round and see if she's in after my next shift.'

Mrs Leggett strode into the room. 'Is there no supper served yet?'

'Lili and I will fetch it,' said Edie, summoning her friend.

In the corridor, on the way to the kitchen, Lili said, 'I'm worried about the kiddies. There was an outbreak of measles in my village a few years back. Killed a few of them it did. Along with a couple of adults.'

'How awful for you all. It doesn't bear thinking about. Freddie and I had it pretty mildly, but our mother caught it from us and she was far worse. But I've never known anyone die from it.'

'And let's hope you never do.'

–

It had been three days since Dorothy had come home with the rash. It now covered her body, while the fever and cough had got worse.

Helen, having not long risen, sat by her sleeping daughter, who had been in her double bed since being diagnosed. Her breathing was noisy, but at least she was resting. Helen picked up the book she'd borrowed from the library, *Sons and Lovers*, by D. H. Lawrence. It was a little depressing, making her wish she'd picked up something lighter.

She'd read only half a page when there was a knock at the door.

'Yes?'

Vera peeped around the door, her brow puckered. 'Mrs Bygrove, both Arthur and Elsie now have a rash.'

Helen groaned inwardly. 'I suppose it was inevitable. Dorothy would have been infectious before she had the symptoms.'

'Poor Arthur's been scratching and is a bit sore, I'm afraid. And Elsie is crying and trying to rub the spots.'

'Oh, poor little loves. You'd better call down to ask someone to telephone Dr Ferngrove, especially as Elsie is so young. I'll go and fetch them in here while you do that. There's no point in them being isolated from us now, and it will be more comfortable in here.'

'Yes, madam.'

Helen rose, checking on Dorothy one more time, before leaving the room.

'Mummy!' Arthur called, still in his pyjamas, when Helen opened the door to his bedroom.

Elsie was in the cot that had been placed in there, next to Dorothy's bed, grizzling. Helen picked her up and joggled her up and down. 'Come on Arthur, you're both coming to sit with me now.'

In the sitting room, Helen placed Elsie on the rug and brought her some wooden bricks to play with. Arthur sat with her and built her a tower. The grizzling became intermittent.

Helen hunkered down. 'I'm so sorry I haven't been able to see you the last three days, Arthur. I was hoping that you wouldn't catch the measles. How do you feel?'

'A bit itchy, Mummy.'

She felt his forehead. 'At least you don't feel too hot. That's something.' She felt Elsie's forehead. It was only a little warmer than usual.

Vera returned. 'Edie's ringing the doctor now.'

'Good. Poor Fanny. We'll have to get someone to locate her. She'll be even more distraught now if Elsie has it. Perhaps I should give her a few days off work to be with her.'

'It's not like she can do anything though, madam. We don't need all of us looking after them.'

'No. I just know how I'd feel if it were me. It was bad enough not seeing Arthur for three days. And although it's December, we don't have as many guests as we would have done. It's something I'll have to think about.'

'I'll go and call down the stairs for our breakfast.'

'Thank you, Vera.'

Seeing the nursemaid leave, Elsie's eyes opened wide and she started to grizzle again.

'Come on, little one,' said Helen. She picked her up, then went over to the shelves and removed a copy of *The Wind in the Willows*. 'Shall we have a story all about Mr Toad, Moley, Ratty and Mr Badger?'

'Yes please, Mummy.' Arthur hopped over to the settee and jumped onto it. At least he seemed in good spirits.

Helen sat down, placing Elsie on her knee, and began to read.

She'd got a few pages in when there was a knock at her living room door. 'It's only me, Mrs Bygrove, Dr Ferngrove.'

'Come in, Doctor.'

He did as requested. 'Hello again, unfortunately. Now let us have a look at these youngsters here.' He lifted Arthur's pyjama top, inspecting his chest, then Elsie's nightie, repeating the action.

'Hmm, yes. I'm afraid they do both have measles. There are quite a few missing from the schools now with it. My advice is the same as I gave for Dorothy. Children under five can get it more seriously, as can adults, so we must keep a particular eye on Elsie. But it's not always the case. With any luck, neither of them will be too unwell. Not everyone is. But call me if you have any concerns, or if they're in pain and you need more laudanum.'

The door opened, and Vera entered with a tray containing two toast racks of triangular slices, a butter dish and a pot of jam.

'Thank you, Vera. If you'd just place them on the table, we'll be over soon.'

'I presume the children do have measles.'

'I'm afraid so... Doctor, could you do me a favour? On your way out, would you go out through the foyer and speak to Miss Moore. According to the rota, she should be on the desk. Would you ask her to find Fanny after her shift and tell her about Elsie? And to tell her that she's to have a couple of days off to attend her daughter.'

'Of course, Mrs Bygrove.'

It was the very least she could do, in fact, the only thing she could do. Fanny's place was with her daughter, just as hers was.

'But first,' said the doctor, 'I'll check on Dorothy while I'm here.'

–

That evening, with Fanny sitting with Arthur and Elsie in the children's bedroom, and Vera having an evening to herself in one of the men's vacant bedrooms, Helen decided she needed to write to Douglas about Dorothy and Arthur. She'd been putting it off, not wanting to commit to paper how ill their daughter was.

She sat at her dressing table so she could keep an eye on Dorothy.

What would Douglas think? Would he be upset, like she was? It made her sad to wonder whether he'd really care. For someone who had been so keen to have children, he'd been quite absent as a father. He'd never been one to lavish affection on them, not even a cuddle.

She pushed the fountain pen and writing pad away, as the tears started to fall. Her poor babies, having a father who always put himself and his own interests first. Even her own father, reprobate that he'd been, had shown her more affection.

Pushing her hand into her skirt pocket, she retrieved a handkerchief, wiping her eyes with it before blowing her nose. This wouldn't get the missive written.

She made the letter short. There was no point furnishing it with any other news, particularly not that of her arrest. With any luck, by the time he came home on leave, that episode would all be over and in the past. But was it likely he wouldn't find out eventually, with Miss Harvey telling everyone? She still wondered how he hadn't heard about it already.

'Mummy?' came a small voice from the bed.

Helen rose and went to her. 'Dorothy, are you all right?'

'I had a bad dream, about school, and a big girl with red spots, hitting me.'

'My poor darling.' She bent over and cuddled her daughter. 'Would you like me to read to you for a while, to cheer you up?'

'Yes please, Mummy.'

Helen picked up *The Emerald City of Oz* from the bedside table and sat on the bed.

—

At early staff lunch the following day, Edie met Lili as they entered the staff dining room.

'Phoebe tells me that there are only a few bookings for the cheap meal today, even though it's a Sunday roast,' said Edie.

'That's right. Some might turn up on the off chance of course, but considering we had full bookings the first two times, and even the last one was half full, seems quite poor it does. As are our outside bookings for the normal luncheon.'

'Do you think word has got around that the children have measles, and people are afraid of catching it?'

'I wouldn't be surprised,' said Lili. 'That, on top of the letters, probably the final straw it is.'

'I can only see it getting worse,' said the housekeeper, entering the room with a tray of sandwiches.

'Don't say that, Mrs Leggett,' said Phoebe, already sitting at the table. 'If this goes on, we'll be losing our jobs.'

'It's better that we expect the worst so we're prepared for it, rather than assuming it will all be fine and being bitterly disappointed when it isn't.'

'That's one way of lookin' at it, I suppose,' said Mrs Turnbull.

Other staff members joined them at the table, but no one was in a talkative mood today. There was little conversation apart from requesting the various trays from different parts of the table.

As Edie rose to gather some of the empty plates, Annie stuck her head around the door. 'Miss Nye's in the scullery and would like a word, Edie.'

'You go,' said Lili. 'I'll clear these up.'

In the scullery, Julia was standing by the back door, her forehead puckered with worry. 'I'm so sorry to disturb you. I was hoping you might have a moment though. There's something I'm rather concerned about.'

'I'm helping with luncheon in a few minutes, but I have a little time after that I can spare, say two-thirty, if that's all right with you.'

'Yes, I'll come back then. I don't know if this is significant, but it might be.'

'I'll meet you by the fountain.'

Julia nodded. 'See you later.' She let herself out, still frowning.

'What was all that about?' said Annie.

'I've no idea.' But it didn't look good, and she had a feeling of foreboding.

Chapter Seven

'Another dull day,' said Edie, as she caught Julia up by the fountain.

'And jolly cold too.'

'I'm sorry for having to get you out twice.'

'No, it's fine. I like to take a walk each day if I can, whatever the weather. How is Dorothy now?'

'Quite poorly still. And now Arthur and Elsie have it.'

'Oh dear.' Julia frowned. 'About a quarter of the children in school have it, so they've decided to close early for the Christmas holidays. Luckily for me, I had it as a child.'

'Is that what you wanted to tell me?' Edie didn't feel that this was something that merited a special meeting.

'No. Shall we head up to the promenade?'

'All right.'

As they walked, Julia said, 'I don't know if this is significant, regarding the libellous letters. It's about one of your newer chambermaids, who was in the staff dining room when I dropped in with the book for Dorothy.'

'Oh dear. We did have our suspicions about Jessie. She left in a huff when she overheard us discussing it.'

'Jessie? No, I don't mean her, I mean the other one. Ada, wasn't it?'

Edie was confused. 'What do you mean?'

'Yesterday afternoon, when I was on my way back from a walk by the beach, I took the route down Selborne Road. I saw Ada going into Miss Harvey's guest house. It was getting dark, but I'm sure it was her. I thought it curious, after all the fuss Miss Harvey had made at the hotel.'

'Goodness, that is rather – odd. She might have been visiting someone who was staying there, of course.'

'I wondered that. Then I remembered Ada mentioning that she lived on Western Road. One of my fellow teachers lived on Western Road until fairly recently, so I called at her house and asked her if she knew Ada, and whether she had a connection to Miss Harvey. She told me that her sister used to be friends with Ada, and that she is Miss Harvey's niece.'

'Her *niece*?'

'Obviously you didn't know that.'

'No. How strange that Miss Harvey would have made such a fuss and risk her niece's job, should the hotel end up closing down.' Edie tried to take it all in. 'Maybe her aunt doesn't even know she works here.'

'I can't imagine she doesn't know, and Ada must know about Miss Harvey's accusations,' said Julia.

'Yes, she must do. Perhaps she didn't mention her aunt because she was afraid she'd be sacked. Or...' Edie was trying to work it out in her mind.

'Or?'

'Did Miss Harvey push her into getting the job to take advantage of the situation, to cause more trouble for Helen somehow? Maybe to gather information to link to the letters and make it seem more likely that Helen was the guilty party? I'm sure she's under the illusion that if Helen went to gaol, they would allow Douglas Bygrove to leave the army and run the hotel.'

'They're unlikely to discharge him for *that*,' said Julia. 'After all, Philip was called up, and he was a detective inspector. But Edie, I think you're missing the point. Someone had the blotting paper and blotted the letters with it, then placed it in Helen's rooms. And then put supposed discarded sheets in her office. Whoever did that *must* have written the letters. So it must have been someone with easy access to Helen's rooms and the office.'

A light dawned in Edie's mind. 'What, you mean Miss Harvey isn't just taking advantage, she's actually *responsible*?'

'That is exactly what I'm saying. I was thinking about it all evening, and long after I went to bed.'

'I know she's rather an unbearable person, and she clearly has a soft spot for Mr Bygrove, but would she be that devious?'

'Someone has been, and given the trouble she's caused, she's the most likely candidate.'

They reached the promenade, looking out over the dull sea that reflected the grey sky. There was a light breeze, but it was chilly. Few other people were strolling here today. On the beach, a few sandpipers were being chased by the frothy waves, pecking at the wet sand as they went.

Edie digested Julia's information for a few moments. It did make perfect sense. Miss Harvey had done a good job of deflecting her guilt by accusing Helen. 'My goodness, Julia, you're not engaged to a detective inspector for nothing. Philip would be proud of you.'

'If I'm right. DI Toshack may not be there on a Sunday, so I will go to the police station first thing tomorrow and ask to speak to him. It's better if I go than one of you, as I'm more removed from the situation and less likely to be thought of as biased.'

'And do you know what? Now I think about it, Ada encouraged us to think it might be Jessie when Gertie suggested it. And she started at the hotel the day that Miss Harvey mentioned the letters to Helen, asking if she'd had one. Thank you, Julia, I'm most grateful for this information. We all will be if your hunch turns out to be right.'

'I wouldn't tell too many people at the moment. Maybe just Helen.'

'I won't tell her just yet as she has enough to deal with. I will tell Lili though. Now, I'd better get back to the hotel.'

'I'm going to carry on with my walk. I'll let you know how my visit to the police station goes. Can you meet up for a little while, tomorrow afternoon?'

'I have a couple of hours off, so yes. I could meet you at, say, quarter past two? At Read's Dining Rooms in Surrey Street?

I could do with visiting the shops for a couple of Christmas presents.'

'Lovely. I'll see you there.'

It had been a busy weekend at the police station. After the burglary in Fitzalan Road at the beginning of December, there had been another the following weekend. But this weekend there had been two reported, at the dairy in Church Street and at a greengrocer's on Beach Road.

Detective Inspector Toshack was examining the notes he'd made, looking for similarities between the cases, when there was a knock at his office door.

'Come in.'

Sergeant Gardner opened the door and leant round it. 'Sir, Miss Nye, a teacher from East Street School, would like a word with you about the letters sent in Beach Town. Seems she might have a lead.'

'I've got work to do, Gardner. I haven't got time to talk to every Tom, Dick and Harry. Just make a note of it and I'll have a look later.'

'Sir, she's well respected in the town, and she is DI Davis's fiancée, so not just some Tom, Dick or Harry, as you put it.'

'I know she's DI Davis's fiancée.' That's what was rattling him. Davis's name came up far too frequently and Toshack felt like he was still in charge here somehow.

'I think you're going to want to hear what she's got to say.'

'The last thing I need is someone thinking they can interfere because they're the former DI's fiancée.'

'But sir—'

'Very well, Gardner,' he said with a strained sigh. 'Show her in.'

'Will do, sir.'

Within seconds, the sergeant was back with her. She was a petite, neatly dressed woman in her twenties, with brown hair pinned up under a small hat.

'Please, take a seat, Miss Nye.'

'Thank you, Inspector.'

When Gardner had left, Toshack turned his notebook over to a fresh page, and lifted his pencil. 'Now, what is this all about?'

'I saw Ada Saltmarsh, a chambermaid at the Beach Hotel, going into Miss Harvey's house on Saturday afternoon.'

'And?'

'She hasn't told anybody at the hotel that she is Miss Harvey's niece.'

'Does she need to?'

'She started working there when the news of the letters began circulating. I visited the hotel then and remember that it was her first day. Edie Moore, the undermanageress there, told me that it was the day that Miss Harvey asked Mrs Bygrove if she'd heard about the letters.'

'Coincidence?' Despite the question, he'd never really believed in them, but he was going to play his interest down. He didn't want her getting any ideas.

'Miss Moore also told me that Ada had encouraged the staff to believe that another new member of staff, Jessie Jessup, might be responsible.'

'Ah yes, I've already spoken to her, and we've eliminated her from our enquiries.'

'Exactly. So why would Ada encourage that belief?'

'She might truly have thought she was responsible.'

'Somebody has gone to a lot of trouble to implicate Helen Bygrove in this crime, Inspector. The blotting paper could easily have been placed in Mrs Bygrove's quarters by a chambermaid. And they could also have taken examples of her handwriting.'

'There are quite a number of people working there.'

'Yes, but the blotting paper and screwed-up letters weren't found until after Ada Saltmarsh started working there.'

Toshack made notes as she spoke, all the while with a creeping sense of unease. Could he have rushed to judgement, being too keen to get the case wrapped up?

'And to be honest, Inspector, I don't believe Mrs Bygrove would do such a thing. She's always struck me as a kind and generous person. And currently, this is the last thing she needs. Did you know she is nursing her sick daughter, who has measles? And her son and a maid's baby daughter now have it too.'

Measles. He hated that word. 'I did hear that there'd been some cases.'

'*Some* cases? It's rampant around the schools. We're lucky so far to have had no deaths.'

Toshack felt like the air had been sucked from his lungs. He took a few seconds to calm himself, displaying a deadpan face so as not to reveal his discomfort. 'I presume it's been reported to the Medical Officer of Health?'

'Yes, all the cases we know of in our school have. I cannot speak for the other schools though.'

'Look, Miss Nye, I've made a note of your concerns and will consider them.'

She looked disappointed, but he was hardly going to admit that it was a good lead.

'That's all I can ask, Inspector.'

As she got up to leave, Toshack rose, asking, 'How is DI Davis getting on? I believe you're engaged?'

'He's still training, but likely to be sent abroad in the new year. I believe you served also, earlier in the war?'

'That's right.' He didn't want to go into that, and regretted, in hindsight, that he'd asked the question. 'Good day to you, Miss Nye.'

'Good day, Inspector.'

When she'd left, he sat back down with a thump. *Measles.* Whenever he heard the word, he wanted to weep. He recalled his younger brother, Lewis, a lively lad. He'd been taken as a four-year-old by a dose of measles. And it had been him who had picked it up from school and given it to his brother. He shook his head.

He had work to do. And that work would help him forget. Forget Lewis, forget Olive, forget his unborn child. Until he was alone once more to mourn them.

But first, he must check the protocol for measles outbreaks in the area with Sergeant Gardner.

–

Edie returned to the hotel after her afternoon tea with Julia and a little shopping. She was taking her hat and coat off in the staff corridor when Lili put her head around the door of the dining room.

'Good, it's you, Edie. How did it go with Miss Nye?'

'Hold on. Who's in the dining room?'

'Just me, Gertie, Phoebe, Mrs Norris and Mrs Leggett.'

'I'll come in and tell you all then, before anyone else turns up.'

As she sat down, Mrs Turnbull put her knitting down. The five women at the table leant in, as if in on a secret. She supposed they were, thought Edie.

'What's all this about then?' said the housekeeper. 'Lili said that there's new information.'

She told them of Julia's discovery about Ada being Miss Harvey's niece.

There were several exclamations of horror.

'Of all the cheeky devils!' said Gertie. 'So Miss Harvey *herself* might be responsible? After all the fuss she made?'

'It makes sense, really,' said Mrs Leggett. 'We should have thought of it before.'

'Julia went to see DI Toshack this morning,' said Edie. 'I'm not sure how well it went, as she overheard him becoming a little irritated about her being DI Davis's fiancée. He said he'd made a note of her concerns, but she wasn't convinced he was at all interested. She reckons he's a bit of a cold fish.'

'He is,' said Phoebe.

'A nice lookin' one, though,' said Mrs Turnbull, with a glint in her eye.

'Bridget, really!' said Mrs Leggett.

'Ada's still on duty,' said Phoebe. 'Do you think one of us should follow her when she leaves?'

'I'll do that,' said Mrs Turnbull. 'Most of you will be on shifts when she goes.'

'Thank you,' said Edie. 'Now, I have a shift on the desk in five minutes as Mr Watkins needs to pop out, so I'd better get ready.'

-

Edie hadn't been on the desk ten minutes, when two angry-looking women shoved their way through the door and into the foyer. She recognised them as proprietresses of nearby guest houses on South Terrace but couldn't recall their names. She sensed immediately that they were not here to partake of the hotel's facilities, but on some contentious errand.

'You there,' called the shorter and older of the two, marching over to the desk. 'I demand to speak with Mrs Bygrove.'

'I'm afraid she is not available at this time.'

'I bet she isn't,' said the other woman, tall and stocky, with an expression of fury. Edie certainly wouldn't have wanted to get on the wrong side of her.

'She is nursing her sick daughter, who has measles.'

'Hm, a likely story,' said the older woman.

'I can assure you it is true. East Street School has had a severe outbreak.'

'We've each received one of her nasty little letters with their slanderous accusations and the most *foul* language.'

'Yes,' said the tall woman. 'Most unbecoming of someone running a first-class hotel. It wouldn't have happened in Mr Bygrove's time as manager as he had her firmly in place. And *her* the daughter of a Knight of the Realm, so we hear.'

'But then Sir Ronald Wright was a drunk and a gambler. His disgraceful behaviour has clearly rubbed off on his daughter.'

'That is enough!' Edie said firmly. 'Clearly you have been listening to Miss Harvey's vitriol. The only so-called evidence that Mrs Bygrove was involved was planted to implicate her. Miss Harvey, who has made it quite clear that she has an interest in Mr Bygrove and was often in his company before he was conscripted, has exploited the situation to blacken his wife's name.'

There was a moment of uncertainty in the two women's eyes, as they glanced at each other. She wouldn't give away that they suspected Miss Harvey of writing the letters herself, but she wanted to put some doubt in their minds.

'But Miss Harvey is a respectable woman.'

'Is she? Paying undue attention to another woman's husband does not seem respectable to me. Nor does accusing somebody of a crime when you have no real evidence. And when, in the six years that Mrs Bygrove has been here, has she ever shown herself to be anything other than respectable? Look at all the charity events she has organised here – and it *was* her who organised them, not Mr Bygrove, as Miss Harvey would have you believe. He wasn't at all keen. Has Miss Harvey been involved in such events?'

'No, but—' started the older woman.

'And why on earth would Mrs Bygrove make it obvious that such letters are from her. She's an intelligent woman.'

'Now *that's* because—'

'She's trying to double bluff people?' finished Edie. '*That* rumour came from Mrs Harvey too, didn't it? And what *motive* would she have for sending such letters?'

The two women looked less sure of themselves.

'Now, if that's all, I suggest you take the letters to the police station and stop harassing Mrs Bygrove who already has enough to contend with and hasn't even had the opportunity to leave the hotel, let alone post libellous letters.'

'She could have got a member of staff to post them,' said the taller woman.

'And the hotel shouldn't be open if there are cases of measles here,' said the older one.

'We have followed Dr Ferngrove's instructions to the letter and they are all completely isolated,' Edie countered. 'The staff and guests here are probably safer than you are walking down a busy street. Now, if you don't mind.'

'Are you encountering some trouble here, Miss Moore?' said Major Thomas, having just come down the stairs, dressed in his overcoat.

'It's all right, Major,' said Edie. 'It's been dealt with.'

He walked to the edge of the desk, hands behind his back, eyeing up the two visitors. 'It sounded like these ladies were accusing Mrs Bygrove of the ridiculous charge of writing the letters.'

Saying nothing further, the two women turned on their heels and left the building.

Edie sighed with relief, but she had a feeling that wouldn't be the end of it. 'Are you off somewhere nice, Major?'

'Just having an evening stroll.'

'You seem to have taken a few recently.'

'I like walking in the moonlight, and examining the stars when there is little or no moon.'

It had been so cloudy the last few days, she wasn't sure how he would have seen either. She hoped that he was all right and not starting to show signs of his age. He'd always seemed bright of mind. Her paternal grandfather had taken to going for walks at odd times when his mind had started to go.

'Don't stay out too long, Major. It's jolly cold. There were even a few flakes of snow earlier.'

'Don't you worry about me, young lady. Hardy as a bull I am.'

He pulled himself up tall and, as if to illustrate his words, marched promptly from the foyer.

—

When it was time for the middle supper for staff, Edie met Mrs Turnbull in the corridor, just coming out of the stillroom in her coat and hat.

'Edie, good. I've just returned from followin' Ada. I don't think she saw me.'

'Where did she go?'

'Nowhere interestin', I'm afraid. Just to her house on Western Road.'

'It was worth a try. And maybe we could make a habit of it, in case she goes –' seeing two of the live-out housemaids enter from the dining room, Edie lowered her voice, '– somewhere more interesting.'

Mrs Turnbull nodded. 'We'll talk about it later, pet.'

Chapter Eight

'Come in, Sergeant, and take a seat.'

Edie showed Gardner into the office, indicating the nearest chair, then went around the desk to sit on the other side.

'How can I help you?'

She wanted to say, *What on earth is it now?* but getting impatient with the sergeant wasn't going to help Helen's case.

'We've heard that you have three cases of measles.'

'Who from? Miss Harvey?' She looked pointedly at Gardner.

'No, Miss Nye. She mentioned it when she came in to tell us about Ada Saltmarsh.'

'Is there a problem with that? Or have you come to offer your regrets?'

'We see that the hotel is still open. I'm here to advise you to close while there are still people who are infectious.'

'Sergeant, Dorothy and the children, along with their nurse-maid, Vera, and Fanny Bullen, the mother of Elsie, are isolating with Mrs Bygrove in her quarters on the middle floor. They are left food on the landing. Then Mrs Bygrove leaves the plates for a couple of hours before cleaning and disinfecting them in her bathroom. She then places them on the landing for someone to collect, after which they are washed and disinfected once more, separately from any other dishes. And the same dishes are used for them again. We are doing everything the doctor, who knows about such things, has recommended. And he hasn't told us to close.' Edie hoped her tone hadn't tipped too far into irritation.

'Miss Nye said that Dorothy was very ill. Why isn't she in hospital?'

'Because Dr Ferngrove says they are already overfull.'

'I wasn't told that.'

'And he said she was better off at home.'

'Right. Do you think I could have a quick word with Mrs Bygrove, just through the door?'

'Have you had measles?'

'A long time ago, but yes.'

'All right. But please don't be long, and do not harangue her, for she has enough to contend with.'

He nodded.

She showed him up the staff stairs, to the first floor. 'That's her sitting room door there. Just knock and call out. She should be able to hear you. And do use the back entrance to go out, please. We don't want more tongues wagging.'

'Very well, miss.'

Downstairs again, she went through the stillroom to the scullery, to have a word with the scullery maids. She was in time to see the postwoman, Clarice, hand the post to Alice.

'Here you are, Edie,' said the maid. 'The top one looks like Charlie's writing.' She smiled and winked.

Edie felt herself blushing, even though everyone knew that she and Charlie Cobbett, a porter at the hotel before he enlisted, were sweethearts.

'I just wanted to make sure that you and Alice can do the extra shifts for the next three days.'

'Yes, we're fine with that.'

'I'm sorry to have to ask you.'

'We don't mind. It's extra wages. And when people's loved ones come home on leave, it wouldn't be fair to make 'em work and miss them.'

'No, quite, but thank you all the same... Ah, the other letter is for Mrs Norris. I'd better let her have it forthwith.'

In the kitchen, Mrs Norris was whipping cream in a huge mixing bowl on the wide table that sat in the middle of the room.

'There's a letter from Joseph.' Edie held it up.

'Ooh!' The cook put down the whisk and wiped her hands on her apron, before scooting around the table to take the offered letter. She tore it open impatiently and took out the single sheet to read. Hopping from foot to foot, she cried, 'He's got leave over Christmas!'

'I wonder...' said Edie. Was it too much to hope for? Only one way to find out. She put her finger through the top of the envelope and worked it open. Taking out the sheets, she skimmed the words quickly, but it wasn't long before she was smiling. 'So has Charlie!' She felt like jumping around like Mrs Norris, but knew she had to show more decorum, especially now she was undermanageress. 'He says it's luck of the draw that he and Joseph got their leave together.'

Mrs Norris beamed. 'What a Christmas we'll have.' Her face suddenly became serious. 'Of course, it could be under better circumstances. I haven't told Joseph nothing about what's been happening.'

'Nor I Charlie. They've got enough on their plates. We'll make the best of it though.'

'Yes, we will,' said Mrs Norris.

—

Helen heard the knock at the door and hoped it was some coffee along with refreshments for the children, though it was a little early.

'Who is it?'

'It's Sergeant Gardner, madam,' a disembodied voice called. 'Making sure everything is all right.'

Helen walked to the door so that she wouldn't have to shout and upset the children.

'In what way, Sergeant?'

'We've heard there are cases of measles, and Inspector Toshack was wondering whether you ought to close, though Miss Moore seemed to think that the doctor thought it unnecessary.'

'Yes, he does!' came another voice.

'Dr Ferngrove,' said Gardner.

'Why on earth are you up *here*, Sergeant, harassing poor Mrs Bygrove. As if she hasn't enough to contend with. You're just picking on her now.'

'No, sir, it's just—'

'I don't care what it's *just*, please desist from bothering her. She has done everything right with the young patients and for the safety of others. The people in the hotel are more likely to get measles from someone sneezing or coughing next to them, or on a busy street. You shouldn't be wasting your time here but sorting out this mess with the libellous letters.'

'I won't take up any more of your time, Mrs Bygrove,' Gardner called.

She didn't reply, instead waiting a few moments as footsteps clomped down the stairs, before opening the door.

'You picked a fortuitous time to turn up, Dr Ferngrove.'

'So it would seem. Now, let's have a look at the patients.'

–

Lili was walking in the dark, a good way behind Ada Saltmarsh, on Norfolk Road. She was shivering and her breath made a cloud in the air. How she wished she'd remembered her gloves.

Ada turned left onto Western Road. Lili was disappointed that the chambermaid hadn't carried on and turned left onto Selborne Road instead, where her aunt, Miss Harvey, lived. Following her would probably be a waste of time again, as Ada would most likely go home, as she had every time someone from the hotel had shadowed her.

She spotted Ada up ahead once more, passing a streetlamp, and her mind wandered as she kept her eyes fixed on her.

There had been some good news today; the doctor was of the opinion that Dorothy was well on the mend. Arthur and Elsie had contracted measles only mildly, and now it had been six days since they'd developed the rash, they would no longer be infectious, and neither would Dorothy. Fanny was back at work, as was Mrs

Bygrove, but the children were going to be in isolation for another couple of days, just to make sure. Lili was thrilled that they'd be able to join everyone again on Christmas Eve, just in time for the celebrations.

It looked likely that Ada was going to enter her own house. How Lili wished she could have reported a breakthrough before Christmas, something to get Mrs Bygrove off the hook.

Ada stopped and turned towards the kerb, causing Lili to dip into an alleyway – one that led to Charlie Cobbett's parents' house. How he'd have loved all this cloak-and-dagger activity. Ada crossed to the right-hand side of the road and was soon heading down North Place.

Lili felt mounting excitement. This short passageway led to Selborne Road. She sent a prayer up to the heavens: *Please, please, please!*

Ada turned left once more, past the Marine Hotel on the corner, in the direction of Miss Harvey's place. Lili dipped in and out of alleyways and doorways, until she saw Ada enter Miss Harvey's guest house.

Lili wanted to rush back to the hotel and let them know she had been successful, but they already knew she was her niece, so it was hardly news. She felt a rush of disappointment. Then what had been the point of following her? Some instinct, however, told her to stay put.

Around five minutes went past, when she saw her come out of the house and turn back the way she had come.

Lili panicked. If she stayed here, Ada would see her for sure, but if she moved away, the girl might spot her. She turned around walking away just like someone else on the street, turning into the first alleyway she came to. She waited, secreted in the dark, until she heard Ada's shoes clomp past. Looking out slightly to make sure she was once more ahead, Lili crept out and followed her.

This time, the girl walked directly to Norfolk Road, and crossed over the end. Lili hunkered down near the corner of Selborne Road, peeping over to the other side of the street. Ada stopped and looked around several times, before heading towards the pillar box. Slowly, Lili stood, to get a better look over the low side wall of the house there, watching as Ada placed several letters into the pillar box, by the light of the lamp on the pavement opposite.

Yes!

Lili turned and walked a few yards back down Selborne Road. She glanced at her wristwatch. Six-fifteen. The next collection was due at seven o'clock. If she hurried, she could get to the police station on the other side of town, and report it, before they were taken away somewhere.

–

Lili was out of breath when she reached the police station on Gloucester Road, behind the railway station. Far from being cold now, she was too warm, her brow perspiring.

'What's all this now then, miss?' said Sergeant Gardner. 'Aren't you from the Beach Hotel?'

'Yes – yes – I am,' she said, catching her breath. 'Is Inspector Toshack here?'

The door to an office opened, and Toshack appeared, brow creased. 'What's all this fuss?'

'Inspector, seen Ada Saltmarsh I have, posting letters, in Norfolk Road. She went to Miss Harvey's guest house, then she went to the pillar box with several letters. I was following her, see. You have to check the letters in the pillar box.' She looked at her wristwatch. 'It's just gone half-past six. They empty it out at seven. I bet she's posted more of them libellous letters.'

'They're probably just Christmas cards, Miss—'

'Probert. No, I'm sure they'll be those letters. I reckon she was the one what put the blotting paper in Mrs Bygrove's quarters, see, and them scraps in her office.'

'There isn't enough evidence—'

'If you're not going to take it serious like, I'll ring up the police station in Arundel, what is in charge of this one, and complain to

122

that Superintendent Crooke that you're not doing your job. DI Davis would have done something.'

She said this, despite knowing that DI Davis was slow to believe Edie's evidence when her landlady had been killed, before she came to the hotel.

'And can't you do fingerprints?' she asked.

'We tried that,' said the sergeant, 'but the person must have been wearing gloves.'

'The general public don't need to know the details,' said the inspector. 'For all we know, Miss Saltmarsh could have been posting them for Mrs Bygrove, and it's coincidence she went to her aunt's first.'

'Why would Ada be part of someone sending libellous letters to her own aunt? And Mrs Bygrove is still occupied with her sick children. And if you don't believe me, ask Dr Ferngrove. Or the sergeant here, since he saw her a coupla days back.'

'That was three days back now,' said Gardner. 'But yes, she was still occupied with them – then.'

'Well, if you won't do anything, we'll have to sort this out ourselves, at the hotel. Like I said, we can ring Superintendent Crooke.'

She twisted round on the spot, about to leave, when the outside door opened. She was surprised to see Major Thomas enter.

'Ah, Lili. How appropriate. I've just come to report that I've spotted Miss Ada Saltmarsh, posting several letters in the pillar box on Norfolk Road.'

'Yes!' said Lili triumphantly. 'I've just reported the same thing.'

'I've been keeping watch quite a few nights now, and I must say, I think your surveillance is woefully inadequate.'

'I think you'll find, Major, that PC Twort has been there the last few nights,' said Gardner. 'You probably didn't see him as he was almost certainly hidden.'

'That's right,' said the inspector. 'We'll have to wait for his report before we do anything.'

'I can assure you he has hardly been there at all,' said the major. 'He turns up for less than an hour every time, always stands where anyone could see him, then skedaddles off down Western Road.'

'He's right,' said Lili. 'We've been taking turns watching from Miss Nye's sitting room, and we've all seen the same.'

Inspector Toshack and Sergeant Gardner glanced at each other, and their expressions were not happy.

'Right. Leave this with us, Major, Miss Probert. We'll deal with it,' said Toshack.

'Mind that you do,' said the older man. 'Lili, I'll escort you back to the hotel, if that's where you're going, seeing as it's so dark.'

'I am, Major, thank you.'

'And make sure you get a look at those letters in the pillar box soon. The next collection is at seven pm.' This was the major's parting shot, before opening the door for Lili.

–

The door closed on Miss Probert and Major Thomas. Toshack turned to Sergeant Gardner. He had a feeling that it was going to be a longer Friday evening at work than he'd anticipated.

'What do you think, Gardner?'

'PC Twort has been reporting every day that there is nothing to report. But it doesn't sound like he's been going the distance. He volunteered for this shift too, saying it suited him to have some time off in the day.'

'It sounds like he's been having most of the evenings off too. But that's not what I meant. We can deal with Twort later. I think we need to act on this, and the quicker the better. Get the motorcar started, Gardner, I'll be out in two ticks.'

'Righty ho, sir.'

He went back to his office to fetch his mackintosh. So much for getting home by eight o'clock. Still, if he got this case sorted out, it would be one less thing to worry about over Christmas, what with another weekend coming up and the possibility of more thefts.

And he had to admit it: he relished the opportunity to clear Helen Bygrove's name.

–

Helen was relieved when the children had settled down for the night. Dorothy had turned a corner four days ago. All of them now being more or less well, but still shut up in two rooms, meant they were rather noisy and wanting constant attention. The fact that it was only three days until Christmas didn't help with the excitement.

Fanny was now taking Elsie back to her own room, finally sorted out in the men's mostly vacant area, so that Gertie didn't have to be disturbed by Elsie's night-time fusses. Vera was also back in her old room at night, which she shared with no one.

Helen sat on the settee, picking up the book that Mrs Turnbull had been kind enough to get her from the library: *Black Beauty*. It was more a children's book really, but it reminded her of her happy days as a girl in South Court Manor, with her own black horse, Ebony. It made her chuckle, realising that it was also the name of one of the three artists staying over the Christmas period. Then she felt sad for those lost days, before her father had descended into drinking and gambling.

She remembered that a letter had come for her in the late post and was still on the dining table. The postmark on it was Shoreham and the handwriting Douglas's; she knew she must read it but had little heart to.

She placed the book down and rose to fetch the letter. An errant thought flitted through her mind, that she hoped it didn't say he was coming home for Christmas. Oh, how wicked she was. The children would love to see him, and she shouldn't begrudge them that.

Taking an ornately curled iron letter opener, one that Douglas's father had made as a blacksmith many years ago in

Amberley, she slit open the back of the envelope. It contained a Christmas card for her and the children, with a note expressing his hope that the children were feeling better. He wouldn't be home, it explained, despite being given the opportunity, because he didn't want to risk catching measles.

What an excuse, thought Helen. She'd have thought he'd have seen it as a perfect opportunity to come home and take charge. Despite her own wishes, she felt bitterly disappointed for Dorothy and Arthur. The disappointment turned to resentment, as she remembered him saying once that he had contracted measles as a child. Had he forgotten this, or did he not know that you couldn't catch it twice? Whatever his reasoning, it would no doubt be self-centred.

Before she settled down to her book and her own distant memories, she would write to him to say that none of them were now contagious, and to remind him of his childhood bout of measles.

She didn't expect it to make the slightest difference to his decision, but at least she would have tried.

–

Toshack turned the corner from Church Street onto Norfolk Road and drove three quarters of the way down, stopping outside the post office.

'I'll speak to Mrs Riddles,' said the inspector as they got out of the motorcar. 'You have a look and see if you can find PC Twort.'

'Righty ho, sir.'

Toshack headed for the post office door and knocked lightly on the glass. Mrs Riddles came quickly, opening the door only a fraction at first.

'Why, Inspector, is something amiss?' She opened the door a little wider.

'I need you to open the pillar box and remove the mail within.'

She turned to look at a clock on the wall. 'There's another five minutes to go yet.'

'And I'm asking you to open it now. We suspect that there are more of the libellous letters inside.'

'Oh my. Very well.'

She retrieved a bunch of keys from her apron pocket and took several steps away from the shop to open it. At the bottom were no more than a dozen letters. She pulled them out.

'Come inside, Inspector, so you can see them better.'

In the shop, she placed the letters on the counter. Sergeant Gardner came in at this point.

'Sir, I can't see any sign of PC Twort within view of the pillar box.'

'Go to his home and see if he's there then. If he is, tell him I want him at the police station now. I'll deal with him when I get there.'

'Very well, sir.'

When Gardner left, the inspector sifted through the letters where they lay. Six of them had been written by the same cursive hand, and he was pretty sure it was the handwriting that had been on the libellous letters.

Chapter Nine

Helen woke up on Saturday morning, two days before Christmas, aware that Dorothy was already sitting up in the gloom.

'Hello Mummy. Can I have some breakfast now? I'm *star*ving.'

Helen heaved herself up and crept out of bed, opening the curtains to a dull daybreak. Looking at the clock on the bedside table she saw that it was already five past eight. She was normally awake long before now.

'My, Dorothy, this is the first time you've been really hungry since you got the measles. Let me light the lamp and then I'll take you to Vera to get dressed. Tonight, you can go back to your own bedroom, with Arthur.'

'Oh. I like the big bed.'

'I know, sweetheart, but you can't sleep here forever. The spots have gone now and you're more or less back to normal. And Daddy will want his space back when he comes home.' Her smile belied the dread she felt at that prospect. His overtures towards her in bed had become cold and functional, carried out purely for his own gratification. It had been a long time since he had been tender or considerate of her needs.

'Is he coming home for Christmas now then?' Her face lit up at the prospect.

'No, sweetheart, but maybe shortly. It's been a week since Arthur and Elsie developed a rash, so you should be all right to mix with everyone today.'

'Can we still have our Christmas lunch with the others, and play games, like you promised?' Dorothy placed her hands in a position of prayer, her face looking hopeful.

'I don't see why not.'

Edie and Mrs Norris had suggested the idea of her and the children eating with the staff on Christmas Day a couple of weeks back, and she'd liked the prospect of the company. She only hoped none of the staff members would resent her being there.

No, she mustn't think like that. She must enjoy it while she could, for who knew what she'd have to face in the new year?

This depressing thought was interrupted by a knock on the bedroom door.

'Mrs Bygrove, Edie's here saying that DI Toshack wants an urgent word with you,' called Vera.

'Would you ask Edie to show him to the office. I'll have to get washed and dressed first. I'll bring Dorothy to you.'

'Very well, madam.'

What now? And just as she was thinking she'd be able to enjoy Christmas. She felt the familiar anxiety crawl across her body.

–

'Detective Inspector, how may I help you?' said Helen, entering the office. 'I'm so sorry to have kept you waiting.'

Edie, whose company she had requested, followed her in.

Toshack was sitting on a chair on one side of the desk, his fedora on his lap. 'And I apologise for the earliness of my call. But I thought it necessary to inform you of the latest news as soon as possible.'

She could hardly breathe as she sat down, wondering how much more guilty she'd been made to look. Edie sat on a chair on the short side of the desk.

'First of all,' said Toshack, 'how are the children?'

'Almost fully recovered. Dorothy is back to her old self, and Arthur and Elsie only ever had a mild bout. And they should no longer be infectious.'

'That is good to hear. Now, I'm pleased to tell you that we made an arrest last night, after a tip-off about more letters being posted in Norfolk Road.'

'Would this be Lili Probert's and the major's tip off, that you initially dismissed?' Edie asked, arms crossed.

'Lili and Major Thomas?' Helen was confused.

'We didn't dismiss it, Miss Moore, but we needed to take a proper look at the evidence first. We have since discovered, during a thorough search of Miss Harvey's guest house, that she herself wrote the letters.'

'Miss Harvey?' said Helen. 'I thought she was just using the situation to, to, well, discredit me.'

'And we've arrested her niece, Ada Saltmarsh, as an accomplice.'

'Ada? Our chambermaid? She's her *niece*?' She couldn't take it all in.

The inspector looked over at Edie. 'Did you not tell Mrs Bygrove about this?'

'No. She had enough on her plate, so we decided to deal with it ourselves.'

'Oh my,' said Helen. 'It seems I underestimated just how much Miss Harvey hates me. It looks like she really was determined to get her hands on my husband.'

'And likely reckoned she'd get her hands on the hotel,' said Edie.

Toshack frowned. 'How would she have done that?'

'She was very friendly with Mr Bygrove. If Helen had been sentenced and sent away, I wouldn't mind betting that he would have put her in as a temporary manageress until his return.'

'My goodness,' said Helen. 'Are you suggesting that Douglas put her up to this?'

Edie shook her head. 'No. But I think *she* might have suggested it to him had you been gaoled. Remember, she said how awful you were at managing the hotel and that *she* would have done a much better job of it.'

'You're right, she did. How could I have been so stupid not to realise it was her?'

'We were all taken in by the way she twisted things and made a fuss, and convinced a lot of the inhabitants,' said Toshack. 'And I can't help but apologise for that.'

'And so you should,' said Edie. 'You should have searched her house long before now. Isn't there a saying about those shouting loudest having the most to hide?'

'So it would seem, in this case,' said the inspector.

'How did you find out that Ada was Miss Harvey's niece?' Helen asked.

'I'll tell you the whole story later.' Edie stood up, looking at her wristwatch. 'I'd better get to my shift on the desk.'

Helen nodded.

When Edie had gone, Toshack said, 'Anyway, you're off the hook now. Hopefully that will help you enjoy Christmas, especially now the children have recovered. I really do apologise for all the inconvenience and trouble this has caused.'

'Inspector, I'm just grateful you got to the bottom of it, however it was achieved. Miss Harvey is a devious and scheming woman, that much is clear. She certainly seems to have wound a spell around my husband who has long considered her a paragon of virtue, by the way he's always spoken of her.'

Helen regretted immediately laying bare her own insecurities and her husband's weakness.

'Anyway,' she continued, 'I hope you will let it be known that I was not guilty of sending the letters, so that I may get back the custom I have lost.'

He nodded. 'I will do all I can. In fact, on my way back to the station I will be dropping in on the offices of the various local newspapers, to tell them the latest development. So this time, any news of the letters published *will* have come from me.'

'I suppose, despite her denial, that it was Miss Harvey who reported my arrest to the newspapers before.'

'I will certainly ask the question when I visit them, along with delivering a warning on the dangers of them reporting misinformation.'

'Thank you, Inspector.' She was about to rise to show him out, when he spoke once more.

'I am genuinely sorry. I had you down as a decent person when we first met, and I've always been intuitive about people, which is very handy in my job. Clearly, I should have kept following my instinct.'

He looked directly at her as he said this, his face creased slightly with concern. She noted his large, piercing blue eyes, which seemed sincere, and the pronounced dimples as he half smiled during the last sentence. His face in this moment seemed a kind one, and inordinately handsome. Certainly a face that she would have noticed across a crowded room.

Had things been different.

There was a moment's silence as they stared at each other. He then rose. 'I must go and leave you in peace.'

'Of course. Good day to you, Inspector.'

'And to you, Mrs Bygrove.'

He put his hat on and left.

Helen closed her eyes and let out a huge sigh. She was no longer under suspicion. Relief flowed through her and she took a moment to enjoy it.

She left it a few minutes before heading to the desk in the foyer.

'He's gone then, has he?' said Edie.

'Yes. He did seem genuinely contrite. I suppose it wasn't his fault that all the clues pointed to me being responsible. That was clearly Miss Harvey's intention. He was only doing his job.'

'You are more forgiving than I am, Helen.'

'What is there to forgive? He did his job, he got there in the end, and I am off the hook. The children have recovered and the season will be a time of joy once more. And you have Charlie coming home for Christmas. Let us look to the future.'

Edie nodded.

'And I'd like to get as many of the staff responsible for endeavouring to find out the truth together, this evening, to say thank you for all you and they have done. I don't think there can be many business owners who have a more loyal staff than I.'

'We don't need thanks. It was in our best interest as well, of course.'

'That's as may be, but it doesn't take anything away from your efforts.'

'Very well. I'll have a look at the rota and see when the best time would be.'

'Thank you, Edie. Thank you for everything.'

Helen smiled at Edie, who smiled coyly in return.

A family of resident guests exited the lift, no doubt on their way to breakfast. Helen took the opportunity to greet them.

–

Helen entered the kitchen late the next morning to what, at first, sounded like an uproar from the staff there. It wasn't long before she realised it was a frenzy of eager greetings.

Charlie Cobbett, the hotel's head porter until he'd enlisted, and Joseph Norris, who'd been head chef before he'd signed up, were in the middle of the room, in their uniforms. They were surrounded by the kitchen staff, all asking questions. Nelly Norris, herself a tall, broad woman, had her arms firmly around her son, who was even taller and broader.

'Look Mrs Bygrove, he's back! My son's back! And Charlie.' The cook leant over to pat him on the shoulder.

'Does Edie know?' said Helen.

'Not yet; we've only just arrived,' said Charlie.

'Hannah, go and fetch her, would you?' she asked one of the live-out cooks. 'She's in the front storeroom with Mrs Turnbull, and it's nearly her lunchtime anyway.'

'Right you are, madam,' said Hannah.

'I'm so glad you've arrived to happier times than were anticipated,' said Helen.

'I was sorry to hear that the littluns have been poorly,' said Charlie.

'You two 'aven't 'eard the 'alf of it,' said Mrs Norris. 'You wait till you hear about the libellous letters and Mrs Bygrove here being arrested.'

'What?' the two men cried out in unison.

'Charlie!' Edie rushed into the room, flinging herself at her sweetheart, who enfolded her in his arms. 'You're earlier than I thought you'd be.'

'We came over the Channel in a ship yesterday evening and spent the night at Dover station. Left first thing and were lucky with the trains. What's all this about letters and arrests though?'

'You can join the staff for early lunch and hear all about it from Edie,' said Mrs Norris. 'If that's all right with Mrs Bygrove.'

'Of course it is.' Helen noticed Charlie and Edie regard each other lovingly and felt a twinge of envy. 'Joseph, we've already decided that you're to stay in your old room and join the staff for meals. This is your home, after all.'

'Thank you, Mrs Bygrove, that's most generous, seeing as I'm not working here at the moment.'

'That's hardly your fault. And Charlie, you would be welcome to stay too, but I believe you're staying with your parents?'

'That's right, madam. And I'm doing Christmas dinner with them, of course.'

'You are still invited to come and share any meals here and are more than welcome to join the staff Christmas meal and celebrations in the evening. We're going to be doing them for the staff in the conservatory for the first time.'

Charlie's face lit up. 'In the conservatory? That'll be posh. And I'll have two Christmas meals. Yep, I could go for that.'

Mrs Turnbull turned up at this point, running in to greet the new arrivals. Helen took the opportunity to vacate the kitchen, taking one last look at Charlie and Edie, his arm around her shoulders.

She was happy for the pair of them. Even though initially so mismatched in class and background, they'd found true happiness. She only wished she had found such lasting bliss with Douglas, instead of the anxiety she always felt in his company now.

Afternoon tea in the conservatory was busier than it had been for three weeks as the news seemed to have spread around Beach Town quickly.

Lili was serving the major a pot of coffee – he never drank tea – and a scone.

'Good turn out,' he said, smiling.

'Yes, Major. It wouldn't have anything to do with you and your mission after breakfast to spread the news around the area, would it?'

She smiled at him and he reciprocated with a sheepish grin. 'Well, m'dear, I always loved a good campaign. I felt like I was going into battle to win the populace back over to Mrs Bygrove's side once more. I dare say Inspector Toshack had something to do with it as well, seeing as Miss Moore reckoned he'd promised to spread the word.'

'I don't suppose he's had enough time today to spread it this quickly.' She lifted her hand to indicate the three-quarters full room.

'I can't participate in the war at my age, so it's nice to be able to do my bit in other ways.'

'Thank you, Major, appreciate it a lot, we do.'

'Anytime, m'dear, anytime.'

Lili moved off, passing Phoebe who was serving the three artists. They were also discussing Miss Harvey's arrest. She heard the distant single tinkle of the bell, indicating that she needed to collect food from the kitchen. As she entered the staff corridor, she thought about how lucky Edie was that Charlie was back for Christmas. How she wished Rhodri could have been on leave too, but he'd reckoned in his last letter that he wouldn't be back before February.

'There you are, Lili,' said Hannah in the kitchen. 'Scones and plum jam for table four, and slices of Yule log.'

'Lovely. Looking forward to trying the Yule log this evening, I am.'

'It's handy that we always use potato starch instead of flour for this, else there might not have been enough refined flour to make it. But don't tell the guests. We don't need them knowing our little culinary secrets.' Hannah winked. 'You ready for the carol concert this evening? Thought it might be a small affair after all that's happened, but now we're so busy for afternoon tea...'

Hannah didn't need to finish the sentence. As if Lili had needed reminding. If there would have been one good thing to come out of the hotel not being popular, it would have been attracting a small audience. She simply smiled and said, 'Of course.'

Picking the tray of food up and carrying it to the conservatory, she felt an attack of nerves once more. She'd been in charge of the choir again this year, and it was twice the size of last year's, despite missing some of the men who'd since been conscripted. Quite a few were live-outs and, although all having decent voices, she'd had to work hard to get them coordinated with the harmonies and counter melodies. And she was the main solo singer. How she'd have loved Rhodri to be there. She might have even persuaded him to sing.

'Are you all right?' Phoebe asked her, as she entered the conservatory. 'You look like you've been told off or something.'

'No, it's fine I am. Just concentrating.' She didn't want anyone knowing how nervous she was.

Lili took the tray over to Lord and Lady Lane, a couple who came to stay once or twice a year.

'Such a shame about all the trouble caused by Miss Harvey,' said Lady Lane.

'And to think people believed the silly woman,' said her husband. 'I hope they lock her away for many years. You don't need her sort around here.'

As he finished the sentence Lili became aware of a fuss at one of Phoebe's tables. Most of the room stopped talking to look around. It was the group of guests who'd arrived that morning, two older couples.

'I don't want your excuses about the war, and I have to complain in the strongest terms,' said the greyer of the two men, who sported a beard. 'This afternoon tea is not up to much with only half a sandwich each, made with *brown* bread. And there's only one undersized scone each, a small mince pie, one thin slice of Christmas cake and a small piece of Yule log. The portions here used to be so much more generous.'

While it was true that the portion sizes had shrunk, Lili still considered them to be a reasonable size, especially compared to other establishments she'd visited in the town.

Major Thomas, two tables away from them, stood up. 'I'd say that you're lucky to get that much, things being as they are. There are shortages everywhere and the prices of goods are going up and up, and it'll get worse, you mark my words. I wouldn't be at all surprised if this new Ministry of Food wasn't tasked with bringing in rationing. As it is, they want to regulate the supply and production of food.'

The man who'd made the complaint looked most put out. 'That's all very well for the man and woman on the street, but *we're* a superior class. We can pay more, so we expect better.'

'It doesn't matter what class you are,' countered the major. 'Shortages are shortages, whatever money you possess. You can't go around thinking you're more entitled than others when there are men dying on the battlefields and at sea. And civilians dying too, like in the coastal bombings and those in London. We should all be in this together!' The last word was said with gusto. 'You'll have to put up with shortages for now. And at least you still have these magnificent surroundings in which to eat.'

'Hear, hear, Major,' said Ebony, clapping along with Hazel and Marigold.

'Quite right,' Lady Lane called over.

The complaining gentleman looked a little embarrassed. His companions said nothing, and his wife picked up the teapot. Phoebe left the table swiftly. The other waitress, a live-out, raised her eyes at Lili as she walked past her.

Lili and Phoebe stood in front of a chest of drawers filled with cutlery, tablecloths and napkins, looking around the room to make sure none of the guests required anything.

'Should we tell Mrs Bygrove about this?' Phoebe whispered.

'No, had enough to deal with, she has. I'll tell Edie, just in case the guest takes it further, and leave it at that.'

'It's probably best.'

'That was a double tinkle of the bell, I believe.'

'I'd better go and fetch it then,' said Phoebe.

—

Early evening had arrived, and Lili was still wondering whether news of Mrs Bygrove's innocence would have got around far enough to increase the numbers they'd initially expected at the carol concert, which was basically only the staying guests. She was now having a last word with her choir in the staff dining room. Among those singing were Mrs Turnbull, Annie and Alice, the youngsters Simon, Bert and Finn, an older part-time gardener, two new chambermaids and Hannah from the kitchen.

Gertie came rushing through the door as Lili was mid-sentence. 'The ballroom's full to the gunwales!' she announced with excitement.

'That's excellent!' said Finn, the scullery lad.

Lili wished she could feel the same confidence. 'But the concert's only going to last forty minutes at the most.'

'People like a good carol concert. And loads of people have said how sorry they were about the miscarriage of justice, so I reckon they're wanting to make amends for believing it. Oh, and Mrs Bygrove said two minutes,' Gertie added before disappearing.

Lili glanced at the clock on the dresser: three minutes past five. 'Right, you know where you've all got to stand, and what the cues are. You all did well in our dress rehearsal.'

'Aye, it was grand of Mr Janus to lend us his pianist,' said Mrs Turnbull. 'Don't worry, lass, it'll all be fine.'

'I'm really looking forward to it,' said Bert. 'Always fancied treading the boards, me.'

'You'll have to see if Mr Janus has got a place for you with the Pierrots,' the gardener joked, causing the others to laugh.

'I think we'd better head out,' said Lili.

They walked in a line through the dining room, where Dennis and Phoebe were laying up for dinner.

'Good luck!' Phoebe called.

'Thank you,' Lili replied, all the while thinking, *I'll need it.*

In the ballroom, despite Gertie telling her as much, she couldn't believe how full it was. Chairs had been moved in from both dining rooms and the conservatory just in case, and Mr Janus had also had quite a few brought over. The choir made their way to the staging, also kindly lent to them by Mr Janus, and carried over during the day by some of his staff. The choir members took their places, with Lili in the front row. When she felt they were all in place and settled, she nodded at the pianist. The introduction of 'Here We Come A-Wassailing' was played, and the choir began.

—

The last chorus of 'We Wish You a Merry Christmas' was in mid flow, with many of the audience joining in. The concert had been a triumph, though Helen, on a seat in the front row, could see the relief on Lili's face when the last, *and a happeee Neeew Yeeear!* was sung. It was followed by enthusiastic applause.

As the applause died down, Helen indicated to Lili to say her bit, thanking everyone for coming. Miss Sophia Perryman, sitting at the other end from Helen, stood as she did so and took to the stage.

'I'm sure you'll all agree with me that the Beach Hotel choir has put on a splendid show. I do hope that, to thank them, you will be generous in your contributions to the Arun Children's Aid Project, for which we are collecting this evening. There will be staff members in the foyer with buckets, should you wish to donate.'

Miss Perryman nodded at the choir who called a rousing, 'Merry Christmas to all, and to all a good night!'

People started to rise and meander slowly towards the foyer, but many lingered a little, speaking to others. It was already a quarter to six, and they would need the way clear before six-thirty, when dinner began. Helen made her way towards the foyer, still nervous about being there with so many of the public, expecting some criticism. It was illogical, but the last few weeks had taken their toll on her.

'Mummy!' called Arthur, as he spotted her in the small corridor between the ballroom and dining room. He was followed by Dorothy and Vera.

'Hello sweethearts. Did you enjoy the singing?'

'It was lovely,' said Dorothy. 'I wish I could be in the choir.'

'I love carols,' said Arthur. 'I wish I could hear some more.'

'I'll get them upstairs, madam,' said Vera. 'It's a bit crowded here.'

'Good idea. Perhaps you could play the two Christmas records we have on the gramophone. I'll be up to see you soon.'

The children clapped their hands with pleasure. Vera took them through the dining room door as a short cut to the staff area.

'Oh, Mrs Bygrove, I'm so sorry about what you've been through recently,' said one of the residents of South Terrace, stopping next to her. 'Such a terrible thing. At least you have Christmas to look forward to now.' She tipped her head to one side.

'Thank you, Mrs Webb-Johnson, it's most kind of you to say.'

The woman moved on, but her place was taken by others, sympathising with her. Helen smiled and thanked each, but wondered whether she should follow the children and avoid having to meet people and suffer their pity.

No, she'd have to face people eventually, and it might as well be now. She strode boldly to the foyer, standing in the middle, wishing people good night and accepting their condolences with good grace. No doubt some of these sympathisers will have believed the lies initially, but it didn't matter now.

'Such a beautiful Christmas tree, so simple and elegant,' said Lady Raynolt, who'd wandered over from the cloak room with her elder daughter Penelope. They had held a ball at the hotel for the twenty-first birthday of their younger daughter a couple of years before.

Her ladyship had on a brown, ermine coat, with a wide collar and cuffs. Her daughter was less conspicuously, though still beautifully, attired in a loose black and white check coat, in the shorter length that had become more popular.

The three of them gazed at the tall Norway spruce in the foyer, with its abundant branches. On it were the blown-glass balls that she and Douglas had bought during their first Christmas here, along with orange slices that had been dried by Hetty and hung with gold ribbons.

'Thank you,' said Helen. 'I hope you enjoyed the concert.'

'It was delightful,' said Lady Raynolt. 'And I believe all those in the choir are employed here. What a talented staff you have. And I have to say, I did not believe for a moment that scurrilous rumour that you were responsible for the defamatory letters that were being sent.'

'It's kind of you to say so, my lady.'

'Now, I will be back in the new year to speak to you about an engagement party for dear Penelope here, who has just become betrothed to the Honourable Alan Dankworth, son of Baron and Baroness Dankworth. The date will depend on when he can get his next leave, of course.'

'Congratulations, Miss Raynolt,' said Helen.

'Thank you, Mrs Bygrove.' Miss Raynolt's smile seemed only superficial. Helen wondered whether the pairing had been arranged rather than chosen.

'Let us away and leave a *generous* donation in one of the buckets,' said her ladyship, with a superior smile.

'Thank you.' Helen didn't care that she was showing off her wealth if it meant plenty of money for the charity.

'Good evening, Mrs Bygrove.'

Helen, surprised by the familiar voice, turned abruptly to face its owner. 'Inspector Toshack. I didn't expect to see you here tonight.'

'I always like a good Christmas concert, and the ballroom is rather a beautiful place to hold one.'

She was surprised by this sentiment from him, maybe because Douglas had always thought such things rather frivolous, even if he wouldn't have admitted that to the guests.

'I'm glad you enjoyed it. And it is for a good cause.'

'I've already given, if that's a hint.' He grinned slightly.

'Oh, no, it wasn't in particular.' She felt a little embarrassed. 'So, what are you doing for Christmas lunch tomorrow? Do you have any family nearby?'

'No, no. They're all in Edinburgh or around Perth. It'll be just another day really. There isn't a lot of point celebrating when you don't have family around.' He looked down frowning, then back up at her, making an attempt at a smile.

She remembered that his wife had been killed during the raid on Hartlepool, feeling an unexpected sorrow for him. The poor man must still miss her. And then he'd lost a leg. To top it all, he'd ended up miles away from home in Horsham, and now in Littlehampton. Had he chosen that, or had he just been sent where they needed him?

Helen had a sudden impulse. 'The restaurant here won't even be half full tomorrow, and there will only be staying guests, so come and have your lunch here. It will be free, as a thank you for helping to clear my name. Between you and the major, you seem to have done a good job of restoring my reputation, and that of the hotel.' She indicated the room with her hand.

'No, I wouldn't be allowed to accept a free meal. It could compromise my impartiality.'

'Of course it would. Sorry, I should have thought about that.' Yet she still didn't like the idea of him being alone on such a special day. Nobody should be. 'In that case, if you wished to dine here for Christmas dinner, at the going price, you would be more than welcome. It will be served at twelve thirty.'

'I'm not sure that—'

'You don't need to decide now. As I said, we'll be nowhere near full, so should you decide on the day, there will be tables free.'

'That's nice of you to give me the option. At least I won't be poring over evidence on yet another weekend burglary case. Unless there's one tonight, of course.' He frowned.

'Mrs Turnbull told me about the burglaries. Three weekends in a row, wasn't it? Have you any leads?'

'That's not for me to say at this juncture. Let's just say it's an ongoing case.'

'Inspector, you did come after all.' It was Sergeant Gardner, accompanied by a woman Helen knew to be his wife. 'It was a lovely concert, Mrs Bygrove.'

'Thank you for coming Sergeant, Mrs Gardner. I've been wondering, what happened to PC Twort? I was told he was found out for not doing the surveillance he was supposed to be doing.'

'He's been dealt with,' said Toshack.

'Inspector, could I have a word?' said a woman Helen didn't recognise.

'Of course. Excuse me, Mrs Bygrove.'

When the inspector had moved away to talk to a couple, Gardner said, 'To answer your question, madam, Twort has been reprimanded and confined to desk duty, and if there's any further misconduct on his part, he'll be suspended without pay. He probably should have been suspended anyway, but we're short of officers.'

'He did look like he was getting on a bit. Perhaps he's too old to be doing that kind of police work?'

'He's fit as a fiddle and perfectly capable. He always was a lazy so-and-so, trying to do the least he could. I was relieved when he retired a few years back, wasn't I Mabel?' He looked at his wife.

'You were dear. Always complaining about him you were, even before you became a sergeant. Right, let's get ourselves home. I've still got presents to wrap for the grandchildren.'

'Good night Sergeant, Mrs Gardner. And a merry Christmas to you both.'

They echoed her wishes and departed, just as DI Toshack returned.

'Funny that you mentioned the burglaries, Mrs Bygrove, for they're the couple who were burgled the first weekend.'

'Poor things. I hope you get somewhere with it soon, Inspector. What with the libellous letters and these burglaries, you've had quite a lot on your plate recently.'

'That's the nature of the job,' he said.

'I suppose it is.'

She really should be talking to other guests, but for some reason, she was loath to let DI Toshack go. No, this wouldn't do. 'Whatever you decide about lunch tomorrow, I hope you have a good Christmas, Inspector, even if it is a quiet one.'

'Thank you, Mrs Bygrove. And I hope you have a good one with your children. I presume your husband's not on leave for Christmas?'

'No.'

He lifted his hat. 'Good evening to you.'

'Good evening, Inspector.'

She watched as he walked to the exit.

'Mrs Bygrove, how nice to see you smiling.'

'Oh, Major Thomas.' She hadn't realised she was, and felt embarrassed. 'Because I think that the carol concert was a success.'

'It was, and it has certainly put me in a festive mood.'

'I'm glad to hear it, Major.'

He wandered off to talk to Lili, who was holding a bucket for donations and to whom she had overheard directed many compliments.

Helen had several short conversations with audience members as they walked through the foyer. There were still quite a few hanging around, admiring the Christmas tree, talking to the staff who were collecting donations and chatting among themselves.

Glancing at the grandfather clock, she saw that it was coming up to six o'clock. There was still a little time before people started arriving for dinner.

She was standing chatting with Mrs Rhys-Pennington, a regular diner from South Terrace, when she became aware of raised voices. There was a middle-aged man, fair haired and small in stature, holding a cap in one hand and wagging the forefinger of the other at Lili. She didn't seem daunted by this, but instead put down the bucket and placed her hands on her hips. As the other people in the room started to realise what was happening, the thrum of chatter slowly diminished.

'I've found out it was you who was following her and got her into trouble,' he said. 'And now here you all are, enjoying yourselves, while I have to raise a pile of money for bail for the poor innocent girl.'

'She certainly weren't a poor naïve girl!' Lili countered, none too gently. 'It's a conniving little madam she were, who acted all nice but lied to us and planted things in the hotel to get Mrs Bygrove falsely arrested. And she tried to make out it were Jessie Jessup.'

Helen walked from the edge of the foyer to where the quarrel was taking place in the middle.

'No, she's a good girl, is my Ada. She wouldn't do that. And now my poor wife is going spare,' said the man, his voice reaching a strangled crescendo.

'Oh, she did it all right. Miss Harvey probably paid her good money to do it, I wouldn't mind betting. And her acting like butter wouldn't melt in her—'

'What is this all about, and who are you, exactly?' said Helen, reaching them.

'I'm Eric Saltmarsh, Ada's father. She was a good worker for you, and you've allowed your staff to hound her and get her arrested for being responsible for these libellous letters. And there'll be no merry Christmas for her!'

'I can assure you, old chap, that—' Major Thomas began, striding forward.

Helen raised the palm of her hand. 'It's all right, Major. I'll handle this.'

He took several steps back, nodding.

'So, who are *you*?' said Ada's father.

'I'm Helen Bygrove, the manageress here, and the person falsely arrested due to Ada's actions. Mr Saltmarsh, I can appreciate that this whole incident must be distressing for you, but you are blaming the wrong people. Although she may not have written any of the letters, Ada was an accomplice to Miss Harvey, who I presume is your... sister-in-law?' Otherwise she'd surely have been Miss Saltmarsh too.

'Yes, my wife's sister.'

'As a chambermaid, Ada planted letters and blotting paper in my rooms and my office, to make it look like I had written the letters that Miss Harvey wrote. And the police know for a fact that Ada posted them for her aunt. And terribly offensive letters they were, too.'

'But, but, if she didn't write them, she isn't guilty of libel.' He clutched his forehead and looked at the floor.

'Shall I telephone the police?' Edie asked, standing near the desk.

Helen looked over and shook her head, before taking a step closer to Mr Saltmarsh. 'Ada knew Miss Harvey was writing them, and, like I said, she's still an accomplice.' When he continued to stare at the floor, now shaking his head, she said, 'I'm sorry for you, Mr Saltmarsh, and your wife. I know Miss Harvey is a bitter, conniving woman, and may well have coerced your daughter in some way.'

'I never did like her.' His words were barely audible. 'Always been jealous of my wife she has.'

Helen glanced around the foyer to see that all attention from the various guests and staff members was focussed on them. It was a shame that Inspector Toshack had already left, but she'd have to do the best she could.

'Then it's her you need to aim your accusations at, Mr Salt-marsh. My staff were only trying to get to the truth so that they could prove it wasn't me sending the letters. I'm sorry that things have turned out the way they have, for Ada was a good worker. I only hope the court will realise what a controlling, despicable woman Miss Harvey is and that most of the blame will be pinned on her, not your daughter.'

Helen wasn't at all sure how naïve or coerced Ada really was, or how well or little this man knew his own daughter, but she needed to defuse this situation.

He was silent for a few moments, before he lifted his head and looked at Helen. 'I'm sorry to have caused a fuss. And I'm sorry you were falsely arrested over this. You are right. This will all be down to my sister-in-law. I should have realised it would be. I will ensure that Ada makes that clear to the court.' He flung his cap back onto his head, his face deadpan. 'Good evening.' He turned and left without another word.

When the door closed after him, people started chatting in subdued tones. Helen took a deep breath. 'Ladies and gentlemen, we very much appreciate your attendance at our carol concert this evening. If I could beg your indulgence now, we will soon be serving dinner, and we need you to vacate the foyer to allow the diners to enter. Wishing a happy Christmas to you all.' She smiled as she turned to take all the guests in.

Quite a few waved and echoed the Christmas wishes, as they left the building.

Edie came to stand by her side. 'That was certainly unexpected.'

'Let's hope it's the last in a long list of unwanted surprises.'

'Indeed.'

Chapter Ten

It was already eleven fifteen, and Toshack still hadn't decided whether to go to the hotel for Christmas lunch. Perhaps he could just sit here for the rest of the day, in front of the warm fire, reading his book. He had some bread, albeit the war bread, with its variety of grains and potato flour, but it tasted all right. He'd managed to purchase some cheese and pickles to make a sandwich. The small portion of chicken he'd bought from the butcher he'd have this evening, with the potatoes and carrots he'd acquired from the greengrocer, not long before they'd run out.

He picked up the novel from his knee once more and started to read again. *Tarzan of the Apes* was entertaining, and he was enjoying it, but he couldn't help but keep looking out of the window of his sitting room. The sun had been coming and going all morning, but at this moment it was shining brightly into the room. Maybe it would be nice to take a walk to the beach. He didn't have to go to the hotel for lunch if he didn't want to. He'd save the sandwich for his return.

Should he leave the house? If he was going to go, he wouldn't bother building the fire back up. Yes. No. Yes he would! At least, he'd go for the walk. He'd decide on the way whether he'd go to the hotel.

He got up to fetch his coat and hat. He was already in his Sunday three-piece suit, with it being Christmas. He'd have worn it even if he'd had no intention of going out.

Leaving his terraced house, he decided to pop into the police station next door, to make sure WPC Lovelock was all right on duty. He should tell her where he was going in case he was needed for anything.

That done, he headed away once more. He'd worked long hours the last few weeks and relished time off. Until he got it, and then he spent most of it thinking about Olive and the future they'd never have.

Last Christmas he'd still been at Netley, at the end of his recovery period. He couldn't have guessed then that so much would change in the next year.

He was soon walking past the railway station and into the town. It was eerily quiet, with not a soul about. He decided to take the route down Pier Road, past warehouses, the river and the fishermen's cottages, and on towards the sea. The sun was still shining when he reached the pier. In the distance he spotted the Beach Hotel, standing magnificently on the common and currently bathed in sunshine. He could spy only a couple of people walking along the promenade, a long way off. He had the sudden feeling of being entirely alone on the planet. It was how he'd felt in the early days after Olive had been killed, even though he'd been surrounded by men at the training camp.

He shook himself. This wouldn't do. It was Christmas Day, and he could do with some company. And he'd told the WPC that he was coming here. He checked his wristwatch. Just after twelve. If he took a slow stroll along the promenade, he should reach the hotel in time for lunch.

—

In the hotel dining room, there was a small Christmas tree by the door with glass ornaments shaped like pinecones and real feathers dyed red. The area was seasonally decorated around the windows and doors, with several different types of greenery, including holly and laurel. The earthy and pine fragrance of the plants reminded him of Christmases back in Edinburgh.

Toshack sat down at the table that Lili Probert showed him to, a table for two by the window, overlooking the garden, on which sat candles and more greenery. She hadn't looked that impressed when he'd walked in, which no doubt had something to do with his reaction when she'd turned up at the police station with the information about Ada Saltmarsh. Still, she'd been polite enough.

Miss Probert handed him a menu and he thanked her. As she walked away, he looked around the room. Sitting nearest to him was a table with three colourful young women engaged in cheerful chatter, and another with a young family. He was glad he'd come yet felt awkward at the same time. Did it look strange, him being on his own?

It was a limited menu, being Christmas Day, with a choice of turkey, goose or partridge for main course, and Hors d'Œuvre Variès to start. There was plum pudding, Charlotte Russe or Chestnut Mont Blanc for dessert.

'May I join you, Inspector?'

Toshack looked up to see Major Thomas smiling down at him.

'Yes, of course, Major.' He wasn't entirely sure if this was a good idea. He hoped the old boy wasn't going to give him a lecture on the recent mistake made in arresting Helen Bygrove. On the other hand, it was someone to talk to.

'Good, good. We can't have you sitting by yourself, especially on Christmas Day.'

'What have you been doing this morning, Major?'

'Been taking it easy, reading a book.'

'Much like myself then.'

'You're fortunate to have Christmas Day off, Inspector.'

'Unless something happens and one of my officers comes to fetch me. WPC Lovelock drew the short straw for desk duty today, and we have a constable on the beat. But I'll be back in the station tomorrow. I'm just glad there wasn't yet another burglary the weekend just gone. They seem to have moved onto Bognor and Chichester – if it's the same perpetrators.'

'*A policeman's lot is not a happy one*, as the song from *Pirates of Penzance* goes.'

'Not when you have people leading you on a merry dance and implicating others in crimes they didn't commit.' The major was bound to mention this, so he might as well get in first.

'Indeed. And the evidence of that is here today.' He indicated the room, only a third full. 'The truth came out a little too late for the hotel's Christmas bookings, but I dare say that will sort itself out in due course, once word gets around properly about Mrs Bygrove's innocence.'

Despite opening up the subject himself, Toshack still felt guilty about the situation. 'Yes, I'm sure.'

'Well, I've chosen,' said the major. 'There isn't as much choice as previous Christmases, but that's not surprising, given the shortages. We all have to make sacrifices.'

A woman came to the table. The inspector was surprised to find that it was Mrs Bygrove, not Miss Probert, and she was in a waitress's uniform.

'Good afternoon, gentlemen. Inspector, I'm so glad to see that you could make it for lunch.'

'So am I,' he said with a smile. 'Are you short of waiting staff?'

'I'm afraid we are. One of our waiters, Dennis, fell off his bicycle and sprained his ankle, so won't be in for a few days. Are you ready to order?'

'I'm having the Hors d'Oeuvre Variès, the partridge and the Charlotte Russe,' said the major.

'And the same for me,' said Toshack, glad not to have to pronounce the French starter.

'And a bottle of the Chateau Lafite Rothschild,' said the major. 'You'll share that with me, won't you, Inspector? It's on me, of course.'

'I'll, um, have a glass or two, thank you.'

'Thank you, gentlemen.' Helen took the menus and walked away.

'She is a good manageress,' said the major. 'She can turn her hand to any job in the hotel. Not like that lazy husband of hers. Goodness knows how he'll do on the battlefield. I hear you were invalided out of the army. False leg, I heard.'

'Aye, that's right.' He didn't really want to talk about it, but he couldn't be rude.

'Which battalion were you in?'

'The 15th Scottish Infantry Division.'

'Didn't you live in Hartlepool by then?'

My, word had got around. He wondered who had found out what and from whom. And how many people knew?

'I did, but I'm from Edinburgh originally and decided to join a Scottish division.'

'Where were you fighting?'

'The Battle of Loos. I was in France barely two months before I was invalided out.'

'Bad business. So many of our boys will end this war injured. Or worse, of course.'

'What about you, Major? I presume you were once in the army.'

'I was in the Royal Sussex Regiment. Spent time in Malta and quite a few years in India. Then fought in the Second Boer War. Retired nine years ago now. I still miss it, but, well, I'm not up to it any more.'

'Did you ever think of going into police work? It sounds like you were pretty persistent with your surveillance, from what I'm told.'

'I like the idea of skulking around, investigating people, but I suspect there's a lot more to police work than that.'

'Aye, there certainly is.'

'Though I reckon I could do a better job than that Twort fellow.'

'You know what, Major? I reckon you could too. But you didn't hear that from me.'

The major threw back his head and laughed. 'Don't worry, I'll keep it to myself.'

—

Toshack was collecting his coat from the cloak room, when he spotted Mrs Bygrove walking towards him, across the foyer. She was no longer in the waitress's uniform, but in an attractive, fashionable green dress, with its shorter hemline that reached above her ankles. There were ruffled panels on the bodice and skirt, and a lace collar. It seemed appropriate for Christmas Day, and something his wife would have loved.

'Inspector Toshack, I'm so glad I caught you. I hope you enjoyed the luncheon.'

'It was delicious, Mrs Bygrove. I hope I haven't overstayed my welcome, but Major Thomas insisted we take the remainder of the wine through to the conservatory to finish.'

'Not at all. We don't serve afternoon tea on Christmas Day, and the guests are welcome to use the conservatory anytime that it's free. Would you come through to the staff quarters with me, as I have something I wish to give you.'

'Very well.'

What could this be? Maybe some more evidence relating to the libellous letters case?

She showed him through to the stillroom, currently empty of staff.

'Here.' She held up a stiff brown paper bag. 'We'd already ordered a little more than we needed for the Christmas meals, with having a couple of late cancellations, so do accept these few bits for your supper, including some of Mrs Norris's excellent Yule log.'

'I did say—'

'I know, you can't accept gratuities. But you've paid for your lunch here, so consider it an extra that's been included. I would hate for it to go to waste.'

'I'm sure the staff would appreciate it.'

'And there's already plenty for them, I can assure you.'

Helen held out the bag, an appeal in her eyes, and he took it.

'Thank you, Mrs Bygrove. I hope you haven't ended up too out of pocket after all the trouble.'

'As long as things get back to normal, we'll soon recoup any losses. But thank you for your concern, Inspector. I'll show you out.'

'That's all right. I know the way out.'

'I've got to go into the kitchen garden anyway.'

They walked into the scullery, where two young maids who had a close likeness to each other were busy by the sink, washing and drying crockery.

Toshack leant forward to open the door.

'After you, Mrs Bygrove,' he said, at the same time that she said, 'After you, Inspector,' resulting in them both trying to get out at the same time.

'I'm so sorry,' she said, as they got wedged in the doorway together.

'No, it's my fault. It should be ladies first.'

He heard the two young women giggling.

'Oh,' said Helen, looking above the doorway. There was mistletoe hanging there. 'That must have been put there for Charlie and Edie.'

He stepped back and invited her to go first. Her face was flushed, maybe because of the mistletoe, which had embarrassed him also.

In the yard, he said, 'A merry Christmas to you and to your family, Mrs Bygrove.'

'And to you, Inspector. And a happy New Year. Hopefully, when we next meet, it will be under better circumstances than it has been most of the times we've met so far.'

'I hope so too.'

He left by the side gate and looked around. He could cross the road and go straight through the town, or back the way he came, taking another walk along the promenade and down by the river. The sun was shining currently, though there were a lot of clouds surrounding it. He'd risk it and go towards the beach.

On the prom he looked over the sand, towards the sea, glinting in parts where the sun was shining on it, yet dark in others. There was a slight but persistent breeze.

He relived the awkwardness of them trying to get out of the door together, and under the mistletoe too. The last woman he'd kissed under the mistletoe had of course been Olive, Christmas 1913.

Almost a year later, on fifteenth December 1914, he'd heard that he was to be on the rota to go home on leave over Christmas. He'd been at the training camp for two months and was looking forward to it, especially as Olive had written in the November to say she was pregnant. He'd felt such joy. And then the following day, nine days before Christmas, came the German raids on Hartlepool.

It had been two days later that he'd discovered she'd been taken, along with over eighty others. And that wasn't counting those killed at Whitby and Scarborough.

Several seagulls flew overhead, calling to each other, as if keening a lament for those lost people.

He felt weary. The half bottle of wine he'd ended up drinking wouldn't be helping. Looking out to sea, he felt suddenly lonely. He was glad he had spent some time today with people. The major had proved entertaining. But now, he wanted to get back to the fireside and to the characters in his book.

He'd seen enough of the beach today. He'd cross back over the common and walk straight home through the town.

–

With the guests' evening buffet over, some were now gathered in the private dining room, which had been converted into a temporary lounge. The fire had been lit, and live-out staff were now serving coffee and drinks there, along with other leftover treats.

After speaking with the guests and gathering that they were more than happy with this new arrangement, Helen returned to the staff area, to see how preparations for the live-in staff's Christmas dinner was going. As she passed the stillroom door, she was reminded, yet again, of the embarrassing moment when she and DI Toshack were wedged in the doorway together, with the mistletoe hanging above.

Eventually it would become something she could laugh about, but for now she still felt discomfort at the memory.

'How are the guests enjoying the lounge?' Edie asked, exiting the kitchen with a tray of condiments and sauces.

'It's proving very popular. I was wondering whether to make it a permanent feature, for we never hold a ball and a private dinner at the same time. Although the conservatory is always available outside of afternoon tea hours, it's not as cosy for the winter months.'

'But where would we place the food for the ball guests?'

'It's something we need to think about. Maybe in the dining room, and put dinner guests in the conservatory? We only ever have staying guests for dinner on those nights anyway. Or build a folding petition in the dining room, to divide it up?'

'My, you have been thinking about it.'

'It's not something I could seriously consider until we are sure of business returning to the hotel. But, since we have no balls or parties booked for the near future, until Lady Raynolt comes to see me, I think we'll keep the guest lounge for now.'

Edie nodded. 'I'd better get this to the conservatory. Our dinner is nearly ready to be served.'

'Wonderful.'

'Mummy!' Dorothy came running out of the door to the stairs, clutching the teddy bear that had been one of her Christmas presents. 'I'm looking forward to eating with everybody. I really enjoyed the games we played in the dining room. I liked being with everybody. So did Arthur.'

'I'm glad to hear it.' It had been kind of Mrs Leggett to suggest this.

'I do miss Daddy though,' said Arthur, catching them up, holding a toy motorcar in one hand and Vera's hand in the other. 'Do you think he would have enjoyed the games too?'

'I don't suppose so,' said Dorothy. 'He never liked playing games.'

It was said in a matter-of-fact manner, as if her daughter accepted it as normal, but it saddened Helen. Perhaps Mrs Leggett had been aware of this and it had formed part of her reason for suggesting the earlier activities. That people had knowledge of Douglas's inadequacies as a parent made her even more depressed. Yet there was an anger there too.

When the war ended and he returned for good, she would have to insist on changes. Perhaps he would be more amenable if she took an interest in some of his hobbies, as much as she had no interest in them whatsoever.

'Off you go to the conservatory and take your places at the table. I'll help with serving.' And she'd forget Douglas for now, and hopefully for the next couple of months, since there seemed no prospect of him turning up on leave any time soon.

–

Edie stood outside the back wall of the hotel, her arm through Charlie's, looking up at the stars twinkling against the black sky. She leant her head against his arm, clothed today in his suit jacket, rather than his rough uniform.

'I never tire of a starry sky,' she said. 'And it's so quiet this evening.'

'Me parents said that sometimes you can 'ear the artillery in France, if you stand on the beach.'

'That's right. I've heard it a few times now.'

'You wouldn't think there was a war going on at the moment though, would you?'

'No. And I wish with all my heart there wasn't.'

'You and me both,' said Charlie.

Edie thought about him going back to it in a couple of days and it was as if her world had come to a standstill. If only it would, then she could keep him here forever. She felt the tears stinging at the back of her eyes, but she didn't want to make their brief time together sad, so she breathed them back.

'I can hardly believe what's been going on 'ere the last few months,' he said. 'How anyone could 'ave believed that Mrs Bygrove wrote those bleedin' awful letters is beyond me. Me mum told me she had an argument with Mrs Riddles at the post office, who was telling someone how Mrs Bygrove had turned out not to be the respectable person everyone thought she was. Mum told her and the customers there that it was all lies and how well she treated 'er staff.'

'That was good of her, to speak up, especially as Mrs Riddles might have refused to serve her in future.'

'Me mum anticipated that, so goes to the post office in Surrey Street now.'

'Mrs Riddles has been over to apologise to Helen.'

'I'll tell Mum that, but I doubt she'll forgive her that quickly.'

'I think there'll be a lot of forgiveness to do, by the time this war is over.'

'At least you're not 'aving to put up with Bygrove. Makes me wish even more I was back 'ere working. Must be so much better without 'im. Just my luck that when I come back, so will he. Providing nothing 'appens to either of us.'

She placed her arms completely around Charlie and hugged him. 'Don't speak like that, darling.'

'Sorry, didn't mean to upset you. Shall we get back in? It's getting a bit parky out 'ere, even it if is pretty. And I fancy that game of charades Jack was talking about.'

'Are you fed up already of being alone with me?' she said in a voice of mock indignity.

'Nah. I'm saving it all up for when we're out alone together tomorrow.'

'I'm looking forward to that.'

'Me too. Come on, I bet I can out do you at charades.'

'Ooh, now there's a challenge, Charlie Cobbett.'

–

Helen had been prepared for a quiet Boxing Day, with their still depleted resident guests and the fact that trade didn't tend to pick up after Christmas until a day or so later. But she was surprised by the number who had arrived for morning coffee, and several telephone enquiries had been made for luncheon.

'My worries about not picking up trade again after my arrest were clearly unfounded,' she told Mrs Leggett, as they went over the staff rotas for January in the office.

'I did tell you after the large attendance at the carol concert that I felt we had turned a corner.'

'So you did, Imogen. I suppose I hardly dared to believe it. As long as we have enough food to accommodate guests.'

'We've still got quite a bit of what we over ordered, so don't worry. And I'm sure 1917 is going to be a splendid year, despite the war.'

Or maybe because of it, thought Helen, since they no longer had to deal with Douglas.

'With any luck, the war might end, and some of our male staff members will be back,' she replied. 'Not all will, of course.' Helen felt anew the sadness of losing three members of staff last August, at the beginning of the Somme battles. It seemed she couldn't have the advantage of the war without some terrible consequences.

There was a knock on the door and Gertie stuck her head around it. 'Mrs Bygrove, there's a visit—'

'I'm perfectly capable of announcing my own arrival,' came a harsh voice that made Helen's stomach lurch with anxiety. She stood up as a figure pushed past Gertie and entered. 'And I'm not a visitor, I'm the owner!'

'Douglas!'

'In the flesh. That will be all, Mrs Leggett.'

'But Imogen and I were—'

'Whatever you were doing can wait. The master's home.'

Chapter Eleven

When the housekeeper and Gertie had left, Douglas shut the door none too gently. She noticed that his moustache was longer than it had been.

'I thought you said you didn't have leave this Christmas?'

'I said I was given the opportunity but couldn't take it because of the children having the measles. But since you sent the letter to say they'd recovered…'

'You do know you can't get measles twice, and you had it as a child.'

'I might still have carried it back to the other men. That wouldn't have looked good, would it?'

She was sure she could have raised an argument against the possibility, but she couldn't be bothered. It struck her that this was a strange kind of greeting between husband and wife, especially when they hadn't seen each other in three months.

'I thought I'd left it too late, but when I explained the situation to my commanding officer, he was very amenable to me having three days leave.'

Helen gathered a new encouragement from this statement. Could it be that, being away from them all for so long, he'd grown to appreciate them more?

'I have some authority, of course,' he added, 'because of my status.'

'Status?'

'Owner of a prestigious hotel.'

Helen wasn't sure what status this would give him in the army, and couldn't be bothered to ask.

'Right, you can show me around the hotel, and fill me in on what's been going on.'

'Don't you want to see the children first?'

'I can see them afterwards.'

'But you're only here for three days. Wouldn't you like to rest?'

'Indeed not. I've been keen to get back to managing the place in person, if only for a while. Come on. Then the guests can see me in my spiffing uniform too.'

In the conservatory, Douglas was quick to speak to everyone, particularly, she noticed, those with titles. Some indulged him, telling him how good he looked in uniform. She trailed behind, trying to look as happy as she could.

'Yes yes, that's right, Major. On leave for three days. I'm off to fight the Hun on the second of January.' He grinned smugly.

The second of January? He hadn't mentioned that to her. Expecting to feel at least a scintilla of dread, she experienced nothing. She felt at once both guilty and numb.

They left the conservatory and entered the dining room. He stood in the middle, looking around. 'Have you rearranged it in here?'

'Only a little. It seems to work better like this.'

'Nonsense. I'll get the waiters to change it back the way it was during tea this afternoon.'

About to speak, she wasn't sure what she could say, and whether it was even worth it. He'd only be here two more days; she'd get the staff to change the tables back once he'd gone.

Walking through the foyer, he went to speak to Mr Watkins, on the desk. Even he didn't look thrilled to see her husband.

'Why, Mr Bygrove, when did you get back?'

'Just now. Isn't it splendid? I'm just advising my wife on a few changes.' He glanced around the desk, as if looking for something else to criticise. 'It looks all shipshape here. Carry on, Watkins.'

'Very well, sir.'

Helen noticed the desk clerk's wan smile turn into a frown as he walked away.

In the private dining room, Douglas's face puckered with annoyance. 'Oh, no no no! What on earth has happened here?'

Luckily, there was no one in the room. 'We turned it into a lounge for the Christmas period. It has proved very popular so far. I did wonder about making it a more permanent feature.'

'It doesn't look very popular to me. Where on earth did the settees come from?'

'The owner of a guest house on Selborne Road was retiring and wished to sell the furniture. Since it was fairly modern, I thought it would be a good opportu—'

'No. We'll have to find somewhere to get rid of it all, but from now on the room is closed to guests, unless they're hiring it for dining.' He glanced at his wristwatch. 'I did say I'd have lunch with some of my old golf chums.'

'When did you arrange that?'

'I rang them before I left Shoreham.'

'You could have rung me, to let me know you were coming.'

'Why did I need to? This is my hotel.'

'Are you going to see the children before you go?'

'I'll spend time with them when I return. If I go to see them now, they'll only make a fuss because I have to go straight away. And I'll be late.'

'Did you bring them any presents for Christmas? I thought you might send something.'

'I didn't have time, and besides, *I* am the present.'

'Not if you don't even bother to say hello to them.'

'That's enough of that now. You seem to forget that I am the master of this family. I'll see you later.'

He marched out of the lounge and across the foyer, back stiff, as if on parade. What a pompous ass he looked.

Helen took a sharp intake of breath. How very impolite of her to think such a thing. Yet he *was* a pompous ass. For herself, she was glad he was going out for a few hours, but she felt miserable for the children. And she was sure the staff would have much to say about the matter, even if they didn't say it to her.

Back in the staff area, she happened upon Edie in the corridor.

'I thought you were spending time with Charlie today,' said Helen.

'I am, but we've come back here for lunch. He's just using the convenience. Annie told me that Mr Bygrove is back on leave.'

'He is. He's just done a tour of downstairs, criticising everything, and now he's gone to have lunch with his golf chums.'

'Nothing changes then. Oh Helen, I am sorry. I shouldn't have spoken out of turn.'

'You haven't. You're my friend, and you've spoken the truth. He never mentioned Isabella Harvey, so I assume he hasn't heard about her arrest. I wonder if I should have told him.'

'I'm sure he'll hear it from these golf chums, since she was in that social group.'

'Then I definitely should have mentioned it first. Oh dear.'

'Don't worry, you're not the guilty one, she is. If he's got any sense, he'll be furious that she could have ruined your business. *His* business.'

'I hope you're right.'

—

Douglas still hadn't come back by nine o'clock that evening.

The children, having overheard that he was on leave, had been upset when he hadn't turned up before their bedtime. It had taken Helen and Vera forty minutes, with several stories, to get them settled down to sleep, since they'd wanted to stay up until he returned.

Helen was sitting in the staff dining room now, with Mrs Leggett, Mrs Turnbull, Edie and Gertie, clutching a cup of cocoa that she'd barely touched. At any other time, the warmth of the fire, the drink and the homemade biscuits would have given her a sense of comfort. At least the subject had not strayed onto Douglas's absence, and for that she was grateful.

It was a quarter past nine when she heard several doors slam, and she knew it would be him.

163

The door to the dining room was shoved open. 'Here you are. I've had an interesting day. A very interesting day indeed.'

Not in a good way, by the looks of it, she thought. He seemed a little unsteady on his feet and she wondered if he'd been drinking. He wasn't usually one for getting tipsy.

Helen stood up. 'Let's take this conversation elsewhere, shall we. The children have missed you, by the way.'

'No, we'll have this conversation here, for no doubt the staff have been in on your tricks and deceits.'

'Whatever do you mean, Douglas?' She felt herself flush, but it wasn't the same as when she'd done so with Inspector Toshack, trying to get through the back door. That had been awkwardness. This was humiliation, to be accused of such things by her husband in front of other people.

'I hear you were responsible for Isabella Harvey's arrest.'

'No, she was responsible for mine. She wrote libellous letters that she made people believe were from me.'

'I heard that someone from here must have framed her, and made it seem like she had done it, by putting incriminating evidence into her home.'

By the way he was looking at Helen, it looked like he thought it might be her.

'That is *not* the case,' said Mrs Leggett, scraping her chair back and standing. 'It was Miss Harvey who got her niece, Ada Saltmarsh, to do the deed here.'

'That's right,' said Edie.

Mrs Turnbull chipped in with, 'It was nothin' to do with your wife.'

'And why else would Ada come to work here and not admit she was Miss Harvey's niece,' said Helen.

'Because she knew you didn't like Isabella,' Douglas barked. 'And you never have.'

'And she has never liked me. I think she had the idea that if I were arrested, you would ask her to run the hotel.'

'What total nonsense! Are you trying to blame *me* for it?'

'No, but I think she might have had that idea as she knows you regard her highly.'

'Goodness knows why,' said Mrs Leggett. 'She's clearly out of her mind. A nasty, jealous piece of work.'

His nostrils flared and he started jabbing his finger forward as he said, 'If I find out anything untoward's been done, I'll have the person responsible out on their ear, if I don't sack the lot of you first for being so underhand with a family friend.'

'She is not a family friend,' said Helen. 'And if you think about it, Douglas, she is no friend of yours either. She could have ruined the business by getting me locked up.'

'But she's not guilty!' he shrieked. 'I am assured of that.'

'By whom?' said Edie.

'Never you mind. And anyone who speaks out of turn again will be sacked.'

Helen took a few steps towards him. 'Let us continue this conversation in our private quarters.'

'I've had a long day. I'm going to bed.'

Helen heard the door to the stairs slam before she turned towards the women. 'I'm so sorry about this.'

'It's not your fault,' said Mrs Leggett.

Then why did it feel like it was? She followed Douglas out, though she had no expectations of making him see sense.

—

'Business as usual,' said Mrs Leggett, taking her seat once more.

'Exactly what I told Helen earlier,' said Edie. 'It's even harder to take his bullying and shouting since we've had so much time without him.'

'At least it's only for two days,' said Mrs Turnbull.

Gertie sighed. 'At this rate, we'll be wanting the war to last longer.'

'Of course we won't,' came from Mrs Leggett, the same time as Edie's, 'Don't say that.'

'I didn't mean it like that, 'cos I have three brothers what I want to come home. But it is, I dunno, I can't think of a word for it.'

'Ironic?' Edie suggested.

Gertie nodded. 'That's the one.'

'I understand,' said Mrs Turnbull. 'War's a terrible thing, takin' our loved ones away, but for us it's been a boon, not havin' Mr Bygrove around.'

They all agreed solemnly.

Chapter Twelve

The third day of the new year, thought Helen, as she did her rounds of the hotel. What would 1917 bring?

The Christmas and New Year guests had mostly gone home, and the hotel was now only a quarter full. That wasn't unusual for this time of year, but she would have welcomed it being busier, if only to take her mind off Douglas's visit. It still plagued her, even though he'd been gone five days now. He'd caused such mayhem during his time here, getting the staff to change things back to the way they'd been before he'd left, poking his nose in everywhere and criticising staff, even in front of guests. He hadn't spent much time with the children either.

Thank goodness he hadn't been here yesterday, when she'd made arrangements with Lord and Lady Raynolt for their daughter's engagement party, booked for Saturday 10 March. It was more than two months away, but still there was much to organise. They'd wanted music in the ballroom and were disappointed to discover that the small orchestra hired previously had now disbanded, due to the war. However, they were pleased with Helen's suggestion of the ladies' string octet, who used to play for Mr Edwards, the old owner. Douglas would never entertain the idea of hiring them since they'd taken over. He'd never said why, but she suspected it was because they were women. He'd never had much respect for female musicians. But she'd seen them play and knew them to be excellent.

The Raynolts also wanted to hire the whole restaurant for the evening for a lavish buffet. That is, as lavish as they could provide in the current time. They would have to serve the resident guests in the conservatory.

Walking through the now empty conservatory, she shook her head. She stopped by a window, looking out at the gloomy day. Douglas would have been sent abroad yesterday. She let the thought sink in for a while. No, she could summon no feelings of anxiety. What a cold and peculiar person she must be.

She made her way through the dining room, only a third full, greeting some guests she was familiar with on the way. In the foyer, she was heading to the desk to speak to Mr Watkins, when the door opened to admit Lady Blackmore. Cecelia was close behind.

'Mrs Bygrove, the *very* person I wished to see.'

Helen couldn't say she felt the same after their last meeting.

Lady Blackmore came bustling over, in her usual out-dated, over-long coat, an umbrella over her arm. On her head was an ornate hat of dark blue mohair with a huge light blue rosette that resembled a sunflower and what looked like a pair of wings sticking out to one side, made of actual feathers.

'What a terrible business, *terrible*.'

What on earth had happened now? She glanced at Mr Watkins, who shrugged.

'Miss Harvey is a snake, a *snake*, I tell you, wheedling her way into everybody's trust and weaving those nasty lies about you.'

'I never believed them,' said Cecelia.

'Do hush, Cecelia. We have come for lunch, Mrs Bygrove, to show there are no hard feelings.'

Helen was tempted to ask her why there should be, since she'd been innocent, and to tell her she was no longer welcome. It wasn't as if she'd even apologised, but then, her sort so often didn't. That wouldn't help business though.

'Follow me, Lady Blackmore, Miss Cecelia.'

As she led them to the dining room, her ladyship said, 'It isn't true, you know, about Cecelia being my daughter.'

'I never believed it was.'

'Good, good. I don't know *where* Miss Harvey got that idea.'

Helen recalled that there was something in the letters that a few people had received about Lady Blackmore and Cecelia having a family resemblance. Looking at them, she realised there was a likeness. Perhaps Cecelia was a cousin? Then why not say so? Unless she was from a poor side of the family, and she was embarrassed.

Reaching the dining room, she met Lili first. 'Would you find Lady Blackmore and Miss Cecelia a table, please.'

There was a moment where Lili's surprised glance shot from one to the other, before she composed herself. 'Yes, of course, madam.'

Relieved to have passed over the responsibility of them, she was about to leave, when young Bert showed Detective Inspector Toshack into the room. Helen went hot, then cold, thinking once more of the doorway incident, before berating herself. She wasn't some silly young girl and it was about time she forgot about it. It was insignificant, so why did it keep popping into her mind?

'Inspector Toshack, welcome. I trust you enjoyed the rest of your Christmas and New Year?'

'It was quiet on the police front, at least. And you?'

How could one describe the brief trauma of Douglas's visit? 'My husband came on leave for a few days, but he's back at camp – oh, well, that is, he's actually been sent to the Front now.' How she wished she had replied much more briefly.

'I'm so sorry to hear that.'

She smiled wanly. 'Unfortunately, Major Thomas isn't here today, if you were hoping for his company, as he has gone to visit an old army chum.'

'That's a shame, but I'm sure I'll enjoy the meal, nonetheless. I see Lady Blackmore is here. She's come back then.'

'Just today yes, as she's apparently forgiven me.'

They exchanged brief smiling glances.

'How noble of her,' he said, raising his eyebrows.

Seeing the humour in it was the only way to go, Helen decided.

'Enjoy your meal, Inspector. Here's Phoebe to show you to your table.'

Toshack had enjoyed his poached cod in egg sauce with the lovely buttery potatoes and parsnips. He was now awaiting the mousse au chocolat for dessert. Going to a premier hotel for a meal was not something he would have indulged in before he'd been posted to Littlehampton, not on his own, anyway. He had taken Olive to a couple of nice restaurants in Newcastle, but nothing as fancy as this. He wondered what she would have made of it.

He looked out at the gardens. Being winter, the flowers were minimal, but it was good to be able to see so much sky. His office at the police station was rather dim and he often had to light the gas lamps.

His attention was taken by a familiar woman's voice, as he spotted Helen speaking to James Perryman, the owner of Haydon's shipyard. She was so much more pleasant to deal with than Mr Bygrove had been. Not that he'd had much to do with the manager, but Major Thomas had known him many years and hadn't spoken well of him. He wondered how his time on leave had gone for Helen, since he did seem such a difficult, controlling man. Still, that wasn't for him to ponder.

Helen was a pretty woman, he couldn't deny that. Beautiful even, with her contoured face and high cheekbones. She had large, slate grey eyes and thick blonde hair that was coiled into a delicate style upon her head.

He looked away from her, in case someone should spot him staring. She did seem to run the hotel well, especially given the burdens she'd recently had to endure – partly inflicted by him. He wondered if her husband appreciated how well she was doing in his absence. He doubted it somehow. And what a loyal staff she had, rallying around to find out who the real perpetrators of the crimes were. He wished that some of the colleagues he'd worked with had been so good catching the culprits. And as for PC Twort…

He couldn't help but look back at her. He hoped people wouldn't wonder why he couldn't take his eyes off her.

Helen, finishing her conversation with the Perrymans, spotted him and smiled. He smiled back, hoping she'd pass him by but at the same time very much wishing she'd come over to speak to him.

'How was your meal, Inspector?'

'The main course was delicious, as I expected. I'm just awaiting dessert.'

'I know our meals aren't as lavish as they were, what with the shortages, but Mrs Norris and her team certainly do the very best with what they have.'

'And I believe you grow your own vegetables. The parsnips were particularly tasty. Do you grow them somewhere in the gardens here?' He'd never spotted any vegetable patches, but they might be around the side of the hotel.

'Only very few in the far corner, where they can only be seen from the private dining room. We don't want to destroy all the flower beds, though it might come to that eventually. Most of the vegetables are grown on what was until recently a tennis court, across the road. Needs must, as they say.'

'I did wonder whether it had been a tennis court, by the fencing.'

'I dare say it will be again, after the war. Do you play, Inspector?'

'Good heavens, no. Football's more my style. Or it was, before the war. I was in a local team in Hartlepool.'

She didn't seem to know what to say to that, maybe conscious of his false leg and the assumption that he'd no longer be able to play.

The door to the dining room opened, and Major Thomas rushed in, a little out of breath.

'Hope I'm not too late for lunch.'

'No, of course not, Major,' said Helen. 'Where would you like to sit?'

'With the inspector here, if he has no objections.'

'None at all,' said Toshack. 'I was told you were out seeing an old army pal.'

'He couldn't stop for lunch in the end, so I decided to come back.'

He sat himself down and Helen brought him over a menu.

'Have you heard about this Rasputin chap, advisor to the Tsar, being murdered in Russia?'

'I read it in the paper this morning,' said Toshack.

'It sounded like a nasty death, but by all accounts, the man was a bit of a menace, with unwarranted influence.'

'I'll leave you to your lunch and conversation,' said Helen, moving away gracefully.

Toshack leant forward to listen to the major's opinion on the matter, relieved to be distracted from paying too much attention to Helen.

–

Helen was disappointed to be leaving the dining room yet couldn't linger there all day. It would look like she was keeping an eye on things, but really she was drawn there by…

She knew what it was but was uncomfortable with the thought of it. How could she be attracted to a man she barely knew, and one who had recently arrested her?

Besides which, she was due to take over from Edie in the foyer soon. She might as well go now and let her get to the late staff lunch.

'Helen, there's a letter come for you. I brought it with me, knowing you'd be here soon. You are a little early though.'

'I know. Don't worry.' She took the letter from Edie. The handwriting was Douglas's. A letter from France already? No, there was a Shoreham postmark. He must have sent it before he'd left. Most wives would be thrilled to get a letter from their husband, but all she could feel was dread.

'Here's the letter opener,' said Edie, passing it over.

'It's from Douglas.'

'I recognised the writing.'

She opened it to find it was a list of instructions. There were no endearments, no messages to pass on to the children, no wishing them all well. Just commands.

'It says much what I'd have expected,' she said sadly. 'It's a list of "orders", as he puts it, and an insistence that I don't change the rooms around again in his absence.'

'Orders?' said Edie. 'And you've already had the private dining room turned back into a lounge.'

'He doesn't need to know that. He reckons he'll get leave in the summer, so we could always change it back before he comes.'

'Providing he tells you this time.'

'I hope he doesn't take over again when he comes on leave.'

'Surely he'll want to rest after fighting. That's certainly how Charlie felt.'

'We'll see.'

—

Helen had been on the desk half-an-hour when DI Toshack entered the foyer from the dining room.

'Have a good afternoon, Inspector,' she called as he made his way towards the door.

He waved and smiled, not stopping to chat, much to Helen's relief. She had already thought too much about the man today.

She noticed the letter from Douglas on the lower part of the desk and pushed it away. The inspector had probably been a better husband to his departed wife than Douglas had been to her. In recent years anyway. She wondered once more whether her husband's love and attention in the early years had been all a show.

It was better not to dwell on it. Whatever the situation, she would have to try to find some way of improving it when he came home from the war for good.

Chapter Thirteen

'Good morning, Clarice,' said Edie, as she took the letters from the postwoman at the scullery door.

'Don't know about good,' she laughed. 'It's jolly cold and looks set to be one of them days where it never seems to get light.'

'At least the days are starting to get longer now.'

'Only just! I'm always glad when January's over, but we've got another three weeks yet.'

'Sadly yes.'

'Anyway, hope everything's all right. Good day to you now.'

'And to you.'

As Edie turned, she wondered about Clarice's parting words. Why would she hope everything was all right today in particular? She looked down at the letters. There were three for guests. One for Lili had Rhodri's handwriting and there was one for Phoebe from Newbury, which would be from Günther.

But the letter at the bottom sent a chill through her. It was from France, with the name and address typed.

'What's wrong?' said Annie, pausing from washing a teapot.

'I need to find Mrs Bygrove.'

'She was in the kitchen five minutes ago.'

'Thank you.' Edie rushed from the room without another word.

–

'That all seems fine, Mrs Norris,' said Helen, thankful once again for her resourceful kitchen staff in times of shortage.

'Mrs Bygrove, may I speak to you please, in the office?'

Helen turned to see Edie in the doorway. She always became official when speaking in a business capacity, but she also looked concerned. *What now?* was a phrase Helen had thought too many times recently. She must learn not to worry too much about each little problem, as there were often minor ones to overcome throughout the working day.

'Of course.'

In the office, she closed the door as Edie placed a letter on the desk. 'This has come for you.'

Helen walked slowly to the desk, then looked down on a letter that had her name on it. It was from France, but Douglas was unlikely to have typed it.

'Oh my.' She sat heavily on the chair, barely able to catch her breath. So soon? All sorts of confused thoughts ran through her mind about how to tell the children, and what she would need to do about the hotel. Had Douglas left a will? She didn't even know that simple fact.

She was getting ahead of herself. How would she know what the letter was about until she opened it?

'Would you like me to leave?'

'No, Edie, please, do stay.' Her hand was shaking as she picked up the letter. She didn't bother about using the fancy opener but tore the seal at the back, then pulled out the single sheet to read.

Casualty Clearing Station
In The Field 7-1-17

Dear Mrs Bygrove,
    You will pardon the liberty I take in writing, since I am a stranger to you, but I have news I must pass on to you.
    Your husband, Private Douglas Bygrove, was admitted here this morning, suffering from shell wounds that fractured both his legs. He is also suffering from minor scratches to his head and arms, but they are of no consequence.

I do not wish to upset you by this news, and he is in other ways unharmed. He is likely to be in this casualty station for a week or so, until he is fit to travel, then will be sent home to England to recuperate in a hospital there. I will duly notify you of this when I have firm news to pass on.

Praying God to comfort you,
I remain your humble servant,

L. Hewitt
Chaplain

'Oh,' was all she could find to say when she got to the end.

'What has happened, Helen?'

'Douglas has been injured.' She didn't want to read it again, so she passed it to Edie. 'Here, you can read it.'

After she'd finished it, Edie said, 'A week? That would make it around the fourteenth that he'll be coming back then. In four days. I wonder which hospital they'll send him to?'

'The chaplain will likely let me know.'

Edie placed the letter back on the desk. 'I suppose it's not unlike Lili's Rhodri. He manages very well now with only a slight limp.'

'It's not unlike Inspector Toshack either.'

'But he lost his leg.'

'And who is to say that Douglas won't? Fracturing both legs could mean simple breaks or… worse.'

'Let us not anticipate that but wait for firm news.'

Helen didn't reply. She was struggling to know how to feel about it, as she had with so many things that had happened recently involving Douglas. She was sorry for him that he'd been through such pain, but it was the kind of sympathy that she would have given to anyone she knew only vaguely.

'Will you let the staff know?'

'There is no reason to keep it from them. I will do it after lunch, then again in the evening, for anyone who wasn't around

176

earlier. And I'll have to find some way of telling the children when they come home from school. That will be the hardest thing. I believe the term for getting a wound serious enough to recuperate back in Britain is a "Blighty".'

'That's right. I've heard Charlie use the term. Though I believe it refers to a more long-term injury, one that guarantees you won't be going back to war.'

'I've read in the newspapers of men who've caused their own wounds, in order to get home.'

'Oh Helen, you're not thinking that Douglas did something like that on purpose, are you?'

'I wouldn't put anything past him to get back here.'

'I understand why you might think that, Helen, but it doesn't sound like the sort of thing a soldier could plan, being involved in an explosion. How would one know when it was going to happen? Or how much damage it might do? In the reports I've seen, the soldiers involved have normally shot themselves, or got in the way of a wagon of some sort.'

Helen stared at the desk, not seeing it but instead picturing Douglas in her mind's eye. 'I don't know, Edie. I suppose I'm not thinking clearly. It is a bit of a shock.'

'Of course it is. Look, there's nothing urgent going on down here. Why don't you go to your rooms and have a rest?'

'I'd rather keep busy.'

'Mrs Turnbull wanted to speak to you, by the way. Shall I deal with that?'

'No, I'll do it now. Thank you for listening, Edie. And not a word to anyone please, until I've had a chance to speak to them.'

'Of course not.'

Chapter Fourteen

It had been an uneventful journey on the train to Southampton, but it had taken nearly two hours, what with that and the motor taxi that Helen had needed to hire from the railway station.

Netley Hospital was a grand but massive building, sitting on the coast of the Solent estuary. She was wondering where on earth to go to find her husband's ward, when she spotted a nurse. The woman directed her around the large main building, to the rows of huts behind. There were a great many of them, but it wasn't long before she found the number written on the brief letter Douglas had sent her.

Inside the long hut she detected the odour of disinfectant and carbolic. There were beds crammed in on both sides, all with a paisley top blanket. There was a window in between each bed and barely five feet in between the ends of the beds on each side. In the middle was a cylindrical stove with a pipe leading up to the ceiling. There were only two other visitors, even though there were – she counted them quickly – sixteen beds here, all with occupants by the looks of it. But she couldn't see Douglas. She spoke to the ward sister there, who pointed her towards a bed on the left at the bottom of the ward.

'Please speak to your husband quietly,' she said, reminding Helen of the headmistress from her school days.

Douglas was lying flat on his back, his eyes closed. His blankets were turned up at the bottom, revealing the splints on both legs. At least he still had his legs. She felt sorry for him, lying there. His left cheek had an almost healed scratch. There was something different about him. The moustache: it was gone.

He opened his eyes, but his expression didn't change much when he noticed her.

'Wondered when you were going to turn up,' he grumbled. 'I've been here five days.'

'I only received your letter yesterday, Douglas. It was lucky I could get the time away so quickly.'

'Hopefully I won't be here too long. I can't stand it,' he growled under his breath. 'There's always someone moaning in pain. And the nurses are so stern and disciplinarian.'

'I thought you appreciated discipline, dear.'

'We're all ill here, not on parade. But you wouldn't think it. When the doctor comes around, those who can stand have to do so with their toes in line with the legs at the foot of the bed. And those in bed have to cross their hands over their chests, like we're dead already.'

'Oh dear, that does sound a little unnecessary.'

'Once I've recovered enough, I'll be sent home to recover for the rest.'

Helen's heart sank. 'Is that what they said?'

'It's what I say. I'm not lazing around in hospital for months on end.'

By the looks of him, that might be a while off yet, thought Helen. And when he did come home, he'd likely be incapacitated for a time. She realised it was a hope more than any knowledge she possessed. And if he was incapacitated, would she end up nursing him? Perhaps Miss Bolton would share the burden, being a trained nurse, for she would have enough to do in the hotel without tending to him also. What a terrible way to think of her husband. But at least the children would be glad to see him.

'What does the doctor say, about your condition?'

'That I'm recovering.'

'Is that it?'

'It's all you need to know. I presume you've kept the hotel as I left it, the dining room and private dining area and so on.'

'It's all fine,' she said, neither confirming nor denying the situation. If he was coming home soon, she'd get it changed back then.

'Who is staying at the hotel at the moment?'

She went through the list, trying to recall them all. Some had been before, but some were new to Douglas. He of course had something to say about them all, whether he knew them or not.

'The hotel is now half-full, and we have received several enquiries about future bookings, so things are looking up.'

'They'll be even better when I get back.'

'I presume when you're fully recovered, you will have to go back to the war though?' She delivered this with, she hoped, worry in her voice, but inside she was hopeful that it would be the case.

'Not if I can help it.'

That didn't sound good, but then, it wasn't up to him whether he was sent back. The tribunal last year, that he'd lost, must have taught him that.

'You haven't asked after the children.'

'I'm sure you'll tell me, regardless.'

'Dorothy came top in an arithmetic test and Arthur's reading is coming on a treat.'

'Right. Now, tell me what the food situation is like, and what you're putting on the menu, so I can give you any advice you need.'

Wasn't he interested in the children at all? Her poor little darlings. Her heart broke for them. This was going to be a tedious visit, but to keep the peace she did as he asked. There were several other questions relating to the hotel, which she dutifully replied to.

'What's happened about Isabella and her niece?'

He was more interested in them than his own children? 'I've no idea.' She knew the trial was in seventeen days' time. She was already dreading it. Mentioning it to Douglas would not help the situation.

'Don't you go giving evidence at the trial, you hear me?'

She already knew she would be. Looking at his condition, he was unlikely to be sent home in that time to find out. Not knowing how to reply to him, she was relieved when a doctor turned up at the bedside.

'Private Bygrove, how are you feeling today?' He lifted the chart at the end of the bed.

'Bored stiff, Dr Matthews. When can I get out of bed and have a try in a wheelchair?'

'Let's not run before we can walk, so to speak. We'll get nurse sitting you up later today, and maybe you could try a wheelchair in two- or three-days' time. There's still a way to go yet though. You're Mrs Bygrove, I presume?'

'That's right, Doctor.'

'Good, good. A visit from the wife goes a long way to cheering a chap up.'

The doctor moved on, leaving Douglas with his mouth tipped down at the sides like a grumpy child.

'I wouldn't be too quick to get up, if you're not keen to go back to the war,' Helen said quietly, as the doctor stood at the bed opposite.

'Don't you worry. I can get well enough to suit myself, not the authorities.'

'I'm not sure—' Helen started, only to be interrupted by a strident voice.

It was a large woman, in a matron's uniform, standing by the stove. 'Visiting time is over. Would all visitors make their way forthwith to the exit. Thank you.'

'I'd better go,' said Helen, relieved. 'I wouldn't want to get on the wrong side of that lady.'

'Miserable old cow.'

'Douglas! It's not like you to swear?'

'What do you expect, being stuck here. And fighting in a war's enough to make anyone start swearing.'

'I don't know when I'll be able to visit again. It depends how long you're here, and whether they send you elsewhere.'

'Goodbye.' He closed his eyes.

She shook her head. It seemed he was also relieved to see her go.

'Come along now, come along,' the matron barked.

Helen left quickly, stopping on the path in front of the hut. She checked her wristwatch. It would be another half-an-hour before the motor taxi she had booked would turn up outside the centre of the main building. Still, it was quite a walk around to the front, so she'd better set off.

About to do so, she noticed that the doctor she had spoken to had come out of the hut, humming to himself.

'Dr Matthews, could you spare a minute?'

'Mrs Bygrove, isn't it?'

'Yes. My husband won't tell me much about his condition. How long is he likely to take to recover?'

'The breaks on his legs weren't too bad, and they did a good job at the field hospital, so I expect him to make a full recovery. He's already mending nicely. We might even be able to move him on in a couple of weeks or so.'

'Move him on?'

'To a nursing home, to recuperate. We'll have to see. I can understand your worry. You want him to recover as soon as possible. That would, however, return him to the Front more quickly too.'

'Is there a chance that he won't get the use of his legs back properly and so won't be returned to the war.'

'I'm sure that's every wife's hope, Mrs Bygrove. The best of both worlds, so to speak, but I don't anticipate any problems. Excuse me, I must continue with my rounds.'

'Thank you for speaking to me, Dr Matthews.'

A nursing home. That sounded like a much better idea than returning to the hotel.

–

It had been a busier journey on the train on the way home than it had been there, with the carriages full of soldiers on leave, but they'd been polite, if noisy, so she couldn't complain. She did, however, have a headache, and was looking forward to a cup of tea and to seeing the children, who would be home from school now. She would tell them that their father had asked after them and was looking forward to seeing them. Sometimes a little white lie was necessary.

She was in the staff corridor, removing her coat and hat, intent on speaking to Edie before she did anything else, when Hetty came out of the stillroom, followed by an all too familiar face.

'Madam, Inspector Toshack here would like a word.'

'Hello, Mrs Bygrove. I'm sorry to disturb you.' He removed his hat.

'You're lucky to have caught me, Inspector, as I've only just returned from visiting my husband in hospital.'

'So Miss Affleck has told me. He's been injured then?'

She hung up her coat and placed the hat on the drawers there before replying. 'That's right. He broke his legs being flung to the ground in an explosion.'

She hadn't meant to, but she glanced at the inspector's leg. He in turn, did the same.

'No chance of him losing a leg, I hope?' he said.

'No, they're apparently mending well.'

'That's good news. Which hospital is he in?'

'The Netley, in Southampton.'

'That's where I was sent, initially.'

'So you know it.'

'I do. They're very good there. I'm sure he'll make a speedy recovery... But what I'm here about is the court case on the fifth of February at the Lewes assizes. I'm going to have to be there at the same time as you, so I could give you a lift, if that would suit you?'

She was about to turn him down, for no good reason, when she said, 'Yes, that would save me petrol, if I could even get enough, or another train journey. Though of course I'd be willing to give you money for the fuel used.'

'That won't be necessary. I'll pick you up at, say, a quarter past eight? That will give us plenty of time to get there.'

'That would be fine. Thank you.'

'And I can also give a lift to Miss Probert and Major Thomas, the next day, as I believe that's when they'll be giving evidence.'

'That's right. I'm sure they'll be very glad of that.'

'I'll leave you to get on. Good day, Mrs Bygrove.'

'Good day, Inspector.'

As soon as he'd gone, she realised she was relieved to have someone to travel with on the day. It might help still her nerves.

It might have been better if it hadn't been Inspector Toshack though.

–

There was a large crowd at the Lewes assizes, the day of Miss Harvey and Ada Saltmarsh's trial. Helen was sitting with DI Toshack among the excited throng, having found out that she and the inspector wouldn't be called until after lunch.

An official strode to the middle of the room and called for silence twice before the crowd's chatter ceased. When the room was quiet, he called, 'All stand.'

A few moments later, the judge and two men she believed to be the Crown Prosecutor and the barrister for Miss Harvey and her niece were brought in, along with the two women. All sat down.

The charge was read out. 'Ethel Mary Harvey and Ada Jane Saltmarsh, you have both been charged under section 63 of the Post Office Act for sending, and attempting to send, postal packets which had thereon words of an indecent, obscene and grossly offensive character. How do you plead?'

Ethel? thought Helen, but she had no time to ponder this before they replied.

'Not guilty,' said Miss Harvey, followed by her niece.

Their barrister, Mr Ward, stood. 'Your Honour, it is my belief that these charges should be forthwith dismissed on a point of law, that being that the letters were never published. Therefore, the people named were only insulted, not defamed.'

'Nice try,' Toshack muttered under his breath.

Helen glanced at him before her attention was taken by the Crown Prosecutor, Mr Randall, as he stood.

'My Lord, the fact that these letters are of an obscene nature means that they still constitute an offence.'

'Quite so,' said the judge.

Mr Randall continued. 'I must remind the jury, and the courtroom…' He looked around at the crowd, '…that this case is not some salacious detail in one of those "penny dreadful" novellas. It is a serious matter. There have been five waves of libellous letters sent, for which Mrs Helen Bygrove was initially arrested and charged, based largely on information provided by Miss Harvey. The charges were dropped when she and Ada Saltmarsh were arrested. We are, however, looking only at the charge of libel today, not that of the slander against Helen Bygrove, though some aspects of that will be pertinent to this case.'

He sat down and Mr Ward stood. 'I call Miss Ethel Harvey to the stand.'

She did as she was instructed. After she'd stated who she was and had sworn on the bible, she was asked to give her side of the story.

'I have absolutely no knowledge of the origin of these letters. They certainly did not come from me. And I received a few myself.' She seemed very confident, speaking clearly. 'I didn't even know initially that Ada had gone to work at the Beach Hotel, for I would certainly have warned against it, especially given the rumours that Helen Bygrove had written the letters.'

'May I remind you, Miss Harvey,' said the judge, 'that you are not here to accuse others, but to answer for the crime you are being accused of.'

'Yes, Your Honour.'

'Miss Harvey,' said her barrister, 'could you tell us what happened on the evening of Friday 22 December 1916?'

'Yes sir. I did not give Ada six letters to post, I gave her one, addressed to my brother in Kent. And it certainly wasn't libellous. I told the police this when they turned up at my house. Of course, it was that Inspector Toshack, who seems rather over friendly with Mrs Bygrove if you—'

'Must I remind you again, Miss Harvey? We simply want the facts, not your suppositions.'

'Sorry, Your Honour. Anyway, I gave Ada just one letter. If she was seen posting others, then it had nothing to do with me.'

Ada's eyes widened and her mouth opened in shock. Even Mr Ward looked taken aback. A muttering began among the crowd once more.

Toshack leant towards Helen, his hand cupped around his mouth to whisper. 'It sounds like Miss Harvey is trying to sell her niece down the river. That's not going to go down well with their barrister.'

Nor Ada's father, thought Helen.

The judge called, 'Order in court!' and brought down his gavel twice.

'No more questions,' said Mr Ward, looking unhappy.

Mr Randall, the Crown Prosecutor, stood back up. 'Miss Harvey, could you tell us, first of all, what job it is you do?'

She seemed pleased about this. 'I am the proprietress of a distinguished guest house on Selborne Road, in Littlehampton,' she announced proudly, as if this alone would vindicate her.

'You said earlier that you have, and I quote, *absolutely no knowledge of the origin of these letters*. Yet you were happy to accuse Mrs Bygrove, on several occasions, of sending them.'

Mr Ward stood up. 'I object, Your Honour. Mr Randall himself has already reminded us that we are not here to consider the charge of slander, only that of libel.'

'If you would indulge me, Your Honour, I am trying to demonstrate Miss Harvey's lack of reliability in what she says.'

'Carry on,' said the judge.

'Miss Harvey?'

'Well, I was… I was only repeating what I'd gathered from others. I wasn't in possession of the facts.' After the brief hesitation, she became confident again.

'I see. You told the courtroom just now that you are the proprietress of a guest house.'

'That's right.'

'Is it not more accurate to say that you are simply the landlady, running it for the owner.'

Her smile slipped. 'Well, yes, I suppose, if you want to be pedantic. But I am the one who makes the business successful.'

'And is it true that, despite claiming to several people that your father was a solicitor, he was actually an ironmonger's assistant?'

'I've never claimed he was a solicitor.'

'That's not what I've been told… Furthermore, on the night that the last libellous letters were posted, there was no letter found in the pillar box addressed to your brother in Kent. How do you account for that?'

After a brief pause, she said, 'Ada, in all likelihood, threw it away and posted the libellous letters instead.'

'I did no such thing!' Ada called out.

There was a rumble of voices in the courtroom, causing the judge to bang his gavel once more and call, 'Order in court!'

'So, you're now saying that, while you had nothing to do with the letters, your niece might be responsible?'

'I don't know. It seems likely though. And she's tried to get the blame put onto me.'

'But the paper, half written letters and blotting paper with incriminating marks on them were all found at your house.'

'My niece often comes to my house. She may well have planted them. She might have done it under Mrs Bygrove's instructions.'

'I did not!' Ada shouted.

'If you do not keep quiet, Miss Saltmarsh, I shall have you charged with contempt of court,' declared the judge.

187

She looked down, her face glum. There was more muttering, in which time Toshack whispered, 'She's a cool customer, Miss Harvey.'

Helen nodded in agreement, hiding her anger at the accusation against herself.

'No more questions for the moment,' said Mr Randall.

Mr Ward stood up. 'I'd like to call Ada Saltmarsh next.'

'This should be interesting,' Helen whispered. This time it was the inspector who nodded.

There had been only a brief lunch period, at noon. Directly afterwards, Helen was called to the stand by the Crown Prosecutor. She was nervous now that Miss Harvey had insinuated that Ada could have been posting the letters for *her*. Ada had denied this strenuously during her time on the stand. In the end, Mr Ward had asked for a short adjournment, and when they'd returned, Ada had changed her plea to guilty, admitting that it was her aunt who'd planned it all. But who knew if the jury would believe her against Miss Harvey.

Mr Randall questioned Helen first. 'Mrs Bygrove, would you like to tell us what part, if any, you had in this affair, and what part you think Miss Harvey might have played?'

'Miss Harvey came to the hotel several times to blame me for sending the letters. The first time she made us aware of the letters though, before she accused me of sending them, was the first day Ada came to work at the hotel.'

'Would Ada have had an opportunity to plant the blotting paper and screwed up letters in your office and your rooms?'

'As a chambermaid, she had access to many parts of the hotel, and sometimes cleaned my rooms. And she was quick to imply that it might be the other chambermaid, who started work the same day as her.'

'Has Miss Harvey some quarrel with you, that would make her fabricate these accusations.'

'I believe that Miss Harvey has an affection for my husband and was trying to take my place.'

There were gasps and several tuts from the courtroom.

'When I say, *take my place*, I mean as manageress of the hotel, as my husband is now in the army.' Though she suspected Miss Harvey would like to have taken her place as his wife too. 'She stated at one point, in front of many people, that she would have made a better manageress than me.'

'Thank you, Mrs Bygrove. No further questions, Your Honour.'

Mr Ward stood up and Helen's stomach squirmed. He was the one who was likely to give her a hard time of it.

'Mrs Bygrove, did you employ your staff, and your permanent guest, Major Aloysius Thomas, to follow Miss Saltmarsh, so that they could invent incriminating evidence against her and Miss Harvey?'

'No, I did not. I had no idea the staff, or anyone outside of the police, was conducting such an investigation.'

'No further questions, Your Honour.'

That was it? Helen stayed put, certain there must be more to come.

'You may leave the stand, Mrs Bygrove,' said the judge.

She nodded and left, relieved but confused. She'd felt sure that he would try to build on Miss Harvey's claim that she was responsible.

As she left, she heard them call Mrs Riddles, the postmistress. She'd leave through the door she'd been guided to, then creep back in the rear entrance to watch the rest of the case.

–

'I'm so glad that is over,' said Helen, coming down the steps of County Hall in Lewes, just after half-past two.

The building was an attractive one, large and cream, in a classical style, and rather grand inside too, but she was not sorry to leave it. The street was busy with people bustling along the pavements, chatting.

'I can understand that, Mrs Bygrove,' said Inspector Toshack. 'I'm going to have to come back tomorrow to give evidence, but hopefully I'll get away a bit earlier.'

'It's nice to see the sun shining at least.'

'We didn't get a chance to have any lunch and I could certainly do with a cup of coffee. How about we find a café before we leave?'

'Yes, I could do with a cup of tea at least.'

'There was a tearoom just along the High Street here, down School Hill, last time I was in Lewes. It wasn't up to the Beach Hotel's standard, of course, but pleasant enough.'

He pointed the way down the hill, and they started walking.

'Sometimes, it's a relief to be somewhere that isn't exclusive and elitist,' she said.

He chuckled, and it was the most relaxed she'd ever seen him. 'I'm sure having the likes of me turning up at your hotel doesn't make it completely exclusive and elitist.'

'You shouldn't put yourself down, Inspector. You're important to the town, in charge of the police station. People respect your position.'

'And I've caused you a great deal of trouble, Mrs Bygrove.'

'I don't blame you for that. And to be honest, I would much rather have you in the hotel than that so-called Superintendent Crooke, who I believe has jurisdiction over the Littlehampton police station, and certainly thinks himself a cut above the rest.'

'You've met him then?'

'Yes indeed. And it was not a pleasant experience. We had a guest a couple of years ago, a Lord Fernsby, who assaulted Gertrude Green, the head portress, when she was a chambermaid. Inspector Davis was going to question him at the station, but Fernsby's cousin, the Earl of Middlesbrough, who was also staying, contacted Crooke and made a fuss. So Fernsby was allowed to leave the hotel facing no consequences, and Inspector Davis wasn't able to do a thing about it.'

Toshack shook his head. 'And that's why the wealthy and privileged think they can get away with misdemeanours. I'm sorry that Miss Green had to suffer that.'

They passed the Town Hall at this point, waiting on the pavement for a horse and cart to go by, before crossing over to take the right-hand road down.

It wasn't long until they came to the tearoom. He opened the door for her and the warmth enveloped her as she entered. It was a pretty establishment, with lace tablecloths on round tables, white china and antique crockery displayed on shelves. The waitresses wore plain blouses and frilly caps, the younger ones having their hair in long plaits with ribbons.

They were shown to a table near the window and given a menu.

'Their choice is even more restricted than ours,' said Helen. 'Only plain scones and two types of cake: meringue or jam tart. I'll have tea and a toasted bun, I think.'

'And I shall have coffee and a jam tart.'

'And I'm paying, to say thank you for driving me here.'

'No, I couldn—'

'Yes you could, and you will.'

'Never argue with a lady, my wi— ...that is, here's the waitress.'

She had no doubt his sentence was going to be *my wife used to say*. Poor man. It must still hurt such a lot to talk about her.

After the waitress had taken their order, Helen said, 'Fancy Miss Harvey not being an Isabella at all, but an Ethel. I suppose she thought Isabella sounded more elegant.'

'Probably. She turned out to be a fraud in so many ways. Hopefully, the jury will take that into account.'

'Indeed. She doesn't even own the guest house on Selborne Place. And I knew she'd claimed in the past to be the daughter of a solicitor.'

'The prosecuting lawyer did seem keen to point all these deceptions out,' he said.

'Not that there's anything wrong with being a blacksmith's assistant.'

'Aye you're right. It's what my father was, before he became the blacksmith himself. He made some beautiful pieces; works of art they were, not just horseshoes and the like.'

'Douglas's father was a blacksmith too, though he did make mostly utilitarian items.'

'And your father was a Knight of the Realm, I hear, Mrs Bygrove.'

'And a noble man he was, deserving of the title, in his younger days, carrying out works of philanthropy with the great deal of money he made from his business. But sadly, alcohol and gambling ruined him.'

'I heard that too. I'm sorry, I shouldn't have mentioned it.'

'I don't mind, as you didn't speak of him unkindly, like many. And please, when we're out and about like this, with no one we know around, do call me Helen. I get enough of hearing "Mrs Bygrove" constantly at the hotel.'

She wasn't sure of the wisdom of this informality, and he seemed surprised. 'In that case, you must call me by my first name.'

'Which is? I have never heard anybody refer to you by anything other than your surname.'

'It's Samuel. Sam. Aye, Sam.'

'Sam. It suits you.'

He laughed. 'I'm glad you think so. I hear it so infrequently these days, that it's easy to forget I've actually got a first name.'

This made Helen feel sad, that he didn't have anyone close enough here to refer to him by his first name. Sam. She wasn't sure she'd get used to calling him that, though it had been her suggestion to be less formal. It might be nice for him to be referred to by something less formal though. Would she go on thinking of him by that name, or go back to thinking of him as the inspector, when he wasn't around? Time would tell.

'Sometimes, when people reveal their first names, they are not at all what you expect. Like Ethel.' She chuckled. 'Sorry, that is a little mean of me.'

'But not undeserved, on Miss Harvey's part. And it struck me, when we searched her house, how cleanliness is not necessarily next to godliness.'

'Was her home particularly spotless then?'

'She became quite distressed that we were treading everywhere and touching things, saying we'd make them greasy with our dirty fingers.'

'How on earth does she cope with guests?'

'I have no idea. And we found an awful lot of cleaning goods in her scullery, much more than seemed necessary to keep in store at any one time. If I'd found those in your stores, I wouldn't have been surprised, but her guest house is a lot smaller.'

'Hm. They didn't include bees' wax, Vim, Jeyes fluid and linseed oil, did they?'

'Sounds familiar, why?'

'We had a few of those go missing while Ada Saltmarsh was working for us. Unfortunately, we suspected Jessie Jessup, the maid I believe you spoke to.'

'You didn't report the thefts to the police.'

'It hardly seemed something you might get involved in. Then when Jessie walked out, and nothing else went missing, we just... assumed.'

'We can't be sure it was Miss Saltmarsh, but it seems likely.'

'Oh dear. Mr Ward didn't seem impressed with Miss Harvey turning on her own niece.'

'Aye, especially as he was representing both of them. It's put him in a bit of a predicament, I'd say. And he did seem to lose interest after Miss Harvey claimed Ada might be responsible... Tell me, why are you not seeking any damages from Miss Harvey, since she's lost you a lot of custom?'

'Because I want to put the case behind me and get on with my life, Inspec— Sam.' Already she was reverting to formality.

'I can understand that.'

They were silent for a while, both regarding the street as a motorcar then a bicycle passed by.

'You said your husband is recovering well, Mrs… Helen. Have you seen him since we last spoke?'

'No, I haven't. Although only in the next county, it's a fair way to travel. I've received a couple of letters though.'

'Is he likely to be going back to the war, do you think?'

'Eventually, most likely. The doctor seemed fairly confident of a full recovery. He'll probably be sent to a rest home for a period of recuperation first.'

The drinks arrived, followed shortly by the food. Helen poured herself a tea whilst Sam poured himself the coffee.

'So, you're from Scotland, Sam.'

'What gave it away?' he said, making his accent more obvious.

'You did mention having family in Edinburgh and Perth.'

'Aye, I did. I'm from Edinburgh originally but moved to Hartlepool in 1900, wanting to broaden my horizons. I'd been in the police force in Edinburgh and had recently become a detective constable. I wasn't in Hartlepool long before I was made a sergeant. It's… it's where I met my… wife, Olive. She was killed in the attack on Hartlepool in December 1914.'

She didn't admit that she already knew that. 'How very sad for you.'

'It happened two months after I enlisted.'

'Did you have children?'

He hesitated for a while, looking down at his coffee as he stirred it, and she regretted asking. It could be that they'd been fostered by someone because he was unable to cope.

'Olive was three months pregnant with our first child when she died. We hadn't known when I enlisted.'

Helen felt the breath sucked out of her at such a tragedy. 'Oh, I'm so sorry to have intruded on your private life.'

'There's no point in hiding it. And to be honest, I've kept it to myself for so long, I think it might be good to talk about it with someone. Mostly I've only had the company of my work colleagues, and I've never felt inclined to share the details with them.'

'I can understand why.' She only wished her private life hadn't been so obvious to her staff.

'There wasn't much time to mourn her. I was given a week's leave from camp, then I was back training. We were sent to France in July 1915. I was only there two months before I was caught in a bomb blast. A bit like your husband, I suppose. But the bottom half of my left leg was so badly damaged, it had to be removed.'

Helen genuinely felt like crying. As if he hadn't been through enough. It wouldn't do to show her emotions over his calamities, so she composed herself.

'That must have been terrifying.'

'I barely knew what was going on. And they knocked me out with anaesthetic. It was rather a shock when I came around though.' He looked into the distance, then closed his eyes, his brow creased, as if he was reliving the experience. After a few moments he looked at her, eyes wide. 'With that and Olive's death, it was not a good period of my life.'

She shook her head, having no words suitable for the situation.

'I was sent to Netley until December, where I was fitted with a false leg, then back to Hartlepool. I was back at work by May last year, having mastered the new leg. But the memories of Olive were too painful, so I asked for a transfer. I'd been an inspector for some years. They sent me to Horsham last June, then to Littlehampton, to replace Davis, in September. And that's my sorry tale.'

She wished she could confess her own sorry tale to him, but now was not the time.

'You've been through a lot. And ending up somewhere you don't know, with no friends or family around you can't have been easy.'

'In a way, no. I did think of asking to be transferred back to Edinburgh, but the idea of family and friends' sympathy was too much. It had been enough living through Olive's parents' grief… I'm sorry to have brought such gloom to our afternoon tea.'

'Don't be. I'm glad you felt you could speak of it. I do believe it helps.'

'It does. But let's speak of something else now.'

'Tell me about Edinburgh. I've never been to Scotland, though I believe it is very beautiful in parts.'

'I haven't seen as much of it as I'd have liked, but I'll tell you about the places I do know.'

He started with Edinburgh Castle, and she listened intently.

–

Helen waved goodbye to Sam as he drove off. He'd dropped her off at the end of Fitzalan Road, on her request, so that people in the hotel were less likely to spot them returning. She didn't want to be bombarded by questions from guests at this point.

She turned onto South Terrace and stared across the common, towards the river. The sky was a mixture of orange and red with clouds. It was like a beautiful painting. A pretty end to an… interesting and mixed day. That was the only way to look at it.

She crossed over and walked to the hotel, taking the path down the side to the staff entrance. There was a stiff breeze now and she shivered. Her mind wandered back to their time in the café. She was surprised how much she'd enjoyed the inspector – *Sam's* – company, considering how badly their initial meetings had gone. It could have been under better circumstances, given the trial, and his story had saddened her, but nevertheless she felt she'd made a friend of sorts.

But she must remember not to refer to him as Sam in the hotel.

As she entered the scullery, Annie was soon at her side.

'Mrs Bygrove, how did it go? Did they convict Miss Harvey and Ada?'

Helen looked at her wristwatch. Just coming up to twenty-past five. 'Staff will be going to the dining room for early supper soon, so I'll go there to give people the latest news, if you'd like to gather up anyone else who can spare the time.'

'All right. Alice and me's on early supper anyway.'

Going upstairs first to see the children also gave her an opportunity to put her coat and hat away and put on a warm cardigan.

Back downstairs in the dining room, staff were already seated and passing around the trays of mackerel and vegetables. It wasn't long before several others crowded in, standing around the walls.

'I'm sure you'd all like to know how it's going at the court,' said Helen.

'Hope they put Miss Harvey away for a very long time,' Jack called.

'And Ada,' Fanny added.

'The court case isn't over yet, of course. Lili and Major Thomas will be going tomorrow, so may have more to tell us. Miss Harvey and Ada both pleaded not guilty initially. It wasn't long before Miss Harvey implied that Ada might have been responsible, possibly instructed by me.'

'What?' said Lili. 'Of all the darn cheek of her. So she's trying to sell her niece down the river now?'

That was exactly what Sam had said, but she wasn't going to tell them that here. 'Yes, you could say that. The inspector has assured me that he will inform us of the verdict as soon as he knows it.'

There was some murmuring and shaking of heads.

'In the meantime, if we could refrain from predicting the verdict, and from discussing it with the guests, I'd be grateful.'

'I shall make sure of it, Mrs Bygrove,' said the housekeeper, standing up from her chair. 'Return to your work now.' She clapped in the direction of those not having supper and moved towards them to encourage them to go.

When they'd dispersed, the housekeeper went to Helen's side. 'Two letters have come for you, from Southampton.' She removed them from her skirt pocket and handed them to Helen.

'Right. Thank you.' Douglas had been at Netley hospital for over two weeks now, so it might be news of where they were sending him to recuperate. One letter had his handwriting, while the other was typed.

She took them to her office to read and had only just finished the missives when there was a knock at the door. Edie entered.

'I heard you'd returned. How did it go?'

'I'll tell you in a moment. I've just had these letters: one from the hospital, and one from Douglas.'

Edie came properly into the room. 'What on earth is wrong?'

'This one's from Dr Matthews, who I spoke to when I was there. It seems they wanted to send Douglas to a nursing home to recuperate, but he is refusing to go and is insisting on coming home to recover. The doctor is not happy about it but can't make Douglas go to the home. The letter from Douglas makes out it was the hospital's idea to send him home. He obviously hasn't realised they've written to me. He'll be back in two days, and has, of course, sent instructions.'

'Goodness me, how will you cope with that?'

'I suppose I'll have to ask Miss Bolton to help nurse him, since she is trained. But it's not ideal.'

'It certainly isn't. Helen, I'm so sorry. I feel this must be yet another burden on you.'

'I shouldn't feel like that. He is my husband, after all. In sickness and in health, and all that.'

'And what about love and honour on his part? I'm sorry, but we both know how difficult he can be, and how disrespectful towards you. I will do my best to support you, as you will still be running the hotel. I can't imagine he'll be up to it for quite some time. And, when he is, they'll presumably send him back to the Front. Or maybe, like they did with Lili's Rhodri initially, send him to a camp in England to help with training.'

'I hope you're right, Edie. I hope you're right.'

Chapter Fifteen

As per Douglas's instructions, Helen had all available staff lined up for his arrival in the foyer. She had summoned them as soon as young Wilf had spotted the motor ambulance from the entrance doors, where he'd been posted. Douglas was lucky he'd arrived between lunch and afternoon tea.

Why they couldn't have been lined up in the staff corridor, she didn't know, though she guessed getting a wheelchair in that way would have been harder. Even better would have been not to line them up at all, but she wasn't surprised that Douglas expected some kind of fanfare.

The major, and a few other guests, having got wind of what was happening, were also in the foyer, standing at a distance.

The ambulance driver was pushing him in a wheelchair by the time Helen got to the front door. She could see he was in his uniform, although the trousers seemed to be cut below the knee and his legs were bandaged. At least they were no longer in splints.

Wilf and Gertie opened the double doors to let him in. As he entered, the staff, as they had been instructed, called, 'Welcome back, Mr Bygrove,' though it was said with varying levels of enthusiasm.

The ambulance driver put down a rucksack. 'I'll leave these with you. I'd better get going.'

'Very well, my good man,' Douglas said, in that superior voice he liked to put on.

'Thank you,' said Helen. 'Your work is much appreciated.'

The driver touched the peak of his cap. 'Thank you, madam,' he said, then left promptly.

'The boss is back,' Doulgas announced, 'so now things will improve.'

Helen saw several members of staff glance at each other, but luckily Douglas didn't notice.

'Mrs Bygrove's been doing a good job, you'll be glad to hear,' said the pastry chef.

'I recognise you from my visit at Christmas. Who are you again?'

'Mr Strong, sir. From the kitchen. Taken on in the autumn.' He beamed. 'Pastry chef originally, but doing whatever's needed now.'

'Well, Mr Strong, that kind of disrespect will get you fired, if you're not careful.'

The chef's mouth opened in shock. 'It wasn't disrespect to you, sir, but respect to your lady wife. You must be pleased that she's kept things going so well in your absence.'

Helen wished Mr Strong hadn't spoken, though she was grateful she had his confidence, after all that had happened.

'Going well? Not from what I've heard. It sounds to me like she nearly got the place closed down.'

'That wasn't her fault—'

'It's all right, Mr Strong,' said Helen.

'Very well, madam.' He raised his eyebrows a little and stared ahead.

'Now,' said Douglas, pulling his back straight and looking around as if he disapproved of everyone. 'I'm going to my office and my wife will bring me up to date with what's been going on, then *I* shall make changes accordingly.'

It was Edie's turn to look askance at Helen. And she knew why. He was supposed to be here purely for rest and recuperation. Goodness knows what the gawping guests were thinking. She didn't look in their direction to assess their expressions.

Helen pushed the wheelchair to the staff area, finding it difficult to negotiate doorways and the narrow corridor to the office. All the while he barked, 'Mind the doorway,' or 'Don't be so clumsy.'

'It's really very cumbersome, the wheelchair,' she finally replied.

'They managed at the hospital fine. It's just you being a clumsy clodhopper.'

Finally in the office, he barked, 'Take me to the other side of the desk. That's my place.'

'Douglas, in his letter the doctor made it clear that you are to rest for several weeks and do nothing.'

'He doesn't know what he's talking about. I'll get well sooner if I do something useful. Enough of that, I hope you've been to the police as I instructed and told them that it couldn't have been Miss Harvey and her niece who were involved in the letters.'

'No, I—'

'Then you will go now, right this moment!'

'Douglas, it's too late. The court case started two days ago. I've already given evidence.'

He tried to swing out at her, but she was too far away. Nevertheless, she drew back a little more, dismayed. He'd been disrespectful of her for many years, but he'd never attempted to hit her before.

'I told you *not* to give evidence.'

Her heart was thumping, and it was a second or two before she could speak. 'I had no choice. Especially if I wanted to properly clear my name. And they *were* guilty. There is no doubt about it. We should know the verdict soon.'

There was a knock on the door. Before Helen had a chance to say anything, Douglas was bawling, 'Who is it?'

Lili peeped timidly around the door. 'Detective Inspector Toshack is here to see Mrs Bygrove.'

'What have you been up to now?' he said to Helen with a scowl.

'It's probably about—'

'He will speak to both of us,' said Douglas. 'Show him in.'

Lili hurried away.

'This gives me an opportunity to put things right and tell the inspector in no uncertain terms that Isabella is innocent.'

She couldn't resist giving her reply. 'Don't you mean, Ethel?'

'Ethel?'

'That's what she's really called: Ethel Harvey.'

'Nonsense! You do make up some rubbish.'

The door was pushed open by Lili once more and DI Toshack entered. *Sam*. She wouldn't be calling him that today.

'Oh, Mr Bygrove. I was under the impression that you were recovering.'

'I am. But I'm up and ready to run this place again also.'

Interesting, thought Helen. He was hardly running it before. What would he do now that he couldn't run away to his various clubs and meetings?

'I see.' The inspector turned towards Helen. 'I thought you'd like to know that they found Miss Harvey and Miss Saltmarsh guilty. Miss Harvey is going to gaol for twelve months, with hard labour, and Ada has been given a suspended sentence, as they felt that Miss Harvey had coerced her.'

'Is this how you always treat invalids, Inspector, by ignoring them?' Douglas bellowed. 'I'm still the master of this place.'

Toshack turned towards him. 'I'm sorry, Mr Bygrove, if I've offended you. I was addressing Mrs Bygrove because it directly concerns her, and it was her I came to see, not you.'

'Then I must tell you that my wife is inclined to exaggerate, so the case should have been thrown out of court. My wife claiming that Isabella wrote those letters and that her niece sent them is a downright lie.'

'Your wife's testimony was only to do with the way Miss Harvey harassed her in the hotel, accusing her of writing the letters and telling everyone that she did. And there were other witnesses to that. The claim that *Ethel* Harvey wrote them, and that Ada Saltmarsh posted them, came from a tip-off by Major Thomas and Miss Probert, who had been following Ada and keeping an eye on the pillar box.'

Douglas glared at Helen. 'You had staff members and *guests* following her?'

'No, I had no idea they were doing so. And the staff apparently had no idea Major Thomas was.'

'Isabella and Ada have clearly been framed by others.' Douglas screwed up his lips and narrowed his eyes.

'I can assure you they haven't, Mr Bygrove.'

'If that's all, you can go. I have a hotel to run.'

'I'll show the inspector out,' said Helen.

'No, you won't. I have work for you to do. Goodbye, Inspector.'

Toshack glanced at Helen with an expression she couldn't quite read.

'Good day, Mr Bygrove, Mrs Bygrove.'

As he left, she felt the red of embarrassment creep up her face. Whatever must he think?

'Get a notepad, Helen. I have instructions for you to carry out and I want to make sure you write them down and cross them off as they are done.'

'Very well, Douglas.'

–

Bygrove had been in the hotel a little over two hours, and already Edie was tired of hearing his voice. It was five o'clock, and, being in between afternoon tea and dinner, he'd called a meeting of all staff. They were now gathered in what had become the guest lounge, outside of which he had already placed a sign that said it was out of bounds.

'I hope this ain't gonna take long,' Mrs Norris mumbled, coming to a halt next to Edie. 'I've got food to prepare for dinner, and it's staff's early supper soon.'

'I wish it wasn't happening at all,' Edie muttered back.

'You and me both.'

Helen wheeled the manager in, who instructed her to take him to the centre of the room. Or rather, ordered her to.

'Now, listen up, you lot. There's going to be a few changes around here now I'm back. Things haven't been running well and a lot of custom's been lost, and I'm now going to put that right.'

'That was nothing to do with how the place was run,' said Mr Watkins, the head desk clerk, boldly.

'That attitude will not be tolerated, so everyone be warned. I will not listen to the lies you've no doubt been persuaded to spout.'

He didn't say who by, but Edie had no doubt he was referring to Helen, and by the look on her face, she thought that too.

'There has been too much underhand activity here, leading to deceits, lies, and even the fabrication of evidence against innocent people.'

Edie looked around the room at the expressions of everyone there, and it told her that they were all feeling as she did. How long before some of them—

'First of all, Miss Moore.'

She came out of her reverie. 'Mr Bygrove.'

'You will no longer be undermanageress as we have no need for one.'

Edie looked at Helen, whose eyes had widened. She looked back at her, shrugging ever so slightly, implying she'd known nothing about it.

'You will become head waitress once again, as you cut an upper-class figure in the dining room. And you will be known as Miss Moreland, not Edie or Miss Moore.'

'Douglas, surely that is Edie's choice, not—'

'I am manager here, and it is *my* choice. She is the daughter of Baron Moreland, and people knowing this can only be good for the hotel's reputation. In fact, we should all call her Honourable Miss Moreland. And she can introduce herself as such to the guests.'

'I'm sorry Mr Bygrove, but that would be an incorrect use of the title,' said Edie. '*Honourable* can only be used when I am referred to in the third person, or on a letter.'

'Oh, well… Then you can still be called that by other staff when they are referring to you.' He wagged his finger as he added, 'And make sure you *do* use Moreland, and not Moore.'

Of all the… There wasn't even an adequate word to describe the man. Who did he think he was? And she'd make sure to tell the staff *not* to refer to her as *Honourable*, when not in Bygrove's hearing, at least.

'And Miss Probert will no longer work as a waitress but will go back to being a chambermaid.'

Edie looked over at Lili, whose expression was one of utter dismay.

'That means one of the current chambermaids can be dismissed.'

The chambermaids looked around at each other with concern.

'Douglas, we're already a chambermaid down after losing Ada. We haven't managed to hire anyone to replace her yet.'

'Then we won't bother taking one on until the summer, when it's busier.'

They really could have done with taking one on, winter or not, thought Edie. In the summer they'd need to hire at least a couple more, just for high season.

'Sir?' Phoebe came forward, raising her hand. 'If anyone should leave the dining room, it's me sir. Lili is above me, sir, so I should go back to the stillroom.'

Edie admired Phoebe for speaking up like that. She always did have a sense of loyalty and of what was right.

'No,' said Bygrove. 'We're not short in the stillroom. Moving on, the food has become too ordinary. There's not enough *haute cuisine* and too many vegetables. I'm going to advertise for a retired head chef to take over, and Mrs Norris will be his under cook, until Joseph returns from the war.'

Mrs Norris strode forward a few steps. With her height and build, she was quite imposing. 'You'll do no better, I assure you,' she said. 'I taught my Joseph everything he knows and I'm a more experienced cook. I don't get to be called "chef", let alone "head chef", 'cos I'm a woman, that's all. If anything's letting the hotel down, and I'd dispute it is, it's not me cooking, it's the lack of food available. It's the wonderful food what Mr Hargreaves and his staff grow on the tennis courts what's saved us. I can get as fancy as you like with the chicken, pigeon and rabbit what's available, but I can't do nothing about the paucity of lamb, beef, veal, pork, and the like.'

Bygrove's face went red and his nostrils flared. He narrowed his eyes and leant forward. 'The tennis courts will be restored and we will get our vegetables from the greengrocers. *I* will sort out a supply of all the meat we require, since my wife seems not to have the skill to do so.'

Helen looked affronted but said nothing.

'That's unfair,' said Will Fletcher, another recent engagement in the kitchen who'd been a sous chef in his younger days. 'It's much harder to—'

'It is *not* unfair, and I suggest you keep your opinions to yourself, Mr Fletcher.'

'Yes, Mr Bygrove.'

If he wasn't careful, Bygrove would have staff walking out, thought Edie. He'd always been on the brittle side, but this was bullying.

'There has been far too much allowing staff to have an opinion since I've been away. Staff meetings will be for management to tell employees what's what. It won't be up for discussion. That is not how to run a business. From now on it's the manager who decides what's best for this hotel, and you will all do as you're told.'

Most people were now looking at the ground, their expressions blank. Edie could see that Lili was biting the side of her mouth.

'One more thing. This so-called guest lounge is to be restored to a private dining room immediately, as I see my instructions were not followed after my leave at Christmas. I don't see why all and sundry should be given leave to enter this room when it is here to be hired. They have luxury bedrooms in which to sit. Dismissed!'

He didn't wait for Helen to take him away. He pushed the hand rims on the wheels, removing himself from the room, barking at her to follow on quickly.

She shook her head as if in dismay. The staff there waited until he'd gone before a murmur of dissent started up.

'Well, we're back to where we started,' said Mrs Norris. 'And if anything, it's worse.'

'It's utterly intolerable,' Mrs Leggett muttered, on the other side of her.

Lili came rushing over to them. 'It's not fair!'

'I quite agree, Miss Probert,' said the housekeeper.

'Me too,' said Fanny, who'd followed Lili over. She patted her shoulder.

'I'm so sorry,' said Edie, who felt guilty about taking Lili's job. 'I had no idea he was going to do that.'

'And I'm supposed to be having this weekend off to see Rhodri while he's home on leave. I don't know how that's going to work with a different rota.' She was almost in tears.

Edie took her hand. 'Don't you worry about that. I'll sort it out with Helen so that Bygrove need not know. If necessary, *I'll* do some cleaning.'

'Me too,' said Mrs Leggett.

'Don't you worry a bit,' said Fanny. 'The cleaning rota is already sorted out for this weekend. You go and see your Rhodri.'

'Thank you.' A tear did now fall down Lili's face. She took a handkerchief from her apron to pat at it.

'If Mr Bygrove feels this able to work already,' said Mrs Leggett, 'that will hopefully mean he'll be well enough to be returned to his battalion sooner rather than later.'

'As much as I hate anyone being sent to war,' said Mrs Norris, 'I have to agree with you. But he will be back eventually.'

They all nodded mournfully, before returning to their jobs.

—

Inspector Toshack wasn't entirely convinced that he was doing the right thing, coming into the hotel for lunch on Saturday, but something had compelled him to. After what could only be described as an *aggressive* reception from Douglas Bygrove yesterday, he found himself worrying about Helen. And the rest of the staff, of course. But Helen most of all.

And why was he convinced that Miss Harvey was innocent and that his wife was somehow implicated? He didn't believe the veiled accusation for a moment. Why would a man want to get his wife into trouble like that? It wasn't as if he'd even been around the last few months to be any kind of witness.

He was surprised to see the undermanageress, Miss Moore, come towards him, in a waitress's uniform. But then, Helen had taken on other roles when necessary, so it wasn't so unusual.

'Inspector, I trust you are here for lunch?'

'That's right. Call it a bit of a celebration, after getting a good result in the court case.'

'Indeed, such good news. Now Mrs Bygrove's name is completely cleared.'

As she showed him to a small table near the middle of the room, he said, 'Are you short staffed today, since you're working in here?'

She took a deep breath, and he wondered what was coming. 'Mr Bygrove has made me head waitress again, as he says he no longer needs an undermanageress. That's now Mrs Bygrove's role once more. I say once more, although she was never called that before he was conscripted.'

He took a seat, wondering if she were trying to make a point. He decided to do a little digging. 'When I visited yesterday to give Mrs Bygrove the news about Miss Harvey, I gathered that Mr Bygrove was in charge once more. I had been under the impression from Mrs Bygrove that he would be recuperating for quite a period.'

Edie put down a menu and looked around. She smiled and lowered her voice. She pointed to the menu as if explaining something. 'So did we all, Inspector. To be honest, he's always been a bit of a bully, but has been worse since he returned. He was supposed to be going to a nursing home to recuperate for several weeks, but refused to go, insisting on being sent home to recover instead. But as soon as he arrived, he took over. He's undoing all the good things Mrs Bygrove did, like insisting the tennis courts are restored and demoting people from positions and swapping jobs. None of it is good.'

She seemed relieved to have got that off her chest, but nevertheless followed it with, 'I'm sorry for my unguarded words. I shouldn't be speaking out of turn, but I am worried for Helen – Mrs Bygrove.'

'Don't worry, I will be the soul of discretion. I was aware of things being a little awkward when I visited yesterday. The way he spoke to her, it's not the way I'd have spoken to my... to a wife.'

'And not a way I would tolerate being treated either, but—' She glanced around once more, still smiling. 'But then, it is complicated between them, with him being the official owner of the hotel, even though it was her inheritance that bought it.'

'I wonder if he has a touch of shellshock, though he was hardly out there five minutes.'

'I think you're being too kind, Inspector.'

'Either way, I do appreciate you telling me this. I'd rather know when things aren't right, in case something happens.'

'What do you mean?'

'If he goes too far with the bullying... and I think I'll have the salmon and mousseline sauce,' he said, regarding the menu.

She looked confused, until she noticed young Simon walk close by.

'Of course, sir. A good choice.' When the young waiter had passed on, she said, 'Is that what you really want?'

He had another look. 'I think it is.'

'Any hors d'oeuvres, sir?'

'I'll probably order dessert instead.'

'And what can I get you to drink?' After another quick glance around, she added, 'It's my experience, with some women I knew in my Suffragist days, that when they report bullying and abuse to the police, nothing is done, because it is accepted that women are under their husband's rule.'

'Times are changing, Miss Moore, and I, for one, don't believe that women should have to put up with abuse. So, if anything untoward happens, please let me know.'

She nodded. 'And by the way, I'm now known as Miss Moreland in the hotel.'

'But I thought—'

'Directive of Mr Bygrove's, to remind people that I'm Lord Moreland's daughter and to give more class to the dining room.' She raised her eyes heavenward.

He frowned. 'I see. I'll just have a lime cordial to drink, as I'm on duty after lunch.'

'Very well, sir.'

He looked around the room, noting that it was fuller than the last time he'd lunched here. That was good for Helen. Poor woman. He was now worried about her once more. Was it his business to be, though? Of course it was; it was his business to look out for everyone. He only hoped that Miss Moore – Moreland – did inform him if anything untoward happened, because he couldn't keep hanging around here.

It wouldn't hurt to come in for the odd lunch though.

–

'How did lunch go today?' Helen asked Edie when she came upon her in the staff corridor that afternoon.

'It was – fine. Several people mentioned they'd heard of Mr Bygrove's return, and asked how he was. I just replied that he was recovering. Phoebe and Simon said much the same.'

'That's about the best answer you could give.' It was also what she'd been replying when asked.

'Detective Inspector Toshack came in for lunch, by the way.'

Helen's stomach did a little twist. It wasn't dread, so what was it? 'He does sometimes.'

'He was concerned with the way Mr Bygrove acted when he visited yesterday. He had the impression you were being... bullied.'

'Bullied? He said that?'

'Yes, he used that word. I think he's keen to, um, keep an eye on the situation.' Edie looked uncomfortable conveying this.

'Oh dear.' Even though she worried about Douglas's deteriorating attitude towards her, she didn't want the police involved yet again. 'As much as I appreciate his concern, it's not something I'd want Douglas getting wind of. It would only make him angrier.'

'Don't worry, he won't hear it from me... I've been wondering, I know it's only February, but will we be doing any activities at Easter, like we did last year, especially the egg hunt and so on that we did for the children?'

Helen had known this would come up eventually, since they'd done so many charity events in the past.

'Not this year no, as much as I'd like to. Douglas has... expressed a wish not to do any at the moment.'

Forbidden it, would be closer to the mark. She didn't want to admit this to Edie, especially as he'd ranted about not having the *hoi polloi* in the hotel.

'That's a shame. I'd better get the conservatory ready for afternoon tea.'

When Edie had left her, Helen leant heavily against the wall and sighed. She stayed there for a few moments, her head back and eyes closed. When she heard Alice's voice get nearer, she pulled herself together.

Douglas had sent her on an errand to collect stamps from the post office in Norfolk Road. She'd better hurry if she wanted to avoid another telling off.

Chapter Sixteen

Helen had managed to make an appointment with Lord and Lady Raynolt, to discuss final arrangements for the engagement party in just over three weeks, at a time when she knew Douglas was having luncheon with a couple of the golf club members in the private dining room. She'd been lucky that he had been in the kitchen, ordering the staff there around, when the telephone call from Lady Raynolt had come through.

He'd have to be told about the party soon, of course, but she'd wanted the details to be finalised first so there was no chance of him taking over.

She was sitting in the conservatory with them now, the menus and timings for the evening's events before them on a table.

'You seem to have it all under control,' said Lord Raynolt, studying the menu once more. 'It's a shame that the war has put a limit on the choice of food, but we'll have to make do. If Penelope and Alan could have just waited until the war had ended...'

'And who knows when that will be?' said his wife.

'Indeed,' he said with a sigh.

'So, you've managed to get hold of the string octet you spoke of?'

'Yes, your ladyship. You won't—'

'What string octet?' said a male voice. 'What's all this then?'

Helen's heart sank as Douglas wheeled himself into the conservatory from the dining room.

'Lord and Lady Raynolt. How nice to see you. Are you arranging another ball?'

'More of a party, an engagement one, for our elder daughter, Mr Bygrove.' Lord Raynolt's expression was one of confusion, as he looked from Douglas to Helen to Douglas once more. He was probably wondering how come the manager knew nothing of it.

'Yes,' she said, turning towards her husband. 'Since you were recuperating, and I'd already started arrangements before you returned, I thought I'd continue. There was no point in involving you when you have enough to do.'

She smiled. Oh, how understanding and noble she sounded, when in reality she was being the opposite. The thought of him interfering at this point was intolerable. With any luck, he would just let her get on with it.

'Let's have a look at the arrangements,' he said, wheeling himself to the table. He picked up the menu and the plan for the evening, looking from one to the other and frowning. 'Oh no, no no no. This won't do for Lord and Lady Raynolt. We can do a much better menu than this.'

'But I thought the shortage of food was a problem,' said Lord Raynolt. 'That's what Mrs Bygrove said.'

'Only if you don't have the right connections. Of course, my wife wouldn't have had those while I've been away.'

'Oh,' said Lady Raynolt, smiling. 'Then you can do better?'

'I most certainly can. Though it would cost a little more.'

'Nothing's too much for our daughter,' said Lord Raynolt.

'And as for this *female* octet,' Douglas continued, 'they are dreadful.'

'But you've never—' Helen started.

'I know of a male quartet who are so much better. Been playing for years they have.'

If he meant the retired string quartet Mr Janus had hired for the charity concert they'd held a couple of Novembers ago, they were certainly a fine group. But she'd already hired the octet now, and she thought them even better.

'That sounds marvellous,' said Lady Raynolt.

'Helen, you can get on with your job now. I came to tell you that Grace's mother came in to say she's unwell, so you'll have to take over her shift at the desk. Mrs Leggett is standing in at the moment, so you'd better hurry. I'll sort out this party with Lord and Lady Raynolt.'

'I thought you were having lunch with—'

'They won't mind waiting while I conduct business.'

She was reluctant to go, but all she could say was, 'Very well.'

There was no point in arguing, especially in front of guests. Once again, she'd have to accept his interference and withdraw with good grace.

—

The day of the engagement party had come. Lunch had finished an hour ago and Helen and all available staff were getting the rooms ready for the evening's events. Even in that area, Douglas had interfered, stating that the buffet would be held in the private dining room so that dinner could take place for the other guests as normal, not in the conservatory. The private dining room was a lot smaller but should accommodate them, just. She only hoped he'd told Lord and Lady Raynolt this.

Helen turned, starting when she found Mrs Norris just behind her.

'Sorry to make you jump, Mrs Bygrove, but I need a word. In private.'

For her to come into the guest area herself to tell her something must mean it was serious.

'I believe my husband is in the office, so let's go to the main storeroom.'

The cook led the way without a word.

The corridor was empty when they reached it. Mrs Norris led the way into the storeroom, her brow puckered.

'This menu that Mr Bygrove prepared for the engagement party...'

'What's wrong?' said Helen.

'We haven't received half of the ingredients we need, what were supposed to come this morning.'

'Maybe they're held up somewhere. Why don't you speak to my husband about it, as he was the one organising that.'

The cook's expression said it all. Helen knew she wasn't the only one reluctant to discuss anything with Douglas.

'All right, Mrs Norris, I'll go and have a word with him. What's missing so far?'

The cook handed her a piece of paper with a long list of ingredients on it, including oysters, veal, venison and quails' eggs. From whom was Douglas planning to obtain those? Below was a list of items they had some of, but not as many as they needed, including eggs and cream.

'Thank you. I'll get back to you in a moment.'

She went around the corner to the office, knocking and entering straight after.

'I didn't say you could come in,' he barked, putting down the telephone receiver.

'This is urgent. Mrs Norris says that a lot of the ingredients they need for the party this evening have not arrived yet. They need time to be able to prepare things.'

She leant over with the list, which he snatched off her. He scanned it quickly, his scowl turning to a frown. 'Leave it with me. I'll contact my supplier now.'

'They'll have to be quick.' She stood her ground.

'Off you go.' He flicked a hand to dismiss her.

'I'll be in the kitchen.'

She wanted to find out what exactly they did have to create a buffet.

In the kitchen, she found Mrs Norris looking through the boxes of ingredients that had arrived.

'With this, and what we already have, we're not going to be able to make 'alf the stuff on the menu,' she said.

'Don't worry. Mr Bygrove is on the telephone now. He'll get it sorted out.'

The cook's expression showed as little confidence in Helen's words as she herself felt.

215

As Mrs Norris was telling her what was possible from the menu promised, Douglas wheeled himself into the kitchen.

'When is the rest of it coming?' said Helen.

'It isn't. There's been a breakdown in the chain of communication, and they're unable to deliver the rest. So, Mrs Norris, you're always boasting that you're a first class cook and can make the best of what you have, so now's the time to prove it.'

With that, he twirled the wheelchair around and left.

'I can't make rabbit taste like veal or chicken like partridge. And hens' eggs ain't small enough to pass as quails' eggs.'

'Then let's sit down and see what you can make,' said Helen. 'I'm sure whatever you conjure up will be just as delicious.'

'A good start would be that menu we created for them to begin with,' said Mrs Norris. 'I've still got a copy in the drawer.'

'You fetch it then and we'll sort something out.'

But it wouldn't be the fancy fare the Raynolts had paid for.

–

The evening's party had begun, and Helen was helping to greet guests in the foyer and show them to the ballroom.

It was the grandest event they had held for a long time. The men were smart enough in their evening suits, but the women had certainly gone to town with their gowns. Rose, mauve, dark green and sky blue seemed to be the favoured colours on dresses that were largely made from crepe de Chine and organza. They had become a lot more daring than before the war, with their calf-length hems and short sleeves. Some were even sleeveless, with thin straps over the shoulders. They had higher waists and hems, while the skirts often possessed two layers or a train. There were a few lace underskirts on show.

The ballroom was lit up by the fashions in a way it hadn't been for a while. Not since the twenty-first-birthday ball of the Raynolts' younger daughter. As spectacular as it was, deep inside Helen felt a little depressed by the scene. She was no longer as fashionable as she had been. She had little time to shop these days, and currently, had little money of her own with which to do it.

She kept her smile in place, deciding to put such selfish worries to one side, as she continued to welcome guests.

The first problem became clear when Lord Raynolt caught Helen as she greeted a young couple she knew to be his cousins.

'I say, Mrs Bygrove, what is the meaning of giving us the small dining room when we asked for the larger one?'

As she was about to reply, Douglas wheeled his way towards them. 'I'm so sorry, my lord, but it was an error on my wife's part.'

'But it was she who originally agreed to us having the main dining room.'

She had suffered enough of being blamed for things. 'Yes it was, and I did say this to you, Douglas, but you said the small one would be big enough.'

'I – I – most certainly did not!' he blustered. 'Helen, return to your work, instead of trying to make excuses to our esteemed guests.'

Helen gave Lord Raynolt an appealing glance, trying to convey that she was not to blame, before heading back to welcoming people.

Not long into the evening, the string quartet arrived, but it was not quite as she remembered it. Two of the older men were still part of the group, but there were now two young lads, one with a cello and the other on violin. Although not a ball as such, there was plenty of room for people to dance. Helen, who was helping to serve champagne, spotted young Penelope and her fiancé, Alan, who was in uniform, holding hands and looking hopefully at the band of musicians.

As the quartet struck up, Helen smiled, but it wasn't long before it faded as it became clear that the two young lads did not have the musical ability of the men they'd replaced. Stress overwhelmed her. She gave the champagne bottle to Edie, who looked equally alarmed, and left the room. To do what, she didn't know.

She found Douglas in the foyer, speaking with a couple who had arrived that day. She waited until they'd headed to the lift, before approaching him.

'How is it going?' he said. 'Splendidly, I should imagine. Though I must speak to you later about your error with the room allocation.'

'It is *not* going splendidly Douglas. The quartet are *terrible*.'

'But they've played here before and were enjoyed by many.'

'It's not the same four musicians. There are two new ones and they are not up to scratch. I don't know how the older two even think they're acceptable, unless they've gone deaf in their old age.'

'Nonsense. I will go and listen for myself.'

As he wheeled himself away, Helen glanced at Mr Watkins at the desk, who must have heard every word. His raised eyebrows confirmed it.

This was a disaster. The Raynolts would never come here again, and would no doubt spread the word about the dreadful evening. She couldn't face going back to the ballroom. She went instead to the small dining room, to double check all was going well there. The canapés, tarts, vol-au-vents, pâtés and various other dishes made with the local fish, seafood, meat and vegetables were exemplary. If nothing else, the supreme effort that Mrs Norris and her staff had put into the food should make up for the shambles so far, even if it wasn't what they had been led to believe would be served.

–

The buffet seemed to be well appreciated by the guests, who had been complimentary about several dishes. Perhaps, as she'd hoped, the food would be the saving grace. But as she listened to Lili explaining to a guest what was in a particular tart, Lady Raynolt approached her, with an expression that did not suggest a compliment was forthcoming.

'After being given an inferior room for the meal, and that very substandard quartet, of which we have another hour to suffer soon, I was hoping for better when it came to the food.'

'It has been prepared to the very highest standards, Lady—'

'There is no doubt of that, and it is very tasty, but it *isn't* what we ordered from Mr Bygrove. I would say, in fact, that it is closer to the menu you originally showed us.'

What could she say to this. 'I am sorry, my lady.'

'My husband has just had a word with Mr Bygrove about it, and he said that you forgot to order some of the food.'

'That is just *not* true, as I didn't even—'

Helen was surprised when Lady Raynolt took her hand. 'Mrs Bygrove, it is perfectly obvious that your husband is responsible for this mess. He did say that *he* was going to oversee the whole evening and use *his* contacts. And it was him who insisted that this quartet was better than the octet you had planned.'

'I'm sorry, all the same, that it hasn't gone to plan.'

'We don't blame you. I recall that you were responsible for organising much of our daughter Isabella's twenty-first-birthday ball, and that went extremely well. I'm only telling you this so that you don't blame yourself, in the way *he* wants to blame you. But sadly, we will forego organising anything at this hotel again for the foreseeable future.'

She nodded. 'I understand.' What else could she say?

—

Helen had been dreading this moment, alone with Douglas in their rooms. She'd been in their sitting room for twenty minutes by the time he arrived. It had been tempting to stay downstairs to have a late night drink with the staff and hope he was asleep by the time she came up, but along with the dread there was fury. He had spoiled an evening that would have run smoothly, had she been left in charge.

When he entered the room, his face inevitably had that sour look that spelled trouble. He brought the wheelchair to a standstill next to where she was standing. She could predict what he was going to say, so she decided to get her piece in first, courage surging through her.

'Douglas,' she said in a hushed tone, not wanting to alert anyone nearby, even though she felt like shouting. 'If you're not careful, you are going to ruin the hotel.'

'Shut up, you bitch.' The muted snarl was accompanied by an ugly twisted expression.

'Douglas!'

'It's not me who'll ruin the place, it's *you*. Because of your negligence, I've had to reimburse the Raynolts some of the money they paid.'

'*My* negligence? I wasn't the one who promised food that wasn't delivered. And *I* wanted to book the ladies' octet, which would have been so much better than that woeful quartet. I don't know what had—'

'They were fine last time I heard them, and *don't* answer back.'

'Yes, they were then, but the new line up seems to be—'

Douglas's fists were clenched as he interrupted with, 'If you had told me of the party in the first place, I would have been able to arrange things earlier and everything would have worked out perfectly fine.'

'You shouldn't have promised food that was difficult to get hold of, especially in that quantity, and we—'

He lurched forward in the wheelchair, punching her shoulder, which caused her to fall back on the settee behind with a small shriek.

'Douglas!'

'Shut up and listen. *I* am in charge here and it's *my* hotel. You will do what I say from now on, all of the time. After all, that's what you promised in our wedding vows, is it not, to obey and serve me?'

'And you promised to love and honour me,' she said, recalling what Edie had said a few weeks back. 'My mother would turn in her grave if she knew what you'd become. She trusted you to look after me, to look after what is, after all, my inheritance.'

'Not any more it isn't. It's *mine*. And you need to be careful, Helen, for I have friends in high places who could make things very difficult for you.'

'What, your friends at the *golf* club?' She made herself say this with confidence, not wanting him to think he could easily scare her. What did he even mean by this claim anyway?

He poked a forefinger almost in her face. 'Never mind who. Now I'm going to bed, and I suggest you do too. I'm going to be keeping my eye on you.' He wheeled himself to the bedroom and let himself in.

She remained on the settee, giving him time to get ready for bed before she joined him. A shudder went through her at the thought of sleeping next to him. But what could she do? She was stuck, and unless some amazing miracle occurred, she'd have to put up with it.

Chapter Seventeen

'Do you think Mr Bygrove's getting any better?' Phoebe asked Edie one morning, as they were re-laying neighbouring tables, at breakfast.

'In what way? His condition, his management skills or his temper?'

Phoebe laughed mirthlessly. 'I think we both know his temper hasn't improved. Quite the opposite. As for his management skills, him taking over the Raynolt party was a disaster.'

'Ugh! Don't remind me. What a terrible evening that was.' It had taken place nearly three weeks ago now, and still it embarrassed her to think about it.

'What I meant was, he's been home seven weeks now, and he's still in that wheelchair. He doesn't seem to have made any effort to get out of it. Didn't Mrs Bygrove tell us that the doctor said he was well on the mend when she visited the hospital?'

Edie had thought the same thing, but when she'd mentioned it to Helen, she'd seemed reluctant to talk about it. In fact, she'd been a lot more subdued since the Raynolts' party.

'For all we know he's doing exercises or trying to walk when he's in his quarters.'

'It's a good job we've got a lift here, otherwise how would he even get there?' said Phoebe. 'There'd be no way of getting that wheelchair up the staff stairs. Still, it seems ironic that he's always forbidden us from going to the staff quarters that way.'

'It is.'

'It's a shame being in the wheelchair hasn't prevented him from interfering in everything and strutting around the hotel like...'

'He owns the place?'

'Yes.' Phoebe chuckled. 'That's what I was going to say when I realised he does own the place. Like he belongs to the upper classes then, which he doesn't. You do, and you don't strut around like him, all high and mighty.'

'I never have done. But some of that class do, and some of them don't, as you must know, working here.'

'True. There's the major,' said Phoebe. 'Is that Inspector Toshack with him?'

'It is.' Edie walked over to greet them.

She felt relief at the inspector's appearance. He'd come for lunch around once a week since their conversation about Bygrove. She felt a sense of security with his regular attendance, like he was keeping an eye on the place and there was someone to report to if she felt things were getting worse. They certainly hadn't got better, but that didn't seem like enough to mention.

'Good morning, m'dear,' said the major. 'Would you have a table by the window for me and the inspector here please? It's nice to be able to look out on the spring flowers in the garden.'

'Of course, Major. You'd already been allocated the one closest to the conservatory, and the inspector can join you. Phoebe will be your waitress today.'

'Very good, m'dear.'

'You don't normally come at breakfast time, Inspector.'

'No, but I've a busy day ahead, and I might not have time later.'

'Enjoy breakfast, gentlemen.'

She turned to greet the resident guests, checking to see which table they had been allocated.

After five minutes, a group of men came in, led by Mr Bloomfield, the chairman of the local council. He was tall and wiry, with a pin-striped suit and greying hair. With him was the vice chairman, Mr Rotherham, and two other men.

'I trust you have room to fit us in for breakfast?' Bloomfield pronounced in an overloud voice. 'We'd prefer a window table.'

No 'pleases' or 'if possibles' were uttered. Not that she'd expect that from Bloomfield, who had always had a high opinion of himself.

'We do, sir,' said Edie, taking them to a table on the opposite side of the windows to the major and Inspector Toshack.

As she placed menus in front of them, she noticed that both Bloomfield and Rotherham had bright blue ties with yellow martlets on, representing Sussex. She'd seen Mr Bygrove wearing the same tie when going to some of his meetings.

'I expect exemplary service today, now Mr Bygrove is back,' said Bloomfield.

'We always endeavour to deliver such service, sir,' said Edie.

'That's not what I've heard.'

Afraid she might show her annoyance, Edie simply said, 'I will be back shortly to take your order, sir.'

More guests entered and were seated and served, most of them residents. Some had left it a little late and she could see they'd have to clear up today beyond their normal time, as occasionally happened.

She was delivering toast to a table two away from the councillors, when Bloomfield put up his hand and clicked his fingers.

'You there, girl. Over here.' He pointed down at his table.

'How rude,' muttered the woman she'd just served.

As she walked to the councillors' table, she noticed the major and the inspector taking an interest.

'This bread tastes like sawdust.' Bloomfield picked a triangular slice out of the toast rack and flung it on the table.

'And the roll I had was not much better,' said Rotherham.

'It might be because of the other grains, the oats, barley, rye, and so on, that are added to the flour now, to make it go further,' Edie explained. 'And we have to make potato rolls for breakfast. It's called "government bread", and we're subject to the rules, the same as everyone else.'

'I am a councillor and *you* are just a waitress and shouldn't be so rude.'

'Then as a councillor, you must be aware of the rules.'

'We are,' said Rotherham. 'But an establishment such as this, serving important people, should be able to source the best food. No doubt this is a hangover from Bygrove's *wife* being in charge.'

The four men laughed.

'Anyway,' Rotherham continued, 'we're not discussing this with a mere waitress. We want to speak to the manager.'

'I will fetch Mrs Bygrove.'

'No, she's just the manager's wife,' said Bloomfield. 'We'll speak to *Mr* Bygrove.'

'Very well, sir. But being in a wheelchair, he may take a little longer to arrive.'

As she walked away, towards the door into the staff corridor, she heard Rotherham say, 'What a cheeky young wench she is.'

Wench? What century was this man from?

Approaching the major's table, she saw him raise his eyes and murmur, 'Shall I tell them who you are, or will you?'

'Neither, Major, if you don't mind.'

She walked on. It was a wonder that Bygrove hadn't already boasted to them about having Baron Moreland's daughter working for him, especially as he'd insisted she use her real surname.

In the staff corridor now, she hoped the manager was in the office, otherwise she'd have to go hunting for him. Luckily, he was.

'What is it?' he barked, as she knocked and entered. 'Councillors Bloomfield and Rotherham would like a word, sir, in the dining room.'

'Why, what has the staff done wrong?'

'It's not the staff, sir, it's the bread. They don't approve of it and have some idea that you'll be able to improve the situation.' She felt herself having to moderate her words, as she was becoming increasingly annoyed.

'I suppose I'd better smooth things over, as usual.'

As usual? This man lived in a fantasy world.

Bygrove had become proficient at wheeling himself swiftly to places and opening doors for himself. Edie walked to the dining room behind him, accompanying him almost to the councillors' table.

She gathered up some plates close by, noticing Bygrove being gestured in closer. They all moved in and spoke quietly together. At one point they all looked around at her. Had Bygrove told them who she was? Next, they looked towards Inspector Toshack and the major. What on earth were they talking about?

Edie took a tray of used crockery to the scullery.

'Do you know where Mrs Bygrove is?' she asked Mrs Leggett, who was inspecting some jars of conserves that Hetty had been making in the stillroom.

'She is on the desk in the foyer, currently. Is something amiss?'

'I'm not sure. I'll tell you later.'

In the foyer, she was relieved to see Helen just finishing with a guest who was leaving that morning. She gave her a quick rundown of what had happened with the councillors.

'Sorry, I wouldn't have left my post, but I only have the Bloomfield's table left now, and, as I said, Mr Bygrove is speaking to them. And I didn't know if I would get the opportunity later.'

'Oh dear. I should be pleased that the hotel has a connection to the council, as it can help sometimes, but I... I don't know. There's something I don't like about this.'

'Me neither. I'd better get back, before they complain about me not being there.'

'Before you go, your father rang the hotel earlier, to say he would be in the vicinity Saturday week and would pop in to see you at eleven. I told him you would ring him back to discuss it, but he said there was nothing to discuss and that you must make sure that you were available.'

'I'm so sorry, Helen. He had no right to speak to you like that. And I realise Easter weekend will be busy.'

'It's not your fault, Edie. I will make sure you are not on duty at that time.'

'Thank you. I'd better get back.'

–

'The councillors were *not* impressed with the way Miss Moreland spoke to them,' were Douglas's opening words to Helen, after he had summoned her to the office.

'She may be the daughter of a baron, but that does not excuse her. Luckily, because I explained she has that position, they did not insist on me sacking her.'

He had to be making this up, surely? 'First of all, Douglas, they are not in a position to tell us who we can and can't employ.'

'You mean *me*, not *we*.'

Already he was starting to sound aggressive. She was glad there was a desk between them. It had been nearly three weeks since the punch to her shoulder, but she was not confident that it wouldn't happen again.

'Secondly, from what I've gathered, they were rude to *her*, not vice versa. Just because they are guests, does not give them that right.'

'That is *not* the case. Miss Moreland is telling fibs.'

'I'm not only going by her testimony, Douglas. Major Thomas and Inspector Toshack came and told me the same thing after breakfast. The inspector, in particular, was not impressed by their behaviour.'

Douglas laughed mockingly. 'What is he going to do then, arrest them for being in authority?'

'It's appalling that they seem to think that the regulations on food don't apply to them. They should be setting an example to the population.'

'They probably do, when in the company of the hoi polloi. But at the hotel, people expect the best. And stop answering me back!'

He gripped hold of the arms of the wheelchair and pulled himself up to a standing position. Helen was taken aback, as she'd not seen him do this since he'd returned. He took a few steps towards the shelves and pulled out a ledger, before sitting back down.

'Douglas, how long have you been able to do this?'

'I've been practising.'

'You're doing well, then. When Dr Ferngrove came to see you last week, you told him you still couldn't manage it, despite the exercises. You should walk more while working. It would build up your strength and—'

'I'm not showing *anyone* else, least of all a doctor, particularly an army doctor.'

'But—'

'No buts! I'm never going back to that war.' He stood once more, carefully, leaning over the desk, wagging his finger and clenching his teeth as he continued with, 'And you'd better not say anything to anybody, otherwise I'll divorce you and keep the hotel and the children.'

He slammed his fist on the desk, making her jump.

'Now, let me get on with giving this hotel back its status.'

From being resentful of his objectionable behaviour she now felt afraid. No, more than that: terrified. She hadn't cared about the threat of his so called 'powerful friends'. But the idea of him trying to take the children away from her? Would he do that? And deprive her of the hotel?

Douglas was not the man she'd married. Or rather, not the man she'd thought she'd married.

And yes, she did think he would do exactly what he threatened.

Chapter Eighteen

On Monday, as Helen stood on desk duty during breakfast time, she heard the squeak of Douglas's wheelchair as he manoeuvred it into the foyer.

Her heart sank. Since the threatening conversation last Saturday, she had felt sick being in the same room as him. She'd also worried every time he'd gone anywhere near the children. Not that his attentions to them ever lasted long.

'I have a meeting in the private dining room today,' he said, 'and there'll be another one on Saturday.'

Is that why he'd been keen to return the guest lounge to a private room, so he could meet up with his cronies?

'Your golfing chums, I presume?' she said lightly, trying to hide that she was probing for information.

He hesitated. 'Um. Yes, yes, they are, and we have committee matters to discuss.'

She resisted pointing out that he couldn't even play golf at the moment, and, if he was going to carry on hiding any progress, he wouldn't for a long time.

'I need to catch up with what's been going on,' he said, as if reading her thoughts. 'They will be arriving at ten forty-five and you will bring us coffee at eleven o'clock on the dot, along with some delicious fancies. Other than that, you are to leave us alone. As is everyone else.' He pushed himself away, back to the staff area.

What was he up to?

Some instinct told her that this had nothing to do with golf.

She was looking forward to Dr Ferngrove's visit the next day. Hopefully he would realise that Douglas was more capable than he was letting on.

Could she speak to him privately maybe, and tell him? There might be something he could do. What, she wasn't sure, but it was worth a try.

–

Helen knocked on the door of the private dining room, just as the grandfather clock in the foyer chimed eleven.

'Enter,' called a voice that wasn't Douglas's.

As she went in with the tray, she recognised the councillors Mr Bloomfield and Mr Rotherham. Two of the other men there were those who had been at breakfast with them last Thursday. Were the councillors part of the golf club? She realised that she knew so little of Douglas's recreational companions.

One of the men whose names she didn't know was speaking of the abdication of Tsar Nicholas II.

'Russian revolution?' Bloomfield snapped. 'I'd hang the whole bally lot of them if they did that here. They'd do better to put their energies into the war effort.'

Like you are? thought Helen, the man who believed that those coming to the hotel shouldn't be under the same wartime restrictions as the rest of the population? What a hypocrite.

'Put the coffee down there and pour it,' said Douglas. 'Then you can leave. Where are the fancies?'

'Mrs Norris has sent biscuits, otherwise we might be short at morning coffee. But they are homemade and quite delicious.'

Douglas narrowed his eyes and she knew this would be something else that she'd be told off about later.

'Ordinary people, what do they know?' said Rotherham. 'We had some residents come to the council offices last week, demanding we increase the number of plots for allotments available in the town, stating that the government has said they need to grow their own food. I told them to use their gardens. They said that they either didn't have them or that they were too small. Is that our fault? They should get a house with a bigger plot of land.'

Helen would have loved to point out that most people in the town rented their accommodation, and those in boarding houses and apartments may not even have access to a garden. But it was more than her life was worth to speak *out of turn*, as Douglas would likely have put it. Such ignorant men. And they called themselves councillors.

Having poured the coffee, she left them to their meeting.

As she was walking back across the foyer, she was aware of someone rushing into the hotel and towards the private dining room door. She glanced at him quickly, noticing the pencil-striped suit, but he had his head down. With that and his green alpine style hat, she couldn't work out if she knew him or not.

She carried on. At least she was guaranteed some time without Douglas barking at her.

–

Dr Ferngrove arrived late morning the following day, going to their bedroom to examine Douglas. Helen stood to one side as he checked his pulse.

'Why are you still here?' Douglas griped. 'Go and do something useful. This is private.'

'Mrs Bygrove may stay if she wishes,' said the doctor.

'No, she may not.'

'I'll be in the sitting room,' Helen said, and left them to it.

She sat on the settee, picking up the book she was reading, hardly able to concentrate. If she could just speak to the doctor in private, maybe when he was leaving. Yes, she'd show him out and talk to him then.

After some minutes, the doctor pushed Douglas back into the sitting room, saying, 'I just can't understand why you can't walk even a little yet, even a couple of steps.'

'It's clearly not as simple an injury as the doctor at Netley claimed,' said Douglas.

'But I was sent the information and the X-rays. Everything looked to be healing well. There's a bit more room here than in the bedroom; let's try and get you up and practising. Mrs Bygrove, you come on the other side of your husband.'

The doctor took hold of one of Douglas's arms and Helen took the other.

'Now, *lift*,' said Ferngrove. 'Try a few steps, Mr Bygrove.'

Douglas thumped his body back into the wheelchair, emitting a loud holler of distress.

'I *told* you I couldn't do it, please, please, it's agony to try.' He put on a big show of being in pain.

'I can't help thinking that you should have gone to a nursing home to recover,' said the doctor. 'I will write a few letters and get you admitted—'

'No!' Douglas shouted, with even more distress in his voice. 'I can't go back to one of those places. I just need time. Time.' The last word was said with a wobbly voice that faded to a croak and then nothing.

What an actor, thought Helen. Mr Janus could make good use of him, with most of his male performers now at war.

'Well, if you won't go to a nursing home, I can't make you. But I do think we should get you into a hospital for a few more tests.'

'I can't leave the hotel. I need to—'

'Nonsense. Your good lady wife is more than capable of running it in your absence.'

'She'd have to convey me to the hospital.'

'Listen, Mr Bygrove, if there are ways we can help, then you should let us. It will probably be a few weeks until the hospital can fit you in, but if you just leave it, then need help once the war is over, you will have to pay for treatment. At the moment, you're considered a wounded soldier.'

'I'm quite capable of paying.'

'I'll look into getting you an appointment anyway. Better safe than sorry.'

'That would be a good idea, wouldn't it, Douglas?' Helen smiled at him, hoping he would see sense.

He said nothing, treating her only to a scowl. She should have known better.

'I'll show you out, Doctor.'

'There's no need for that,' said Douglas. 'He knows the way. I need you to help me get changed into my good suit so I can greet the committee from Rustington who are hiring the private dining room for lunch.'

She tried to come up quickly with some reason to do as she'd suggested, but nothing sensible came to mind.

'Very well, dear.'

Gone was her chance to talk to the doctor. For now.

—

Edie entered the foyer two minutes before her father was due on the Saturday. He'd always been a punctual man and expected the same in others.

It seemed that, on this occasion, he had arrived early, and was just backing out of the private dining room.

'I beg your pardon,' her father said to those in the room. 'I seem to have been sent to the wrong place.'

'Aren't you Lord Moreland?' came Adrian Bloomfield's voice.

'That's right. I'll leave you gentlemen to your meeting.'

'Father,' Edie said, hurrying towards him, knowing Bygrove had said that the people in the private dining room were not to be disturbed.

He closed the door. 'Ah, Edith, there you are.'

'I'm so sorry,' called Grace English, the part-time desk clerk. 'I assumed you were one of Mr Bygrove's expected guests.'

He lifted a hand as if to indicate it was fine.

'Would you like to come to the ballroom?' said Edie. 'It's empty and there are some seats there to sit on.'

'No, let's take a walk while it's still sunny,' said her father.

As they were almost at the outside doors, Bygrove rushed across the foyer in his wheelchair and entered the private dining room.

'What's wrong with him?'

'That's the manager,' said Edie. 'His legs were broken in the war and he's still recuperating.' Even though he didn't seem to have got any better.

'I recognised a few chaps in that room, including a couple of the councillors here in Littlehampton, I believe.'

'That's right. Mr Bloomfield and Mr Rotherham.'

'Yes, those were their names.'

'How do you know them?' Now outside, Edie took her father's arm and they made their way to the gate.

'Saw them in Brighton a while back, in a meeting about impending food shortages and how the county should manage them. They were of the opinion that those with sufficient money should be given priority over the poorer members of society. It didn't go down well with most, including me.'

'I'm glad to hear that, Father. That is, that you disagreed with them.'

'Of course I would. We're in a war situation. We all need to stick together.'

She wondered whether her mother agreed with her father. It was ironic that she was of humble stock, having married into society, and yet was much more of a snob than her father. But it seemed so often the case with those who'd clawed their way up the ranks of society.

Out of the gate, they headed for the common.

'I'm not surprised,' said Edie. 'The week before last, they were in the hotel for breakfast, complaining about the war bread, and how those coming to the hotel should expect better.'

'They haven't changed then. I also noticed – look out!' He pulled her out of the way as a bicycle came careering down the pavement. 'Ride on the road, you fool!' he called to a man in a boater. He turned towards Edie. 'Are you all right?'

'I'm fine. What were you saying?'

'I've lost the thread now. Never mind, it couldn't have been important.'

'I'm so glad to see you, Father. How is Mother?'

'Much the same as always. Organising her committees. Fretting about your brother.'

'I've had a few letters from Freddie. He is coping better with the war than I anticipated.'

'I suppose you just do the best you can, under the circumstances. With any luck, it will be over a bit more quickly than it would have been, what with the United States now declaring war on Germany. Had you heard the news?'

'I read it in the newspaper this morning. It is good news for us. Not so good for the Americans, I imagine.'

'Hardly surprising though, with the German submarines sinking American merchant ships in the Atlantic.'

Edie wondered whether, rather than bringing the war to a halt, it would simply get bigger and bigger, involving more and more countries. She knew better than to start a political debate with her father though.

'That looks rather fun for the youngsters,' her father said, pointing to the goats pulling small carriages with children in. 'You would have loved that as a child.'

'I did like it a lot, as did Freddie. Our governess, Miss Langley, used to bring us here on holiday, if you recall.'

'Of course she did.'

'Is there a particular reason you've come today, Father?'

'Simply because I haven't seen you for so long, my dear. I'm trying to talk your mother around to seeing sense, but she's very stubborn. She did have her eye on a couple of very eligible bachelors for you.'

'Which is one of the reasons why I left.'

He huffed out a breath. 'I know dear, I know. You're under-manageress at the hotel now, I understand from Lucia.'

So, Freddie's wife was passing on the things she wrote in letters to her. Not that she minded. Clearly her father wanted to know how she was getting on, even if her mother didn't.

'I *was*.' She told him the story of Bygrove's arrival home, and how he'd become even more controlling. 'I worry for Helen. And it was better run when she was in charge. But he won't accept that she's been running it well in his absence and thinks he knows better about everything and does rather bully her.'

'I know a few men like him. I can't imagine what would happen if I tried to bully your mother.' He chuckled and she joined in.

'I wouldn't try it if I were you.'

'Not that she has any official say in the business, but she has some good opinions, and I do listen to them.'

'The staff here are very loyal to Helen, and we're keeping an eye on the situation.'

'Sometimes, that's all you can do.'

They'd reached the promenade by this time. There were several rows of deckchairs lined up on the beach in front of them, where people were sitting watching a Punch and Judy show.

'Have you time for a walk by the beach, Father?'

'I have no urgent need to get away, so yes. Do you have time for me to treat you to lunch?'

'I have until afternoon tea off, so yes. I know a nice tearoom by the river on Pier Road, run by a lovely Italian family. It's not the Beach Hotel, but it's very pleasant, all the same.'

'Perfect. I'll look forward to it.'

—

Back at the hotel, having got dressed in her uniform ready for afternoon tea, Edie went via the foyer, knowing Helen would now be on duty there.

'I trust you had a good visit with your father,' Helen said as she spotted Edie. 'As you are smiling.'

'I was dreading it, but we had a nice walk and an enjoyable lunch. Thank you again for allowing me the time off to see him. I hope it didn't cause any trouble with your husband.'

'It didn't. Mrs Leggett was able to reorganise the rota without him knowing. He's still in there, with his *friends*.' She pointed at the door of the private dining room. 'Then he insisted on having luncheon served to them all in there. He could have said something—' The telephone rang and Helen lifted the receiver. 'The Beach Hotel, Littlehampton.'

Edie left her to it and was heading towards the conservatory when the door opened from the private dining room. Mr Rotherham came out. She carried on, but, on spotting her, he caught her up, just inside the door of the public dining room.

'So, I hear that you're Lord Moreland's daughter. Bygrove's been boasting about it to us. Seems to see you as an asset. I saw him here earlier, Moreland. What on earth does he think of you working at a hotel?'

Since it had become more common knowledge, she'd had to answer this question several times, so had a ready reply, even if it wasn't quite true. 'My father encourages his children to find out what the real world is like and to show they can make their own way in it.'

He looked around, pulling a face. 'And this is all you wanted for yourself? You can't be earning much money. I don't think any potential husband would be too impressed with you having been a waitress.'

'Then they would not be the right husband for me,' she replied.

She turned away, hoping that was the end of the cross-examination, but he stood in her way. 'You could earn a little more if you were willing to do a few favours.'

'I beg your pardon?'

'You're a good-looking woman, elegant and classy. And nobody need know, unless you'd want me to pass your name on to colleagues. Classy women are very popular, if you get my meaning.'

She held herself tall and straight backed, as her mother had taught her that a lady should stand, and looked him in the eyes. 'No thank you. And I can't imagine that Mr Bygrove would be thrilled with you soliciting his staff.'

'Soliciting?' He threw back his head and laughed. 'I don't recommend that you tell him, otherwise I could make life difficult for you, baron's daughter or not. I'll just say you're a liar, and who do you think he'll believe? A baron's fallen daughter, or a respected councillor who's also a solicitor?'

'I'm not a fallen woman. Absolutely not.'

'They'll believe you are, once I've finished my story.'

He twisted on the balls of his feet, and walked away, heading towards the lavatory.

She shivered. Fancy him thinking she'd do *favours* for *him*.

Once he'd disappeared, she decided to go back to the desk, and tell Helen what had happened, despite Rotherham's threats. But as she was about to do so, the rest of Bygrove's party exited the private dining room.

She'd have to wait until later.

—

Late that evening, after Edie and Phoebe had finally finished serving dinner, they entered the staff dining room to find other colleagues there chatting excitedly, with Jack giving a little cheer. With him was Fanny and Gertie, Miss Bolton the nurse, Mrs Leggett, Mrs Turnbull, Mrs Norris, Hetty from the stillroom, Lili and the children's nursemaid, Vera.

'What's all this then?' said Phoebe. 'Has the war ended?'

'No such luck,' said Jack. 'But we are celebrating the United States' declaration of war on Germany, so maybe the end won't be too far off. Shame it's only tea we've got, but it'll have to do.'

'It will not have to do!' said Mrs Norris, swivelling off the bench seat. 'I've got some beer left from Christmas. Only a few bottles, but we can share it around.'

'Come and sit next to me,' Lili called to Edie. 'I haven't seen you all day. How did your father's visit go?'

'I'll tell you later, in our room.' It might be an opportunity to tell someone what Rotherham had said too. She hadn't had a chance to speak to Helen, and she was beginning to question the wisdom of doing so when she had so much to worry about already.

Mrs Norris was soon back with the bottles and some glasses on a large tray. Mrs Leggett helped her place it on the middle of the table.

'Right, share the glasses out,' said the cook. 'Jack, you open the bottles. I reckon there's enough for half a glass each. If ya don't want that much, I'm sure others'll drink it up.'

Once they'd all served themselves, Mrs Leggett stood up. She held her glass out, that was only a quarter full. 'Here's to a speedier end to the war, now the Americans have joined,' she announced.

'Hear, hear!' called everyone around the table. They all lifted their glasses, then took a mouthful of the beer.

'Let's hope it *will* mean a swift end to it,' said Mrs Norris, 'and then my Joseph, Charlie, Lorcan, Günther, and all the other men can come—'

She hadn't finished the sentence, when the door was kicked further open and Mr Bygrove wheeled himself in, his face like thunder. 'Günther? Did you say Günther? I am never having that Hun back working here ever again. And whoever thinks he should come back is a traitor and can leave my employ.'

'But Günther was a good worker, sir,' said Phoebe. 'And he has no sympathy for the Kaiser.'

'You're fired!'

'What?'

'Mr Bygrove, she was only telling the truth,' said Mrs Norris.

'No, she was not! He is a traitor.'

'I write to him, sir, and I know he hates what's happening and—'

'That is enough! You are fired, and that is that. Get your things. Now!'

Phoebe looked around the staff, who all stared back, with shock on their faces.

'She can't go now, sir,' said Edie, feeling someone had to speak up. Since Bygrove seemed to be so proud of having her working here, he was less likely to sack her. 'It's night time, and her parents are in Angmering, and there's no way to get there now.'

'I could not care *less*,' said Bygrove. 'She can sleep on the street for all I care. She's a traitor and I should report her to the authorities. Günther is a nasty, stinking little Bosch. He should have been put before a firing squad.'

Edie couldn't believe the vitriol coming out of his mouth for a man who had been a well-respected waiter at the hotel for several years and in whom there was no harm. 'Mr Bygrove I don't think—' Edie started.

Phoebe stepped over the bench. 'Don't worry, I wouldn't stay a moment longer where someone would use such vile words against a decent man. My sister lives on Duke Street. She'll put me up for a night.' She stood in front of Bygrove. 'If anyone in this place is a nasty, stinking person, it's *you*, Mr Bygrove.'

He kicked out his foot, but she moved before he could reach her. 'I will be waiting in the corridor, to make sure you do go.'

Lili got up and followed Phoebe.

Mrs Leggett then got up, going out to the corridor. 'I don't think this is wise when we are already short of staff, sir,' they heard her say.

'We'll get more staff. Better ones. I've got connections. And don't think you're exempt from being dismissed, Mrs Leggett, just because you've been here so many years. I'm sure I could find a better housekeeper. Perhaps I'll get Miss Harvey in, once she's finished her year in gaol. That was all down to you lot as well. I should sack the lot of you.'

'I can assure you that was down to her, and her alone.'

'Shut up, before I sack you too.'

Everyone in the dining room looked around at each other, eyes wide. Mrs Leggett returned, her face pinched in anger.

When they heard Phoebe return to the corridor, Edie rose and joined her and Lili.

'Get out, get out now!' Douglas shrieked, as he pushed her on with his legs.

'Here, stop that,' she shouted.

He didn't stop until she was out of the scullery door, Bygrove shouting, 'And don't come back.'

Edie and Lili were looking at each other, when they were both kicked out of the way by Bygrove. They watched him go, shouting about belligerent staff, until he was out of earshot. When they returned to the dining room, everyone there looked gloomy, heads on hands or looking at the floor, their beer undrunk.

'I swear that man is going to come to no good,' Mrs Leggett muttered in a low voice. 'He is going to get on the wrong side of the wrong person, and he will come off worse, mark my words.'

'If one of us doesn't see him off first,' said Mrs Norris. 'Speaking to us like we're bits of dirt on the floor.'

'Only if any of us are left,' said Edie. 'At this rate, he'll have no staff.'

There were nods and mumbles of agreement.

'It is a little odd though,' said Edie, picturing the scene she'd just witnessed. 'The way Bygrove kicked out at Phoebe. His legs seemed to work well enough to do that, yet he claims not to be able to walk.'

'You're right,' Lili agreed. 'But maybe he just has difficulty putting any weight on them.'

'Perhaps.'

'Let's be thankful he can't walk,' said Mrs Norris, 'else our lives would be made even worse.'

Several people picked up their glasses of beer and drank them, but it was more in the manner of solace than celebration.

—

Helen had been waiting for Douglas to arrive at their rooms for a late lunch on Easter Sunday. Since his return from hospital, he had forbidden her or the children from eating with the staff. Consequently, Helen often found herself eating alone when the children were at school, as he was invariably late, if he turned up at all.

He finally turned up at a quarter to three.

'Where are the children?'

'They've finished already. Vera has taken them to the beach as there will be donkeys there today, and several children's entertainers.'

'Hm, they could have waited until I arrived.'

'To be honest, I'm rather glad to be here alone with you.'

He sat back and pulled a face. 'Why is that?'

She hoped to goodness he wasn't expecting some romantic overture on her part. Her wording should maybe have been a little clearer.

'Come and get settled first.'

He wheeled himself to the middle of the room, then got out and limped to the table, where he sat opposite her. He pulled the plate of quartered sandwiches towards him. 'These could be fresher.'

'They have been waiting here for you nearly an hour... Douglas, I've not long heard what happened last night, with Phoebe.'

'Nasty little bitch, answering me back.'

'You never used to swear. Is this what being in the army has done to you?'

'Oh, I've always sworn, up here.' He tapped a finger against his forehead several times.

'The trouble is, she should have been on breakfast and lunch shift today, as well as afternoon tea and dinner later, and they've had to do a last-minute reshuffle, bringing Lili back into the dining room. Did you not think to try and sort something out? I wish someone had told me before.'

'Who's been snitching about it?'

'It's hardly snitching, telling me that a staff member has been dismissed, especially when they assumed you would have told me.'

'I'm the boss here. It's none of your business.'

'If you're not careful, Douglas, they will all leave, as there are other jobs they can do now.'

'What, the women too?' he sneered.

'Especially the women. Like Amanda Lovelock, who left to become a WPC at the police station here. Then there's factory work, munitions and office jobs where they're short of men. Women are having to do all sorts of work done by men in the past, as we know well enough in the hotel.'

'Huh, that lazy bunch of idiots won't leave here; they've had it too easy. And they have accommodation.'

'Some of them have family nearby. We are already short of staff, and this will get worse come the summer. Phoebe has always been an excellent worker, as most of them have, despite what you say. I've got her address and I will go and see if I can persuade her to come back.'

From what she'd heard from Vera of their conversation, and the insults dealt by Douglas, she wasn't at all confident that Phoebe would want to come back.

'No you won't. I won't put up with it.'

Something occurred to Helen, which emboldened her. 'What are you going to do, get out of the wheelchair and run after me, and show everyone you can walk?'

Albeit with a limp, but it would still reveal his deception to one and all.

'In the meantime, Lili had better stay working in the dining room. It will make us short of a chambermaid again, but we can see to that later.'

He looked set to argue but seemed not to be able to find the words. 'We will leave it at that, for now,' he said eventually. 'But I'm looking into replacements, via my contacts.'

Helen wondered whether this was through the councillors he seemed to have struck a relationship up with. How could they help though? Or was it just another boast with no substance? He'd said this several times, but nothing had yet come of these contacts.

'And have a word with Hargreaves about re-seeding the tennis courts again,' he said. 'He keeps telling me they'll have to wait until the vegetables have all grown and been picked. He's not taking a blind bit of notice of me.'

It was a wonder he hadn't threatened to sack him too, but then, Mr Hargreaves had been there many years, longer than any of the other staff, and he had a lot of experience. Douglas would be afraid to lose him.

'He knows what he's doing. It would be a shame to waste the vegetables growing there.' He didn't need to know that the head gardener was continuing to sow new seeds. 'It's not like you can play tennis at the moment anyway.'

He glared at her, his eyes narrowed and his lips pinched in.

'I'll take the dirty plates down to the kitchen and make sure the rota is sorted out for the waiting staff.' She had no desire to remain in his company longer than she needed to.

She carried the tray to the landing and closed the door. Leaning against the wall she let out a huge sigh. Five minutes in Douglas's company was enough.

Chapter Nineteen

Helen entered the kitchen at the end of morning coffee on the Easter Monday to speak with Mrs Norris.

'Hello there, Mrs Bygrove,' said the cook. 'Think it's been even busier today than yesterday, and we've 'ardly begun yet.'

'There have been some new bookings for lunch too. It is a lot sunnier today, which has encouraged people out, but it is still rather nippy.'

'That's why people want to get themselves indoors here. Now, is there anything in particular I can do for you?'

'I just wanted to check—'

She was interrupted by Douglas rolling into the kitchen so fast that he almost knocked into Hannah as she was chopping leeks at the large table.

'Out of the way, woman!' he shouted.

She said nothing, looking peeved as she took the chopping board and vegetables around to the other side of the table.

'Douglas!'

'Shush now. The order has arrived!' he announced with a flourish.

'What order?'

'Mrs Norris,' he said, 'it's too late to change the luncheon menu, so we will add a couple of special dishes. And we *will* be changing the dinner menu.'

'It's a bit late to add more dishes to lunch,' said the cook.

'Nonsense. They will be announced to each table by the waiting staff. I will go and tell them when I've left here.'

Mrs Norris looked at Helen, a query in her eyes.

'Douglas, what order is this?'

'One I made with my connections, like I told you. Veal and also some steak today, so we'll be able to offer filet mignon. And there'll be other meats in the coming days, as there's more where they came from. Things you've struggled to get hold of, but *I've* been able to source, like extra cream and milk, and some proper bread for afternoon tea. And there are other things, fruit and the like. They're all in the scullery currently.'

'Good gracious, Mr Bygrove, that's wonderful news,' said the cook. 'The best I've heard for ages. Where have you managed to get all that from?'

'If you have the right skills as a manager, you can get what you need.' He gave Helen a derogatory glance, letting her know he considered her not up to the job.

'Get young Finn to bring it in, sir, and we'll work out a new menu for this evening. And add the coupla dishes you want for lunch.'

Mrs Norris was over the moon, almost dancing as she spoke. Hannah, who was chopping once more, didn't look quite so impressed. Helen wondered if she was thinking along the same lines as herself. Where had Douglas got this food? And how had he got it delivered on Easter Monday?

Hannah glanced up at her and Helen smiled. She didn't want her getting suspicious and maybe going home and telling someone outside of the hotel.

'How nice to have more choice on the menu,' said Helen, before leaving the kitchen. What she'd had to say to Mrs Norris was now redundant.

—

Edie was glad to have Lili back in the dining room, but she wished so much that it hadn't been at the expense of Phoebe. It was now lunchtime, and although it wasn't as hectic as it had been over the Easter weekend, they were still quite busy today for a Thursday in Easter week.

'Mrs Rhys-Pennington on table ten just told me she'd heard that there was more choice on the menu now, so that's why she's come in,' said Lili, stopping by the drawers to collect some cutlery.

'It's good to be able to offer such a premium menu again, but where is Bygrove getting it from?'

'Have you spoken to Mrs Bygrove about it?'

'I tried to, but she said it's to do with his connections and nothing to do with her.'

Lili took several napkins from an already open drawer. 'She doesn't seem to take him on as much as she used to, before he went to war.'

'No. And that in itself is worrying.'

'Oh dear, there's Inspector Toshack,' said Lili. 'I hope he isn't here because he's heard anything.'

'I'll show him to one of my tables.'

Edie greeted the inspector and sat him on a table by the window with a menu, but was soon waylaid by Lady Blackmore, two tables along.

'Compliments to the chef on the filet mignon,' she announced rather primly and precisely. 'There hasn't been such a good choice of food for a while, has there, Cecelia?'

'No, Lady Blackmore.'

'Is this anything to do with Mr Bygrove's return?'

How Edie hated giving the man any credit. 'Just erratic availability, I believe,' she replied.

After a while she returned to take the inspector's order.

'I seem to have picked a good day,' he said, still perusing the menu. 'I'll have the veal chops périgourdine, please. And a lime cordial, thank you.'

'Very good, Inspector.'

—

Inspector Toshack placed his cutlery on the plate and dabbed his mouth with his napkin. He had enjoyed the veal chops, but something niggled at him. It was probably nothing, but he couldn't help thinking that there should now be less available on the menu, not more. Perhaps, as he'd stated to Miss Moreland, he'd simply managed to pick a good day to come to lunch. After all, food was in short supply, not totally unavailable.

He hadn't spotted Helen today, and he felt the disappointment deeply. He knew that was wrong, especially now that her husband was home. It was only that she'd become a friend, of sorts, someone he could talk to. And he was short of those. Yes, that was it. He'd enjoyed her company in Lewes, despite the circumstances.

He looked around the room, trying to distract himself. There was a young couple, holding hands over the table. The man was in uniform, so presumably on leave. Even though he didn't know them, he hoped with all his heart that they'd have a future after the war.

His attention was taken by the grating tones of Lady Blackmore nearby, berating her companion for spilling water on her plate. Poor Miss Wilson. He recalled her ladyship storming into the hotel during one of the waves of libellous letters, leading a group of local residents. He felt relieved anew that Helen had been absolved.

'Have you finished, Inspector?'

His attention came back to the present, to find Miss Moreland beside him. 'Yes, yes. Thank you.'

'I'll clear away your plate then.'

'That was delicious.' He was going to leave it there, but that niggling doubt urged him to make a little gentle enquiry. 'I haven't seen it on the menu before. Very rich. Lovely flavours. What exactly was the paste over the top made of?'

'I believe it's bacon, cloves, shallots and parsley, sir.'

'It's the best dish I've had here so far. Veal is quite hard to get hold of at the moment.' He smiled, hoping that his expression didn't reveal any hint of suspicion.

'But not impossible,' she replied, smiling in return.

'I suppose, with there being a couple of farms and a dairy nearby, it makes it easier to obtain some of the meat and dairy products.'

248

'Probably easier than for a restaurant in a city.'

He nodded. 'Is, um, everything going all right?' he said in a quieter voice. This enquiry would at least be valid.

'In what way, Inspector?'

'You know, with Mrs Bygrove. Is she coping well with her husband's return?'

'She's coping admirably. Things seem a lot better now than they did before.'

He was surprised at this, and not totally reassured. 'I'm glad to hear it. I'll forego dessert and just have coffee, thank you.'

'Very well, Inspector.'

She walked away and he was relieved that the rather stiff exchange was over. Either there was nothing to worry about – on the food and Bygrove front – or Miss Moreland was keeping things close to her chest. Maybe the two things were linked? He wasn't sure where that thought had come from. Since he had no proof of anything, he'd endeavour simply to enjoy the rest of his time at the hotel.

–

Helen was walking down the staff corridor after the lunch period, when she met Edie coming out of the stillroom.

'Helen, could I have a word in private?'

'Of course. I believe the dining room is empty.'

What was this going to be about? Was Edie going to announce her departure too? She wouldn't blame her if she did leave. She'd been waiting all week for people to resign after what happened to Phoebe and was surprised that nobody had so far.

In the dining room, they stood by the fireplace, as far from the door as they could.

'This seems very cloak and dagger,' said Helen, now doubting it had anything to do with Edie leaving, but dreading what it might be.

Edie looked towards the door before saying quietly, 'We had DI Toshack in for lunch, and he was asking questions.'

'What sort of questions?'

'They weren't suspicious questions, exactly. He enjoyed his meal and mentioned that veal was hard to come by now. I said, but not impossible. And Lady Blackmore made some comment about there being more choice too, in his hearing. Anyway, the inspector said having farms and a dairy nearby must make it easier for us, and I left it at that.'

'Was he digging for information?'

'I don't know. It might have been a perfectly innocent conversation. I think, had it been with anyone else, I would not have been that worried, but, with a policeman...'

'And how long before he does suspect something? Oh dear. I was pleased when he started coming in regularly, as I felt he could keep an eye on things, what with Douglas having such a temper.'

'He's not hitting you, is he?'

'No, no.' Helen didn't want to admit to the punch he'd given her shoulder, which had resulted in a nasty bruise, the night of Penelope Raynolt's party. She had doubts now about carrying on, but she needed to tell someone at least some of it. 'But, he has threatened to divorce me and take the children and hotel away if I don't do as he says.'

'Oh Helen! When did he say this?'

'A couple of weeks back.'

Edie placed her hand on Helen's shoulder. 'Why didn't you say anything?'

'I didn't want to get anyone else involved. And with him going on about getting supplies through his contacts, and these secret meetings, or whatever they are, with his so-called golf chums.'

'Do you think the councillors have something to do with it?'

Helen shrugged her shoulders. 'I don't know. But if there is something going on, how long before Inspector Toshack suspects something?'

Sam. She'd tried to stop herself thinking of him by that name. It was best forgotten.

'My thoughts exactly. And if your husband is involved in something illicit, we might all get into trouble, and the hotel might be shut down.'

The door was kicked open, making both Helen and Edie start.

'There you are, Helen,' said Douglas, wheeling himself in. 'What's all this skulking in corners.'

'Edie was telling me about her latest letter from Charlie.' That had been three days ago, but it would serve as an excuse.

'Charlie who?'

'Cobbett, Douglas. Charlie Cobbett. Who was head porter here.'

'Oh, him. He was only head porter because Alan Drew enlisted before him. Hope he doesn't think he's coming back to that position. Anyway, I'll have another head porter installed before any of them get back from the war, and certainly none of your head *portress* nonsense. That'll teach him and all the other men who enlisted when they didn't have to.'

'Was there something in particular you wanted to talk to me about, Douglas?'

'No. Just wanted to say I'm going out now.'

'Out? Where? How?' He had not tried to leave the hotel until now.

'To the golf club, to see the rest of my old chums. Councillor Bloomfield has been kind enough to offer to take me in his motorcar and help me in and out.'

'But you struggle with getting in and out of the wheelchair as it is, just to go to bed.' She couldn't afford to reveal his deceit to Edie, in case he found out and made things even harder.

'I'll manage. But thank you for your concern,' said Douglas, in a sarcastic tone.

When he left the room, Helen went to the door to watch as he wheeled himself to the foyer door and out of it. With him gone, she returned to Edie.

'Listen. Douglas has taken the safe keys away from me, which means I have no access to the money.'

'That's terrible.'

'He gives me the odd allowance to buy things I need, and that's all. But I really need to find out what he's up to. With him gone for the afternoon, I'm going to have a look for the keys.'

'What if he's taken them with him?' said Edie.

'He probably has done, but there is a spare set. If I can open the safe, I might find something that gives me a clue to what's going on.'

'Good idea. I'm on the desk for a couple of hours this afternoon. I'll keep a look out for him returning early.'

'Thank you, though, if the past has taught me anything, it's that he's more likely to be back late,' said Helen.

--

In their bedroom, Helen searched Douglas's wardrobe first. She doubted he'd be daft enough to keep the keys somewhere so obvious, but it was a start.

It wasn't long before she felt something cold and metallic in one of his suit pockets.

Eureka!

He really wasn't as bright as he believed himself to be. Or, he underestimated her intelligence. Both may well be true.

She was tempted to rush to the office, but it might look odd if she came across any staff members. And she didn't want even a hint of what she was up to having any chance of getting back to Douglas. Instead, she walked sedately down the stairs and through the staff area.

In the office she shut the door and locked it. It's what Douglas had done on several occasions recently, when she'd needed to get in. He'd called out each time she'd knocked that he had important telephone calls to make and didn't want any distractions.

The first thing she did after she'd got into the safe was take the cash box out and open it with another key on the fob. She was alarmed to see that there wasn't much there. They must have made a good deal of money at the weekend, and it wasn't as if Douglas could have taken it to the bank. Maybe he'd got a member of staff to do so? It seemed unlikely. One of his friends then?

Next, she pulled the accounts book out of the safe. He'd insisted on dealing with them in the last four weeks, when she had dealt with them herself recently. There seemed to be an awful lot more spent on food than there should have been. They would be bankrupt if they kept this up. And how would staff be paid?

Was it possible he'd hidden money elsewhere, in case she'd got hold of the keys? Who knew how his mind worked these days? Or how it had ever worked?

She wasn't sure now whether she should let Edie in on this. If there was anything to be let in on. Maybe it wasn't what it seemed.

But if it was, the stupid fool was going to ruin them all!

Chapter Twenty

Helen didn't get to visit Phoebe until the following Monday, but the trip had been fruitless. It was mid-afternoon and she was now entering the office, to tell Douglas this.

'Don't bother sitting down,' he said. 'You're not stopping, as I need to get on. Just say what you came to and go.'

'Phoebe isn't coming back. She's joining the Women's Land Army and will be working on one of the local farms.'

'What a waste of your time and my petrol. I *told* you I didn't want her back.'

'I went by train, Douglas.'

'It was a waste of my money then.'

'The point is, Douglas, that we will need to keep Lili in the dining room, as she has the experience, and, with the season getting busier, we'll have to employ another waitress and at least two more chambermaids.'

'Are you trying to tell me how to run *my* business again, Helen? Considering what a mess you made of it while I was away. And after I've told you to keep *out* of it.'

Helen felt her anger rising. She wasn't sure how long she could put up with this browbeating from him. If it came to it, would he be seen as a fit father to look after the children? Wouldn't the staff back her up on this? But he might still get the hotel, meaning she'd end up with no means of supporting herself and the children. Would it be a good idea to ask her solicitor, Mr Burtenshaw's advice? So many questions. How she wished she'd insisted on joint ownership of the hotel.

'No, Douglas, I did not make a mess of the business. In fact, I had several compliments about how well I was running it while you away. Any mess was caused by *Ethel* Harvey, trying to implicate me in the writing of those libellous letters. She set out purposefully to ruin me. I wondered at the time why she would risk ruining your business in the process, as she is clearly besotted with you, but then that made me wonder, whether she hoped to be put in my place by you. And then that made me wonder, in turn, whether there was even more to it.'

Douglas stood slowly, piercing her with a glare. '*What* are you trying to say?'

'I wondered whether you'd planned it yourself.'

He took a step back, his mouth and eyes widening. For the first time, he didn't look so sure of himself. 'And how could I have planned it? I was in Shoreham, training.'

'By letter, Douglas, giving her instructions, the same way you were giving me directives on running the hotel.'

'It's true she wrote to me, but I only wrote to her once. I hope you didn't say any of this to the police because it isn't true. I don't want them hauling me off.'

'You once told me you'd rather be arrested than go to war. But no, I didn't say that, not to the police anyway.' She was doubting, by his reaction, that he had been involved with it, but she wanted him to believe that she'd spoken to someone else, just in case. In case of what, she wasn't sure.

He thumped heavily back into the wheelchair. 'Then make sure you don't. Miss Harvey is a silly woman; I don't know what she was playing at. She didn't imply I was involved at the hearing, did she?'

'Not that I am aware. And I'm sure the police would have paid you a visit if she had. So you do believe it was her who wrote the letters now, do you?'

'I've no idea.' He stared ahead a few seconds during which his usual, sneering expression returned. 'That's enough of that. It's in the past and we don't need to dwell on it.'

'Shall I go to the newspaper offices and get the hotel positions advertised?'

'No. I will deal with the staff shortages. Dismissed.'

'I'm not a school pupil, Douglas.'

He stood once more, coming around the desk to stand close to her, looking down at her with a sneer.

'Now you listen to me, and you listen well.'

–

'That was a busy afternoon tea, despite the wind,' Edie said to Lili as they undid their aprons, walking along the staff corridor.

'I couldn't believe that Lady Blackmore was in yet again. Been in far more since she started coming back than she did before, she has.'

'She probably feels guilty for accusing Helen of writing the letters and is trying to make up for it.'

Mrs Leggett and Mrs Turnbull came rushing out of the still-room and almost bumped into Edie and Lili.

'Have you seen Mrs Bygrove?' said the housekeeper. 'Alice says she returned some twenty minutes ago.'

'We've only just finished serving in the conservatory. Did Alice say whether Phoebe's coming back?'

'No, that's what we're trying to find out. Alice reckons Mrs Bygrove went to the office.'

Mrs Leggett led the way down the passageway. As they neared the door, they could hear Bygrove's voice shouting. The house-keeper put her finger to her lips and they all crept towards the door to listen.

'I make the decisions around here. Your time as *manageress* is finished. In fact, I'm considering dismissing Vera so that you can spend all your time looking after the children.'

Edie and the others looked around at each other, with various expressions of dismay.

'But Douglas, I—'

'And as I said, *I* will deal with staff employment, as your decisions have been faulty. Eventually I hope to replace most of the staff here who don't have enough respect for me, and that seems to be most of them.'

Something needed to be done about that man, thought Edie. But what?

'Douglas, I don't—'

'And if you argue, you'll be sorry, oh yes you will.'

The women looked at each other again, alarmed by the threats they had heard.

—

Helen had heard enough. She wasn't staying here to be threatened by the man who had sworn to love and cherish her, till death parted them. A terrible thought passed through her mind, that she wished he had died on the battlefield, not simply suffered an injury. God help her.

She started to turn to leave, but before she had a chance, he'd grabbed the collar of her blouse. He was holding it so tightly that it was squeezing her neck.

'D – Douglas, please,' she gasped, afraid she was going to choke.

'I told you, I have powerful friends, you stupid woman, and if you're not careful, they'll make you disappear.'

The door flung open and Helen was confused, until she saw Mrs Leggett, Edie, Mrs Turnbull and Lili storm in.

Douglas let go of her, tumbling backwards with a cry of anguish. 'You see, I can't walk, I said I couldn't, and you can't keep threatening to throw me out just because I'm not the man I used to be.'

'What on earth is going on?' said the housekeeper.

Helen did up a button on her blouse that had come undone. She was having trouble getting her breath back. She tried several times before she could say anything, and then her words were shaky. 'I m-most certainly did *not* s-say that.'

'We heard you, Mr Bygrove,' said Mrs Turnbull. 'You were threatenin' Mrs Bygrove with your powerful friends.'

'Yes, we all heard you we did,' Lili added.

Bygrove grabbed hold of the desk and pulled himself around it on his knees. Helen noted that none of the women tried to help him. Reaching the wheelchair, he pulled himself into it, groaning.

'No, no, you misheard,' he said, once he was seated. 'I was telling my wife what happened to me in the army. That's why not being able to walk is a blessing in disguise, as I won't have to tolerate the bullying.' His posture drooped and he covered his face with his hands, shaking his head.

Helen looked at the other women, who didn't seem impressed, or persuaded, by his performance.

'I've got w–work to do,' said Helen, making her way through the women there, still trying to take a full breath. She hid her shaking hands behind her back.

As she left the passageway, she decided to telephone Dr Ferngrove. She would tell him that Douglas could walk but was refusing to. Where that would lead, she didn't know, but exposing his deception had to be better for her than these constant threats. She might even mention that his behaviour was giving her cause for concern. Not able to use the telephone in the office, she carried on to reception. She'd got her breath back by the time she reached it.

'Excuse me, Mr Watkins,' she said, on reaching the desk in the foyer, 'but I'm just going to use the telephone.'

'Of course, Mrs Bygrove.' He moved to the opposite side.

Having been put through to the doctor's surgery, she asked the receptionist there for a home visit.

'I'm afraid Dr Ferngrove is fully booked until tomorrow after-noon,' she said.

She'd rather not have waited that long but said, 'That's fine,' and agreed a time.

Four o'clock, she thought, as she put the telephone receiver down. Almost a whole day of having to put up with Douglas. With any luck, the fact that Mrs Leggett and the others overheard him, would make him refrain from further threats.

'Is everything all right, madam?' said Mr Watkins. 'I couldn't help but overhear you calling the doctor.'

'I'd just like to do a routine check of my husband's condition, that's all.' She tried to smile. 'But he doesn't like the fuss, so keep it to yourself, please.'

'Of course, madam.'

She didn't want Douglas getting wind of the visit and cancelling it. From now on, she was going to make more effort to get some control of the situation.

–

Edie, Lili and Mrs Turnbull went to the staff dining room for the late afternoon break, all in a sombre mood. Mrs Leggett joined them after a few minutes with a pot of tea.

'I didn't believe Bygrove for a moment,' said Edie. 'He was clearly threatening Helen, not relating a story. And I don't believe it's the first time. He's already taken the safe keys away from her, and she's been worried about where all this extra food we're getting is coming from.'

The housekeeper poured them each a cup of tea. 'I've been wondering that myself.'

'And he clearly said he was going to replace us all,' said Lili.

'Aye, and there was that bit about her being finished as manageress,' said Mrs Turnbull. 'That couldn't have had anything to do with his time in the army either.'

There was something else bothering Edie, but she couldn't quite put her finger on it.

'Are you all right, lass?'

'Yes, yes, Mrs Turnbull. Just thinking.'

'Hello,' called Hetty, entering the room, stroking back her hair, which was in a bun. 'I am ready for a cup of tea after almost being blown off my feet.'

'It's still windy then?' said Edie.

'It's even worse than it was earlier. I popped over to Norfolk Road to see if there were any sweets available at the confectioners.

I managed to pick up a few mint humbugs at least, for my troubles. It was hard walking against the wind.'

Mrs Leggett frowned. 'I hope there's no structural damage to the hotel as a result.'

'That's all we need,' said Hetty. 'I bet the waves'll be quite dramatic though. I'd have gone and had a look if I hadn't been afraid of being blown over.'

'One of the guest rooms on the second floor facing that way is free,' said Mrs Leggett. 'You'll get a good view from there. Go and have a look after tea.'

Edie still couldn't believe how much more relaxed Mrs Leggett had become since she'd first met her. She could still be very strict and authoritative but had let her softer side show through more recently.

'Great!' said Hetty, leaning over to help herself to a bourbon.

–

'My, I've never seen the sea so choppy,' said Edie, as she, Lili and Hetty stared out of the guest room window.

'It's quite mesmerising, watching the waves crash onto the sand,' said Hetty. 'When I was a child, I used to love jumping up and down over large ones as they came in.'

'A bit big for that these would be,' said Lili. 'You'd have to be careful not to be swept away. There were a woman what drowned here a few years back, just after I arrived. No one knew whether it were an accident or not. It were windy that night too. And look at that sky! The clouds are almost black over the sea.'

'Looks like they're coming this way, and quickly,' said Hetty.

'It's fascinating to watch the whole spectacle from here,' said Edie, 'but I wouldn't fancy a walk on the beach right now. No wonder it's empty. Look, even the sand is being whipped up. There already seems to be quite a lot on the promenade.'

Hetty pulled up the window a little. It rattled as they all listened. 'Hark at that roar. The sea sounds jolly angry.'

Edie shivered. 'Brrr, better close it quickly, otherwise the bedroom will get cold. It's a shame we don't have shutters that we can put up. We had them on my parents' house.'

'Mr Hargreaves has removed anything loose in the garden,' said Lili. 'And the guests have all been advised to stay in.'

Hetty tugged the window back down. 'Hopefully it'll have died down by tomorrow.'

'We won't get many customers from outside if it doesn't. Let's hope nobody gets hurt going out in it.'

Lili and Hetty nodded, and they all left the room.

Chapter Twenty-One

Helen had found it hard to get to sleep that night, with the wind buffeting against the windows. At times it became extra fierce, whistling and howling in the air. She was surprised the children hadn't been up, crying that it had woken them.

The fact that Douglas hadn't come to bed didn't help. He always made a noise coming in the room and whilst undressing, often lighting the lamp, and the expectation of this disturbance happening any minute was not relaxing. At least he hadn't expected any intimate attention from her since he'd returned, that was a relief.

What was he doing till this time, for it must be nearly one o'clock now?

Despite the noise and the worry, she eventually fell into a fitful sleep.

When she awoke once more, it was still dark. She put her hand out tentatively to see if there was anyone next to her. No, it was empty still.

What time must it be now? She got out of bed and felt for the matches on the bedside table, before lighting the oil lamp. The clock said a quarter past two. She looked towards Douglas's side of the bed: he definitely wasn't there.

Could he have become too tired to wheel his chair to the lift and fallen asleep at the desk? There was only one way to find out. She put on her dressing gown and made her way downstairs with the lamp.

In the office, the gas light was still on. The wheelchair was behind the desk, but turned on its side. The papers on the desk were strewn everywhere, and there were some on the floor. Could he have knocked the wheelchair over in a fit of pique, and the papers too? It wouldn't surprise her if he'd gone to the bar to drown his sorrows. It's not like he would have gone out anywhere in this storm.

She didn't want to keep walking around the hotel in her nightclothes. She might as well get back to bed. No doubt she'd see him in the morning. She pulled the chain on the lamp and left.

—

Helen awoke at a quarter to six, to silence. The wind could no longer be heard, and for that she was grateful. Douglas was still not beside her. She could only assume that he'd got to bed late and got up early. His side didn't look slept in at all though. Maybe he'd fallen asleep in the bar. Considering his wheelchair was in the office, he'd give himself away to staff. That would be an excellent outcome, and at least he wouldn't be able to accuse *her* of giving his secret away.

She got out of bed and opened the curtains. All looked peaceful outside, though there was a lot of debris on the common, blown from who knew where. She washed and dressed, then went to look for Douglas.

In the office, the wheelchair was still on the floor. She went to the bar next, but he wasn't there. Bert, who was on early porter duty, hadn't seen him. She did a tour of the downstairs, but he was nowhere to be found.

By this time, the live-in staff were down for breakfast. Helen went to their dining room and wished them good morning but said nothing of the situation.

'Edie, would you come and see me in the office when you've finished breakfast?'

'Of course, Mrs Bygrove.'

Helen waited in the office, sitting on a chair by the desk, but not behind it, where the wheelchair was still on the floor.

Something told her she shouldn't move it, or tidy the papers. She stared at the wall, unable to conjure up the energy to do any work. And what was there to do? Most jobs had been taken from her.

Eventually there was a knock at the door, and she called, 'Come in.'

'Helen, why are you sitting there?'

'Edie, something strange has happened.' She stood up and went around the desk, pointing at the papers and then down at the wheelchair.

Edie followed her around. 'Why is it on its side?'

'I don't know. Douglas didn't come to bed last night. I awoke at a quarter past two and came down to look for him, but all I found was this mess.'

'It looks like he got angry. Or...'

'Or what?'

'Or there was a struggle,' said Edie. 'We should call the police. He can't walk, so how on earth would he get out of the office by himself, let alone the hotel?'

Helen was on the brink of telling Edie he could walk, but, not sure it was the right thing to do, stalled. 'Yes, we should call the police.'

–

Detective Inspector Toshack turned up just after eight o'clock with Sergeant Gardner and WPC Lovelock. Helen greeted them at the back door in the scullery, having been told by Bert that he'd seen the police motorcar arrive.

'I didn't expect this to be the province of the DI,' she said, showing them in.

'If Mr Bygrove couldn't get out of the hotel by himself, then it sounds serious that he's missing. And with that storm overnight, it makes it even more worrying.' In the corridor he turned to his colleagues. 'You two talk to employees in the staff areas about when they last saw the manager and whether he said anything to indicate what he was doing. Don't go into the public areas yet.'

'Very well, sir,' said Gardner.

The staff were going to find out he was missing without her having to tell them. She was relieved about that, not knowing how many times she'd be able to tell people before she sounded like she didn't care.

'If you'd like to show me where the disturbance is?' he said to Helen.

She showed him down the passageway to the office door and indicated he should go through. 'This is how I found it.'

The inspector hunkered down awkwardly, his left leg unbent, and examined the wheelchair. When he stood, he said, 'Shouldn't his legs have healed enough by now for him to be able to walk at least a little?'

How to reply to this? 'How long did it take you to be able to walk?'

He looked down at his limb self-consciously. 'It's hardly the same as I didn't have a leg from the knee down and had to learn to walk with a false one.'

'You do it very proficiently.'

'That's as maybe, but that doesn't answer the question as to how your husband got out of the hotel without a wheelchair.'

She knew she'd been stalling again, not wanting to admit he could walk, but not wanting to lie. How would it look though, if she admitted she knew and hadn't said anything?

'No, you're right, it doesn't. Sorry.'

–

There was something wrong here, thought Toshack. It wasn't just that the wheelchair was tipped up, the papers strewn and Bygrove nowhere in sight, it was something to do with Helen herself. She didn't seem upset as much as... uncomfortable. It was as if she were holding something back. He'd seen it enough times to know the signs.

But he couldn't keep thinking of her as 'Helen'. This was official business.

'We'll need to have a word with *all* the staff eventually,' he said.

'Quite a few are on duty now. I'd rather not alert the guests to anything being wrong yet.'

'I'd have thought you'd have been more concerned about locating your injured husband,' he said, frowning.

'I am, but, well… Douglas had quite a temper on him. He'd also started disappearing off with friends once more, as he did before he went to war. I can't help feeling this might just be him getting into a rage for some reason and going off somewhere with his chums from the golf club.'

'In the middle of the night, without his wheelchair?'

She shrugged, her expression becoming worried. That was more what he expected from a missing man's wife. Maybe she'd been brought up to be stoic in such situations.

'I want this room locked and left undisturbed by anyone, until we can examine it properly. Now, let's see how the sergeant and WPC are getting on.'

Mrs Bygrove nodded, leading him back to the corridor.

He met Sergeant Gardner, coming out of the kitchen. 'There you are, Inspector. Nobody here has seen Mr Bygrove since yesterday evening or had any indication that he was going anywhere or being taken anywhere by anyone. I wondered if it would be worth WPC Lovelock and I having a walk around the area, in case he went out and got knocked over by the wind and hurt himself.'

'Gardner, the man couldn't walk.'

'With all due respect, sir, he must have got out somehow, if he's not here.'

'You're right. Of course you are. Yes, you and Lovelock go and do that.'

The telephone could be heard ringing in the office.

'I'd better answer that,' said Mrs Bygrove. 'It might be him.'

As she rushed away, a middle-aged woman came out into the corridor. 'I hear Mr Bygrove's gone missin' from the hotel.'

'That's right,' Toshack told the woman. 'Is that a Tyneside accent I'm hearing?'

'That's right. I'm Mrs Turnbull, the storekeeper. I'm sorry if this sounds like talkin' out of turn, but with any luck, Mr Bygrove is lost for good, treatin' us all like dirt, especially Mrs Bygrove, poor lass.'

He didn't approve of the sentiment, but it might be interesting to dig a little deeper, after what Miss Moreland had told him previously. She hadn't come up with any other information, so he'd assumed things had got better in the last couple of months.

'He wasn't a good employer then?'

'Why don't you come and have a sit in the dinin' room, Inspector, and I'll pour you a cup of tea.'

He didn't really have time for tea, but it might be worth it for some extra information that maybe Mrs Bygrove was reluctant to tell him.

Inside the room, he headed for the chair at the end of the table. He didn't fancy having to lift his leg over the bench seat.

'Milk and sugar, Inspector?'

'Yes please.'

'We heard him threatenin' Mrs Bygrove yesterday,' she said as she poured.

'Mr Bygrove did?'

'That's right. Mrs Leggett the housekeeper, Edie, Lili and myself. We'd heard she'd got back from tryin' to persuade Phoebe to come back, after Mr Bygrove was rude to her and dismissed her. He was more than rude, I'd say. Tried to kick the girl as she was leavin' with her things. I mean literally kick her.'

'Was he standing up?'

'No, course not. He was goin' along in his wheelchair, kickin' his leg out.'

'I see.' Toshack took a sip of his tea.

'Mrs Bygrove came back yesterday, after visitin' Phoebe to ask her to return, and we'd heard she'd gone to the office, so the four of us went to find out what Phoebe had said. But before we got there, we heard him, Bygrove, threatenin' the poor lass. When we got to the door he was sayin' somethin' about not having her as manageress any more, and that he'd replace most of us, 'cos we didn't have enough respect for him. Then he told her she'd be sorry if she argued and he had *powerful friends* that could make her disappear. It was then that Mrs Leggett opened the door and we all went in.'

Now this was getting interesting. 'Did you confront him with what you'd heard.'

'Oh yes. When we entered, he was fallin' backwards and complainin'. He tried to say that Mrs Bygrove had tried to get him to walk, and he told her he couldn't, and that she couldn't throw him out just because he wasn't the man he used to be.'

'Go on.'

'Mrs Bygrove denied she'd said that. When I said we'd heard him threatenin' her, he tried to make out he'd been relatin' a story about being bullied in the army.'

'But you didn't believe him?'

'Not for a second. No.'

'And what happened about—' Before he could carry on, Mrs Bygrove entered the room.

'There you are, Inspector. I'm sorry, that was one of my husband's friends and he took a lot of persuading that Douglas wasn't available to speak. I didn't want to tell anyone outside the hotel anything yet.'

'That's wise,' said Toshack.

There was a clatter of distant doors, and loud voices in the corridor. Toshack was about to go and investigate when WPC Lovelock charged into the room.

'Inspector!' She looked around, spotting the two women. 'Could… could you come outside. I'd like a word.'

'What's happened?' said Mrs Bygrove. 'Have you found him?'

'I just need to speak to the inspector in private.' Lovelock widened her eyes as if to convey the urgency of the situation to him.

'Very well, I'll speak to you outside. I shall be back presently,' he told Mrs Bygrove.

He and Lovelock were outside the side gate before she stopped and turned towards him. 'Sir, we've found him, lying on the beach, and it doesn't look good.'

'Mr Bygrove? Are you sure?'

'Oh, I'm sure. Remember, I worked for the old so and so – so I know it's him. And the sergeant agrees.'

He took off his fedora and ran his fingers through his hair, heaving out a sigh. Replacing the hat he said, 'You'd better show me then.'

They walked in silence, straight across the common to the promenade. There was rubbish strewn far and wide, pieces of cardboard, bits of wood and cloth, all bearing witness to the terrific winds overnight. Several people were already out, clearing up the debris. It was chilly, and the sky overhead was still gloomy; he hoped that it didn't rain before they'd got any evidence they needed from the body and surroundings.

On the prom, Toshack could already see the debris on the beach, including deckchairs and tarpaulins. The beach tents had fared badly. In the distance, closer to the pier and lighthouse, he could see men on the beach clearing up the odds and ends that had been blown there, making their way slowly towards them.

WPC Lovelock ignored the steps and jumped onto the beach, close to where Sergeant Gardner was keeping guard. Toshack took the steps down.

On the beach, right near the promenade wall, was a large, tangled tarpaulin on the ground. To the right of it was a body. Even though he'd only seen him a couple of times and he was partly covered with sand, he could tell it was Douglas Bygrove.

'I'm surprised someone hadn't already found him and reported it,' he said.

'Not exactly the weather for a morning stroll, sir,' said Gardner. 'And them men clearing up haven't reached here yet. He wouldn't be easy to spot with all this stuff around.'

'I don't suppose the sand will have helped with any of the evidence we might gather. How on earth did he get here though, given that his wheelchair is in the office?'

'Beats me, sir.'

'Could he have drowned and been washed back up onto shore?'

'Could be, sir, he is quite wet.'

Toshack leant over to take a closer look at the body. There were some blue and yellow fabric strands caught under Bygrove's fingernails.

'We need to gather any forensic evidence we can. WPC Lovelock, you stay and guard the body and don't let anyone near it. Gardner, get back to the station and ring Dr Ferngrove and then the coroner. Then come back and bring PC Flower with you. Contact the photographer to come and take photos. Tell him it's urgent. Have a look around for any important clues and bag any evidence you find.'

'Yes sir,' they each replied, half a second apart.

'I'll have to go and break the news to Mrs Bygrove.'

He wasn't looking forward to that.

–

Mrs Bygrove was kissing her children goodbye when he reached the side door into the staff area. He guessed they were on their way to school. He felt a sadness for them, poor little mites, losing their father at such a young age.

Toshack waited until their nursemaid had taken them through the gate, before speaking.

'Could we go somewhere private?' he said.

'Since we can't go to the office, you'd better come to our quarters.'

He was led through the staff area and up the stairs. She didn't seem aware that he might be about to impart bad news. His stomach clenched; this was the part of his job he hated the most. To make it worse, it always reminded him of when the detective chief inspector in Hartlepool had broken the news of Olive's death to him. Even though the Bygroves may not have been a match made in heaven, this wouldn't be pleasant.

They ended up in what looked like a sitting and dining room combined. Mrs Bygrove invited him to sit down. He declined.

'You may want to sit down though,' he said.

'Why?' She did now look concerned, but remained standing, nevertheless.

He took a deep breath. 'I'm so sorry, but a body has been found on the beach, identified as Mr Bygrove by WPC Lovelock and Sergeant Gardner.'

Her face crumpled and she bent over, holding her arms around her waist. He didn't know what to do, until she wobbled and looked in danger of falling over, when he stepped forward and caught hold of her. He held her as she continued to grip onto herself. It wasn't long before he saw the tears start to fall down her cheeks.

He had the most unsettling feeling, holding her in this way, something he couldn't quite describe. It was probably because he hadn't held a woman like this since Olive had passed away.

'Come on now, let's get you sitting down.'

He led her to the settee, where she put her head into her hands and then onto her lap.

'D – did he drown?'

'We don't know, at present, until he's examined.' He avoided saying, *until his body's examined*, knowing, from experience, how cold and uncaring it would sound.

She started sobbing.

'I'm going to have to leave now, so I'll fetch someone to sit with you.'

'E – Edie Moore if p – possible.'

'Very well. You will have to officially identify him soon, but we can leave that until later, when – that is, I'll contact you.'

He rose and left, feeling downhearted. It was almost as if he'd lost someone too. But he had no feelings whatever about Bygrove's death. It was his wife's grief that was distressing him.

He wasn't sure what he'd expected. Maybe she cared for the man more than he'd thought. Or more than she'd thought.

In the corridor, he came across Edie Moore, or Moreland. He was confused now as to what to call her. With her was the storekeeper.

'What's goin' on, Inspector?' said Mrs Turnbull.

'Mrs Bygrove needs somebody with her. We've found a body on the beach we believe to be her husband's.'

Both women drew in a sharp breath.

'I know I said he'd be better off lost for good, but I didn't mean dead.'

'Of course you didn't.' Miss Moore rubbed the older woman's shoulder.

'She needs someone with her, and has asked for you, Miss Moore – or Moreland?'

'Moore will be fine, thank you.'

'I'd rather this news didn't get out at the moment. Tell as few of the staff as you can, and only those who can keep it to themselves.'

'Of course, Inspector,' said Mrs Turnbull. 'I will need to tell Mrs Leggett and Mrs Norris. Edie, you go and see to the poor lass. I'll ask Mrs Leggett to be in charge down here. And we'll find someone else to fill in for mornin' coffee.'

'I'll be back later,' said Toshack, leaving them to their arrangements.

As he walked out of the side gate and back over the common, he wondered how a woman could feel so sad for a man who appeared to have been abusing her. Maybe it was to do with looking back to better times together, if they'd ever had any. It wouldn't be the first time he'd seen this though, and no doubt it wouldn't be the last.

–

Back on the beach, Toshack saw that Dr Ferngrove had arrived and was kneeling by the body. WPC Lovelock was standing on the promenade in front, keeping guard with PC Flower, another constable who'd come out of retirement. Several people passing by were peering over to see what was happening.

Sergeant Gardner was standing next to the doctor. 'The photographer's been and gone,' he told Toshack as he came down the steps.

Toshack nodded. 'Good… What's your verdict, Doctor?'

'He might have drowned, Inspector, but I doubt it. There are also these marks on his neck, indicating some kind of injury, particularly these two oblong marks.' He moved the head slightly to show them. 'And there's a scratch at the front of his neck. They may have happened post-mortem, from the wind or the waves, but equally they might not.'

'What do you make of those blue and yellow threads caught in his fingernails?'

The doctor took a look. 'They're not really part of my expertise, though I'd say he'd been clawing at something. The coroner should be able to tell you more.'

'At the hotel, they claim he couldn't walk, and his wheelchair was found tipped up in the office.'

'So Sergeant Gardner informed me. I'm not even sure why he couldn't walk at least a few steps by now, if not a lot more. I was sent copies of the records from Netley Hospital. Bygrove sustained only minor fractures and the X-rays they took indicated that the bones had been welding back together nicely before he even left the place. It's been well over three months since it happened, and well over two since he came home. I really don't understand it. Unless it was psychosomatic. That's when an illness is aggravated by anxiety and—'

'I know what it means, Doctor.'

'Right, of course. I think it's best to see what the coroner says after the post-mortem… I guess I won't be having to make the home visit this afternoon. At least, not for Mr Bygrove. How was his wife when you left her?'

'Distraught.'

'She might be glad of a sedative then.'

'Why were you making a visit today, Doctor?'

'Mrs Bygrove rang yesterday and asked for me to come. I didn't speak to her, but my receptionist had the impression that she was concerned about his lack of progress.'

A motor ambulance drew up slowly on the promenade, causing even more interest from those passing by.

'Good, we'll be able to move the body now,' said Ferngrove.

–

'I'm sorry, I – I must be k – keeping you from your work,' said Helen, as Edie held her hand, sitting on the settee next to her.

'I wasn't supposed to be on duty until morning coffee, and Mrs Turnbull's going to organise a replacement, so don't you worry about that.'

'I'm a terrible, *terrible* fraud you know, and a terrible person.'

'Of course you're not.' Edie rubbed her back. 'Why would you say that?'

'Because these tears, oh, they're no indication of how I feel, personally, about Douglas's demise. In fact, I feel – numb. Nothing. I can't raise a single emotion for him. And that worries me. For although my marriage to Douglas has not been perfect the last few years, I used to love him. No, my tears are for my children. And they are selfish tears too, for I am dreading telling them.' She took a strangled breath in and let out a sobbing whine. She tried to stop it, but she couldn't.

'There, there, of course you're upset for them.'

'How do I tell an eight- and seven-year-old that their father has died? And under such *awful* circumstances too.'

'You don't have to tell them how it happened. Just say it was an accident. Because it probably was. Somehow he got outside – who knows, maybe he could walk and didn't tell anyone – and he got caught by the weather.'

Helen felt her stomach roll and felt a little dizzy. She did know he could walk, though she had no idea he'd been able to walk that far. But the longer she didn't tell anyone, the harder it was becoming to come clean. What a fool she'd been. What if they discovered somehow that he could walk? Could she just say he'd kept it from her?

No, it would be deceitful. But how would it look if she confessed it?

'I'm sure, once the story gets around the town, that the children will hear from others at school how he was found. I will have to tell them a little more than it was just an accident.'

'We don't even know what happened yet, so it's probably best to tell them that for now.'

'Yes. Perhaps by the time they return from school, we will know more.' Helen took a handkerchief from her skirt pocket and blew her nose. 'We're going to have to close the hotel, to outside guests at least. We shouldn't even be doing breakfast or morning coffee.' She stood up and composed herself. 'I'm going to do that now. I'll get the porter on the door to explain to people that there's been a – a – death in the family. The staff will only have to deal with those staying.'

'Are you sure? You don't need to do anything. We'll run things while you're sorting yourself out.'

'No, it wouldn't be right, to remain open to all when Douglas has…' She rubbed her forehead roughly with the tips of her fingers and squeezed her eyes shut.

'How long for?'

Helen opened her eyes. 'Just for the day. It's not like we can survive as a business if we close any longer. Douglas would understand and do the same himself.'

She had no doubt that he'd have remained fully open if their positions had been reversed.

It would be too easy to sit here and do nothing, worrying about the children and about what people would say. The place had been plagued with misfortune recently. But she needed to get on with things, not wallow in self-pity.

'I'd better go down and sort things out.'

275

Chapter Twenty-Two

Helen stood in the staff corridor and pulled on a pair of gloves, dreading the next hour, when the children would have to be told the news about their father.

The hotel had been closed to all but those already staying, who had been informed only that there had been a death in the family. They had been assured of the same high quality of service by Edie, who had made a point of speaking to each group of guests herself. Helen had not been out of the staff area at all today but had gathered from Mrs Leggett that everything was running smoothly.

How many of the staff were aware of what had actually happened she didn't know, and at this moment, didn't care.

'Are you ready to leave, madam?' said Vera, a pained expression on her face.

'I am. It seems quite cold out there, considering we are in the midst of April.'

'It is, madam. And the skies look rather ominous.'

Cold and ominous. Rather like her life right now.

About to enter the stillroom, she heard her name being called by Edie.

'Helen, I'm sorry, but we've got a bit of a problem. Mr Bloomfield is in the foyer with Mr Rotherham, *insisting* on seeing your husband. They seem to think that I'm lying when I say that he isn't available.'

'Did they not see the sign?'

'Yes, but Bloomfield is claiming that Mr Bygrove rang him last night in distress, and that they've come to see how he is, having not heard from him again.'

'I wonder if he has some clue about what might have occurred then? Edie, tell them what has happened, but ask them to keep it to themselves for now. And suggest that they take any information they have to the police.'

'All right.'

Helen was about to carry on with Vera but came to a sudden decision. 'Edie, I think it might be better if we closed for the week to outside guests. I know it won't be good for trade, but hopefully people will understand, once they find out what has happened.'

'Very well.' Edie hurried back down the corridor.

'Come Vera, we have a grim task ahead of us.'

–

Edie was not convinced that it was a good idea to tell these men what had happened at this time. As councillors, they might be used to keeping some things confidential, but she didn't like their general attitude. And Mr Rotherham, who had done nothing short of proposition her before, had showed himself up as anything but honourable. Bloomfield did not seem much better.

In the foyer once again, she felt her skin crawl on spotting the two arrogant men. Rotherham was questioning Gertie, who was on porter duty, and she was replying and shaking her head. Edie only hoped he wasn't trying to proposition her too.

'Gentlemen,' she said as she approached them, thinking them anything but. 'I have been instructed to tell you the situation.'

'We asked to see Mr Bygrove, so where is he?' said Bloomfield, his jaw stiff. '*He* can tell us the *situation*.'

Edie glanced at Gertie, who took several steps backwards, maybe guessing what was coming.

'I'm afraid it is not possible to see Mr Bygrove, as he was found this morning, on the beach.'

'How did he get there?' said Rotherham. 'He couldn't walk. Is he all right? I would imagine he's a little battered after the wind last night.'

She had tried to put it delicately, but it didn't look like either of them had understood as they both looked cross as they waited for her reply.

'No, gentlemen, he is not all right. I'm afraid he is – dead.' She couldn't put it straighter than that.

Both men opened their mouths in shock and looked at each other. Bloomfield's hand flew to his chest and he stumbled back a little. Rotherham's hands shook as he put them to his mouth. Edie found it rather melodramatic, like something she might have seen in a music hall act. It almost seemed... rehearsed?

'B – but like I said, I spoke to him l – last night, on, on the telephone,' said Bloomfield. 'W – what happened? Did he... drown?' His eyes widened.

'Or was he knocked unconscious by the wind?' Rotherham added.

'Nobody knows at present, sir. The police are looking into it. In the meantime, the family are in mourning, and we will be closing the hotel to outside guests for the next week.'

'Of course, quite right, quite right,' said Bloomfield. 'Come, Rotherham, let us leave these people in peace.'

'Oh, one more thing, gentlemen,' said Edie. 'Mrs Bygrove has requested that you tell the police anything you know. So the contents of the telephone call might help in their enquiries.'

Bloomfield nodded, looking solemn, and then the two men walked out, standing tall as if they were immensely important. Rotherham, at the back, didn't bother shutting the door.

'Arrogant buffoon,' Edie mumbled as she went to close it. The cold air made her shiver. Or was it the sight of them marching away in that superior manner? She went over to Gertie, who was now standing by the desk.

'What was Mr Rotherham saying to you?' Edie asked.

'Just that it was unacceptable that they'd been blocked from seeing Bygrove, as he'd told Bloomfield on the telephone last night that he needed to speak to them urgently. As if *I* 'ad any say in the matter.'

'I wonder what that was all about?' Edie was still staring at the outer doors, even though the men were now out of sight.

'We'll never know now.'

'You're probably right.'

–

Detective Inspector Toshack had been worrying about Helen for the last three days. He'd returned to the hotel later on the same day Bygrove's body had been discovered, only to collect the evidence available from the office, but hadn't seen her at all. He'd seen Miss Moore though, who had revealed something interesting she'd remembered about Bygrove.

When Helen had gone to identify the body, she'd been accompanied by Dr Ferngrove, so he hadn't seen her then either.

He could do with asking her a few more questions, and now would be as good an opportunity as any. He wasn't sure why he felt apprehensive about seeing her again, but he knew deep down it was because he had a personal motive for wanting to see her, that was not at all professional – nor appropriate under the circumstances.

On this occasion he went through the foyer, which was empty. He'd heard that she'd closed the hotel to outside guests for a week, so he wasn't surprised. At the desk was the rather stern Mr Watkins, who had clearly taken a dislike to him.

'Good afternoon,' said Toshack. 'I would like to speak to Mrs Bygrove.'

'I doubt she's in any mood to talk to you, but I suppose you'll insist on it anyway.'

'I'm trying to solve this case,' he said, calmly, despite the man's attitude. 'And to do that, I need as much information as possible. I'm sure Mrs Bygrove would appreciate that.'

'Yes, well, she's in the office. You know where that is.'

A guest had come from the lift by this time, and Watkins was already turning to greet them.

At the office he knocked and called, 'It's Inspector Toshack.'

There was no reply for a while, but then the door was opened, and Helen stepped back to allow him in.

'Good afternoon, Inspector. Take a seat.'

She closed the door and went to the other side of the desk to sit down. It had been tidied since he last saw it, and on it was a large ledger and several pieces of paper that looked like bills or receipts.

'I'm trying to sort out the accounts that my husband had insisted on doing himself, and it seems he wasn't quite as good at it as he made out.'

'You could do without that. Isn't there anyone else who could do them?'

'I'd rather sort them out first, then I'll employ a new accounts person, since you now have the benefit of the one we had.'

'Ah, WPC Lovelock, of course.'

'Have you come to tell me the results of the post-mortem?'

'No, that isn't complete yet. These things take a few days. I've come, firstly, to see how you are.'

She leant on the desk and looked down. 'The hardest part was telling the children. They had the following day off but went back to school yesterday. It's better that they're occupied. I'm just worried what the other children will say to them when it becomes general knowledge.'

'But how are *you* coping?'

She looked him squarely in the eyes. 'As cold as it sounds, Inspector, I don't miss him. I realised, when you told me what had happened, that I hadn't loved him for a long time. No, that's not true. I'd known that for a while. But it became even more apparent when he was found dead. I apologise for breaking down in front of you the other day.'

'You don't need to apologise.'

'The only reason I did so was because of the children. Despite his careless way of treating them, they loved him. And no child should lose a parent so young. As for me, I didn't even miss him when he was conscripted. It was a relief that he was gone. He was so often out when he was supposed to be running the hotel, and I ended up running it. He never did anything with the children, nor anything with me. He spent all his spare time with his golfing, tennis and bowls chums. And...'

'And?'

'I suspect there might have been something going on with Miss Harvey too. Though, it may only have been in her mind. She was clearly fond of him. He claimed not to have felt the same way. I asked him, you know, whether he had put her up to writing the letters and implicating me. He seemed so genuinely taken aback, even scared that such an idea would be considered, that I do think he knew nothing about it.'

Interesting, thought Toshack, for he had wondered the same, and would have bet good money on Bygrove being involved. Still, they'd found only one letter from him in Miss Harvey's house when they'd searched it, and that was to ask her to keep an eye on the hotel as the woman had apparently reported to him that it was being badly managed. He wouldn't say this to Helen though. Not yet, at least.

'Does it make me a terrible wife, that I really have no feelings about his death? He'd become a stranger to me. I felt more sorrow on hearing of the death in battle of some of our staff.'

'It's understandable, after what he put you through,' he said. 'I, um, also understand that he attacked you, the day before he was found, then made out you'd been bullying him into walking.'

She looked surprised. 'How do you—?'

'Mrs Leggett and Mrs Turnbull mentioned it.'

'Ah, of course. Yes, he did.'

'And is it true that he threatened you with powerful friends?'

'He did. He also grabbed my neck, but they wouldn't have been aware of that, as he stumbled backwards as they entered.' She pulled down the high, lacy neck of her blouse to show him the red mark and scratches that were still visible.

'He must have got out of the wheelchair to do that. Miss Moore told me, when I came back to examine the office, that your husband had crawled around the desk afterwards, to get back to his wheelchair. She wondered how he got to you in the first place.'

Helen went quiet for a few seconds, fiddling with her fingers. 'To be honest, Inspector, and I realise I should have been in the first place, he could walk fairly well. He didn't want anyone to know, least of all the doctor, because he didn't want to go back to the war.'

Toshack put his head back and let out a huff of frustration. 'I wish you had told me this on the day we found him. It might have helped to explain how he got to the beach. It might also have implied that it was an accident, not an attack.'

'I'm sorry, Inspector. He'd told me not to tell anyone, otherwise he would divorce me and deprive me of the hotel and the children.'

'But he couldn't do that any more, once he was found dead.'

'No. I didn't know what it would look like, me being in on his lie. And the fact he'd threatened me, might have made it look like I'd killed him.'

'Please, tell me anything else you can think of that might be relevant, whether now, or if you think of it in the future.'

She nodded, looking so wretched that he had the overwhelming feeling of wanting to hold her. He took a deep breath, attempting to put that emotion to one side.

What's the matter with you, man? The woman's just become a widow.

He tried to imagine what he would have felt like, had a woman he barely knew tried to hug him when his wife had just died. But he'd loved his wife and had missed her terribly. That wasn't the case here.

Still, it was an unacceptable emotion on his part.

'There – there was the extra food Douglas managed to get hold of. I was worried that it wasn't all above board, you know, something underhand, like the hoarding or profiteering that's been mentioned in the newspapers – or worse. Perhaps those shop thefts that have been happening in the area.'

Now that was an interesting theory. He had wondered himself how the menu at the hotel had improved recently. Could this be connected to his so-called 'powerful friends'?

'That's all I can think of, for now,' she said.

'Thank you. I had better let you get on.'

–

Helen was able to hold in her emotions until the inspector left the office. Once he'd gone, she put her head on the desk and let the tears slowly build up. She was soon sobbing, not because of any sense of loss, but due to other, unacceptable feelings. What a terrible woman she truly was, for what she would have liked most at this moment, was for Inspector Toshack, *Sam*, to have held her, like he had in her sitting room, the day that Douglas was found.

After a few minutes she pulled herself up and wiped the tears from her eyes with a handkerchief. She wondered how he had felt when his wife had died, how he'd reacted. They'd both died under tragic circumstances, yet, even being unaware of the details of Douglas's death, she knew the two cases were so different, for a lot of reasons.

She pulled herself together and looked at the ledger, bills and receipts in front of her. It didn't add up, and the most startling aspect was what was missing, not just money, but the receipts for many of the goods that Douglas had acquired recently.

What a mess. And she'd have to be the one to sort it out. She had better contact her solicitor about how to get access to the bank account – and about the will, if there was one. She only hoped Douglas hadn't been malicious enough to make things difficult for her.

Chapter Twenty-Three

It wasn't until five days later that the post-mortem report was delivered to the police station. Inspector Toshack and Sergeant Gardner were now standing in his office, looking down at it.

'Strangulation,' said Toshack, experiencing a feeling of ominous inevitability. 'That would explain the marks on his neck. So we *are* looking at murder.'

'And it looks like he was put in the sea post-mortem.'

'Those marks either side of his throat suggest the perpetrator had a heavy ring on each finger. And the yellow and blue thread imply he clawed at some fabric that colour.'

'And look at the X-ray report, sir. It appears that his legs had healed so well that it's likely he could walk, if he tried. So, did he just not try, or did he, like the doctor said, have psychosomatic problems?'

How to put this so he didn't sound like Helen was implicated in anything. 'Mrs Bygrove told me that she suspected he might be able to walk, but he'd also said he was never going back to the war, so it sounds like he was hiding it.'

'Oh dear,' said Gardner, sounding weary. 'So, we're looking for a murderer now. Let's hope they don't strike again before we catch 'em.'

'Could it be someone who's struck before? What about those two murders and the attempted murder you had here in 1914 and 1915, involving Miss Moore?'

'They were committed by the same man, Gordon Hadley, and he's um, been hanged, sir.'

'Yes, I know. I read the case notes when I first arrived. I was thinking about the suspected accomplice though, a Jim someone, who was never apprehended.'

'We never did find out his surname, and Lord knows where he disappeared to. But he had no known connection to Douglas Bygrove that I can remember.'

'Apart from Edie Moore, who Hadley also tried to murder.'

'True enough, sir, but I'm not sure how that would involve Bygrove?'

'Maybe not.' Toshack thought again of Helen's worry about the extra food, and wondered if this Jim might have taken on a new illegal occupation. 'It's something to consider though.'

There was a quick knock on the door before WPC Lovelock popped her head around it. 'Sir, there's an Adrian Bloomfield to see you.'

'Send him in.'

He'd barely finished the sentence when the door was pushed open and a man entered, almost knocking the WPC over.

'That would be *Councillor* Bloomfield from the Littlehampton Urban District Council. I knew Douglas Bygrove. I need to speak to you.'

'Gardner, Lovelock, I'll speak to you both in a few minutes.'

The pair left and Toshack invited the councillor to sit down. He did so, removing his trilby.

'Do you have some information that would help in our investigation, Councillor?'

'I don't want to talk out of turn, that's why it's taken me a few days to come in. Of course, Douglas's demise may have been an accident, I don't know if you've had any more information on that score, Inspector, but, well...' He crossed his legs and picked off a piece of fluff from the knee of his pincheck trousers.

He hoped that Bloomfield had something useful to tell him. He needed a lead in a case that might prove impossible to unravel.

'Douglas told me that his wife was very resentful of his disability and bullied him. And, with him unable to walk, she'd be able to *bully* him very easily, if you get my meaning. Obviously, I don't know the ins and outs of the situation, but I felt the police should know, in case it's significant.'

Toshack had no doubt that Bygrove had given this impression to his friends so that he'd look like a victim, and to back his story up that he couldn't walk. But it sounded like Bloomfield was implying that Helen might have done something to her husband. He was angry with the man, for believing Bygrove's lies, and despised him for trying to implicate an innocent woman, for he had no doubt that Helen *was* innocent of any wrongdoing.

He probably should be keeping details of the post-mortem to himself for now, but it wouldn't hurt to reveal one little fact, and it might prevent the man from spreading his poison around the community.

'That's very interesting, Councillor, but the fact is, Douglas Bygrove *could* walk. The post-mortem has proved that. If he said he couldn't then he was lying. So, if a woman tried to tackle him in any way, I dare say he would have got the better of her. Especially someone of his height.'

'Well, keep it in mind anyway, Inspector. She is an awful woman who made his life a misery. She wasn't happy when he came home injured and threatened to throw him out on several occasions. Maybe that's why he pretended he couldn't walk, so she wouldn't be able to. Yes, that would be it.'

Toshack needed to get rid of this man before he said – or did – something he'd regret.

'Thank you for the information, Councillor. I'd advise you to keep it to yourself. Now, if you don't mind, I have a lot to get on with.'

'Of course, Inspector. Do bear in mind what I've told you though.'

'Good day to you, Councillor.'

'Good afternoon, Inspector.' He put his trilby back on and left.

Gardner was soon back. 'What would you like me to do now, sir?'

'Come in a minute, Sergeant, and close the door.'

When he'd done so, Toshack told him what Councillor Bloomfield had said.

'I don't believe it for a moment, sir. Besides which, she wouldn't be strong enough to drag him out and strangle him, even if he hadn't been able to walk, let alone if he could.'

'I agree, Gardner. It seems one of the least likely scenarios. I hope he doesn't go spreading his theory around. Poor Mrs Bygrove has had enough to deal with recently. No, we need to look at other avenues.'

Helen could hear his voice in the passageway before Edie knocked on the door and peeped around.

'The inspector is here to see you.'

'Bring him in.' She felt a sense of relief at his presence, especially when he said, 'We have some news.'

'I'll leave you to it,' Edie said, closing the door behind her.

They sat either side of the desk, both leaning forward, each with their fingers interlocked and resting on the wood.

'You know what happened?'

'Possibly. I can't give out any details at this point, but we got the post-mortem results back this morning, and it looks like it wasn't an accident.'

'Murder?'

'Do you have any idea who might have had a motive to kill him?'

She laughed mirthlessly. 'The whole of the staff here disliked him as he treated them appallingly, but that doesn't make them murderers.'

'No, but we can't discount anybody at this stage.'

'Including me?' she said.

He couldn't tell her he didn't believe it was her, as that wouldn't be professional. He changed the subject instead. 'Have you been to the solicitor to sort out the inheritance? I presume everything was in joint names so should be fairly easy to sort out.'

'I have been, but it wasn't in joint names, only in his. He only gave me access to the hotel bank account when he was conscripted, but he wouldn't let me near the money once he came back.'

'Is that going to cause problems?'

'Luckily not. I was afraid that he had done something stupid and made a will leaving the hotel to someone else.'

'To Miss Harvey?'

'Something like that,' she confessed. 'But he hadn't made any kind of will at all, which makes it much simpler than I thought it would, with me being his next of kin.'

'Hopefully it will go smoothly then. Is there anything I can do for you?'

There were a few things that sprang to mind, but none were appropriate. How she wished for his company, not in his capacity as a policeman, but as a… friend. He was so much easier to talk to than Douglas had been the last few years, or maybe, ever.

'All I can ask is for you to find out what happened, and quickly. I'm afraid if he was murdered, that I might be targeted next, or the children. Or that people might assume – again – that I am guilty.'

'I can't imagine that you or the children would be at risk. I would think that, whoever it was, had something specific against him. But if you become at all worried about anything, do contact me.'

'I will, thank you.' She extended her arms across the desk and took his hands in hers. 'I do appreciate it.'

She lingered maybe a second too long, then let go. He looked as embarrassed as she felt at her impulsiveness.

'I must go and make more enquiries.' He rose and headed for the door.

She stood and followed him. 'And I must get ready to greet the children. They haven't had an easy time of it at school in the last few days, since the news got out.'

'I'm sorry about that.'

As he opened the door, she said, 'You know, when I met you, I thought you rather curmudgeonly and maybe a little anti-women.'

He looked taken aback. 'Really?'

'But I realised eventually that you're a good man who cares about his job.'

'If a job's worth doing, it's worth doing well. Which reminds me. We will have to come back and question the staff, not just those who were here on the night. They might remember something, even insignificant, that could help. I will endeavour to solve this case as quickly as I can.'

'Thank you, Inspector. That's all I can ask.'

There was one last lingering look before he walked off down the passageway.

Once he was out of sight she went back to the desk. Could any of the staff have got so angry with him that they'd finished him off? One of the men might have managed it, though most were a good few years older than Douglas, but not one of the women, surely? What if a few of them had got together to do the deed? It wouldn't be the first time they'd got together to help her and the hotel. And, as she'd pointed out, they all disliked the way he'd treated them.

She shook her head at an idea that had more in common with the plots of detective novels she'd read as a younger woman than real life. She just hoped that the police got to the bottom of it soon.

Toshack and the sergeant had been back the following morning to question staff once more. He was sitting at his desk now, looking at the notes he'd taken. All the evidence still pointed to the last sighting of Bygrove being at around nine o'clock on the night of his death, at which point he'd been seen wheeling himself to the office. All who'd seen him in the last hour or so had attested to him being in a bad mood and rather rude to them. But that wasn't out of character, by all accounts.

The porter on night duty, a young lad called Wilf, had not been aware of anyone coming or going, not through the front entrance at least. They could have come in the side door, through the scullery, and no one else in the hotel would have been any the wiser after the staff there had finished for the evening. And the wind had been so noisy, it would have been more difficult to hear any rumpus going on in the office, especially as the porter had claimed to be sitting on one of the chairs near the front doors.

Maybe nobody did come in. Perhaps Bygrove had tipped up the wheelchair in anger himself, and scattered the papers, then gone out to meet his assailant. But even by nine o'clock, the wind had been blowing a gale.

At this point he heard what seemed like shouting, outside his door, where the main desk was.

Now what?

He rose to see what was going on, but before he'd left his desk, the door was flung open, and there, in the doorway, was the tall, imposing figure of Harold Crooke, the superintendent from Arundel, carrying his cap in his hand.

'Toshack! I've not long had a call from Councillor Bloomfield, complaining that he gave you a big lead in the Douglas Bygrove case, but that you didn't seem to have followed it up.'

'Superintendent, I—'

'It seems his wife is the most likely suspect, as spouses usually are, but she still seems to be at large.'

'Sir, I discounted the theory, and that's all it was, as unlikely on several counts, one being that his wife wouldn't have been strong enough to have inflicted the wounds on him and drag him to the beach.'

'But you told Bloomfield that you'd discovered that Bygrove could walk.'

'Exactly, so he'd have been in a better position to defend himself. And I was told, not only by Mrs Bygrove but also several of the staff, that it was *him* who bullied *her*, and had threatened her.'

'So, the staff are all taking her side. I've heard that he wasn't popular with them, because they were all lazy and disrespectful and he was trying to lick them into shape.'

'Where did you hear that?' It was undoubtedly true that the staff didn't like him, but he didn't for a moment believe they were lazy or disrespectful.

'Never mind, I have my sources.'

He wouldn't mind betting that this so-called information was from Bloomfield as well.

'So that's obviously what happened. A couple of the staff, maybe more, must have helped her, maybe the men as there are a few older ones there still. Yes, that's how she got him to the beach and did away with him.'

Toshack was tempted to slap his palm against his forehead in frustration but knew Crooke wouldn't be impressed.

'And contrary to what the staff told you, Inspector, Bloomfield told *me* that it was Mrs Bygrove who bullied *him*.'

'No, I don't believe that to be true, sir. One time when I went to the hotel to speak with Mrs Bygrove, he'd just come home, and I witnessed myself his rather patronising attitude towards her. And staff members told me that they heard him threaten her. She told me herself that he threatened her with powerful friends if she told anyone he could walk. And the post-mortem confirmed—'

'What nonsense!' said Crooke. 'That sounds like the fantasy of an unhinged woman who's persuaded her staff to lie. And I'm told she was arrested before, for sending libellous letters.'

'Only because she was framed. We caught the real perpetrator, who is now in gaol.'

'Is that so?' The superintendent didn't look impressed. 'And what did Mrs Bygrove do to make someone want to frame her, huh?'

'The guilty party, Ethel Harvey, was in love with her husband it would seem, so it was likely jealousy.'

'Sounds like supposition to me. I would say that it's almost certain that Mrs Bygrove was the murderer. I've crossed swords with her before, so I know what she's like. Tried to accuse an upstanding member of the aristocracy of assaulting one of her staff. Got quite annoyed she did. I could tell then that she had a temper on her. I was brought in to sort it out, since your predecessor, Inspector Davis, was too ready to believe her and was going to arrest Lord Fernsby, the son of the Earl of Scunthorpe. Can you imagine!'

Toshack remembered Helen telling him this story. Trust Superintendent Crooke to suck up to the aristocracy. He was starting to like the sound of this Inspector Davis.

'Sir, that is in the past now. As for Helen Bygrove murdering her husband, apart from anything else, the marks on her husband's neck indicated an assailant who was wearing a heavy ring on each hand. Mrs Bygrove has only an engagement ring and wedding ring on one hand.' He'd purposely looked for this on his visit after receiving the post-mortem report.

The superintendent clenched his teeth and went red in the face. 'She could have taken it off since then, to fool people. Or worn it only while strangling him to have the police come to the same stupid conclusion *you've* come to. Or got one of her staff to strangle him. If you are not going to do your job, then *I* will have to arrest her, and I'll take some men to search the place and question the staff. And I'll need the name of guests staying at the time.'

'Sir, we did all that, thoroughly, and—'

'You obviously didn't do it well enough! I'm going to organise this now, today, as I have a meeting first thing tomorrow, then I'm off for the weekend to Chichester, sailing.'

'Sir, I have to protest in the most—'

'I couldn't care less what you have to do. You haven't been doing your job, and now *I* am going to be in charge of this case, and you will do what *I* say.'

Superintendent Crooke spun on the soles of his shoes and marched out, yelling, 'Sergeant Gardner, get me the Arundel station on the telephone, *now*!'

Toshack leant against the wall next to the door and closed his eyes. If he didn't do something, Helen's life would be ruined for good, as Crooke seemed to be determined that it had to be her.

Maybe *he* was wrong and Helen had fooled him. No, he didn't believe that. Then he'd better come up with something to prove her innocence – and that of any of her staff Crooke tried to implicate.

Chapter Twenty-Four

This had to be one of the worst days of Helen's life, and recently there had been many bad days.

She had just been marched to her quarters by Superintendent Crooke, a man she'd despised the first time she'd come across him, a couple of years ago now. He was firing questions at her, barely allowing her to answer before he interrupted. In tow was Inspector Toshack, looking a cross between unhappy and angry, and she wasn't sure if that expression was aimed at the superintendent or at her.

Reaching her sitting room, Crooke shouted, 'And *I* believe you told people that your husband could walk, so you could claim that it wouldn't be possible to drag him to the beach. He probably ran to the beach to get away from you, and that's when you attacked him.'

Toshack's narrow eyed expression suggested he thought that Crooke had gone mad, which gave Helen the confidence to state firmly, 'I can assure you that my husband *could* walk, and fairly well. He practised every day. He was pretending he couldn't because he didn't want to go back into the army.'

'Sir,' Toshack interrupted, 'the post-mortem did show that the bones in his legs had healed well.'

'You didn't tell me this before.'

'You didn't ask.'

'Have you not read the post-mortem report yourself, Superintendent?' Helen asked.

'I am questioning *you*, not the other way round!'

'My husband told me that if I told anyone—'

'I've heard all this already. If that is the case, I reckon killing him would be a good way to get yourself out of the situation.'

'No, I would never do that,' said Helen. 'Not to anyone.'

'You probably didn't have to. You've got a hotel full of staff who could have helped, including a couple of tall men.'

'What?' Helen glanced at Toshack, who was shaking his head.

PC Flower entered the open door of the sitting room and headed towards Toshack. 'Sir, I found this in the wardrobe. It's got coloured threads the same as were found under Bygrove's fingernails.' He held up the bright blue tie with yellow martlets on.

It was the first Helen had heard of this.

Superintendent Crooke snatched the tie from Flower, gaping at it as if it were something alarming.

'I've seen that before,' said Toshack.

'It was a tie that Douglas often wore when he went out with his golfing friends,' said Helen.

Toshack nodded. 'That's right, I remember seeing it on the councillors when I was lunching at the—'

'I'll ask your opinion if I want it,' said Crooke. 'So this is what you strangled him with. Or got one of your staff to.'

'Look at it, Superintendent,' she said. 'It is pristine. Does it look like it's strangled anyone, or lost any of its threads?'

Crooke reached down to the coffee table, picking up some darning she'd been working on. 'You're clearly skilled in such matters and probably mended the tie before washing and ironing it and putting it away as if nothing had happened.'

'Surely I would have got rid of it altogether, had it been the murder weapon?'

The superintendent pulled his mouth into a wide grimace and narrowed his eyes. 'I've heard enough of your lies. Helen Bygrove, I am arresting you on suspicion of the murder of Douglas Bygrove—'

'But sir, you can't—'

'Shut up, Toshack, and keep out of this.' He grabbed Helen's arm and rammed it up her back.

'Ahhh!' she hollered, as the pain shot up her arm to her shoulder.

'Sir, you can't do that!' said Toshack, his hands lifted as if about to come to her defence.

PC Flower came forward with, 'Sir, I have handcuffs on me. That might be better.'

'Then put the things on this damned woman.'

The constable came forward cautiously, then gently placed the handcuffs on Helen as Crooke let her go.

Helen felt dizzy and frightened. Why on earth had the superintendent even got involved? Had the inspector called him in because he doubted her innocence? Yet, he didn't seem to like what was going on.

'What about my children? I can't leave them.'

'You have plenty of staff here to look after them, including a nursemaid, I believe. And if necessary, they can go to an orphanage.'

'No, you can't do that!'

'And you won't be getting any bail this time,' Crooke said. 'Oh yes, I've looked at your record. I'll have to open the libel case up again too, as I've heard your husband was convinced you'd actually framed Miss Harvey and her niece, not the other way round.'

'No, that's not true!' she howled.

'What's going on?' said WPC Lovelock as she rushed into the room. 'Mrs Bygrove, are you all right?'

Crooke put his hand up. 'Stop there, young woman, and keep away from this criminal.'

'Mrs Bygrove's no criminal!'

'I will deal with your insubordination back at the station – and yours, Inspector.'

'Sir, Ada Saltmarsh was *seen* posting the letters after going to her aunt's house,' said Toshack, who seemed not to care about Crooke's threats.

Crooke glared at him. 'Says who? An employee of Mrs Bygrove's and one of her long-standing guests? Not exactly impartial then.'

'But sir, we searched—' Toshack tried again, only to be halted by Crooke's hand being held up once more.

'Enough, Inspector! You two constables, take Mrs Bygrove to the motorcar. And take her through the foyer, to make an example of her. She'll be in the cells in Littlehampton over the weekend, then I'll arrange for them to take her to Portsmouth. In the meantime, we'll find out exactly who's been aiding and abetting her.'

Crooke looked gleeful, thought Helen, as if he'd just won a prize. It frightened her even more to think that this man seemed to consider this as some kind of game.

He started to march off ahead, looking pleased with himself, but stopped briefly to bark, 'There won't be enough room for you in the motorcar, Toshack, so you'll have to walk back.' He glanced at Toshack's leg and smirked.

The rotten, stinking… Helen didn't finish the sentence in her head, knowing the final word would be extremely rude.

When Crooke had got ahead, humming to himself, Helen whispered to Toshack, 'It wasn't me, Sam. It really wasn't.'

'I believe you, Helen, and I'll do all I can to help.'

'So will I,' said Amanda Lovelock, leading Helen along gently. 'I don't believe you, or any of the staff, did it for a moment. And we'll collect your coat on the way out and put it over your shoulders, so people can't see the handcuffs.'

PC Flower, who didn't look very happy about the situation either, nodded. 'Wish I'd never found the tie now. The man's a—'

'Constable!' the inspector warned.

She was grateful for their support, but against the might of Superintendent Crooke, she had no hope that it would make the slightest bit of difference.

-

In the foyer, several of the guests were looking on curiously as Helen was led away towards the door.

'What on earth is going on, old chap?' said the major, waylaying Toshack, as he lagged behind.

'Mrs Bygrove wants to speak to us about a few more things that might help us catch Mr Bygrove's killer. You can tell the other guests that if they ask.' He indicated the onlookers with a nod of his head.

'Good luck, Inspector.' As the major strode away, the door from the staff area opened once again, and Miss Moore hurried out, looking anxious. He halted her before she called out to Helen.

'Inspector, what's going on?'

'Keep your voice down, Miss Moore. I've just told the major we're simply interviewing Helen – Mrs Bygrove – to get a few more clues. But Superintendent Crooke has actually arrested her for her husband's murder.'

She gasped but kept calm. 'But why?'

He waited a few moments, until Helen and the constables had left the building. 'Councillor Bloomfield told the superintendent that Helen was abusive towards Bygrove.'

'But it was the other—'

'Yes, I know. They've twisted it. Or Bygrove did.'

'Helen wouldn't have done that. She couldn't.'

'I agree, but unfortunately, she is currently the main suspect. Crooke is convinced that staff members helped her carry out the deed.'

'No, that's nonsense.'

'I think you're right. I believe that Bloomfield might have something to do with that accusation. Unfortunately, the superintendent is very keen on statistics, so he likes to get cases wrapped up rapidly, any way he can… Miss Moore, what do you know about the blue tie with yellow martlets on? The councillors were wearing them at lunch when I was sitting with the major once.'

'Yes, that's right. I've seen Mr Bygrove wear the same tie, usually when he's going out to meet his golfing chums, though he's only been out once since he got back. Oh, and he was wearing it the times they came here with other men and spent a couple of hours in the private dining room.'

'They had meetings here, with Bygrove?'

'That's right. Inspector, did Helen tell you about the extra food that Bygrove managed to get hold of?'

'She did.'

Two more guests entered the foyer, going to the desk.

'Would you step into the staff area, Inspector.'

He nodded and followed her.

Edie shut the door and they stood in the corridor. 'I have wondered whether the food was something to do with Bygrove's friends, a few of whom were councillors, including Mr Bloomfield and Mr Rotherham. And they turned up the day Bygrove's body was discovered, insisting on speaking to him. Bloomfield claimed that he'd had a telephone call from him the night before, and he had been 'distressed.'

'So Bloomfield told you that on Tuesday 17 April. But he didn't come to the police station with his concerns until yesterday, more than a week later, and he'd mentioned nothing about a distressed telephone call. Leave it with me, Miss Moore, and don't talk to anyone else about this.'

'I won't. But why exactly has the superintendent arrested Helen?'

He told her as succinctly as he could what had been said since Crooke had turned up at the police station. He probably shouldn't have done, but since the superintendent had handled it all so badly, in his opinion, he didn't care.

'His conclusion that Helen is guilty, along with some of her staff members, doesn't seem to be based on anything very concrete,' she said.

'I agree. I'd better go and make sure that Helen is being treated well. I'll go out the staff entrance. We don't want anyone else wondering what's going on.'

As he left the side gate, heading back towards South Terrace, it occurred to him that it was odd, Bloomfield and Rotherham turning up the next day like that, insisting on speaking to Bygrove. It was almost as if they were creating an alibi by pretending to not know he was dead.

He needed to make a few of his own enquiries.

–

Edie hadn't relished telling the staff about Helen's arrest, and, as she'd predicted, they were outraged and shocked. This was also the first time they had heard about Bygrove being able to walk.

'Superintendent Crooke's whole case seems to be based on contradictions,' said Mrs Leggett. 'If Mr Bygrove could have walked, he'd have been a match for Mrs Bygrove. If he couldn't, how on earth would she have dragged him to the beach, the size of him compared to her?'

'Well,' she said, hesitating. 'It seems Crooke thinks that some of the staff might have helped her.'

There were several exclamations of indignation.

'I believe that Councillor Bloomfield might have put that idea in Crooke's mind.'

'It sounds like those councillors want to get Mrs Bygrove in trouble for her husband's death,' said Gertie.

'I've never liked that pair,' said Lili. 'Nor the other two what come in with them. But Mr Bloomfield and Mr Rotherham in particular are horrible, always treating the waitresses as if they're nothing.'

'My father didn't think much of them either,' said Edie. 'He recognised them when he went into the private dining room by accident, the day he visited me here. They'd been at a meeting he'd attended in Brighton about the food shortages, claiming that those with money should have priority over the poor.'

Mrs Leggett shook her head. 'What shocking arrogance. I wonder, Miss Moore, whether your father would know anything else about them? For it seems to me that it was Bloomfield's telephone call to the superintendent that caused this problem. What has the councillor got to gain by this accusation?'

'That's a good point, Mrs Leggett. I shall telephone him forthwith.'

She left the room, going to the office. Looking around, she realised that she'd be in charge for the next few days. Or maybe longer. Would they be allowed to run the hotel in Helen's absence? And what about her children? Could they keep them here, or would they be sent to an orphanage? Surely they could look after them in Helen's absence? They'd been told when Vera had collected them that mummy had needed to visit her cousin Eleanor for a few days.

What a mess!

She sat at the desk and picked up the telephone receiver. She requested to be put through to her father at his work telephone, hoping he'd still be there. When she was put through, she was relieved to hear his voice.

She told him briefly what had happened. 'So I was wondering, what you might know about Mr Bloomfield and Mr Rotherham.'

'Not a lot more than I told you at the time. The pair of them, but particularly Bloomfield, are more concerned with making sure their own interests are met than that of the town. They like the status. Just look at the people they associate with. Like Superintendent Crooke up at Arundel police station, who's no different.'

'You know him? It was he who arrested Helen, because of Bloomfield's telephone call.'

'He was at that meeting in Brighton I told you about, and also that one I interrupted at the hotel, the day I came to see you.'

A shock ran through Edie. 'He was there? I don't recall seeing him.'

'He wasn't in uniform, so maybe that's why.'

'So Superintendent Crooke knows Bloomfield well.'

'Indeed.'

'And also knew Bygrove.'

'So it would seem,' said her father. 'Is that significant?'

'It might be. Thank you, Father, you've been a lot of help. I'd better go. Love to Mother, whether she appreciates it or not.'

'Don't be a stranger, Edith.'

'I'll try not to. Goodbye Father.'

What to make of this latest revelation? No wonder Crooke took Bloomfield's word for it. She must go to the station first thing tomorrow and tell Inspector Toshack, always assuming he didn't already know.

But first, she'd tell the staff.

Chapter Twenty-Five

'Thank you for seeing me, Inspector,' said Edie, as she sat in the chair opposite Toshack at his desk early the next morning.

'I'm open to any useful information you can give me, Miss Moore, to clear Mrs Bygrove's name.' He removed a notepad from a drawer and took the lid off a fountain pen, making notes as she spoke.

'My father, who you probably know by now is Baron Moreland, has come across Councillors Bloomfield and Rotherham before, along with Superintendent Crooke. They apparently all know each other. He saw them at a meeting in Brighton a while back. And, all three of them were at a meeting at the hotel, with Bygrove and others, what, three weeks back. My father visited me at the hotel and walked in on their meeting by mistake.'

'Superintendent Crooke was there too? You didn't mention this yesterday.'

'I didn't know yesterday. I rang my father to see what he knew about Bloomfield and Rotherham, and he mentioned Crooke as well.'

'What was the meeting about, at the hotel?'

'I assume it was members of the golf club. That's what Bygrove always told Helen when he met with them.'

'And what was this meeting in Brighton that your father attended?'

'It was about food shortages in the area. Bloomfield and Rotherham were apparently of the opinion that people with money should have better access to food than the poor.'

Toshack pinched in his mouth. 'Seriously?'

'My father was appalled by the attitude. And, well, not to cast aspersions, but, as you know, Bygrove had been getting hold of food that we hadn't been able to source for a while and...' She wasn't sure how to finish this, and whether it was unfair to connect the two things. But then, the inspector could judge for himself.

'You were wondering if they had anything to do with some kind of profiteering scheme?'

'And I read there had been thefts from various food shops and providers in the area.'

'Mrs Bygrove mentioned this too, but we shouldn't jump to conclusions,' he said.

'Of course not. And I'm not necessarily implicating Superintendent Crooke in that part, by the way. Just wondering if he's not being impartial because he knew Mr Bygrove.'

He nodded, making another note.

'There is one more thing,' she said, tentatively. 'I don't know if this has any bearing on the case at all, only that it maybe shows a flaw in Mr Rotherham's character.' She told him how he'd tried to solicit her on the day of Bygrove's meeting with his friends.

'You're right, it may have nothing to do with it, but it's atrocious behaviour nonetheless and shows much about his character.' He closed the notebook. 'Thank you for the information, Miss Moore.'

'Would it be possible to see Helen, Inspector?'

'Probably better not today, I'm afraid. We've had *orders* from the superintendent. But if you come back tomorrow, I'll see what I can do.'

'I will do that. You have to wonder why he wants to isolate her from everyone.'

'She's not isolated from me, Miss Moore, and I will make sure she's looked after while she's here.'

'Thank you, Inspector.' She rose. 'I'll see myself out.'

—

After Miss Moore had left, Toshack went to the front desk.

'Sergeant Gardner, would it be possible to apply for a warrant to search the council officers and Councillor Bloomfield's home today?'

'Is that wise, sir? And what would the superintendent say?'

'He hasn't left any orders about that. And he's in a meeting this morning, before going away for the weekend, so now would be the best time.'

'Leave it with me. I know the judge responsible as I helped catch a thief what robbed him, so he's been eternally grateful ever since. I'll sort it out.'

'Thank you, Sergeant. *I* will be eternally grateful if you can do that... Has Mrs Bygrove been given her breakfast yet?'

'Lovelock is just sorting it out, sir.'

Toshack went to the kitchen to find the WPC serving scrambled eggs on a plate that already contained toast.

'For Mrs Bygrove, I assume?'

'Yes, sir. It won't be up to the Beach Hotel's standard, but I reckon it will be tasty enough.'

'I'll take it in to her, Constable. Is there any tea?'

'Already given her a cup, sir.'

'How was she?'

'Miserable, sir.'

—

Helen had hardly had a wink of sleep, worrying to the point that she felt sick. The cell smelled of damp and ammonia and wasn't the warmest of places. There was only a small bucket with a lid for her calls of nature, which she found immensely degrading, not to mention cumbersome.

They'd been very kind to her at the police station – after Superintendent Crooke had left – giving her an extra pillow and blanket from another cell. It had still been cold though. Both Toshack and Gardner had checked several times to make sure she was all right, and Amanda Lovelock had brought her a couple of magazines to read, *A Woman's Life* and *Home Chat*. She didn't normally have time to read periodicals, but they at least helped keep her mind occupied.

She was sitting on what passed for a bed now, which she had made up, and was sipping at her tea when the cell door opened. Inspector Toshack came in with a plate.

'Good morning, Mrs Bygrove. I hope you slept well.'

'No, Inspector, I did not.'

He placed the plate down on the small table by the bed. She didn't much feel like the eggs and toast, even though they looked well cooked, but thought she ought to make an effort.

'Am I allowed visitors today?' she asked. 'Or is the superintendent's ban meant for today as well?'

'He's definitely otherwise occupied today, and I believe Miss Moore will be calling in to visit.'

'I need to know how the children are.'

'Of course you do.' He sat on the bed, next to her. 'I am really sorry, Helen, about all of this. We do have certain information that has come to our attention, and I'm hoping it will help. I will do my utmost to vindicate you.'

He took her hand and squeezed it gently. Cutting across her anguish and fear, the warm touch of his hand provided a small jolt of contentment. And hope. Yes, hope. It was what she needed to keep her going.

'Thank you, Sam.'

'I'd better leave you to your breakfast, before it gets cold.'

He let go of her hand before standing and moving towards the door. She felt a tiny moment of loss.

Turning, he said. 'We'll get to the bottom of this, I promise.'

After he'd gone she ate a forkful of the eggs. They were already cold, but she needed to keep her strength up. The promise was surely empty, for he couldn't possibly know if he'd be able to find the real murderer. She guessed he was trying to keep her spirits up. But what if he couldn't solve the case?

She couldn't think like that. She needed to stay positive. Closing her eyes, she tilted her head to the heavens, sending up a desperate prayer.

-

Toshack's first job that morning was to go to the telephone exchange, which was at the post office in Surrey Street. Any information he could get on this telephone call that Douglas Bygrove had allegedly made to Councillor Bloomfield might be valuable, like the time it was made. He didn't have much hope of anyone remembering that from eleven days ago, so it was a long shot. He could ask Bloomfield of course, but something about the man told Toshack that he wasn't a reliable witness.

'The telephonist on duty that evening would have been Miss Harrad,' said the supervisor, after Toshack's enquiry. 'You're lucky: she's been away a few days but has just arrived for a shift now, but you'll have to be quick if you want to speak to her.'

He was shown into an office, and a woman in her thirties soon opened the door cautiously and stepped in, a notepad in her hand. 'I'm Miss Harrad. You wanted to speak to me about the evening of the sixteenth?'

'That's right. I was wondering if you remember a telephone call from the Beach Hotel, telephone number Littlehampton 55, to a Councillor Bloomfield, telephone number Littlehampton 76.'

'We have to keep a list sir, and I've brought mine with me. Let me have a look.' She set her notepad on the desk there and flicked through the pages. 'Here we are. Yes, I remember it now, as the caller sounded rather bad tempered.'

That would maybe fit in with Bygrove being distressed, though it wasn't the same as bad tempered.

'But that's not quite right,' she said frowning.

'In what way?'

'Because it wasn't the Beach Hotel ringing Councillor Bloom-field, it was the other way round. See?'

She showed him the note she had made, that clearly stated that Bloomfield, at Littlehampton 76, had requested to be put through to Mr Bygrove at the Beach Hotel on telephone number 55.

Why would Bloomfield have claimed it was the other way around?

'And you're absolutely certain that it was Mr Bloomfield who telephoned Mr Bygrove?'

'Oh yes, sir, for I am very thorough.'

'Did you hear any of their conversation?'

'Oh no, sir, we're not allowed to listen in.'

He bet some of them did though. 'Did you hear that Mr Bygrove had been found dead?'

She slapped her hand against her mouth. 'Oh, was it him? I've been at my poorly mother's in Bognor the last few days and only heard something about someone at the hotel being found dead this morning.'

'I'd appreciate it if you'd keep the information about the telephone call to yourself, please.' He didn't want her spreading it around all her friends and risking Bloomfield getting wind of the fact he'd found out. Not until he was ready.

'Of course, Inspector. My job's all about privacy.'

'Thank you, Miss Harrad. I'd like to keep this notebook for now.'

'I'd need to ask the supervisor about that, as he'll have to give me a new one.'

He closed the notebook and picked it up. 'Don't worry, I'll take care of that.'

—

The conservatory had been quite busy that afternoon with guests, especially from outside, and Lili wondered how many of them were here as gawkers to the tragedy. Some had obviously heard the excuse that Mrs Bygrove was helping the police gather more information and had asked how she was. Lili and the rest of the staff had already agreed among themselves to say she had returned and that she was spending a few days resting in her rooms. People didn't need to know she was in a cell at the police station.

'Poor Mrs Bygrove,' said Lady Blackmore, as Lili placed the tray of tea down in front of her and Cecelia. 'So many troubles laid at her door recently. I was saying to Cecelia, that I hope she has some tremendous good fortune come her way soon, wasn't I, Cecelia?'

'Yes, my lady.'

'Hear, hear to that,' said Major Thomas, sitting at the next table.

There were several nods and murmurs of agreement from those sitting nearby.

Lili was moving away from the table when the door from the dining room was pushed open wide and Ada Saltmarsh entered.

Young Simon, passing by, said, 'She surely hasn't come here for afternoon tea. What a cheek!'

'I think I'll ask her to leave,' said Lili, hoping she wouldn't cause a fuss if she did so.

The fact that Mr Watkins was hurrying in after Ada made Lili even more determined to waylay her.

She hadn't quite reached her when Ada stopped in the middle of the room and announced, 'You should all be ashamed of yourselves! My aunt might have written some libellous letters, but at least she didn't kill her husband.'

'That's enough of that,' hissed Watkins, catching her up.

Lili saw Simon, out of the corner of her eye, rush to the door to the staff area.

'That is a scandalous and slanderous accusation, young woman,' said the major, standing. 'You might have got a suspended sentence for aiding and abetting your aunt, but you'll be carted off again if you keep casting these aspersions.'

'They're not aspersions, you stupid old man. Mrs Bygrove was arrested yesterday afternoon.'

'Be quiet you, and leave immediately,' said Watkins, trying to move her along, but Ada resisted.

'I thought she was just providing some information?' said a rather prim young woman, who was staying the week with her husband.

'No, she was taken away and locked up,' Ada shouted.

Lady Blackmore stood and came a few steps towards them. 'You have already proved to be a liar and a scoundrel, so no one is going to believe you.'

'Indeed,' said another regular customer from South Terrace.

The other guests were mesmerised by the exchange, though some had expressions of uncertainty.

'*I'm* a liar,' said Ada. 'What about you? All this nonsense about Cecelia being your *companion*.'

'If you're going to spout that lie about her being my daughter, you can just stop there. I am fifty-eight years old, and Cecelia is forty-eight. How could she possibly be my daughter, you stupid girl?'

'Oh, I know she's not your daughter. Aunt Isabella just exaggerated the story to make you hate Mrs Bygrove even more, for it's all she deserved.'

'Hush your nonsense and be gone,' said Lady Blackmore, turning to sit back down.

'No, she's not your daughter, but she *is* your sister. And look at the appalling way you treat her, like a servant.'

Lady Blackmore halted and glared at Ada. Cecelia was wide-eyed, her mouth slightly open. Neither confirmed nor denied the claim.

'Come Cecelia, we are leaving.'

Cecelia said nothing as she rose and followed on, her expression concerned.

Edie rushed through the staff door, Simon behind her, as Ada was saying, 'And I swear on my life that it's true they've arrested Mrs Bygrove, for Councillor Bloomfield's wife told me.'

'Is this true?' called a man from Surrey.

Edie stopped and looked around. 'It is true that she has been mistakenly arrested by Superintendent Crooke, from the Arundel police station, who knows *nothing* of the case. The police in Littlehampton, who do know the case, do not believe she is guilty.'

'He must have some reason for arresting her,' called out another guest.

'It's over some nonsense that Councillor Bloomfield told the superintendent about Mrs Bygrove bullying Mr Bygrove, but in truth it was the other way around.'

'But the poor man couldn't walk,' said the guest from South Terrace.

'Yes, he could. He was only pretending not to so he wouldn't have to go back to the war.'

'True that is,' said Lili.

The Surrey guest rose and indicated to his wife to do the same. 'I don't think it's a good idea to stay here until the whole murder thing has been proved one way or another.'

Three quarters of the guests mumbled agreement and did the same.

Lili noticed Ada look around and smirk, then follow the guests out. She obviously thought she'd achieved her aim. Watkins followed her, calling, 'Don't think you'll get away with this, this, *slander*, young woman!'

Simon and Edie joined Lili, who said, 'What are we going to do?'

'We're going to tell Inspector Toshack what's happened,' said Edie, 'and make sure Ada gets what she deserves. Causing trouble like this must be a breach of the terms of her suspended sentence.'

'I can't understand it, after her aunt tried to get her blamed for all the libellous letters at the court case,' said Lili. 'Jolly angry I'd be if an aunt had done that to me, and I certainly wouldn't stick up for her.'

'I agree. It seems odd that Councillor Bloomfield's wife should have told her about Helen.'

'You don't think she's been told to make a fuss by them, do you?'

'It's possible,' said Edie. 'I think there's more to this than meets the eye. It's almost like everything leads back to Councillor Bloomfield.'

'What are we going to do about the hotel?' Lili swallowed the urge to cry.

'The best we can,' said Edie, 'and hope to goodness that they find the real murderer.'

'Let's hope they do it in the next couple of days then, before they send Mrs Bygrove off to Portsmouth gaol. And before they start dragging some of us off.' Lili took a deep sigh. 'And we'd better clear up these afternoon teas that don't look like they're going to be paid for.'

–

'Oh dear, oh dear, oh dear,' said the housekeeper, standing in the stillroom as Edie told her the latest disastrous news. 'I'm not sure what we can do now that people outside the hotel have found out.'

'Nor me, Mrs Leggett. I was hoping that the inspector might have been able to clear her name before it got out.'

'If he is even *able* to clear her name.'

'Don't say that, we've still got to—'

Edie's words were interrupted by two children wailing loudly in the scullery. It could only be Dorothy and Arthur.

Sure enough, Vera, looking distressed, brought through the two distraught children, stopping in the middle of the stillroom when she spotted Edie and Mrs Leggett.

'They were told at school,' she said.

'W – we were bullied in the playground and the children called us murderer's children so M – Miss Nye took us in and we had to spend p – playtimes indoors with her,' said Dorothy. 'And a girl in my class k – kept kicking my chair, and when Miss Nye told her off she said her big brother would come and punch me.'

'Children in my class kept poking their tongues out at me when the teacher wasn't looking,' said Arthur. He thrust his bottom lip out.

'Take them into the staff dining room, Vera, and calm them down,' said Mrs Leggett. 'We'll get them some nice cups of cocoa and find some biscuits for them.'

When Vera had gone, Edie said, 'It might be a good idea to keep them down with us as much as possible, to keep their minds off things. We'll have to find out what they've been told and see if we can limit the damage.'

Mrs Leggett nodded. 'And we'll need to consider what we're going to do with them if Mrs Bygrove doesn't come home. It might be better not to send them to school next week. I'm sure Vera could do some school work with them if necessary. Miss Nye might be able to advise us on that, as Dorothy's teacher.'

Edie's head ached with stress. If this was the end of the hotel, most of them would be able to find jobs elsewhere, especially with the men away, but goodness knows what would happen to Fanny and little Elsie. And there would be no chance that the children could stay at the hotel with them all gone. They'd go to an orphanage for sure.

Douglas Bygrove might be dead, but he was still causing a great deal of trouble.

–

The middle of the following morning, there was a frantic knock on Toshack's office door, and Gardner stepped in looking eager. 'Sir, the warrants for the council offices and Bloomfield's home have arrived.'

'Well done, Sergeant. Let's waste no time. I don't want anyone getting wind of anything before we get there. Round up three of the constables – not Twort – and bring them into my office. You and one of them can go to Bloomfield's house on St Catherine's Road, and I'll go with the other two to the council offices.'

'Righty ho, sir.'

Having briefed them, each party set off on foot to their destinations. Toshack and his team reached the council offices on Beach Road, near the junctions that split the road in two, just after eleven o'clock. He opened the gate into the tiny courtyard in front of the two-storey red brick building.

In the reception area, the secretary greeted him, a neat little woman in her forties with round, metal rimmed glasses. She looked concerned when she realised there were two uniformed police officers with him.

'We have a warrant to search the premises,' said Toshack, holding up the piece of paper for her to look at.

'Oh, I had better—'

'What's going on here?' said Councillor Bloomfield, coming out of an office that faced the front of the building. He must have seen them coming in.

Toshack repeated his words, showing the warrant to Bloomfield.

'This is unacceptable. I'm not allowing you to do anything until I've been in touch with Superintendent Crooke.'

'I'm afraid he's away for the weekend, and this is a legal document which gives me and my officers every right to search the premises right now. We'll start with your office.'

Bloomfield stood in the way of his door. 'But what is all this to do with?'

Constable Flower, being taller and broader, moved him to one side. 'Out of the way, sir.'

'It's to do with certain information we've received,' said Toshack, not explaining any further. 'Constable Lovelock, would you start on the next office, please?'

'Very well, sir.'

The councillor followed Toshack in. 'I hope this has nothing to do with Bygrove's murder. You already have the killer locked up for that.'

He didn't reply to this. He didn't have to tell this man anything. 'Unlock these drawers please, and then wait in the reception area,' is all he said.

'This is preposterous. You wait until I get hold of Crooke. I'll make sure he sacks you. You're an incompetent nincompoop!'

'The drawers, sir.'

Bloomfield took a key from his pocket and unlocked them, all the while mumbling under his breath, before stomping out of the room.

Toshack and PC Flower searched the room thoroughly, during which time they heard the telephone in reception ringing. They found nothing of interest.

'Let's move on, Constable.'

The councillor was putting the telephone receiver down as they re-entered reception. Bloomfield's eyes were narrowed and he'd gone red in the face. 'What the hell are you up to? That was my wife to say that you have officers searching my home. Oh, you will be so sorry when you find *nothing* and Crooke fires you for your arrogance and incompetence.' He rushed off upstairs.

'Follow him, Flower.'

'Yes, Inspector.'

The secretary had her head down, typing something, but looked anxious. It wasn't long before Councillor Rotherham was hurrying down the stairs.

'What's all this? You've got no right—'

'Yes we have,' said Toshack, weary of having to keep saying it. 'We have a warrant. And before you say you'll take it up with Superintendent Crooke, he's away. Now, I suggest you keep out of our way, Mr Rotherham, and we'll be finished more quickly.'

Between the three of them, they spent an hour going over all the rooms, searching any drawers, checking files on shelves. Bloomfield had tried twice to get hold of Superintendent Crooke on the telephone at the Arundel station and at his home too, by the sounds of it, but he'd clearly had no luck.

Finally, having searched every room there, Toshack had to admit defeat. If they were hiding anything that could incriminate them in any way, it was not here. He hoped that Gardner was having better luck at his home. Perhaps they should have got a warrant for Rotherham's house too. If they tried at this point, it might get blocked by Crooke.

Toshack and the two constables were gathered in the foyer now, ready to leave.

'So, you didn't find anything then,' said Bloomfield, looking smug.

Rotherham sniggered with scorn. 'Don't forget to close the door on the way out.'

'And you won't find anything at my house either,' Bloomfield added. 'Don't get comfortable back at the station, for you won't be there long once Superintendent Crooke hears about this.'

The two men regarded each other with triumphant smirks, before going back up the stairs, laughing drily.

Toshack watched them as they went, wondering what his next move could be. For now, it would be to see if Gardner had turned up anything during his search, despite Bloomfield's confidence that he wouldn't.

'Let's go.' Toshack took a step towards the door.

'Wait a moment,' said the secretary, so quietly that he almost missed it. She looked towards the stairs, then beckoned him towards her. 'Have you tried the basement?' she whispered.

Toshack indicated to the other two not to leave. 'Where's that? I didn't see any doors to one.'

She stood quietly, making sure her chair made no noise, then went to the wooden panelling under a flight of stairs that twisted at a right angle halfway up. She pressed against something, and part of the panel opened a little.

'But you didn't hear it from me,' she muttered. 'I feel that there are things going on here that I don't agree with.'

He nodded and indicated for the other two to follow him. Behind the panel opening was a flight of steps down.

As the three of them started their descent, WPC Lovelock leading the way, there was a thumping of footsteps coming down the stairs from the first floor.

'Are you still—?' Bloomfield started, then, seeing where they were heading, shouted, 'Where the *devil* do you think you're going?'

'To the basement that I've realised you must have,' said Toshack, hoping not to implicate the secretary.

'You can't go down there; it's old records, private and confidential ones, and you're not allowed to touch them. Miss Jarsdel, why did you not tell us what was happening?'

Before she had a chance to reply, Toshack said, 'I told her to keep quiet. And I advise you to keep your distance.' He put his hand up to halt him.

Rotherham came down the stairs next, looking equally alarmed. 'You can't go down there!'

'We can, and we will. Constable Flower, stay up here and keep an eye on these two.'

'Yes, sir.'

As they headed down, Toshack could already smell the food. It was like entering a grocery store. There was light coming in from a back window, but it was still gloomy. Despite this, they could see that there was enough evidence here to convict the pair of them for stealing. Some of the items were on shelves, while others sat on the floor. There were sacks of sugar and flour on one side and, further along, crates of vegetables. There was even a box with a couple of large meat joints, which presumably they were planning on moving on that day. Where these so-called confidential records were, he had no idea.

'Do you think some of these will be things that have been stolen, Inspector?' asked Lovelock.

'Absolutely no doubt. And look at this.' He indicated a container in one corner that held other items. 'I'm sure some of these were on an inventory given to us by the owners of the house burgled on Fitzalan Road. Right, you'd better stay here and log it all, and I'll get the photographer over to take photographs before we remove it all as evidence.'

Back upstairs, Toshack picked up the telephone receiver on the secretary's desk and got put through to the station. He was relieved to hear Gardner's voice. 'You're back, good.'

'Yes sir, and I've found something very interesting.'

'Me too,' said Toshack, looking at the councillors, who were sitting scowling at him. 'Bring the motorcar around to the council offices would you, Sergeant? I'm bringing Bloomfield and Rotherham in.'

'You can't do that!' said Bloomfield, standing.

'Sit down,' growled Flower.

'And contact the photographer, Gardner, and get him over to the council offices right away.' Toshack hung up and walked over to the councillors. 'Adrian Bloomfield and Michael Rotherham, I'm arresting you on suspicion of criminal activity involving the illegal acquisition and selling of stolen items. For now. There may be more charges to come, once we've examined the contents of the basement more closely.'

Bloomfield snarled, 'You'll regret this,' as PC Flower placed handcuffs on him.

It was in that moment that Toshack noticed the two heavy rings the councillor was wearing, one on each hand. He said nothing, but watched as Rotherham was cuffed by the constable.

'I don't suppose you'd like to tell me how you came by all the food items in the basement here?'

'What food items?' said Bloomfield, with an attempt at a surprised face that wouldn't have fooled anyone. 'Has someone been storing food in our basement? Miss Jarsdel, do you know anything about this?'

'Of course I don't,' she said, affronted.

'And what about the non-food items?' Toshack continued. 'Some of which match descriptions of items stolen from properties.'

'Nothing to do with us,' said Rotherham.

The front door started to open. Toshack was just thinking how quick Gardner had been, when three other men came through the door. He recognised them all as members of the council.

'What on *earth* are you doing, Inspector?' said the short, blond one, who Toshack knew to be the Inspector of Nuisances. 'Mrs Bloomfield rang us with great concern.' He noticed at that point that his colleagues had been handcuffed. 'What is the meaning of this?'

'It's an error of judgement he'll live to regret,' said Rotherham.

'It's no error of judgement, after the commodities we found in the basement, which you were keen we shouldn't enter,' said Toshack. 'And since you three have turned up to defend them, am I to assume you're in on it too?'

They looked at each other, alarmed. 'In on what?' said the blond man. 'Bloomfield, what have you been up to?'

'Nothing. And Superintendent Crooke will deal with this matter when he comes back.'

The three men's surprise looked genuine enough. This group didn't include the two other men he'd seen with Bloomfield and Rotherham at the hotel, but Toshack would need to look into them too, eventually.

'I suggest you uncuff the men, Inspector,' said the blond man. 'They are the chairman and vice chairman of the council.'

'That makes no difference if they've committed a crime. But if you want to keep on arguing about it, we can take you to the station too. I'm not sure how you could work so closely with them and not know what they're up to.'

The three men stepped back, almost in unison. 'I can assure you, Inspector, that we have no idea what's going on.'

The door opened once more. Toshack was relieved to see that it was Gardner this time.

'Right, time to go. Gardner, you accompany Mr Bloomfield to the motorcar. Flower, you take Mr Rotherham.'

Toshack turned and lifted his hat in the secretary's direction. 'Good day to you, Miss Jarsdel. One of my officers will be remaining here for now, and I dare say a few more will be back later.'

'Very well, Inspector.'

He turned to the three remaining councillors. 'Gentlemen, I suggest you find a new chairman and vice chairman for the council. Good day to you.'

—

Bloomfield and Rotherham were now locked up in the two remaining cells at the police station, still making a lot of fuss about being falsely arrested. Toshack would have liked to check on Helen next, but he was keen to see what Gardner had found.

'All right, Sergeant, what have you got?' he said, returning to the front desk.

Gardner unlocked a drawer and took out a brown paper bag. He shook it against the desk, and a bright blue tie with yellow martlets on slithered out. Toshack recognised it as the one he'd seen the councillors and Bygrove wear. It was snagged and stretched — and it had blood on it.

Toshack couldn't believe what he was seeing. 'Where did you find this, Sergeant?'

'Under the wardrobe in Bloomfield's bedroom, sir. I could see something when I looked underneath it. Took a while for us to shift the wardrobe, but there it was.'

'Why would he risk leaving it somewhere it could be found?'

Gardner shrugged. 'I guess he didn't reckon on anyone checking under there. Pretty stupid of him, but lucky for us he did. There were also three good ties with the same pattern hanging up in the wardrobe.'

'Why would he have more than one?'

'No idea, sir. To give out to friends? Oh, by the way, I meant to say this morning. I went around to a neighbour's house last night, one who works at the golf club, to ask about the tie. He reckons it's nothing to do with the golf club.'

'That's what Bygrove claimed to his wife.'

'I reckon it's just for them what belongs to some special club of Bloomfield's, or whoever's in charge. Anyway, I reckon this is what we've been looking for. This is surely where the threads under Bygrove's nails came from. I'll send it now to be examined and to get the blood type identified, but I bet it'll match the victim's.'

'Gardner, you're a genius.' He slapped him on the back a couple of times.

'Just doing me job sir.' He was beaming all the same. 'I'll get onto that now.'

'And I've got a little job of my own to do,' said Toshack, feeling a weight drop from him.

He marched back to the cells and unlocked the one with Bloomfield in.

'Coming to let us go already,' said the councillor. 'I should damn well think so.'

'No. I've come to arrest you, Bloomfield.'

The councillor huffed out a laugh. 'In case you hadn't noticed, Inspector, you've already arrested me.'

'Not for murder.'

'What!'

'We found the tie, under your wardrobe, the one with the threads missing that we found under Bygrove's nails. And with blood on. Adrian Bloomfield, I am arresting you on suspicion of the murder of Douglas Bygrove…'

–

There was a terrible fuss going on when Helen's cell door opened and Toshack stepped in.

'What has all the noise been about?' she asked.

'We arrested a couple of the councillors for stealing and selling on food earlier. Probably including the food your husband got hold of.'

'I thought I heard Councillor Bloomfield's voice.'

'You did. And the other is Mr Rotherham.'

'Oh my.'

'And… Bloomfield has also this moment been arrested for your husband's murder.'

Helen took a deep, sudden breath and held it there, not quite believing her ears. 'Mr Bloomfield?'

'That's right.'

'But – how did you find out?'

'That's a story for another time.'

Another time. She looked forward to spending time with Toshack. *Sam*.

'Why did he kill him?'

'That, we've yet to establish.'

As she took another long breath in, she realised she was crying. She put her head down in embarrassment, only to find herself being held by him. She leant against his chest as she sobbed. 'I – I'm sorry. How silly of me t – to cry.'

'It's all right, it's fine. It'll be the relief.'

He held her a little more firmly. Her enjoyment of the sensations it caused made her even more embarrassed. And ashamed. She should pull away, but she couldn't. He was so kind, so considerate, so gentle with her.

He finally loosened his hold on her. 'Come on, you're free to go. Let's get your things and take you home.'

As they left the cell, they could hear another rumpus, but it didn't sound like it was coming from the next cells. It was from further away. They went up the stairs and down the corridor to the desk to find Superintendent Crooke raving at Sergeant Gardner. He was out of uniform, in brown trousers and a wool jumper, with a green alpine style hat.

'There you are, Toshack. I had a call at my hotel in Chichester from my wife who'd had an urgent call from Bloomfield's wife to say he was very angry because you were interfering for no good reason in the council offices. I don't appreciate being called away from my weekend. And what is *she* doing out of the cells! Being transferred to Portsmouth, I hope?'

'No sir. She's no longer the suspect for the murder. I've arrested Bloomfield and Rotherham for stealing and selling on food.'

'Nonsense! Someone's framing them, it's obvious. And what's that got to do with Bygrove's murder?'

'It's not nonsense. We found a load of food in the basement of the council offices. And other items clearly stolen. WPC Lovelock is there now logging it all, and the photographer's been called.'

Crooke didn't look so sure of himself for a moment. He then rallied to shout, 'Get this mad woman locked back up!'

'Bloomfield has also been arrested for Bygrove's murder. Sergeant, show Superintendent Crooke the evidence.' He turned to Helen. 'You may want to turn away.'

But she didn't. She wanted to know what had happened. Gardner opened a drawer and took out a bag, from which he extracted a bloodied tie, one that was in bad shape.

'It was found under Bloomfield's wardrobe and is almost certainly the one that was used during the murder of Douglas Bygrove, sir.'

Crooke blinked rapidly and rubbed his chin. He took a step backwards. 'Um, well, good work, Toshack. Yes, good work. The man's obviously a clever bleeder. Had me fooled, I can tell you. You'd better check up on the rest of his colleagues.'

'That's our next job, sir.'

'Yes, yes. Keep up the good work. Now, I'm driving back to Chichester, and I don't expect to be disturbed again.'

He marched quickly to the door and left forthwith.

PC Flower appeared from the door to the cells. 'Sir, Mr Rotherham says he'd like to make a statement.'

'Does he realise that Bloomfield's been charged with murder?'

'Yes, sir. I think that's why he wants to do it.'

'All right, Flower. I'll deal with that when I return.'

–

Toshack opened the door of the motorcar for Helen, before striding around to the driver's side. While he was delighted to have released Helen and have caught the real perpetrator of the crime, something still bothered him. Why had Crooke backtracked so suddenly? He hadn't argued, hadn't tried to suggest that the tie might have been planted, which is what he'd expected.

Was he afraid that, being friends with Bloomfield, he might be implicated in some way if he continued to support him? Had the accusation of murder been just too much? But what if he were involved, with the stolen items, if not the murder?

'This is very kind of you, to take me home,' said Helen, as he started the engine. 'I'm looking forward to changing and tidying myself up, apart from anything else. I didn't even have time to bring a hat. At least I could have hidden my hair under it.'

'Taking you home is the very least I can do after all the trouble we've caused you.'

'All the trouble Superintendent Crooke caused, you mean,' she corrected.

'We're not entirely guiltless though, are we?' He raised his eyes at her briefly before driving off, down Gloucester Road.

A chug and hiss of a train was heard, and he spotted one pulling into the station as they headed off, on the rail that ran alongside the road.

'I think I might take the children to Brighton on the train next weekend, just to get away for the day,' Helen said. 'I haven't been able to spend much time with them recently with all that's been going on. Or take them to see my cousin Eleanor in Arundel, who I haven't seen for a while.'

'That's a good idea.' He wished he could join them, but then, what would the children make of that?

They were silent for most of the short journey to the hotel. They were passing the River Arun and the fishermen's cottages on Pier Road, when Helen said, 'I can't thank you enough, Sam, despite what you say about not being guiltless. You could have taken the easy route, one that would undoubtedly have been better for your career where the superintendent is concerned, and not pursued Bloomfield and Rotherham.'

'That would be dishonest, and I'm not, nor ever will be, a dishonest policeman, even if that means remaining a detective inspector for evermore.'

'I know, and for that I am truly grateful.'

He turned onto South Terrace, looking over Oyster Pond and beyond at the vast common on his right. In the distance he could spy the Beach Hotel. He was about to drop Helen off and who knew when he'd see her again? Maybe occasionally, while wrapping up the case, and perhaps when it went to court she'd have to be there. He was relieved to have proved her innocence, but this might mean he'd rarely see her again. He wouldn't even have the excuse of dining at the hotel in order to keep an eye on things.

He pulled up on the far side of the hotel, assuming she'd want to go in the staff entrance while not looking her best. In her eyes, anyway. She'd unpinned her blonde hair overnight and it was falling down her back in waves, which he found more attractive than her pinned-up hairstyles. He admonished himself. He shouldn't be feeling anything other than relief at releasing an innocent woman.

'My next job is to visit the newspapers,' he said. 'To make sure they print the latest news on this case. And I'll contact the general Sussex newspapers as well.'

She looked around outside for some reason, and he wondered whether she was waiting until there was no one around to get out. There didn't seem to be anyone in the immediate vicinity, so he went to open the door, but was surprised to find her leaning towards him. He'd barely begun wondering what she was going to do when she planted a kiss on his cheek. He stayed still, staring at the steering wheel, not knowing what to say or do.

'I'm sorry, I've embarrassed you. And myself.' She gave a shy chuckle. 'It's not at all like me to do such… spontaneous things like that normally. I don't know what came over me, except a profound relief at being free, and an appreciation of your efforts.'

'It's all right. I can understand your relief. I honestly don't mind.'

They were both silent for a while, before she said, 'I owe you a lot of free meals after what you've done.'

He did now look at her, 'But we're not allowed to—'

'I know what you're going to say, but if you came to my own quarters as a family friend, and had the meal there, it would surely be seen as just that.' She said nothing for a moment, before adding, 'Sorry, I seem to have embarrassed you, again. I didn't mean to. I wasn't suggesting anything improper.'

He pulled his confused senses together. 'I didn't think you were. You'd better get inside now and let your children and friends know you're home.'

'Yes. Home. It's amazing how much you appreciate the word after an experience like this. And it's interesting that you referred to them as friends, not *staff*, for they have been good friends to me.'

'They have indeed. I'll keep you up to date with anything I'm able to on this case.' He got out of the motorcar and went around it to open her door. 'Farewell, for now, Helen.'

She stepped out delicately and said, 'Farewell, Sam.' She smiled at him before moving off towards the hotel.

He watched her for some moments before getting back into the vehicle. There was a word for what he was feeling, if only he could think of it.

Discombobulated.

Yes, that was it. He started the engine and drove away, ready for whatever the rest of the day would bring.

–

When Helen arrived at the scullery it was empty, as was the still-room. Where was everybody? Entering the corridor, she could hear voices in the dining room. Some staff would be on late lunch. She entered to find it was much fuller than it would normally be at this time. The aroma of good home cooking was very welcoming, especially after the fetid stench of her cell.

'Mrs Bygrove!' called the housekeeper, spotting her first and rising to greet her.

There was a chorus of welcome and surprise.

'They've let you go then?' asked Edie. 'On bail?'

'No, no, for good. They've got the killer.'

The staff gathered around her. 'Who was it?' Lili asked.

'Councillor Bloomfield.'

There were gasps of amazement from most of them there.

'Well, I'm not surprised,' said Edie. 'I always thought there was something not right about the man, and particularly Rotherham, not to mention the other two men who tended to hang around with them.'

'It would appear that they were also responsible for my husband getting hold of the extra food. Illegally.'

Mrs Norris folded her arms under her bust. 'I was thrilled with that food to begin with, but then it seemed a bit too good to be true.'

'It certainly was, Mrs Norris.'

Edie placed her hand on Helen's shoulder. 'So, what exactly happened?'

'I only know the bare minimum myself at the moment, but I'll tell you all that later. How has the hotel been doing?'

There was a lot of sighing and hanging of heads.

'That Ada Saltmarsh gave the game away,' said Lili. 'She came in during afternoon tea yesterday and told everyone you'd been arrested. We'd told people you'd come back from helping the police and was having a rest for a few days. A lot of people walked out and quite a few checked out too.'

'It's been very quiet since, which is why so many of us are here now,' said Edie. 'There's not been a lot to do.'

'Oh dear.' Helen shook her head. 'At least Inspector Toshack is going to notify the newspapers about the mistake made and tell them they've arrested others. But there'll still be work to do, building up our reputation again. Even if I hadn't been implicated in the murder, the fact that a murder has taken place here is not good for the hotel's status.'

'We're all behind you, Helen,' said Edie. 'And we'll do our very best to get the hotel back to where it was.'

'Hear, hear!' called the rest of the staff.

'Thank you, everyone, I'm very touched by your loyalty and all your hard work. We've still got Douglas's funeral to get through, and, although I'm sad to say that our relationship had not been one of pleasant companionship for quite some time, he is my children's father, so we will make it as solemn and respectful as we can.'

'Of course we will, lass,' said Mrs Turnbull. 'Talkin' of which, I believe there are two sad little scraps upstairs, waitin' for their mummy to come home.'

Before she'd finished the sentence, the door opened and the children stood there, wide-eyed, with Vera behind them, beaming.

'Mummy!' Dorothy and Arthur called as they ran towards her. They each clutched a side of her waist and held on tightly. She hunkered down to hug them properly.

'It's wonderful to see you back, Mrs Bygrove,' said Vera.

'It's wonderful to be back,' said Helen, smiling.

Chapter Twenty-Six

Two days had elapsed since Helen had been set free, and already word had spread rapidly around the town.

'I can't believe how busy we are for a Monday morning,' said Edie, sitting opposite Helen in the office. 'It looks like the newspapers will be behind the times by the time they're published.'

Helen nodded. 'I can't believe people have been so quick to return. I thought some would be sceptical, or that the very thought that something so awful had taken place here would put them off. I suppose that there is probably a little element of, I don't know, morbid curiosity?'

'Maybe war and the many deaths endured have hardened people to such things. Which is sad, of course.' Edie hung her head and tutted.

'Or they see it as a real-life version of one of those penny dreadful novels. I suppose it's human nature to be curious.'

'Whatever the reason, I suppose we should be thankful that you still have a viable business.'

Helen knew Edie was right, but it seemed sinful to be thankful about this when her husband had been killed, however awful a person he'd become.

She must have shown this sentiment in her expression, as Edie leant over the desk and took her hand, giving it a squeeze. 'You can't do anything about Douglas's death. The important thing now is to look to the future, for you and the children.'

'Yes. Yes, you're right. And it's for that reason that I asked you in here. Now that I am the permanent manageress – and proprietress…' She still couldn't quite believe the latter title. 'I

329

will need a permanent undermanageress. And since you did such a good job before, the position is yours again. If you want it.'

Helen was relieved by Edie's wide smile. She'd been an asset to the hotel and she would have hated to lose her for any reason.

'Of course I want the position. I'm delighted you still have confidence in me. I presume it's until the war is over and the men come home?'

'No, I'd like you to do the job permanently. I can't think of a better person to fulfil the role.'

'Thank you, Helen.'

There was a knock on the door and Mrs Turnbull came in. 'Mornin' coffee, ladies, and you have a visitor. Come in lad.'

Behind the storekeeper came Sam, looking smart in a three-piece suit and no mackintosh today. He lifted his hat. 'Good morning, ladies.'

'Come in, Inspector. Mrs Turnbull, would you fetch another cup and saucer, please.'

'Already have.' She put the tray down and left.

'Do sit down, Inspector.' Helen pointed to the empty seat. It seemed strange now to refer to him by his title and not his name, but she didn't want to give Edie the wrong idea.

'Thank you... I wanted to come and tell you the latest news.'

'Let me pour us all a coffee first,' said Helen.

Edie and Sam discussed the weather, and how pleased they were to see the sun appear after a cloudy start. It was such a trivial subject, yet she was glad of its normality.

'There,' she said, passing the cups around. 'Now, you were saying, Inspector?'

'The test shows that the blood on the tie is confirmed as the same type as your husband's, and the threads under his fingernails are a match for the ones in the tie found under Bloomfield's wardrobe. Also, the fingerprints found on the food packaging are a match not only for Bloomfield and Rotherham, but also the other two councillors who were often with them, so they've all been charged with receiving stolen goods.'

'And the evidence of the tie will be enough to convict Bloomfield of the murder?' asked Helen, who hoped there was no way of him wriggling out of the charge.

'That, and the fact that Rotherham panicked and confessed that Bloomfield had told him about the murder.'

'Sorry, can we go back a bit. Bloomfield left the tie under his wardrobe?' said Edie, incredulous. 'That wasn't very smart.'

'My thought too. Bloomfield told Rotherham that he didn't realise until he was in his bedroom that it was stained and torn, and his wife was coming up the stairs, so he shoved it under the wardrobe. He was trying to decide the best way to dispose of it, and obviously didn't get around to it.'

'So why did he do it?' said Helen.

'According to Rotherham, Mr Bygrove had threatened to report them all if he didn't get the stolen food for a cheaper price. Bloomfield had decided to deal with him, and that's what the telephone call that night was about. And Bloomfield had telephoned *him*, not the other way around. He'd then come secretly to the hotel to confront him around midnight, but when Mr Bygrove wouldn't give in, and threatened again to report them, he... did the deed, using first the tie, and then his bare hands. Rotherham reckons it wasn't planned, only a situation that got out of hand. Bloomfield then dragged him to the water's edge, hoping the fierce waves would sweep him away.'

'He must have been mad,' said Helen. 'He could have been washed away himself, or been blown away.'

'Mad or desperate,' said Toshack. 'When he related to Rotherham in a panic what had happened, they conspired to make you look like the guilty party. Rotherham doesn't want to be implicated in the murder, which is why he's told us. And it will probably go in his favour at court.'

'Well, well,' Edie said. 'How the mighty have fallen.'

'There was something else that Rotherham said.' Toshack paused for a moment to take a sip of his coffee. 'It was Bloomfield's idea for Miss Harvey to write those letters and implicate you, Mrs Bygrove. He apparently persuaded her by saying that your husband would be most appreciative and place her there as manageress when you were arrested.'

Helen couldn't quite comprehend what had been going on. 'But how would it help Douglas, who was his friend, if the reputation of the hotel went downhill? Surely my husband wouldn't have agreed to that, for his own sake alone, if not mine.'

'According to Rotherham, he knew nothing about it.'

'That makes sense at least. But it still begs the question of why Bloomfield would do that to his friend's business.'

'Because he wasn't his friend. Although your husband clearly didn't realise that.'

Helen and Edie looked at each other, brows creased in confusion.

'Rotherham reckons that Bloomfield's ultimate goal was to get his hands on the hotel at a cheap price, and that he could do that if he ruined the reputation of the present owners, that is, you and Mr Bygrove, with him being abroad and unable to do anything.'

'What?' Helen and Edie exclaimed in unison.

'Then he had a plan to advertise it as under new management and build up trade again. When Mr Bygrove returned, and didn't look set to be gone again, doing away with him was useful, even if Bloomfield hadn't originally intended it.'

'And Rotherham told you all this?' said Edie.

'Oh yes. Once he started talking, it was like he couldn't stop. I suppose he thought, the more he told us, the more it would look good for him.'

'Goodness.'

'Oh my. I can hardly believe what I'm hearing.' Helen stared at the desk, trying to take it all in.

'I don't suppose Superintendent Crooke can argue with any of that,' said Edie. 'Which reminds me. Ada Saltmarsh was in here on Friday causing trouble. She came into the conservatory and told our guests that Helen had been arrested. She said her mother had heard from Mrs Bloomfield. Most of our guests left afternoon tea, and quite a few checked out.'

'From Mrs Bloomfield? Interesting. Anyway, I'm so sorry about that. I'd say that Ada has definitely broken the terms of her suspended sentence and will have to go to court again. What a silly young woman, spoiling her second chance, especially after her aunt seemed determined to get the letters pinned on her.'

'I wonder if she'd been put up to it, to make it worse for Helen.'

'It's a possibility. I will deal with that after I've left here.'

He seemed wearied by the thought. Helen couldn't blame him; the last few days had been rather hectic.

Edie put down her cup and saucer and checked her wrist-watch. 'I'd better go to my shift on the desk. Thank you, Inspector, for coming in to update us on the situation.'

'I would appreciate it if you'd keep it to yourselves for now.'

'Of course.'

After Edie had left, Helen said, 'What about Superintendent Crooke?'

'What about him?'

'Do you think he might have had something to do with the receiving of stolen goods and was making some money on the side?'

He half smiled at her. 'Are you trying to do some detecting of your own?'

'He just seemed very eager to protect them. To begin with, at least. And he was very keen to take their word for it about my guilt, with no tangible proof. And, Edie tells me, he was part of the so-called golf club group.'

'Well, that may well be an investigation for another day, but for now, I have no evidence of such a thing, and it would be wise to keep such thoughts to yourself.'

Helen nodded, suspecting he agreed with her theory but knowing his counsel was wise.

'I'd better get on,' he said, standing. When she stood too, he added, 'It's all right, I'll see myself out.'

'Bye-bye Sam. And thank you again.'

He reached the door before he turned to look back at her. She wondered if he was going to suggest something, by the look on his face. But all he said was, 'Bye-bye Helen,' before he opened the door and left.

She was disappointed, yet relieved. There'd be time, in the future, when all this was behind them, to get to know each other better.

Chapter Twenty-Seven

It had been a busy July Sunday at the hotel, with all the rooms booked and a full restaurant and conservatory at luncheon and afternoon tea. Helen was now walking down the promenade, towards the pier, lighthouse and coastguard cottages, admiring the sunset hanging over the river and West Beach. The sky on the horizon was a reddish-orange, getting lighter as it went up to a light golden pink, and then to a pale pink before merging as a lilac band into the barely darkening blue sky.

Gentle waves were lapping onto the sand about halfway down the beach. The tents and huts of the summer businesses running along the top of the sand, next to the promenade, were all closed for the day now. There were a few people out still, mainly couples, taking advantage of the clear, colourful evening with its warm breeze. She detected a faint whiff of briny sea air as she took in a deep breath.

This time of the day, outside by the beach, always felt so tranquil to Helen, even with the insistent calls of the seagulls overhead. She noticed the lamplighter, with his wick on a long pole, lighting the streetlamps along the promenade.

Looking forward again, she spotted a familiar figure coming towards her. She couldn't help but smile. He did the same.

They both came to a standstill when they reached each other, next to a shelter.

'Good evening, Sam.'

'Good evening, Helen. Which way would you like to walk?'

'Towards the river, I think.'

She thought for a moment that he was going to take her arm, though it was probably more a wish than any indication on his part. He was, however, quite close to her as they walked.

'I'm glad you could make it this evening,' he said.

'It's such a relief after a hectic day. And the cooler air is welcome.'

'With the court cases over, and the four councillors convicted, how do you feel?'

'Reassured. I was relieved when they arrested Councillor Bloomfield, but with his conviction for Douglas's murder, I feel fully vindicated. I know it sounds rather heartless to say I'm relieved, after what happened to my husband.'

'It's understandable after the way he treated you.'

'I used to wish he'd maybe just run away to a new life and sign over the hotel to me.' She knew, even as she said it, that he would never have done that. Had he wanted to leave her and the children, she had no doubt that he would have sold the hotel and taken the money.

Sam's 'Hmm' suggested he thought the same.

'What will you do now?' he said.

'Run the hotel and bring up the children. And care for my loyal staff. If it hadn't been for them, I might still be locked up for libel. And if it hadn't been for your diligence, I might still be locked up for murder. I reckon that's worth a few free meals at the hotel, even though you're resistant to the suggestion.'

'If you want to pay me back—' he started, then said no more. They'd reached the end of the promenade, between the pepperpot lighthouse and pier.

'What?' she asked.

'Shall we walk by the river?'

'I'd like that.'

They turned right, walking by the sloping riverbank. They'd passed the old gun battery mound and reached the Casino Theatre and windmill before Helen said, 'You started a sentence, but didn't finish it.'

'I did, didn't I.' He seemed reluctant to say any more.

'I think it was to do with me paying you back?'

'It was, but I'm not sure it was the right way to word it.' He stopped, looking towards the oyster pond a few yards away. 'Nothing to do with you paying me back, for I don't require that. It's my job to make sure the innocent aren't arrested and the guilty are. But, if you ever have the time, and the inclination, to have dinner out with me one evening... or, if you have a day off and would like to take a trip to Arundel, or somewhere else... well, I'd be – um – I'd very much enjoy your company.'

She bit her bottom lip as she considered her answer, looking him in the eyes, wanting to say yes, but not knowing if she should. Or how she should.

'I'm sorry, I've clearly embarrassed you,' he said. 'It was very insensitive of me. You've been a widow barely over two months. I should know how that feels.'

He went to walk away but she grabbed his arm. 'No, it was not at all insensitive, it was very thoughtful. Douglas never had time to spend with me, only with his chums at his various clubs. And do you know what? I think I might deserve a treat for a change. I feel like I lost Douglas a long time ago, and I'm not going to be one of those women who wears black for a year. It would be an empty gesture. So yes, I would love a trip out with you.'

He stared at her, his full lips parted, looking pleasantly surprised at her reply.

'Good, aye. Very well. I'll telephone you tomorrow, give you a chance to look at your diary, and we'll organise something.'

They continued to walk. As they entered Pier Road, reaching the riverbank opposite the Nelson public house, Helen noticed something coming down the river, towards the mouth. She faced the water to observe it.

'It's one of the naval dazzle camouflage ships,' she said. 'I still haven't got used to them. They don't have the elegance of the sailing ships, which we sadly see fewer of these days.'

He took a couple of steps to stand next to her, watching as it approached. She slipped her arm through his and he looked down at her briefly, smiling.

When the ship had passed, they stood there, silent, watching the river. Her gaze rested on two swans, tinted blood orange by the low sun, gliding gracefully up the river, side by side. There was nobody else about now.

'The light's fading. I'd better go,' she said.

'Aye, me too.'

They began to turn but ended up facing each other. A compulsion overtook her, to hold him tightly, which must have seized him too. She felt safe in his arms, and at the same time, free. Had she ever felt this exhilaration in Douglas's arms, this dizzy swirl of emotions? She knew she hadn't. They stayed in this position for some seconds, before separating a little, staring into each other's shadowed eyes. There was a moment's hesitation before their faces moved forward and their lips touched. They kissed for some seconds. As they did, she caressed his cheek with her thumb, feeling the slight stubble and the small hollow of his dimple.

When they separated, he said in a low, emotional voice, 'Until tomorrow, Helen.'

'Until tomorrow, Sam.'

They both turned away at the same time. Helen walked back towards the pier, looking forward to tomorrow, and all her tomorrows.

A letter from Francesca

Thank you to all the readers who have contacted me to tell me how much they've enjoyed both the Beach Hotel and the Wartime in the Valleys series.

This time, it's the turn of manageress, Helen Bygrove, to have her story told. The libel investigation she finds herself involved with is based, albeit loosely, on a real case, known as the Littlehampton Libels, which took place in the early 1920s. It had several more stages and was far more complicated than that portrayed in the book, but had a similar character scenario. It was fascinating reading about it in Christopher Hilliard's book, *The Littlehampton Libels*, and I knew it would make a great storyline.

At this time in history, many women would have had to step up to managerial positions, especially if the businesses their husbands, or other male relatives, were involved in were not seen as essential and they'd been sent to fight.

I hope, in most cases, that the men were grateful to their wives, family members, or maybe even just their staff, for keeping the businesses going, even if it wasn't so in Douglas Bygrove's case.

At the end of the war, it must have been hard for some women to have to give up that authority, and the chance that had been given to them to show that they could run a business as well as a man, whatever society thought.

Helen is a competent manageress, but that doesn't mean that things always go smoothly for her (it wouldn't make for a good story if it did!). I dare say there really was a good deal of resentment from some quarters, that women had gained such control, especially as the powers that be were quick to put women back in their places as soon as the war finished, despite some winning the vote. However, the First World War was certainly the start of a brighter future for women.

If you'd like to contact me to discuss the novels, or discover more about them, I'd love to chat to you on social media here:

Website and blog: www.francesca-capaldi.co.uk/
Facebook: www.facebook.com/FrancescaCapaldiAuthor/
Twitter: @FCapaldiBurgess
TikTok: @francesca.capaldi.author

Best wishes
Francesca xx

Acknowledgements

A big thank you to Keshini Naidoo and Jennie Ayres, at Hera Books.

Grateful thanks to author Elaine Everest, for starting me off on my publishing journey, and to all the writers I've met along the way who have been encouraging and helpful.

A big thank you to the Bygone Littlehampton Facebook page. It's an excellent community history page and has on it so many wonderfully evocative photographs of old Littlehampton.